Praise for Megan Hart

"While Hart's writing has many strengths, including some refreshingly real dialogue, she really shines with her sensory description. Whether the scene is gruesome, sexy, or sometimes even both, she will put you in that moment with her skillful description. I'm definitely looking forward to reading more from this author!"
—Rob E. Boley, author of *That Risen Snow*, on *The Resurrected*

"Hart's beautiful use of language and discerning eye toward human experience elevate the book to a poignant reflection on the deepest yearnings of the human heart and the seductive temptation of passion in its many forms."
—Kirkus Reviews on *Tear You Apart*

"A tense look at dark secrets and the redemptive power of truth; not perfect, but compelling."
—Kirkus Reviews on *The Favor*

"Riveting, poignant, and powerful…"
—Publishers Weekly on *Tear You Apart*

Samhain Publishing, Ltd.
11821 Mason Montgomery Road, 4B
Cincinnati, OH 45249
www.samhainpublishing.com

Little Secrets
Copyright © 2016 by Megan Hart
Print ISBN: 978-1-61923-399-7
Digital ISBN: 978-1-61923-087-3

Editing by Don D'Auria
Cover by Kanaxa

First Samhain Publishing, Ltd. electronic publication: February 2016
First Samhain Publishing, Ltd. print publication: February 2016

Little Secrets

Megan Hart

SAMHAIN PUBLISHING

Dedication

This book is for the ventriloquist dummy sitting on my office shelf. Please don't come to life and kill me in my sleep.

Chapter One

A fresh start.

That's what they needed. A new house, new jobs, new hobbies, new friends. Even her haircut was new, shorn to the shoulders instead of hanging halfway down her back. And her body was certainly getting newer all the time.

Ginny Bohn stepped out of her old car into her new driveway. She put her hand on the roof for a minute, the metal chilly under her fingertips, and looked at the house. Brick with black shutters. There'd been a garage at one time, according to the realtor who'd sold them the house, but a fire had destroyed it years ago, and the previous owner had never rebuilt. It had been replaced with a small fenced garden, bare now, but Ginny could easily imagine it filled with flowers—assuming she became the sort of woman who took the time to plant seeds and make things grow.

"Honey, just got a call from the movers. They'll be here in about half an hour." Sean had pulled up next to her and was out of his car. He stretched, cracking his back and neck in the way that always made her cringe. He came around the front of his car to hold out his hand to her. "Careful. The walk's a little wet. It could be slippery."

It was sweet, his hesitation, his desire to make her something fragile. It almost made Ginny want to grab his arm and have him guide her along the slightly buckled sidewalk as though she were somehow incapable of navigating it without his help. Almost.

She did take his hand, though, linking their fingers. They kissed matter-of-factly. That's how it had always been with them. Matter-of-fact, familiar kisses they shared almost every time they were close enough for their lips to meet. This time, she put her arms around his waist when he tried to get away and hooked her fingertips into his belt loops. Ginny held her husband closer, just for a moment, her head tipped back so he could kiss her more thoroughly, though Sean was too busy laughing to really do justice to the smooch.

"You want to give the neighbors a show, huh?"

Ginny smiled, not giving a damn about the neighbors, just wanting to feel the pressure of his mouth on hers again. Taste him. Feel his breath on her face and maybe the beat of his heart against her. She stroked the fringes of hair that always fell in front of his ears, no matter how he had it cut. His bangs were longer now too, but she kept herself from ruffling them because she knew it irritated him when she messed with his hair. "I love you."

"Love you too." His kiss lingered this time, not as long as she'd have liked, but with a little more heat. His hands fit against her hips. He nuzzled her nose with his, a gesture she'd told him a hundred times she hated, but that he never seemed to remember.

From the backseat came a sudden, irritated yowl. Sean ducked to look through the back window. "Noodles sounds pissed."

Ginny sighed. "She doesn't like the carrier. Can you grab the litter pan and stuff? I'm going to put her in the upstairs bathroom until we can get everything settled."

Sean nodded and got them from the trunk as Ginny pulled out the carrier and looked at Noodles's furious, furry face. "Shhh. You act like you're getting killed in there."

Noodles, unimpressed with Ginny's scolding and Ginny in general, yowled again. Ginny balanced the carrier, which rocked in her arms as Noodles shifted, and followed Sean up the curving brick path to the cute-as-a-button front porch with its white-painted railing and double swing hung on chains from the roof. The front door was black, sober, the gold handle surprisingly ornate and old-fashioned, compared to the rest of the outside decor. It was the kind of handle that looked as though it used a fancy skeleton-type key, not the small and freshly cut generic silver sort they'd copied from the equally small but tarnished key the realtor had given them.

A fresh key for their fresh start.

It slipped into the lock with a faint clinking sound, and Sean glanced at her over his shoulder before he twisted his wrist. The click was louder this time, but the door didn't open. Sean took the key out. Blew on it, which made Ginny laugh. Tried again. Waiting, the carrier too heavy, she set it down and held out her hand. Noodles yowled from inside, then went quiet.

"Want me to try?"

Sean handed her the key, which slipped into the lock without effort. The handle creaked when she turned it, and then the door was opening with a squeal of hinges. Before she could step inside, Sean put out an arm to stop her.

Ginny had no time to protest or even prepare herself before Sean bent to sweep her into his arms, one beneath her legs and the other around her back. She let out a startled squeak and clung to him. He took two normal steps over the threshold before his foot hit a throw rug that had been placed a little too far away from the threshold. It started to skid out from under him.

For a sickening moment, Ginny was sure they were going to fall. Her body tensed, muscles going tight in anticipation of the pain. She bit her tongue and let out a yelp. Her hands slipped on Sean's back as he grappled and kept her from toppling onto the floor… just barely. He put her down, stepping on her foot as the pair of them stumbled forward another few steps, dancing to some routine neither had practiced.

Heart pounding, breath catching sharp in the back of her throat, Ginny ended up straddling the errant throw rug, one of her hands on the wall and the other still clutching at the back of Sean's shirt. Her nails dug so deeply into the plaster they'd have broken if she still kept them long, but she'd given up her manicures months ago. It was the first time she'd looked at her hands with clipped nails and been grateful for it.

"You okay?" Sean laughed nervously. His hand shifted on her waist, and he looked over his shoulder at the rug. "We should throw that away. It could be dangerous."

Ginny took a slow, calming breath and rubbed the toe of her ballet flat along the polished wood floor. She found her balance, caught her breath. "It's ugly anyway."

It was. Hideous, in fact. Fluffy yarn of alternating green and brown and orange stripes, with a contrasting flowery border. Nothing like she'd ever have chosen. Now that she looked around the hall, she saw a lot of things she didn't recognize, including an ugly telephone table. "I thought Bonnie said she was going to have someone come and get rid of all this stuff, except what we specifically requested to be left in the contract."

George Miller, the former owner, had died—in the hospital, thank God. Ginny didn't consider herself superstitious, but she wasn't sure she'd have been able to get past the idea of someone actually expiring in her house. They'd never met his son, Brendan, who'd inherited the house but whose lawyer had handled all the details. Brendan Miller had offered to let them take anything they wanted. Everything in the house, as a matter of fact. She'd asked only to keep the ugly but still serviceable barstools in the kitchen, a few of the lighting fixtures and the custom-made drapes in all the rooms, which were as hideous as the throw rug but better than the nothing she owned to replace them with.

"Yeah…she was supposed to."

The rug and the telephone table hadn't been on the list, Ginny knew that for sure. She tugged the small handle on a drawer meant to hold a pen and paper or a phone book and found instead a jumble of junk. Coins, paper clips, a bunch of old buttons, some tiny carved wooden figures. She lifted one, a thick wooden peg in a vaguely female shape without a face or limbs, the hash marks from the whittling knife still cutting deep into the wood. George Miller had been a carpenter. She tossed the peg back into the drawer. Cell phones and cordless handsets made tables like this irrelevant and unnecessary, though Ginny could vividly remember one similar to this that had been in her grandparents' front hallway. Different phones over the years, but that same table. With her finger, she pushed against the wood and the table rocked, one leg slightly shorter than the others.

"You okay?"

Ginny looked up at Sean. Found a smile that quirked her lips without much true humor. "Fine. Just a little shaky."

Maybe it was from almost being squished within the first five minutes of entering her new home. More likely it was because she hadn't eaten in a few hours. Low blood sugar. She couldn't decide if she was hungry or on the verge of nausea.

"Do you feel sick? Should I get you something to eat? Some saltines? Shit. I don't think we have any."

There was that sweet concern again. In the first weeks of her pregnancy she'd spent more time hunched over the toilet than anywhere else, and Sean had been right there with her, holding her hair. Rubbing her back. Bringing her flat ginger ale and crackers and wet cloths to press along the back of her neck. He'd meant his concern as comfort, though she'd told him over and over that she hated any kind of attention on her when she was sick, and had suffered it only because it had taken too much energy to keep asking him to leave her alone.

"No." She shook her head. The dizziness wasn't fading, and the thick, throat-closing nausea was rising. "I just need to sit down. Get a drink and something to eat. I'll be fine."

He hovered over her all the way down the hall and into the kitchen, where she let him ease her onto one of the barstools she *had* wanted to keep. She let him chafe her hands too. But beyond that, there wasn't much Sean could do to help her since the brand-new fridge they'd already had delivered was empty and so were the cupboards.

Sean opened one anyway and pulled out a vintage Looney Tunes glass adorned with Tweety Bird. "Hey. Look at this? You want some ice water, honey? I think the fridge's hooked up."

Their old fridge had an ice maker but not one that dispensed through the door. The new one had both cubed and crushed ice, and also filtered water. They'd really splurged.

Sean rinsed the glass at the sink, then pressed it against the dispenser. Nothing happened.

"Shit." He opened the fridge to reveal an empty interior, shadowed without the automatic light to illuminate it. "Damn it."

He flicked the switch on the wall on and off a couple times, then looked at her. "I thought you said you'd handled the electricity."

If her head hadn't been spinning, Ginny would've shaken it. As it was, all she could do was blink. "I did. I called and told them we'd be moving in today, and that everything should be turned on."

He flicked the switch again, then once more. "Well. They didn't. Are you sure you talked to the right person?"

She could argue with him about it, or she could keep her lunch in her stomach. Ginny chose the latter. She breathed slowly in through her nose and out through her mouth, closing her eyes to push away the dizziness. She heard running water and looked up to see Sean at the sink.

He gave her a triumphant look, then offered the glass with a flourish. "At least we have running water. Walla."

The term was actually *voilà*, but Ginny didn't point that out. She just took the glass of water and sipped it, grateful for the way the liquid slipped down the back of her throat, nice and cool. This house had a well and septic system, not like the city water and sewer at their old place, and the water actually had a flavor.

Sean rubbed her shoulder briefly. "Be right back. I'll grab you a snack from the car."

"Oh! Bring Noodles too!"

She was a lucky woman. Sean was a good husband. She breathed slowly, fighting another wave of sickness. She should get up, call the electric company and figure out what happened with the power. But for now, all Ginny could manage was to sit and sip the water her husband had poured for her.

Sean came in again with a handful of granola bars and the cat carrier. "Where do you want her?"

She took one of the snacks from him and tore it open, eyeing the carrier in which the cat was now growling. "Oh Lord. She's going to pee on everything. Can you put her in the upstairs bathroom, with the litter box, and the door closed? And oh, put a sign on it so nobody opens it. I'll take care of getting her set up later."

Ginny heard the sound of a big vehicle in the drive. The movers must've arrived early. She'd have to get up in a minute to greet them herself, direct them where to put the boxes and furniture. "I hear a truck, good. I was thinking we wouldn't be finished before it got dark, and I really want to at least get our bedroom set up before night."

"Yeah," he said. "Especially since we won't have any lights."

It wasn't her fault, Ginny wanted to say. She'd spoken to the power company and made the arrangements for the electricity to be turned on today. Cable television, phone and Internet too. Trash next week. She had all the information in a folder still in the car, with the dates and times she'd called, the names of the customer service reps she'd spoken to. It was not her fault that someone, somewhere, had forgotten to do their job and flip a switch.

She said nothing, biting her tongue and hiding her grimace with another sip of water.

Sean started toward the stairs with the carrier. "I'll get them started. You sit."

She did for another few minutes, not out of laziness or some sort of Lady of the Manor attitude, but simply because pushing herself off the barstool still required more of an effort than she felt capable of making. Her head still threatened to keep spinning if she didn't take some deep breaths, and she wasn't certain she wouldn't puke. And no wonder, she thought as she nodded and smiled at the first of the movers who brought in a box of dishes and settled it on the counter before heading back out for another load. She was exhausted, operating on little to no sleep over the past few days as she'd fretted over the final details of the sale that had seemed too good to be true. She'd stayed up late packing and making lists, paying bills, making sure everything in their new life was going as smoothly as possible. No sleep, not enough to eat… Her hands went protectively to her belly for a minute.

The doctor had assured her that a history of miscarriage didn't necessarily mean she couldn't carry to term. That everything about this pregnancy looked healthy and normal, no cause for alarm. Still, Ginny thought of the almost fall and the subsequent dizziness, and she forced herself to nibble away on the granola bar and sip water until it passed.

By five o'clock the truck was unloaded, the movers paid and tipped and sent on their way. The electricity had been restored, the culprit a blown circuit breaker, as it turned out, which Ginny discovered when she called the power company and was told that, indeed, their house was supposed to be fully supplied. Sean hadn't apologized for doubting her, but he had gone into the basement to fiddle with the fuse box, and the fact they had lights was enough to make it easy for Ginny to forget that she'd been angry. Noodles had been petted and loved up and generally soothed with a can of fancy cat food and fresh litter, though she was still confined to the bathroom until Ginny could get more of the house arranged and find a place to put the litter box.

Pizza was ordered and delivered. Ginny flipped open the cardboard box and breathed in the pepperoni-scented steam as Sean popped the top on a can of caffeine-free cola for her, a beer for him. She'd found a candelabra that had been a wedding gift, never used, along with a set of semi-melted red candles and a half-dozen votive holders. They were eating on paper plates since she hadn't yet unpacked the dishes, but Sean had discovered another couple of those Looney Tunes glasses in the cupboard.

"Cheers." Sean tipped his glass to hers. "To our first, but not last, romantic dinner in our new house."

"*Salut.*" Ginny sipped bubbly cola, relishing the sting of the carbonation in the back of her throat and the sweetly spreading glow of sugar. It would've been even better with caffeine, but Sean had read an article that said pregnant women shouldn't touch it.

Even with the candles, it was far from the most elegant dinner they'd ever had. No flowers in crystal vases, no glittering silverware or gold-rimmed china. But he was right, it was romantic. Ginny downed a third slice of pizza without guilt over calories and listened to Sean wax philosophical on the benefits of hiring a landscaping service in the spring versus trying to get the yard in decent shape all by themselves. He was making plans for the future, she thought. And that was good.

All of this was good.

Chapter Two

All of this was bad.

Ginny woke, eyes wide, heart pounding, coughing at the sting of bile in her throat. She swallowed hard and pressed a fist between her breasts in a futile attempt to relieve some of the pressure as she sat up against the headboard. She'd gone to bed in a soft flannel granny gown, the house chilly enough to warrant the heavier pajamas since she'd been unable to find the boxes containing either the extra blanket or the flannel sheets. Slick sweat coated her now. She tossed back the comforter and let the cool air cover her instead.

Heartburn. Nobody to blame but herself since she'd been the one to shove that third slice of pizza down her gullet. Ginny pressed her fist harder against her chest. Beside her, Sean slept the sleep of the guiltless, arms akimbo and one leg hooked outside the blankets. Despite the sweat still running rivers between her breasts and down her spine, Ginny was now cold. Her teeth chattered a few times as she forced herself to swallow, then again, hoping to at least get rid of some of the burning taste at the back of her throat.

What had woken her? The heartburn, yes, but before that she'd been happily dreaming. Perhaps not so happily, considering the content of her dreams—they'd been full of running and searching. Lots of losing, but not so much finding. Sometimes Ginny clung to dreams, but tonight she was more than happy to have been pulled from them.

But there. There it was again, the faint scritch-scratch of something in the ceiling. She strained, listening, but didn't hear it again. Shit. Mice. It wasn't entirely unexpected. They lived in an old house in an old neighborhood that backed up onto a farmer's field. There could easily be mice in the house.

This sounded much bigger than a mouse.

There were squirrels in the backyard, she'd seen them. They made a weird chittering sound she'd thought at first was birds. The scritch-scratch came again, softer and farther away.

The home inspector hadn't turned up any evidence of rodent infestation, but as she'd discovered when she tried to shower before bed, the guy had also completely somehow missed that the hot-water heater wasn't capable of providing enough water for a quick shower, much less a luxurious one. Forget about filling the old clawfoot tub in the master bathroom. He'd also passed the fuse box, which was obviously not operating up to standards since the power had gone out once more during the move. Ginny supposed she wouldn't be surprised if the entire house turned out to be overrun with Mickey and his buddies.

The noise didn't come again, but between it and the heartburn and the lingering dreams, Ginny was in no way going to return to slumberland. She stuck a tentative bare toe off the bed and felt for the edge of the vent in the floor, hoping for a tickle of hot air. Nothing. The house had been empty long enough that the heat had probably been set at a minimum, and because the temperature had been fine during the day, Ginny hadn't touched the thermostat before coming to bed. Sean probably hadn't either. It would've been fine if she were still snuggled up under the comforter, but not wide awake with the pizza sitting like a stone in her gut and reflux climbing her throat.

Ginny got out of the bed, which was placed much closer to the wall in this house. Their old bedroom had been bigger, laid out differently, though it lacked the attached master bath and dressing room that had sold her on this house. This room had more windows, one of them a cute dormer she intended to somehow transform into a reading nook or something equally as interesting, if only she could figure out how. Now her hand tapped along the wall and hit open space—the dormer. She peeked into it but saw only darkness and felt an even cooler puff of air on her cheeks. Maybe the window at the end of the narrow space was open or needed some better insulation. She eased past the opening until her hand found the wall on the other side and oriented herself toward the door to the hall, blinking rapidly as though that would make her see better in the blackness.

She hadn't slept with a night-light since childhood, but wished for one now. All the small details of this house that she hadn't yet learned threatened to trip her worse than the slippery throw rug. She moved blindly, hands outstretched and feet shuffling along the wooden floor. The hardwood had seemed so appealing in the light of day, easy to keep clean and giving the house such a classic feeling. In the middle of the night, with cold bare feet, all she could think of was putting a rug big enough for the bedroom at the top of her mental "gotta get" list.

She bumped into a tall cardboard box, hitting with both her hand and foot at the same time. It moved when she hit it, lightweight. The wardrobe box, then, one of the few she'd managed to completely empty since the closet here was bigger than their old one and far better equipped with built-in shelving and rods. Sean let out a series of snuffling snorts and shifted, making the bed creak, but didn't wake. If she remembered correctly, the box was in front of the still-open closet door, which was between the bathroom door and the bedroom door, both of which should also be open.

She'd remembered wrong, obviously, because though she took a couple cautious steps, hands out, she found nothing but air. One more step and her fingertips grazed the wall, found the doorframe. She oriented herself again and discovered she'd also been wrong about the bedroom door being open, when she rammed into it with her face. She'd reached with both her hands, so the muffled thud of her nose hitting the wood wasn't loud, and she managed to bite back her cry of pain so neither noise woke Sean.

With her palms flat on the wood, Ginny pressed her forehead to the door, eyes watering. Cautiously, she felt her nose, but there was no blood and the pain faded rapidly. Her hand slid down the cool wood to the knob—this one, like the one on the front door, was elaborately constructed of an ornate metal plate, a crystal knob and a real keyhole the realtor had promised was for show, since the door actually locked with a small button on the inside of the handle. Her fingers toyed with it as she twisted the knob, the hinges stuttering.

Sean muttered and snorted again, rolling around and probably tearing all the blankets up from the foot of the bed. Ginny froze, waiting to see if he'd woken. She really didn't want to wake him. Sean had to work in the morning, which felt like it could be a million or only a few hours in the future, she had no idea since she hadn't looked at the clock. And more than that, if she woke him, he'd want to make sure she was all right. He'd want her to stay in bed while he went downstairs and checked the thermostat, or brought her some water, or rubbed her feet, or rummaged around in the boxes in the bathroom to find her some antacid.

The last thing in the world Ginny wanted right now was to have Sean hovering over her, no matter how good his intentions.

More cool air washed over her as she eased herself into the hall. She took a second or two just to relish the fact they had an upstairs with a hallway—their townhouse had been two-story but the second floor had been completely made up of their bedroom, a tiny guest room and shared bathroom. This house was so much bigger, so much a real house, not some rinky-dink starter home. Ginny took the time to savor this, until her teeth chattered harder and she had to wrap her arms around herself to keep warm.

It seemed they'd been looking at houses forever, unable to make the leap, until the housing market made it impossible not to go for it. They'd looked at this house four times before making their offer. The seller had accepted immediately without haggling, though they'd come in low the way the realtor had suggested. Four times Ginny had toured it, making sure she could imagine herself in just this spot, before she felt she could commit to it for what she knew didn't have to be the rest of her life, but surely felt like it.

Standing outside her bedroom door now, Ginny could imagine the placement of every other door. Six of them—four other bedrooms, empty because they didn't have enough furniture to fill them. A bathroom, inside which she could still hear Noodles's faint, annoyed meowing. A linen closet. In front of her, the railing surrounded the open space around the stairs, with the entrance an equidistant walk to the left or the right of her, depending on which way she felt like going. The movers hadn't closed the doors after putting the labeled boxes in them, and some light filtered in through the one directly to her left. That would be the nursery, and like the master, faced the street as well as the yard on the other side of the house. Blinking, her eyes adjusted to the dark. She could make out the faint shapes of open doors, a window at the other end of the hall.

And something else.

On the far side of the hall, something in the shadows moved. She was sure of it. Something low to the ground, but not Noodles, because not only was the cat still locked up, this was bigger than a cat. Which meant it was bigger than a mouse. Bigger than a squirrel too. Way bigger. Oh God. What if it was a raccoon or something, come in from the attic? Didn't raccoons carry rabies? Ginny reached for the railing, smooth and cool beneath her fingers. The wood creaked as she squeezed. Whatever it was, whatever she'd seen, didn't move again.

She blinked hard, then again, eyes straining against the darkness. Something took shape in the place where she'd seen movement. A box, a pile of sheets and towels on top of it. She remembered it then. The movers had asked her if she wanted the box in one of the empty bedrooms, but she hadn't wanted to move it again. They'd left it by the linen closet, right there—that's all it was. A stack of linens that probably hid her flannel sheets and the extra blanket she was missing.

Ginny had been holding her breath but let it out now on a long, low hiss that became a self-conscious laugh. Silly. Seeing things. New house, new life, all of it new, and of course she wasn't used to getting up in the night and seeing things move that should be still. And she was still cold, no heat sifting up from the registers.

Ginny went to the left, past the nursery and toward the linen closet, her hand on the railing to keep her from stumbling. Shuffling, one foot sliding in front of the other, bare toes on bare wood, without ever really lifting fully. She didn't want to bump into anything or step on something unexpected.

Just before she got to the stairs, her sliding foot encountered what felt like a splinter. A faint, small sting had her pause and hop to rub it, her toes cold against equally chilled fingers. She couldn't find the splinter in her sole, and when she put her foot down gingerly the sting seemed to have gone.

She added a hall runner to the "gotta get."

The thermostat was in the front hall, just at the bottom of the stairs. Unlike most of the house's fixtures, the thermostat was brand-new. Electronic. It had been replaced, along with the furnace, shortly before the previous owner passed away. It lit when she flipped up the cover to get at the buttons, and the green light that would be barely visible in the daytime was like a beacon to her night-sensitive eyes.

Ginny squinted against the sudden glow and leaned forward to push the button once, twice, again. The digital numbers changed from sixty-two—way too cold, to sixty-five. That wasn't that much better. She pushed it a few more times, bringing the temperature to sixty-eight. Sean would grumble about the heating costs, but, dammit, she was cold. At least until they had some sort of idea how much this house would cost to heat she could claim ignorance in her desire for comfort.

She'd changed the temperature, but there was no rumble from the basement of the furnace kicking on, no welcome burst of warmth from the vents. To the left of the front door, she went through an archway and into what the realtor had called the "front room." It connected to one of equal size through a set of pocket doors. Both rooms had fireplaces, as did the small parlor across the hall, though only the fireplace in the front room still worked. In the months leading up to this night, Ginny had imagined a hundred different ways she'd furnish this place, but for now the movers had simply put their old furniture and all the boxes marked "Living Room" into the front room.

Most of the rooms had no overhead fixtures, just switches that operated certain outlets, and she hadn't yet figured out exactly where she wanted the lamps or which outlets worked from the switch. There was enough light from the front windows to direct her to the leather couch pushed up near the front window. She wove around the boxes and chairs to snag the afghan thrown over the back and wrap herself in it, then took a minute to peer through the front windows hung with lace curtains she'd never have chosen but had asked to keep anyway. Those curtains were hers now.

This place was hers.

She ran her fingers along the leather couch. The back of the overstuffed armchair. The cardboard boxes still crammed full and taped shut, guarding everything they owned. This house, this brand-new place, this fresh start…it began in chaos and confusion but would settle. It would. Ginny stood for a minute in the middle of the room, eyes closed, breathing in the smell of this new place. Her nose was cold. Her toes were cold. She hugged the afghan tighter around herself and waited to get tired. Waited to be warm.

Well, the afghan was helping with the latter, but though every muscle ached, weighted with exhaustion, she was very far from sleepy. Mindful of her splinter-stuck foot, this time she didn't slide her feet while walking. So of course, two steps away from the couch, she stepped on something hard enough to make her gasp and hop with pain. The heavy thud of whatever it was moved along the floor as she kicked it, and though she tried to see what it was, shadows consumed it.

Damn, it hurt, her sole bruised. Ginny added a pair of slippers to that ever-growing mental list—clearly, she couldn't be shuffling around in her bare feet until everything had been unpacked and cleaned up. Instead of traversing the maze of boxes and possibly stubbing her toes or stepping on some other bit of moving detritus, Ginny decided to head for the kitchen via the hallway.

From behind her, when she got to the doorway, came another sound of something clinking on the wood floor, so faint that though she turned her head toward it, she could easily convince herself that she'd imagined it. Or maybe that it had been her rings clicking on the wall as she gripped it to pause.

She listened.

Nothing. Only the sounds of an old house settling; sadly, still no huff and puff of hot air from the furnace vents. She felt a little warmer, though, under the blanket like a cape. Ginny's gran hadn't crocheted it. She wasn't the sort to spend her time in what she called "handicrafts." But the blanket reminded Ginny of her. Gran had been a late-night wanderer, often with a blanket wrapped around her just like this. Checking the doors and windows to make sure they were locked. The stove to make certain all the burners were off. Gran had been one to bend over her sleeping children and grandchildren, holding her fingers under their nostrils to make sure they were still breathing. Ginny had woken many times in the night to see the shadowy figure looming over her, to hear the sharp pant of breath or Gran's grunt of approval when she figured out Ginny was still alive.

Ginny shivered at the memory, more from emotion than the chill. Gran's house had been similar to this one, full of nooks and crannies and delightful built-ins. A great place for kids to play hide and seek. A wonderful house for parties with neighbors, family and friends gathered around to eat, drink and be merry. Gran's Christmas Eve parties had been legendary, but only those closest to her knew how much effort and frustration she'd had in the planning and execution of even the simplest bits of the planning, how she'd worked herself into a frenzy with the preparations and how hard she'd crashed after. Those manic highs and lows had been the reason why Ginny's own mom had never thrown any parties, not even for birthdays. Maybe it was why her mom had never crept into her bedroom at night either, to make sure her children hadn't died in their sleep. Ginny couldn't say she minded that bit, but she had always loved helping Gran get ready for the Christmas Eve celebration.

Maybe she'd have her own Christmas Eve party, Ginny thought as she moved through the dark hall past the small parlor. It didn't matter that she and Sean had always celebrated the holiday with no more fuss than a tabletop tree, a few gifts and dinner at the Chinese buffet—unless they went to his mother's house. They'd get a real tree, floor to ceiling. Garland and tinsel and twinkling lights, with mistletoe in all the doorways. Gran's eggnog in the big crystal punch bowl she'd given Ginny when she moved into the nursing home and had distributed all of her "treasures." It would be a lot of work, but Christmas was a couple months away and, besides, after that, the baby would be here. There'd be no time for parties after that, at least not for a while.

And as for the other…would she be the sort of mother to creep around at night on cat-soft feet, always afraid? Or the other sort, so determined to let her kids go she didn't cling to them fiercely enough? Only time would tell.

Ginny made a pit stop in the powder room, her five-months-pregnant bladder reminding her that even without heartburn, sleeping through the night had become a thing of the past. She had to squint from the bright-white glare of the single, hideous fluorescent fixture. A new bathroom light went on the list. She peed forever, the jingle of urine splashing in the bowl sounding extra loud in the tiny room.

From her spot in the light, the hall seemed extra dark, the shadows even thicker. There was an alcove beneath the rise of the stairs and in it, something moved. No flash of light to indicate eyes, no pale glimpse of a face, but nevertheless, the shape moved with a purpose. No random shift of light and dark, nor a mimic of her movements spilling into the hall and making the illusion of something else there.

In the dark, something moved.

Ginny froze, a crumpled wad of toilet paper in her fist, her bladder already loose and now looser with fear. She wouldn't have been able to stop the flow even if she wanted to, but the mortifying horror of being found dead on the toilet, with her faded and stretched-out panties around her ankles, forced a sudden startled laugh out of her. It also sounded extra loud. She cut off the noise by closing her mouth tight; in the next moment she finished peeing and that noise stopped too.

She waited, listening, trying to see what would loom up out of the shadows to get her. Of course, nothing did. She waited another thirty seconds before finishing on the toilet, pulling up her underpants and washing her hands while she stared hard into the mirror to make sure nothing came up behind her. And of course, nothing did.

In the doorway she put a hand out into the hall, searching for a light switch. None to the left. None to the right. There was one in the kitchen, she knew that. And one by the front door. But none here. She could stand here in the light forever, or she could venture out and face her fears.

It would be another box, she thought. A pile of something in the shape of a person, maybe a slowly toppling pile of curtains or tablecloths that had finally given in to gravity just when she happened to be looking at them. She stepped forward, into the hall, the alcove just a step or two in front of her and slightly to the left.

"It's just a jump to the left," she murmured and laughed again. "And then a step to the right."

She didn't need a time warp. Two or three more steps in the direction would take her to the kitchen and the light switch, but for now she just blinked to let her eyes adjust again to the darkness. And then…she remembered. When they'd looked at this house, the alcove had been used to store the broom, a mop with its bucket and the vacuum cleaner. The basement door was there too.

Just a leaning mop that had probably lost its precarious balance from her thundering weight as she walked. That was all. Nothing else.

Still, that was twice in one night that Ginny'd let herself be scared into seeing things that weren't there. Understandable, she guessed. New house, still so unfamiliar. Everything in her life had been turned upside down. Nothing was the same. She let her hand rest on the slight bump beneath her nightgown. Nothing would ever be the same.

But this house was their new start, hers and Sean's. This was where they'd raise a family. God willing, they'd grow old together, still interested in sitting on the fabulous front porch in rocking chairs, holding hands. They'd make every cliché and stereotype of a happy family come true, she thought with grim determination as she stared fiercely into the alcove, daring the shadows to shift in front of her again.

Of course, nothing did.

In the kitchen, Ginny shuffled across the linoleum to open the fridge, squinting again as she pulled out a carton of orange juice they'd picked up from the convenience store. She really wanted a cup of hot tea but had no clue where either the kettle or the mugs were. Or the tea bags, for that matter. She poured a paper cup of juice and sipped at it as she looked around the humped shapes of stacked boxes on counters and the floor. They had put their old dining room table in here. In the townhouse, the table had seemed immense, but here the kitchen dwarfed it. She ran a finger along the clean modern edge, thinking maybe she'd hunt for something antique for the new dining room. Or at least something that looked antique, not another sleek but flimsy thing Sean would have to put together using one of those little wrenches that came in the box.

Sean had made some noise about turning at least one of the bedrooms into an office, but so far anything that might someday go into such a thing as a home office was still packed up in boxes that had been distributed to other rooms. However, her laptop was plugged in and charging on the table, she knew that for sure, because earlier she'd gone online to make sure the Internet was working and to check her email. She'd never had a desk. She'd always done all of her computer work at this very table in their minuscule dining room in the townhouse.

Investigating insurance fraud was never as exciting as most people would imagine, but there had been some occasional physical stress to it. Sometimes a stakeout, watching the man who'd claimed his back hurt too much to stack boxes do the tango with his wife in a backyard they hadn't secured from every line of sight. Or asking that seemingly innocent young woman to help her reach something on the top shelf of the grocery store, when the woman had claimed her injuries kept her from doing her job as a retail clerk. But most of Ginny's job was spent writing reports and making sure her facts were straight, that she had proof of the fraud that couldn't be disputed, that all her t's were crossed and i's dotted. She'd spent lots of late nights bathed in the glow of the laptop, a mug of hot tea and a plate of cheese and crackers next to her if she was being good, a piece of cake or some cookies or a bowl of ice cream if she wasn't.

Most of those late nights, she wasn't being good. But that was all over now, and though she let her fingers drift across the laptop's polished-metal lid, detecting the smoother outline of the sticker she'd applied—a zombie Snow White with her hands posed to hold the Apple logo—Ginny didn't open the lid. She didn't check her email or surf the gossip sites or buy things she wanted but didn't need and couldn't really afford. She didn't log on to her Connex account, and she had no reason any longer to snoop around figuring out what other people tried to keep hidden. She was finished with that. This was their new start, and she wasn't going to ruin it by old habits.

Ginny climbed the stairs in the dark, one hand on the railing to ensure she didn't trip or fall and plummet to her sprawling, awkward death. She moved through the upstairs hall, also in the dark, found her bedroom door and crept into her bed, all without turning on the lights, all without anything jumping out at her. By the time she wiggled under the blankets and curled onto her side, the first edges of morning light were beginning to peek through the windows. When Sean's alarm went off, she sighed, dreaming, and snuggled back down beneath the comforter, finally able to sleep.

Chapter Three

The screams of children woke her. Ginny's eyes flew open and she clawed out at the air, her fingertips not close enough to skim the curtains but moving them a bit in the breeze her startled motion left behind. She gasped.

Kids playing outside, that was all. She could hear the shush-shush of feet rustling in leaves and the singsongy chant of some childhood rhyme she'd recognize when she woke up a little more, or it would drive her crazy until she could remember it. Like the night before, she was coated in sweat, her nightshirt sticking to her back. Her mouth tasted sour.

She didn't force herself to get up right away. She rolled onto her back for a minute or so, remembering with a bit of melancholy how once, not so long ago, she'd spent every night flat on her back with her hands crossed over her chest. Vampira, Sean sometimes called her, but that had been her favorite sleeping position since childhood. She missed it. Though her belly was barely bumped, her muscles and joints had already started going loose, and she needed a complicated arrangement of pillows and positions to keep her back from hurting. Her inevitable aches eased briefly when she switched positions, but in another few minutes they'd start up again and worse, if she didn't move. For now, she let herself relax into the mattress as she stared up at the ceiling.

Watermarks, faint beneath a coat of paint, but still there. Some cracks in the plaster. This wasn't a new house, so she shouldn't be surprised, but after the townhouse's smooth, pristine and flawless ceiling, this view was far more interesting. Ginny thought again of her gran's house. For all her eccentricities, Gran had loved having her grandchildren come to stay, and Ginny and her female cousins had always bunked up in the "rose room." Floral-patterned wallpaper and sheets, two double beds along one wall and a twin tucked under the eaves. It had been Ginny's aunt Patty's room growing up and still bore the marks inside the closet door where she'd used a pen to keep track of how tall she and her siblings had grown. The ceiling in the rose room had been plastered in swirls that made faces if you looked just right, and Ginny's cousin Dana had been the queen of telling stories about them.

This ceiling didn't have those swirls, but Ginny looked for faces anyway. One pattern of cracks and shadow made a man with a walrus mustache. Another a lady in a floppy hat. A smaller configuration looked more like letters, though she couldn't quite make out what word they spelled. Staring, she started to doze before another series of childish shrieks slammed her awake again.

"Brats," she muttered, without real anger, just before a patter of something like gravel pinged the window over the bed. Then she scowled and rolled herself upright to pull back the curtain and stare down into the front yard.

A little boy and a little girl, both blond and in matching red coats, stared up at the window. When the curtain twitched, the boy screamed again, backing away so fast he tripped himself up and landed on his butt. The girl's mouth opened wide, her eyes wider, but she didn't move. Frozen by fear, maybe, Ginny thought as she shook a finger at them. The glass had cracked, cold air seeping in, but remembering the chill from the night before, she wasn't sure she could blame the kids for breaking it. It looked old, if it were possible to tell how old a window crack was, but the lines of it were dirty. Still, why the hell were they tossing pebbles at her window in the first place? She shook her finger again, shooing them, and the girl reached down to pull the boy by the hand. The pair of them ran off across the yard and disappeared around the right-hand corner, leaving behind an assortment of toys. A wagon, some sort of trike. A ball.

Ginny sighed. "Great."

She didn't exactly hate kids. She liked her nieces and nephews well enough, and her cousins' kids. And she'd love her own child, of course, she thought as she cradled her belly for a moment. More than love. She'd cherish her own child.

But random kids? Random, ill-behaved, screaming, rock-throwing and trespassing kids? Not a fan. Besides, what were they doing in *her* yard anyway? The house they'd run toward was bigger than this one, with a matching yard that looked manicured and maintained. She thought she remembered a swing set in the back too.

Her own childhood hadn't been so long ago that she couldn't remember how exciting it was to do the very things your parents didn't want you doing. The house next door might have a swing set and perfectly mown grass, but Ginny's backyard had a giant tree with a rope that probably had once been a tire swing hanging from it. It had a gentle slope in the back, just right for rolling down, and the creek that edged their property took a sharp bend away from that other house. Ginny's backyard had knee-high grass that would need to be mowed sooner rather than later and a big collection of leaves perfect for jumping in, if anyone bothered to rake them. The appeal of her backyard wasn't so strange after all. But they hadn't been in the back, they'd been in the front, and even so, she didn't want strange children carousing on her property, especially if they were prone to screaming and throwing stones at her house.

In the hall bath, she took some time to give Noodles more food and fresh water, though she didn't scoop the box. Sean had read an article about how cat poop could be toxic to fetuses, and while Ginny was more than happy to give up the chore to him, he had to be reminded to do it on a daily basis. It was already starting to stink, worse than usual since she was keeping the bathroom door closed.

The cat had calmed, at least a little, though she nipped at Ginny's fingertips when Ginny tried to scratch behind her ears. Not that Ginny blamed her, at least not too much. She'd be cranky too if she'd been locked up for two days. Then again, if Ginny peed all over everything, she wouldn't blame anyone who locked her in the bathroom.

"You stay," she told the cat who tried to sneak out after her. "Just another day or so, boo-boo, so I can get everything set up for you. So you don't pee on stuff."

The cat gave her a bland look that somehow also managed to convey how supremely insulting she found the insinuation that she ever voided her bladder inappropriately. Then she shook herself so the bell on her collar jingled. She turned and blatantly gave Ginny her back.

"Well," Ginny said as she got up, joints creaking, "don't look at me like that. You know you do."

In the kitchen, she found a surprise—a counter and floor sticky with juice dried into a gluey puddle. Her jaw clenched, and the giveaway throb in her temple told her that her blood pressure had spiked.

Ginny took a few calming breaths that did nothing to calm her. Muttering a few choice curse words made her feel better as she stood with her hands on her hips, staring down at the spill any reasonable adult would've cleaned up...but she knew what Sean would say if she confronted him about it. He was busy. Late for work. Didn't mean to do it.

"Whatever," she said aloud.

Getting onto her hands and knees to scrub the spill was far easier than getting up. In fact, for a few strained minutes Ginny was sure she wasn't going to get up at all—she tried to stand too fast and the world began to spin. She had to crawl to the table and push herself up on one of the chairs, where she let her head drop onto her hands. She breathed slowly in, slowly out. The dizziness abated, but then her stomach lurched and she barely made it to the sink in time to heave out a mouthful of bitter bile. Ginny clung to the sink for a minute, with the water running to wash away the sick. When she felt a little better, she bent to take a long, slow drink, letting the water fill and overflow her mouth to rinse it before she swallowed.

She lifted her head at the sound of childish laughter, but could see nothing through the window over the sink. By the time she managed to get herself to the back door to look out into the yard, they were gone. Maybe they'd run around to the front of the house again to collect what they'd left behind. Maybe she should go out and give them a scare, be the mean old lady from next door who shouted "get off my lawn!" and shook a broom. The one who gave out pennies and apples for trick or treat, instead of candy.

She laughed aloud at that thought and settled for opening the back door to lean out a little farther. Unlike the front of the house with its gorgeous porch, the back had only a set of cracked and crumbling concrete stairs and a crooked metal railing. The flagstone patio had been long overgrown with weeds, the stones themselves sunken into the dirt and covered with moss, but Sean had already announced plans for a big deck that would take advantage of the sloping yard and view of the creek, what there was of it. She'd only looked at it the first time they saw the house, and the summer had been dry enough to make it rather unimpressive. Enough to dip your toes in, maybe, no more than that. All she'd cared about was how far the water was from the house, and if the basement had a sump pump—which it did. Also, according to the realtor, that creek hadn't flooded in over twenty years, and only then after an unusual inland hurricane.

"You'll never need to worry about water from that creek," Bonnie had said. "But you have the sump pump downstairs in the basement, just in case."

Ginny took one step onto the concrete stairs before deciding she wasn't about to go tumbling down into the yard just to chase after a few noisy kids. If it kept up, she'd have to go over and talk to their parents, and "bitchy" wouldn't be the best introduction to the neighborhood. She listened for the sound of rustling leaves and the screaming laughter, but all she caught was the scamper of a squirrel in the tree and the sound of a truck in the street out front.

She lifted her face to the fresh autumn air. Took a long, deep sniff. This was her favorite time of year. Sean always said he didn't like fall, when the days got shorter. He said there was never enough time to do everything you wanted to in a day when the winter came, but Ginny'd always liked the sorts of things you did in the dark anyway.

Her cell phone rang from her pocket, the ringtone telling her without even looking that it was Sean. She debated for half a second about not answering—the call reminded her of the juice spill, which annoyed her all over again. But if she didn't answer, he'd call back or send a text, and if she didn't answer those… Well, she didn't want to find out what her husband would do if he couldn't get in touch with her at once. If there was any worse introduction to the neighbors than bitching to them about their wayward spawn, a police car, fire truck and/or ambulance screeching up to the front of the house would be it.

She went back into the kitchen as she thumbed the screen to answer the call. "Hi."

"Hey, it's me. What're you up to?"

"Nothing. What's up?"

She glanced at the clock. Nearly noon, and she hadn't yet eaten. That was no good, even if she had woken just past eleven. Typically, the nausea had passed and she was ravenous. The problem was, did they have any food? Pizza, after the heartburn of the night before, was completely unappealing. She tried to remember the few groceries she'd brought along and drew a blank. Baby brain, her sister had called it. The inability of a pregnant woman to retain information of current importance.

"…so do you need me to get you anything?" This was Sean, who'd been talking for a good few minutes while Ginny stared into the fridge and mentally checked off everything inside it as unappealing.

Her stomach rumbled. She reached for a string cheese and tore the plastic. Took a bite. "We're out of everything. As soon as I get something to eat and clean up the kitchen, I'll run to the store."

"Don't work too hard," Sean warned. "You should take it easy."

Maybe if he hadn't spilled the juice and left it for her to clean, she wouldn't have been so immediately irritated by his admonition, but as it was, Ginny had to count to five before saying, "All this stuff won't unpack itself, Sean."

"But, honey, you know you need to be careful."

"I'm careful."

"When we talked about you not going back to work, I didn't mean you had to take on everything at home, that's all."

She heard the concern in his voice, knew he was being sincere and not trying to be overbearing or patronizing. Just like she knew that if she didn't organize the house, it would not only take him forever to even get started, but once he did, he'd put everything in all the wrong places.

Ginny tried to keep her voice light. "What am I supposed to do, Sean? Sit around all day eating bonbons and watching the soaps? Do they even have soaps on anymore?"

Silence ticked between them. She'd probably hurt his feelings. She tried again. "I have to do *something*, okay? I'll go slow; I won't lift anything heavy. But if nothing else, I need to be able to get the kitchen organized so I can go to the store and buy us some food. We can't survive on takeout."

Well. *They* could. Their budget was another story. Even as she thought about the grocery store, she remembered the fast-food burger joint in the parking lot. She could just about murder a burger, fries and milkshake. The worst food always made her feel the best.

"You could get your studio set up," Sean said after another half a minute. "That's not too strenuous."

Ginny laughed softly. "Not physically, no. Mentally…"

"You're a great painter."

"Sure. Of walls." She looked around the kitchen. "Speaking of which…"

"No," Sean said. "No way. Don't even think about it."

"I could just stop at the paint store…look at colors."

"I told you we could go this weekend." Now he sounded as irritable as she felt, which in turn only made her all the more annoyed. "I don't want you lifting heavy paint cans, and besides, Ginny, I know you. You'll go to pick out colors and come back with all the stuff, and I'll find you up on a ladder when I get home."

She couldn't really argue with him, since that was true. Still, it didn't sit well with her to be lectured that way, even if he had good intentions. "You worry too much."

More silence. Now she'd hurt his feelings for sure. He always clammed up when he was upset, and she stifled a sigh. She settled for a halfhearted apology instead. "I'm sorry."

"I worry. Of course I do. Am I not allowed?"

She rubbed the space between her eyes with the tip of her finger. "Of course you are. But—"

"I'll stop and pick up something for dinner on the way home," he told her. "It's Friday. We can just relax tonight, and tomorrow we'll hit the grocery store, the mall, the paint store, whatever you want. Okay? I'll be there to do the heavy lifting, and you can pick out the colors. I can paint Sunday, before anything gets unpacked. Easier that way, we won't have to cover the furniture or anything."

When he put it that way, made it sound so reasonable she couldn't argue, there was no way for her to reply with anything but a murmured "fine."

It was far from fine, but as usual, Sean didn't appear to hear the frustration in her voice. "Good. What do you want for dinner?"

"If you're going to pick it up," Ginny said in a clipped tone, "you should just decide."

"Okay, good idea. I'll surprise you. I'll be home a little later than usual, then. Are you good for now, though? Should I have my mom—"

"No. If I need anything, I'll tell my sister to bring it over." She couldn't tell him enough times that she didn't need his mother to help her do the things she could do on her own, or with the help of her own mother or siblings. Or friends. Sean's mother meant well, but she was an easily flustered, flighty and sort of useless kind of woman with whom Ginny had never really connected. It was going to be bad enough that she had to tippy-toe around the mess in her house while she waited for her big, strong man to help her with tasks she could so easily accomplish twice as fast and perfectly well on her own. She didn't need a hovering, cooing mother-in-law there to second-guess and wring her hands fretfully over every choice.

"I gotta go. Lunch meeting. Paul's picking up Chinese."

"Well," Ginny said drily, because how could she stay angry in the face of Sean's clear delight, "I guess I know what you *won't* be bringing home for dinner then."

He laughed, and after a moment she did too. They exchanged I-love-yous, his coming first but hers at least sincere, and she disconnected. It wasn't so much that she wasn't angry anymore as it was that she was making a deliberate effort—a choice, if you will—to tuck that annoyance away and focus on the positives. She didn't have to cook dinner. That was a plus. Her husband loved her. Another plus. They'd just bought a new house, and she could be a lady of leisure in it. No more job. Didn't have to unpack. Bonus, bonus, bonus. Everything she listed eased her irritation into a smaller, tighter package, until she was able to get rid of it altogether.

That was until she wanted to drink some juice and it was all gone, and when her stomach growled because she still hadn't eaten, and when she wanted to at least have a peanut butter sandwich and there was no bread, only saltines, and she had to use a spoon because she couldn't find a knife to spread it with.

"Fuck this," Ginny said aloud. Then again, just because she could, as loud as she wanted, no neighbors with their ears pressed against the walls to hear her. Or at least she presumed so, unless she screamed at the top of her lungs or those kids were hanging around on the porch, nobody would hear her. "Fuck this with something hard and sandpapery."

It felt good to have let off just that little bit of steam, but when she had to resort to eating her saltine crackers over the sink because the table was too crowded to set down a plate, Ginny knew there was no way she could wait until the weekend to at least get some part of the kitchen unpacked and organized. She finished her lunch and dusted her hands free of crumbs, then lifted the lid of her laptop to turn the music on since, of course, she hadn't yet found either her iPod or the speakers that went with it.

She'd learned to be fastidious about shutting down her browsers, cleaning her cache, signing out of her email and social media sites. Sean had his own computer, but that never stopped him from "just hopping" on to hers if it was more accessible or faster or just plain nicer than his older model desktop—and the laptop almost always was all of those things. No matter how many times she'd tried to explain that the entirety of her job was contained on that laptop, that not only was all the information she gathered confidential—legally— but that when he went in and tried to fiddle around, closing tabs she'd left open on purpose or signing her out of whatever she'd been doing, he was potentially screwing her investigations. She'd thought about setting up a user account for him, except she knew he'd never use it because he only ever intended to do something "real quick" and would see no point. And now, she supposed, since she was no longer working, it wouldn't matter. He'd been on here this morning though; she could tell because though the laptop powered up to the login screen, the lid itself was slightly sticky. Like from juice. Frowning, she ran her fingers over the metal.

Sticky.

Not like someone had spilled juice right on it. More like someone with juice-coated fingers had touched it. She tried the keys, but they all seemed fine. The screen too, which was a good thing, because if Sean had not only spilled juice and left it for her to clean up, but also had gotten it all over her computer, paying hell would be less expensive than totaling up Ginny's expense report.

Moments ago she'd been on fire to get something done, but the inertia of pregnancy settled her more firmly into her chair as she opened iTunes and clicked Shuffle to play through her entire music library. She didn't *have* to check her email or anything else…but she was going to. Why not? Sean had said she was supposed to take it easy, and fooling around on the Internet, not even pretending it was for work, was as easy as it got.

She checked her messages, answered one from her mom, marked one from her brother as unread so she'd remember to answer it later, deleted a slew of fluffy kitten glitter angels and urban legend warning forwards from Sean's mom, who obviously never visited Snopes.com. Ginny logged in to Connex and skimmed the updates, wished an old college friend a happy birthday and thought about resisting the allure of starting up a word challenge game with some random strangers, but didn't. She loved and hated those games because despite her large and eclectic vocabulary, she sucked spectacularly at the sort of strategizing necessary to make the most of the double-word and letter tiles. This time, she started off with a seventy-six point word that made her whoop aloud with glee.

With half the day already gone, her stomach momentarily at least sated if not full and a house full of boxes silently cajoling her into opening them, Ginny moved to log out of everything but the music program. And then...the way it always happens, a song shuffled up. At the first note she froze, fingers on the trackpad twitching so the cursor flew around the screen.

This song.

Oh, this song.

She hadn't let herself listen to it in months, though there'd been a time when she'd played it over and over again on Repeat, barely a break in between. On her laptop, in the car, through her headphones as she exercised or shopped or sat on the beach and pretended to read. That song had been a punch in the gut every single time, and yet she'd done that to herself on purpose. She'd let it cut her open so she had to sew herself back up again, over and over and over, and gained some sort of sick satisfaction from it. Some measure of...relief, she guessed.

Some closure.

The problem with doing something you don't want anyone to know about is that when it all goes wrong and you sit at your kitchen table and put your face in your hands and cry because you're hurting even though you have no right to ache...you can't talk to anyone about your pain.

This pain was hers to carry alone, and that was all right. She deserved it to be that way. Heavy, with nobody to help her carry it. Sharp enough to cut.

She ought to have deleted the song from her music library entirely instead of just taking it off her playlists, but the fact was that even now, months later, a year later, maybe a fucking lifetime later, this song would always have the ability to cut her open. She would always find a way to sew herself up; that was who she was. It was what she did. So now when it started and she sat at her old table in its new place and stared all around her at the unfamiliar patterns of light streaming through the windows, all Ginny could do was sit and listen.

And when the song ended, though she knew she needed to get up and get to work, Ginny hit Replay.

Chapter Four

"It's cold in here." Sean set the paper bags of takeout food on the table. "Has it been this cold all day?"

Ginny didn't turn from the sink where she was washing her hands. She'd spent the rest of her day wiping out the cabinets and cleaning the counters and cupboards so that when Sean unpacked the dishes he could put them on clean shelves. She'd given the floor a good mopping too. For a house that hadn't been lived in for a long time, there'd been a lot of dust. Now she ran the water as hot as it would go, scrubbing under her nails to get them clean of grime.

"I don't know. I guess so." She shrugged, still not looking at him, still a little tender from her earlier self-indulgent, emotional binge. "It wasn't that cold out today, was it? Turn up the thermostat."

Sean disappeared into the hall and came back a few minutes later. "It was already set at seventy. That's warm enough. Doesn't feel like seventy in here."

Her hands clean, she crossed the kitchen to greet him with a kiss. Pushed all the residual emo down, way down, made it invisible. "Mmmm. Your nose is cold."

He laughed, but his brow remained creased. "Aren't you cold?"

"I was busy working today. Want a sweatshirt?"

"Yeah," he said, finally focusing on her face. When she tried to pull away, he kept her close with his hands on her hips. "Hey, you. I thought you were going to take it easy."

"Sean…"

His smile tipped the corners of his lips but left his eyes uncrinkled. "I just want you to be careful. That's all."

Ginny sighed but didn't try to pull away from him. "I know. And I was. I took my time. I didn't overdo anything. And look how nice the kitchen looks, you didn't even notice."

Sean didn't look around. He kissed her instead. "You could've let me help."

Enough. It was too much. With a sigh, Ginny pushed out of his embrace. "It was fine. Let's eat."

He didn't move from behind her as she went to the cupboard to pull out a couple of plates. "I don't like it when you walk away from me like that."

"Yeah, well, I don't like it when you lecture me." She turned. "I couldn't wait for you to get home to help me clean the kitchen, Sean. Okay? It had to be done, especially since there was juice all over the place. You think I should've just, what, walked over it all day? C'mon. That's crazy."

He tilted his head just a little. "What happened with the juice?"

"What do you mean, what happened with the juice?" She put the plates on the table, then went to the drawer for forks and knives. "You spilled it all over the floor."

"I didn't spill it."

She paused, silverware in hand. She'd expected excuses, not outright denial. "Well, I sure didn't."

"I didn't even come in here this morning, I was running late. Had to stop at the Green Bean for coffee." He glanced at the fridge, then her. "What juice?"

"Certainly not the juice I bought at the grocery store today, since I was forbidden from going." He gave her a blank look. Ginny sighed. She put the forks and knives on the table next to the plates, then her hands on her hips. "The orange juice we picked up from the convenience store. I woke up in the night and came downstairs and had some juice…"

Ginny trailed off, trying to remember if she'd put the juice back in the fridge. Sean smiled just a little. She frowned. "I didn't spill it. I'd remember that."

"Like you remembered leaving your purse on top of the car? Or when you put your phone in the fridge and the butter in your tote bag?"

"Totally different," Ginny said crossly.

Sean said nothing, but this time his smile did crinkle the corners of his eyes in that way she loved so much. It made her want to trace his eyebrows, so finely arched she sometimes teased him that he had a secret waxing habit. It made her want to pull him close and open his mouth with hers and taste him, and if nothing else, she was grateful for that sudden, trip-trapping beat of her heart. There'd been a long, long period of time when she feared she'd forgotten what it was like to want him that way.

"Maybe I left the juice on the counter," she conceded. "But I didn't spill it."

"It was probably Noodles."

Ginny frowned. "She doesn't jump up on the counters."

"So you say," Sean told her. "She just doesn't do it when we're around."

"She's locked in the bathroom," Ginny pointed out just as a familiar, plaintive cry meeped out from under the door to the pantry.

Sean went to the door and turned the knob. Noodles slipped out nonchalantly, wound around his legs a few times and then sat to lick her paw. Sean looked at Ginny, who frowned.

"I didn't let her out," Ginny said. "And I sure didn't lock her in there."

"Maybe she snuck in there while you were cleaning, and you closed the door." He opened it wider and looked inside.

The narrow space, about four feet wide but easily eight feet deep, had floor-to-ceiling wire shelving Ginny hadn't even touched. She peered around his shoulder at the inside, but aside from a few dust balls matching the dirt caught in Noodles's whiskers, she saw nothing. At least the cat hadn't crapped or peed on the floor. Sean was talking, but Ginny ignored him to push into the small room. She looked up, down, side to side. At last, admitting defeat, she turned.

"...just tired," Sean was saying. "You know she's an escape artist. Remember when she got behind the furnace and wouldn't come out?"

This was true. Since kittenhood, Noodles had found her way in and out of places where she wasn't supposed to be. But this time, it didn't feel right. Ginny had shut the bathroom door firmly behind her this morning, and she hadn't gone into the pantry at all...had she? She looked again. It was dirty. She hadn't cleaned it. But it was possible the door had been open, even the smallest amount, enough for a nimble and mischievous cat to slip inside and hide before Ginny pulled it shut during her kitchen makeover.

"Sure," Ginny said and bent to lift Noodles. She stroked the soft fur as the cat butted her head against Ginny's chin. She smelled musty, and the white patches of her calico coat were smudged with grime.

The cat let out a warning growl and struggled to get down, and Ginny let her go. Noodles ran out of the kitchen through the arched doorway into the dining room. Ginny thought about chasing her, but sighed, figuring she'd just open up the hall bathroom door until she could get the litter box into the basement. And, of course, convince the cat to use it there.

"I'm going to set up the TV and stuff so we can watch something. I think we're behind on a few episodes of *Runner*." Sean pulled her close to kiss the top of her head, and before she could protest, followed the cat into the dining room.

Ginny looked around the mess in the kitchen—dirty dishes, rice and beans left over from the Mexican takeout spilled on the table. So much for not having to take care of everything around the house, she thought and went to the doorway to peek through to the living room, where Sean had started pulling open one of the boxes and had his hands full of wires. So much for not unpacking anything until they painted the walls.

So much, she thought, for all of that.

Chapter Five

Ginny runs.

One foot in front of the other, never faltering, she runs and runs, dodging and weaving through a landscape that looks like something out of *The Terminator*. Scorched earth. Dark skies.

Her heart pounds, her fists pump, but this feeling is not harsh or bad. It's glorious, working her body this way, like she never does in her real life. Ginny runs. She jumps. She stretches her arms; she grows wings.

She flies.

And she falls.

* * * * *

Gasping, Ginny woke again coated in sweat, again with her throat burning from reflux. Mexican food. She'd stayed up too late trying to make sure she didn't go to bed with her stomach too full, and she'd even managed a long, relaxing bath, which was a pleasant surprise considering the water heater's sporadic offerings. Yet still her body rebelled against the spicy food and here she was, sitting straight up in bed with her eyes wide and the dream of all her bones breaking still vivid enough to keep her from wanting to go back to sleep.

"You okay?"

"Yeah. Go back to sleep."

"What time is it?" Sean pressed the button on his clock radio and bathed the room in cold white light. "Shit. Late."

It felt like she'd gone to bed hours ago, but it had only been about forty-five minutes since she'd slipped under the covers beside him. Ginny yawned with her hand over her mouth, hoping nothing else came up and out. The light from Sean's clock dimmed, then went out, but not before she caught a flash of something in the hall. Something bright, reflective. Something like eyes.

"Turn that light on," she whispered.

Sean had already fallen back to sleep, or mostly, and he let out a muffled "hmmph?"

Ginny rolled over to turn her bedside light on, which made Sean grunt and throw an arm over his face. "I saw something in the hallway."

Sean sat up at once. "What?"

Her pumped-up heartbeat wasn't helping the reflux. "I saw something like…eyes."

"The cat."

"No," she said. "Unless Noodles is now the size of a Great Dane and standing on her back legs on a box."

Sean got up and went to the half-open door and pulled it all the way to show the empty hallway. "Nothing there. Probably something reflecting off of something. Or the window at the end of the hall. Or the night-light, maybe it was that."

She knew he was right, of course he was. The quick, bright flash might've even been her imagination or a quirk of the shadows. It could've been some light coming in through the window, splitting shadows she hadn't yet come to know.

Sean's warm hand on her back reminded her of how chilly she was, and Ginny turned off her light to snuggle back under the blankets. The reflux was fading with every swallow, just like the memories of her dream. She rolled to face her husband, who was sprawled on his back with one arm flung over his head. His slow, even breaths soothed her. She put a hand on his belly, first on top of the soft T-shirt, then slipped her fingers underneath to lay them on the warm skin beneath. Then, lower.

"Oh yeah?" Sean sounded sleepy, but amused. Beneath her fingers, he responded.

"Yeah," Ginny said. "Definitely."

She moved to pull him on top of her, but Sean resisted, rolling her on top of him instead. "Don't want to squish…you."

The baby. He meant the baby. Ginny sighed, straddling him. It felt awkward now. Unwieldy, when she'd simply wanted him to move inside her, but now she had to do some sort of gymnastics routine to get things going. She kissed him when he pulled her down to his mouth, but all at once she couldn't stop thinking about the landscape from her dream and the inconsistent amount of hot water and the errands they needed to do the next day, which would come way too early the longer they were awake.

"No?" Sean murmured into her ear, his breath warm. He pushed a hand between them, but the position wasn't quite right and the pressure against her was more pain than pleasure. "I thought you wanted to."

But it was lost, and she didn't want to tell him so because she'd been the one to start this. It would be unfair to back out now. So she took him in her hand and shifted to slide him inside her, and she moved the way she knew he liked her to move.

And when it was over, in the dark, she listened to the sound of his breathing slow and deepen beside her. She listened to Noodles's rhythmic purring. She listened to the soft scritch-scratch of something inside the walls of her house, and it was that sound that finally soothed her into sleep.

Chapter Six

The exterminator was much cuter than he had any right to be. Over six feet tall, dark hair, ice-blue eyes. Dimples in both cheeks when he grinned, which he did the second Ginny opened the door and wished she'd put on something nicer than a pair of yoga pants and one of Sean's old college sweatshirts.

"Mrs. Murphy?"

Technically, she was not Mrs. Murphy since she'd kept her maiden name, but it was easier to nod than explain. She stepped aside to let him in. "Yeah. Come on in. Thanks for getting here so fast."

"No problem. It's my job, right?" He turned in a slow half circle, looking up at the ceiling before focusing on her. "I'm Danny."

He held out a hand for her to shake, surprising her. Ginny's hand was engulfed inside his fingers. "Ginny."

"You have mice?" Danny asked as he let go. He set down the tool bag in his other hand and put both hands on his hips. He wore a dark-blue coverall with his name on a patch over his heart. Big black boots.

"I think so." Ginny tried not to ogle his ass when he turned again to look up, but didn't manage very well. It was a pretty stellar butt, hard to ignore even in the baggy coveralls. "I've heard things in the walls and ceiling. We just moved in—"

"Yeah, I thought you must be new. I've been doing this neighborhood for a few years now, but this is the first time I've been called to this house."

Something in the way he said "doing this neighborhood" made her think of housewives clad in leopard-print robes, martini glasses in hand, standing on top of chairs and screaming while cartoon mice ran around them. "We've been in for not quite a week."

"Guy who owned this place before never had a contract with us, not even just the standard maintenance. Your husband signed you up for that, so I can take care of that for you today too. If you want." Danny's grin made Ginny think he'd take care of lots of things she wanted.

She shoved that idea away as absurd. She was easily at least ten years older than him, face bare of makeup and inadequately showered. And pregnant. And married, she reminded herself. Still, looking wasn't touching, and she admired Danny's dimples again.

"Did he?" she remembered to say. "What does that mean?"

"Means I'll come out every three months to treat your place for spiders, bees, wasps, check for termites. Whatever you need. And if you have any other problems, I'm your guy to take of that too. Like mice." Danny winked.

Ginny blinked.

Danny pulled a flashlight from the tool bag and shone it along the crown molding. "Termites usually aren't a problem in this neighborhood, but you get a lot of spiders and silverfish. Being so close to the creek, you can get millipedes and stuff in your basement too."

"But…you'll take care of all that. Right?"

Danny clicked off the flashlight and gave her another of those grins. Ginny wondered if he practiced them. "Yep. All of it. If you want to show me into the basement first, I can take care of you from the ground up."

Oh, I bet you could, Ginny thought. Top to toe too. She bit the inside of her cheek to keep a straight face and pointed down the hall. "Basement door's to the right there, in that alcove. I have a cat. You won't put anything down that's poisonous to animals, right?"

Danny shook his head. "No, ma'am."

Jesus. *Ma'am.* It should've made her feel old and possibly respected, but instead made her flash on a vision of herself in librarian glasses and a pencil skirt, with her hair in a bun and a ruler in her hand.

She pointed the way toward the basement, but didn't follow him down. She was in the middle of not only a cutthroat game of online Scrabble, but also finishing up some final files she needed to send in to the company she no longer worked for. The word game was winning her attention, because while the files were important, they were also the last link she had to her job. As soon as she turned them in, she'd have no more reasons to think of herself as a working woman.

She got so engrossed in trying to figure out where to use her Q, U and Z tiles for the best results that she didn't hear Danny until he appeared in the kitchen suddenly enough to make her scream. "You scared me," Ginny said unnecessarily, one hand on her heart. "God."

"Sorry." Danny looked serious. "I need to talk to you about your basement."

That sounded bad. Ginny hadn't actually been in the basement since they'd moved in. She remembered it as being unfinished and dry, the only thing she'd really cared about. Sean had talked about making it into a rumpus room, a place for a home theater. Sean talked about a lot of things.

"My husband has big plans for it," she said. "Aside from that, what's the problem?"

"It's your ductwork. Oh hey, puss." Danny crouched to offer a hand to Noodles, who sniffed it with disdain but let him pet her. He stroked the cat's fur, then looked up at Ginny. "It's all over the place down there."

"Umm...?" Ginny had no idea what ductwork was supposed to look like.

"Plenty of places for rodents and pests to hide. Basically, like a little superhighway for mice. But it's okay. I put some glue traps in there, and I'll add some bait traps in the attic. That's where you heard them, right? But you'll have to be sure your cat doesn't go up there."

Ginny looked at Noodles, busy licking her paw, and then at him. "She doesn't go in the attic. Hell, right now she doesn't even go into the basement. The door's always closed."

Danny frowned. "You'll have to check the glue traps, which, honestly, I don't love. Bait traps are more effective, for sure. But you do risk the chance then that they might not go all the way outside to..."

"Die?"

He nodded. For an exterminator, Danny seemed awfully delicate.

Ginny sighed. "So what, then? They'd get stuck inside the wall someplace and... rot?"

Danny nodded again. "But, you know, mice. They're small. It would only stink for a little while. If you had a squirrel or something bigger, a raccoon, say..."

"Jesus," Ginny muttered. "Do you think we might?"

"I won't know until I go up and check. This close to the creek, you might get rats." Danny made a pow-pow gesture with his fingers. "But it's probably just mice. You heard noises in the walls?"

"And ceiling. Yeah." For a moment she thought about mentioning the shape she thought she'd seen that first night here. The eyes. "Rats...they can get pretty big?"

Danny smiled. "Sure. Huge, some of them. When I was working in the city, I'm not even kidding you, I once saw a rat that was bigger than a Chihuahua."

"Jesus."

"Yeah." Danny nodded, eyes wide and serious for a moment before the grin was back. "But around here? Nah. You'll get field mice and squirrels, sure. Sometimes a raccoon. Sometimes bats. But even if you do get rats, they're probably not that big."

Not Great Dane size anyway. That was only in the movies. Ginny frowned. "But you'll put out enough poison to take care of whatever it might be?"

"Yep. If you'll show me the attic, I can get up there and take a look around. Do I need a ladder?"

"No. There's a pulldown."

Upstairs, she showed him the door in the ceiling and he pulled the cord, dropping the stairs. Ginny had left Sean to inspect the attic, but watching Danny's feet disappear into her ceiling, she decided to follow him. She stayed on the stairs, and stuck only her head through the hole. There was no floor up there, just a few boards placed across the beams, and the steeply pitched roof made it impossible for anyone but a child—or a super tiny adult—to stand upright except in the center.

"I thought it would be bigger," Ginny said. "Like the size of the house."

"You have those gables and dormer things." Danny shone his flashlight into the corners, but didn't move more than a step or two from the hole in the floor. The beams creaked under his boots. "Crawl spaces, right?"

"Oh. Yeah. But still…" Ginny gestured, though he wasn't looking, "…I guess this isn't what I was expecting."

He grinned at her over his shoulder. "Could be worse, right? You could've come up here and found something really creepy."

"Yeah, like Gary Busey."

Danny obviously missed the reference to the 80s horror classic *Hider in the House*. Busey had played a crazy guy who built a secret room in Mimi Rogers's attic, then stalked her. Ginny had meant it as a joke, and if her brother, Billy, were here he'd have laughed. He'd watched that movie with her so many times they could both quote the dialogue back and forth. Ginny thought briefly of explaining, but couldn't muster the effort. Danny shone his light around the room, pausing to spotlight a round vent at one end. Then one on the other side, identical except for the mesh covering.

"There's part of your problem. That vent should have the same protection on it. That's how stuff can get in."

Ginny had a hard time believing mice would climb up the side of the house and in through a vent, but she supposed squirrels could. Or bats. She grimaced. A bat had flown into her college apartment once. All she could remember was some drunken frat boy her roommate was screwing going after it with a tennis racket.

"Can you fix that?"

Danny shook his head and pointed the light at the beams under his feet. "Sorry. I can only spray for bugs and put down bait traps. But I'll do that up here. I see some droppings, not a huge amount, looks like mice. Kinda old, but, still, definitely some evidence that you have something going on. I'll put some glue traps in here too, along with the bait, okay?"

"Sure. Yes. Perfect, thanks." Ginny backed down the rickety stairs carefully.

Danny was there for about another hour, during which time Ginny managed a crushing win in her word game, but also completed all her final files and sent them off to where they needed to go. All done. All gone. She was officially unemployed for the first time since she was fifteen years old.

When he came in one more time, Danny found her at the kitchen table, staring at her laptop's blank screen. A tiny bouncing icon alerted her to her sister Peg's instant message, but Ginny was ignoring it for now. She had her hands folded in front of her, not touching the keyboard or even the mouse she used because the laptop's small trackpad drove her crazy.

"Ma'am?"

Ginny turned. "Finished?"

"I put the traps out. I found a few places out here your husband will want to check out too. Your house has a brick front, but the rest is aluminum siding. The places in the corners of the house where the siding comes together, those are open on the bottom. Sometimes they're capped, but the caps fall off. Rodents climb up in there, that's how they get in the walls. Just have him shove some steel wool up there. That should solve it."

Ginny pushed her chair back with a long screech on the linoleum. "Thanks."

"You writing a book or something?"

Taken aback, she looked at the laptop. "Huh? Oh. No. I'm not a writer."

"Oh. So you're the painter?"

This took her even more aback, literally, as she stepped back. Her calves hit the chair. "What?"

"The easel and stuff, I saw it upstairs when I was putting some traps in your crawl space. You sure your cat won't get into them, right?" Danny, bless his pretty face, looked worried. "Even if she gets into the crawl space, she shouldn't be able to get into the bait, but…"

"It'll be fine." Ginny wasn't sure how to feel about him not only helping himself to her crawl space, which, honestly, was what he was there to do, but also noticing her… stuff.

"My girlfriend took a couple art classes this summer. She's really into watercolors. What do you paint?"

"Nothing," Ginny said too fast. "Well. Nothing lately."

"Did you do the ones in the basement?"

This stunned her so much she sat down. "What?"

"There were a bunch of canvases in the basement. Mostly flowers and stuff, big flowers." Danny demonstrated by holding his hands apart, shoulder width.

"Yes," Ginny said after a moment. "Yes. Those are mine."

"They're pretty good. You ever think about showing them in a gallery or something?"

"No. They were just for fun."

Danny nodded like this made total sense, then paused to look at her more solemnly. "So…it's not fun for you anymore, or…?"

"I just haven't had time. That's all. I'll get back to it," Ginny told him, but from his look she thought he didn't believe her, any more than she did herself.

As soon as she closed the front door behind him, cutting off his cheerful reminder that he'd be back in three months to "squirt for bugs," Ginny went to the basement door. Noodles was suddenly at her feet, winding around her ankles and meowing plaintively—the cat had put on too much weight when they let her eat at her leisure, and she was reminding Ginny it was overdue time for her to be fed now. Ginny bent to pick her up and scratch her under the chin, then tossed her gently toward the kitchen and opened the basement door to squeeze through it. Noodles managed to run after her anyway, barely missing getting the tip of her tail caught. Bell collar jingling, she rocketed down the stairs in front of Ginny, who at least wanted to wait until she'd turned on the light.

She didn't have to go far to see the paintings. Someone had stacked them up against the wall closest to the foot of the basement stairs. Carelessly, without so much as a single sheet of bubble wrap or anything between them to protect the canvases from getting scratched. The movers must've done it, she thought, since she surely wouldn't have packed them that way. She hadn't packed them at all.

For a moment, Ginny saw herself crossing the short distance and flipping through those paintings, which represented not only hours of her time, but an entire rainbow of memories in every single shade of gray. She saw it so clearly—how her hands would shift and move them, separating them into chronological order or by color scheme or theme. She closed her eyes and saw every single painting she'd ever done that had been worth saving.

The problem was, just like she hadn't packed them, Ginny hadn't saved them, either.

Chapter Seven

Don't forget, I have class tonight.

Sean had sent the text that morning, but though once not so long ago Ginny'd carried her phone around with her like it was attached by an umbilical cord, she'd gotten out of the habit now that she wasn't working and also home full time, where she could be reached on the landline. She'd have remembered about his class when six o'clock arrived and he didn't come through the door, but it was good he'd reminded her. She could have a dinner of leftovers while she watched TV and tried to ignore the mess in the living room. At least the boxes made it easy for her to find a place to put her plate.

Pasta with roasted red peppers, hearts of palm and a sprinkling of olive oil and grated parmesan cheese. That was her dinner, along with a couple of crusty French rolls. Her craving for a nice glass of red wine was like a physical punch, but Ginny didn't even give the bottle a longing glance. Her previous doctor had told her a glass of wine a day was perfectly fine; this time around, she hadn't asked the ob-gyn's opinion. Better to just avoid it, the way she avoided caffeine and secondhand smoke, and baths that were too hot or showers that were too cold, artificial sweeteners and caustic chemicals. She cleaned with organic products or old home remedies like vinegar and baking soda. She looked both ways at least twice before crossing the street.

"Because I'm not taking any chances," Ginny told the cat, who couldn't be bothered to even glance her way. "Nope. Not a single one."

Her eyes had been bigger than her stomach, no small feat these days. With only half her dinner finished, Ginny took her plate to the kitchen and set it on the counter, intending to scrape it before putting it in the dishwasher, but discovering instead that once again, Sean had taken out the trash without replacing the garbage bag.

A quick search of the cupboard beneath the sink turned up no box of trash bags, and she'd already learned from sad experience that this older-model dishwasher couldn't handle dishes that weren't already mostly clean. But Ginny, mindful that anger raised her blood pressure, didn't fume. Instead, she took her daily dose of vitamins, minerals, anti-nausea remedies and a potent cocktail of homeopathic tinctures that were supposed to guarantee her optimum health and that of her unborn child. Some went down easier than others, no doubt about that, but she forced herself to take each pill or liquid slowly.

She wasn't taking any chances.

Noodles's bell collar jingled, and Ginny turned to greet that cat. "What do you think, Noodles? Should I have that…chocolate cake… Noodles?"

Ginny scanned the doorway to the hall, then the arched one leading to the dining room, expecting to see the cat sitting there, giving her the normal bored look. She'd heard the collar, the jingle of bells she suspected Noodles, should she ever find a voice, would disdain in favor of a collar with spikes. Yet…no cat.

"Noodles?"

Slowly, Ginny moved toward the hall, ears cocked for any sound of the bell. There it was, but far away and faint now. Upstairs. Ginny heard the sound of something rattling against the still-bare wooden floors up there, and the soft patter of paws. She climbed the stairs, one at a time, her hand there to pull her along like she was eighty years old and a hundred pounds overweight, which was sort of how she felt most of the time. At the top, she psh-pshed for the cat and listened again for the sound of the bell.

Nothing.

She called the cat's name again, but unlike a dog or even a cat with a pleasant personality, Noodles had never come when called. The sound of a can of food opening would bring her running as fast as her legs could carry her too-tubby body, but to the sound of her own name she was deliberately deaf.

From the room Sean liked to call the office but Ginny thought of as the library came another faint jingle and the rattle of something on the wood floor. Ginny peeked in the doorway, but the cat was gone. The room was warm, though—that was a bonus. Inside it on the floor, she found what the cat had been playing with. Bending to pick it up made her head spin a little, dammit, so she made sure to stand very, very carefully.

It was a small wooden figure. A lady. The paint had worn off, but her carved features were pretty. She wore forties fashion, an animal stole and peplum jacket. She was the size of Ginny's pinky and matched the ones she'd found that first day in the telephone table drawer. Ginny looked her over. The wood was warm in her palm.

This room had a fireplace that matched the one in the parlor below it, though like the one in the dining room, it had been blocked off, unusable. It also had a set of beautiful, floor-to-ceiling built-in bookcases that went from the fireplace to the opposite wall and around the corner. Gorgeous crown molding. On the other side of the fireplace was a dormer window like the one in her bedroom, but much larger. Inside the dormer area, one of those crawl-space doors.

Her easel leaned against the wall in that dormer, surrounded by the boxes of her painting supplies. She hadn't put it there. Like the paintings in the basement, Ginny hadn't even packed any of this stuff. The last she'd seen it all was in their garage in the townhouse after not even looking at it for months before that.

Ginny rolled the figure in her palms, back and forth. Whoever had carved it was an artist, of sorts. How long had it taken him to create this tiny figure? To carve the details in the fox stole, the dress, the expression on the woman's face that, the longer Ginny looked at it, seemed to be a smirk? Had he loved this work, or had he spent the time on it because it was better than facing something else?

Ginny put the figure on one of the shelves. "Noodles?"

Stricken by the thought that the cat had somehow wormed her way into the crawl space and found the bait Ginny had promised exterminator Danny she'd keep her away from, Ginny moved toward the small door. It was a little ajar, cold air blowing in around the edges. Ginny swore she heard Noodles's bell jingling. With a low cry, she tugged the door open to find…

Nothing.

Well, not totally nothing. She found some mouse turds and a few of those glue traps, along with a black bait box. Tattered pink insulation. Some weathered cardboard boxes she didn't recognize and refused to open. Oh, and a shit ton of frigid air wafting up from the open spaces under the eaves.

"Shit." If the cat got in there, she could easily get hurt. Ginny shoved the door closed extra tight and made a mental note to ask Sean about weather stripping around the door. Maybe even putting a lock on it to make sure it didn't blow open again.

In the kitchen, she found a smug-looking Noodles on top of the kitchen table and shooed her off, then thought better of it and picked up the protesting cat to give her a snuggle. Noodles might be a bit of a bitch, but they'd had her since she was a kitten.

"If something happened to you…" Ginny kissed the cat's head, ignoring for a minute the way Noodles squirmed. At least until the cat made that low, warning growl that meant she was going to bite. Then Ginny put her down fast.

Affection turned to annoyance quickly enough when she went to put her plate in the dishwasher, though. The cat had helped herself to all of Ginny's leftovers, even licking the plate clean in wide stripes. Great. Now she not only would pee on stuff they left lying around, she'd probably puke too. And in just the right spot for Ginny to find it with her bare feet in the middle of the night.

"Brat cat," Ginny said aloud, but Noodles had once more disappeared.

Chapter Eight

Ginny had fallen in love three and a half times in her life. Well, two half times, so maybe that counted as one whole time? So. Four times. She'd fallen in love four times, with five different men, one of whom she'd married.

As soon as she saw the crimson-upholstered fainting couch with carved wooden legs and accents of gold thread, she knew she had to have it. She'd never wanted anything so much at first glance, not ever.

Well. Maybe once before, but that had been a man and not a piece of furniture.

This was the first time an inanimate object had moved her to such instant, almost-feral desire. She touched it with reverent fingers, testing the upholstery. It was old, not in the best shape. It didn't even look comfortable, really, unless maybe you were a Victorian lady used to corsets and sitting stiffly upright. It was definitely not the sort of couch you were supposed to loll upon.

"I want it," she said.

Sean turned from where he'd been looking at a display of old Looney Tunes glasses in a locked cabinet. "Hey, look. Like the ones we found in the house. Jesus, they're like five bucks apiece. My mom had the whole set of these. I bet we could get them from her."

"Good luck with that." Sean's mom had lots of things tucked away in her cupboards, on shelves, stored in boxes. She wasn't apt to give anything up, though she was fond of making lists about who was going to get what when she inevitably passed away. Which, according to his mother, could be at any moment.

Ignoring the sign that said *Please Do NOT Sit*, Ginny lowered herself onto the couch, testing the firmness. The legs didn't wobble. A puff of dust came out, tickling her nose. She looked at him. "I want it."

Sean's mouth pursed. "That? Why?"

"It's perfect," Ginny said simply. There was no other answer. This couch was perfect, she wanted it. It didn't matter the cost or how they were supposed to get it home.

Sean scratched his head and cupped the back of his neck with a hand while he gave her a squint-eyed look. "Where would you put it?"

"The library." Already she could imagine just how she'd angle it in front of the bookshelves. The pendent lamp from the living room, an end table, a warm and cozy throw. She stroked a hand over the upholstery. "It'll be my Christmas present."

Her husband held out a hand to help her up. He pulled her into his arms, held her close and nuzzled her nose before kissing her lightly. "It's old. Since when do you like old furniture?"

"Newsflash," she said. "We live in an old house now. The kind that antiques look good in. And it's good for the environment. You know. Reduce, reuse, recycle and all that."

Sean looked dubious. "Okay. If you really want it."

"I do. I want it. It's so gorgeous, and it will be perfect in the library." She ran a hand over the fabric again.

* * * * *

"I thought you were going to use it as a studio," he said in the car after they'd made arrangements for the couch to be delivered.

Ginny'd been staring out the window, thinking about telling him she wanted to stop someplace for an early dinner even though she'd just blown their budget, and something in his tone of voice kept her looking through the glass instead of at his face. "I never said that."

"I thought, when we looked at the house, you said what great light that room had, how it would make a great place to paint."

"I don't remember saying that."

"I do," Sean said.

Ginny looked at him. "It's not like I couldn't paint in a library, if I wanted to. What difference does it make what we call it? It's got all those bookshelves, it seems like a library. There's room for a desk in there for you, if you want to make it an office, which is what I thought you wanted it to be."

"No. The little room is going to be the office."

She distinctly remembered him calling the room with the bookshelves the office. She supposed it was too late to convince him to take her out for dinner too, since they were pulling up the street to the house. Sean parked, then peered upward through the windshield.

"Wish we had a garage." He pointed, frowning. "Wonder why he never rebuilt it after the fire."

Ginny also looked through the glass toward the empty space where Sean's coveted garage had once stood. It was strange to see a house bare of a garage in a suburban neighborhood like this. Every other house on the block had one. Even their townhouse, tiny as it was, had had one. Here there was plenty of room in the driveway for at least four cars, but the trip from the car to the house wasn't even sheltered by a breezeway. It was on the ten-year plan, along with landscaping and finishing the basement.

"Who knows. Money, probably. Isn't everything always about money?"

"Not everything," her husband said.

Ginny got out of the car. She went to the house and straight to the fridge to get a snack. She'd been looking forward to something ooey-gooey—cheese sticks or chili fries, something like that. Instead, she had a choice of organic yogurt and granola or a handful of almonds. Totally not satisfactory. She found some ice cream in the freezer, contemplated a bowl, decided to eat it straight from the carton. Because she was only going to have a bite or two...right?

Sean must've had the same idea, because the carton was almost empty. Ginny frowned but scraped the cardboard sides with her spoon. So, she'd have to finish all of it; that was no big deal. She had the spoon in her mouth when Sean came into the kitchen behind her.

"What's for dinner?"

Ginny, metal still tucked against her tongue, looked at him for a long half a minute before she slowly removed the spoon. "I don't know. What *is* for dinner?"

"I don't know." Sean opened the fridge. Looked inside. Looked at her. Closed the fridge. "Are you going to make something or...?"

"There's plenty of lunchmeat and deli rolls in there. Macaroni salad." Ginny scraped the last bit of ice cream and licked the spoon clean, then went to the trash to dump the carton. Through the back door, she caught a glimpse of two red coats. Blond hair. Those kids from next door were in her yard again.

"I thought you'd cook something."

"Did you?" she said absently, trying to see exactly what the kids were doing.

Sean was quiet for another minute. "No."

"Have a sandwich," Ginny told him and went out the back door.

"Where are you going?"

"I'm going to chase those kids out of our yard," she told him and let the door close behind her.

In the side yard she found a soft-foam football on the grass and a battered wooden wagon half-hidden in the leaves. No kids, though. They must've ducked through the hedge. The yard itself was a mess even without the abandoned toys. Their yard had only the two big trees, but both had completely shed their leaves and none of them had blown away. The grass was also ankle high, brown and dead instead of lush and green, but overgrown just the same. Ginny scuffed through the piles made by the wind shoving the leaves against the hedge and the house, kicking her feet the way she had as a kid.

This was the side of the house with windows into the basement, and lined up along the window well, Ginny found a set of carved wooden figures. Like the lady in the fur stole, the figures wore clothes of past fashions, and their sizes ranged from the length of her pinky to match the rest of her fingers too. The weather had worn some of these harder than the ones she'd already found. How long had they been here? Ginny bent as best she could to peek into the window, but could see only dirty glass until she reached to rub a circle clean. Then, still nothing. She stood without moving the figures, wondering what sort of game the kids next door had been playing.

In the yard under the big tree, she tugged the rope that had once been a tire swing. It needed to come down. The tree itself needed a good pruning. And the leaves… Oh God. All the leaves.

Ginny looked toward the house. Sean had promised her he'd take care of the yard. Just like inside the house, he'd made her promise not to unpack the boxes, not to move the furniture, not to exert herself with all the tasks he was going to do. Yes, they'd had a lot of rain that made it hard to work outside. Yes, he worked long hours and had the responsibilities of school too. But he'd not only promised, he'd insisted that she promise him she wouldn't rake or mow or put stuff away. And now what? They were living out of boxes, never able to find anything when they needed it. The yard was a trash heap.

She would not be angry.

She would not lose her temper.

She would not say things that could not be taken back.

Instead, she went to the shed and found a rake and the box of garbage bags she'd bought especially for the leaves. She took them into the yard and started raking. It would be dark soon, and her hands were cold, but so far Sean hadn't bothered to come out and see what she was doing, so she was going to keep doing it. It wasn't hard work, not even for a pregnant lady. Holding the bag open while she put the leaves inside and fought the frigid wind that had sprung up proved to be a lot harder. Frustrated, she looked toward the house, the windows in the parlor glowing faintly golden. Upstairs, the light in the master bedroom was on, and also the one in the hall, which touched the windows in the library—it *was* a library, she thought fiercely.

Ginny's nose had begun to run with clear snot she didn't want to wipe with her bare hands. She dug in her pocket for a tissue and found only a few crumpled receipts. The dark had truly fallen by this time, and the temperature had dropped. She had no mittens or scarf, and the wind bit at her. This suddenly seemed a fool's task. She'd half filled one bag.

Leaning on the rake, Ginny looked toward the house. Sean stood in the library, silhouetted in the window. How long had he been watching? Ginny waved, certain it was too dark now for him to see her, but after a moment he returned the gesture.

Screw this, she thought. Tomorrow she'd remind him again about the yard and insist he let her help him, even if was just to hold the bag open for him. They'd halve the job and would be spending time together. Two birds, one stone, all that.

She did want to put the rest of this small pile into the bag, though, if only so the wind wouldn't scatter the leaves she'd already taken the time to gather. Ginny leaned the rake against a tree and bent to scoop the leaves, shoving them into the bag as fast as she could with numbed fingers. Her teeth chattered, more snot ran, and she was just about to give it up entirely when her fingers sank into something soft.

The leaves had been crunchy, rustling, brittle, but whatever this was clutched and clung to her fingers. Ginny yanked her hand back, shaking it, but it was coated in… something. She screamed and scraped her hand along the grass. When she turned, her shadow turned with her, no longer blocking the light. She didn't have a clear view of what she'd just grabbed, but it was clear enough.

Temperatures were cold, but not yet freezing. The past few weeks had seen rain, a lot of it. The squirrel into which she'd just sunk her fingers was both mushy and saturated, its belly bloated. It stunk. Its eyes were gone, she could see that much, and its little mouth gaped with teeth that were too long. Ginny backpedaled with her hands out in front of her, her shriek locked in her throat.

In the kitchen, Sean sat at the table with a towering Dagwood sandwich in front of him. She pushed past him to the sink, where she ran the hot water aggressively and scrubbed at her hands. More soap. More scrubbing. *Oh God, so gross. So gross.*

"What the hell are you doing?"

"I was bagging up leaves, and guess what I found. A dead squirrel. A rotten dead squirrel. And guess what I found it with, Sean? My hands!" She shuddered, repulsed, but laughed too at the absurdity of it. "It must've gotten into the bait and gone outside to die, just like the exterminator said."

Sean crossed to the sink to grab her hands. "What? Jesus Christ, Ginny, what the hell were you thinking? Are you okay?"

"I didn't puke, so yes, I guess so." She shuddered again, but the disgust was fading as the hot water and soap washed her clean. She tried to tug her hands from Sean's grip, but he held her tight.

"Get something," he said.

"Something like what?"

"Hand sanitizer. Alcohol. Something! No, I'll get it." Incredibly, he grabbed a bottle of whiskey from the lower cabinet and spun the lid.

Ginny stared. "What are you going to do with that? Light my hands on fire?"

Sean looked at the bottle, sighed, put the cap back on. "Maybe I should drink it."

"Sean…" Ginny turned off the water and dried her hands on a towel. In the yard, knuckle deep in rotting squirrel, she'd screamed. Here in the bright kitchen with her hands clean, she didn't want him to keep fretting. "It's not that big a deal. Really. It was gross and startling, but that's all."

"You shouldn't have been out there at all. Raking leaves? In the dark?"

"I didn't start when it was dark," she pointed out. "And the leaves needed raking. It's not a big deal."

Except that it sort of was.

"I thought I heard you go upstairs," Sean muttered. "I didn't know you were still out there, I'd have come out and helped you."

Ginny pulled a bottle of hand lotion from the cupboard and rubbed it carefully into her skin. "What do you mean, you didn't know I was out there? You saw me go out the back door."

"I thought maybe you came in the front."

"You thought I came in the front door," Ginny said. "How on earth could you think I came in the front door? You saw me from the window upstairs."

"I didn't see you." Sean went back to the table and scraped his chair back to sit again in front of the sandwich.

Ginny's fingers curled so tight into her palm her fingernails dented the skin. Not quite painful—not yet. But the potential was there. "I saw you. In the window upstairs. I waved. You waved."

"I was in here making myself something to eat since you weren't cooking dinner."

Oh. No. He. Didn't.

"Yeah well, I was outside raking the leaves since you weren't doing *that*." She eyed the table. "I notice you didn't make *me* a sandwich."

"How was I supposed to know you wanted one? You were upstairs. I figured you were pissed off at me, so you went upstairs to…you know. Be pissed."

Incredulity kept her speechless for a minute as her mouth worked without finding words. And, ah yes, there was the bright sting of pain in her palms. Ginny focused, eased her grip. "Sean. Seriously? You are kidding, right?"

He looked at her, eyes narrowed. She couldn't tell if he was challenging her or genuinely oblivious. "No."

"I saw you," Ginny said. "Upstairs. In the window."

"I wasn't up there." He bit into the sandwich, spoke around a mouthful of sloppy lettuce and mayo. "You want some of mine?"

She didn't want any of his. She'd starve before she ate any piece of that dripping mess. Plunging her hands into a dead and bloated squirrel hadn't made her vomit, but that sandwich might.

In times past, she'd have raged at him until he turned his back and gave her the silent treatment, but this was supposed to be a fresh start. Right? All of this, everything new and fresh and different than it had been before. Every fucking piece of it.

Sean cut off a piece of the sandwich and held it aloft, ignoring the slide of tomato seeds and mayonnaise over his hand. "Here. It's good. Eat some."

Ginny sat at the table across from him. "Yes, okay," she said. "Thanks."

Chapter Nine

This would be the baby's room.

Ginny had never wanted to know the gender of her child in advance. So few surprises in life were truly wonderful, and she'd always imagined the moment of birth to be the perfect time to discover if she was the mother of a daughter or a son. Because of her previous problems, this time around she'd been subjected to every possible test and what felt like an insane number of ultrasounds. You could get them in 3-D now, a scarily vivid image of your unborn child's face presented to you on a piece of photo paper or on disc to upload to the Internet and show off to all your friends. It was hard to make sure the techs didn't slip up and give away the baby's sex, even though most of them were genuinely eager to help keep the secret. Ginny thought Sean knew, though. She'd heard him murmuring to the tech once when she was getting dressed. Something about "if you could make a guess."

She thought it was a boy.

That didn't mean she was decorating this room in any shade of blue, though. Both her sister Peg and sister-in-law, Jeannie, had done up their nurseries in pastels, with babycentric designs, and then complained when the kids got older and the rooms needed to be redecorated. Ginny had decided to go with a fun jungle theme, using vinyl stickers against brightly painted walls. The stickers could be pulled off later and replaced. The bedding could be changed as a child of either gender graduated from a crib to a bed, and the colors she'd chosen would work for even an older child. Two walls lime green, two a rich chocolate brown. This room also had a dormer. She envisioned benches with cushions, a cozy place to read and play. Maybe some curtains to make a cave or castle, depending on the kid's personality.

For now, it needed a thorough cleaning and all of the fixtures and trim taped off. Sean had forbidden her from doing any painting, but he hadn't been able to argue too strenuously against her taping things. At least so long as she promised not to get up on a ladder.

This pregnancy had been hard on her physically, but mentally Ginny had taught herself to feel better than she ever had. Less worried, for one thing. The more she'd learned about the possibilities of mental and physical defects, the less frightening having a child with special needs seemed.

For Sean, on the other hand, the more he knew, the more uneasy he became. The facts and statistics she devoured unsettled him. Sean didn't think he could balance a checkbook or clean a strange stain off a shirt or organize a surprise weekend away, and in the fourteen years they'd been married, Ginny'd never been able to convince him otherwise. There was no way she could convince him he could be a good father to a baby with problems. All she could do was not take chances. Reassure him. Let him fuss over her. Ginny had learned not to tell him what she discovered from her online research.

She'd learned not to tell him lots of things.

With her music playing, this time from a carefully chosen playlist that contained nothing to sneak-attack her emotions, Ginny gathered her bucket of supplies, all organic or nonchemical based because Sean had insisted he didn't want her breathing in toxic fumes. They'd had a cleaning service come through the house before they moved in, but she hadn't been particularly impressed with the job they'd done. It was bad enough that more of the former owner's belongings had been left behind than they'd wanted, but knowing the dust balls and finger smudges were someone else's grime…gross.

Sean's mom, Barb, had offered to come over and help, but that would've been more of a nightmare than trying to get water stains out of a tub without using bleach. Besides, Ginny had been looking forward to cleaning. Maybe it was all that time spent with Gran, who'd not only had a "hired woman" for most of her life but also spent more hours on her knees scrubbing the floors than she ever had in church.

Ginny's mom had been a terrible housekeeper, in direct response to her upbringing. Just like she'd never host a party, Christmas or otherwise, Ginny's mother also had never done more than the bare minimum when it came to keeping them from living in squalor. Beds unmade, dishes in the sink, dust everywhere—that was Ginny's house growing up. It wasn't exactly like living in the pigsty Gran called it, but it wasn't quite as tidy as most of her friends' houses either, with moms who stayed home and presumably spent their days making use of old toothbrushes to keep their grout from going gray.

"I have better things to do with my time," Ginny's mom always said, and as a working woman herself, Ginny had often found that to be true. The kind of clean Gran had

demanded took a lot of time and/or money to maintain, and though Ginny always made sure to make the bed in the morning and put dirty dishes in the dishwasher, she also sometimes left her laundry in the basket for days on end before folding it and putting it away.

Now, of course, she wasn't working and had nothing but time, and the combined clutter of a just-moved-into house with her being home all the time to actually see the mess…well, she understood now what her gran had meant when her fingers itched to "get to fixing things."

This room wasn't in terrible shape. Mostly it bore the touches of time and disuse. Cobwebs in the corners of the ceiling—she got those down easily enough with a broom. Something that looked like shavings in a couple of the corners, possibly from the insects Danny was supposed to have taken care of. She swept the room quickly, then drew a bucket of hot water from the bathroom and mopped the wood floor. They hadn't yet shopped for furniture, though she'd gone through a couple catalogs and picked out what she wanted. They'd need a carpet in here too, or maybe a couple fun throw rugs.

She looked around the room, envisioning it painted and furnished. There in the corner, a rocking chair. Her sister swore by a glider, but Ginny had seen a bent-cane rocker at one of the Amish markets a few summers ago. When she pictured herself with a baby in her arms, it was always in that chair. The crib could go here, she thought, away from the windows and the drafty cubbyhole door. The dresser, there. A bookcase in that corner, because her child would certainly be a reader. And in the closet…

"Ugh." She stopped, nose wrinkling when she opened up the double wooden doors. The dust in there was palpable, along with the acrid tang of mouse droppings. Old mouse shit was still shit, she thought with a grimace, and grabbed the broom.

In the closet, when it was clean, she planned to install a set of wire shelves and hangers to store toys and clothes. Like most of the others in the house, including hers, the one in this room was deep but narrow. Not really a walk-in. Almost like an afterthought. This one had nothing but a single bar running from front to back and a shallow wooden shelf above it. Lots of functional space made useless by that old-fashioned setup. She'd make it better.

For now, Ginny concentrated on sweeping out the dust bunnies and mouse poop and dead beetle shells. It was a good thing Barb wasn't here to help her out. Sean's mom would've screamed and tossed up her hands at even the hint of a little poop, no matter how ancient. Ginny laughed a little guiltily at the image. Barb meant well; it wasn't her fault Ginny found her mother-in-law as useless as the shelf in this closet.

Her broom bumped that shelf as she worked, rattling the wood on the pegs holding it up. As it turned out, the shelf wasn't one long piece of wood, but three or four foot-long sections. She figured that out when she bumped it again and only part of it lifted, sending down a drift of more dust and pellets.

Gross.

She'd promised Sean she wouldn't exert herself or climb on ladders or lift heavy paint cans, but there was no way she could leave the filth. From downstairs, she brought the pantry step stool and set it up. That was only two steps; surely he wouldn't get on her case about that. Armed with a roll of paper towels and squirt bottle of vinegar and water, Ginny stepped onto the bottom step. Then the next. The ceilings in this house, including the closet, were a luxurious nine feet, but that meant that even with the stool, she wasn't quite tall enough to see all the way to the back of the shelf, or all the way to the end.

"A little at a time, baby, just a little at a time." Gran's words again, used for all manner of tasks that had seemed too daunting. One jar at a time while canning the endless supply of tomatoes from her garden, one pan of cookies at a time when she got to baking for the Christmas party, one stitch at a time when she was working on her embroidery. Ginny supposed the same held true for cleaning dirty closets. One wipe at a time.

The first paper towel she swiped across the top came away black with dirt and speckled with dead ants. Her swipe also brought along a couple ant traps. That explained the shavings in the corners. She dropped the paper towel. Spritzed more cleanser. Wiped again. This time was better.

Ginny used six paper towels to clean that section of the shelf, another four for the next. Then she had to get down and move the stool over a few inches. As she did, above her, the wood creaked. She straightened, looking, but saw nothing. Heard nothing. She looked around the closet and saw nothing there, either.

Ginny took a step back, looking upward again. Set into the ceiling was an attic access panel similar to the one in the hallway, though in here there was no room for a pull-down ladder. Ginny held her breath, listening, but the sound didn't repeat.

"Right," she said aloud, slapping her dirty hands against each other and wishing she'd thought to grab some rubber gloves. "Come out, Gary Busey, wherever you are."

The joke didn't seem so funny when she herself had just moved into an old house with a sort of creepy crawl-space attic. And she was alone. And she'd heard a weird noise.

Ginny wasn't in the habit of talking to herself, at least not out loud, but more words slipped from her lips as though speaking them instead of just thinking them gave them the power to be true. "It was nothing. Just like the nothing you saw in the hallway. Just like the nothing you saw in a window. Shadows, that's it. And old houses creaking. That's it, Virginia Eloise."

That's what her gran had called her, ever so formally. Nicknames, she said, were for people who didn't have beautiful names. She'd never referred to Ginny's mom by her name, always calling her honey or darling or sweetheart, affectionate terms that had curled Ginny's mom's lip because she said they weren't meant fondly but as a way of pointing out how unbeautiful her name was. Gertrude, named after Gran's mother-in-law. Ginny's mom went by Trudy and had been careful not to name her own daughters after any relatives.

Saying it aloud that way settled something inside Ginny. Almost like Gran had said it herself, which was impossible, both because Gran wasn't here, and also because Gran had been incapable of saying much of anything that made sense for the past few years. She didn't talk much at all, in fact. She mostly sat and stared out the windows of the nursing home, even when Ginny came and brought her special treats that she wasn't supposed to have on her diet.

For the second time since moving into this house, emotion blindsided her. Ginny put a hand on her heart, mindless of the dirt on her white shirt, although it left a smudge she'd have to fuss with later and which would never quite come entirely clean. She closed her eyes, her other hand on the back of the stool for balance as she bent over with the force of her sorrow. Gran was old and had always been a little wacky, but to see her losing her mind…to watch her actually lose all sense of not just the people around her and where she was, but of herself…

Ginny'd been ignoring it for a long time. Her monthly visits were filled with forced cheer and lots of bright, one-sided conversation, and she pretended the headaches that always came home with her were from the stink of the cleaning chemicals in the home, not from the stress of smiling so hard her face hurt. She hadn't allowed herself to think fully on Gran's condition, or how it made her feel, and now it all swung up and hit her in the face like a stepped-on rake.

Bam. Slam. Right between the eyes, the pain sudden and fierce enough to make her gasp as she fought against tears and lost. Heat slipped down her cheeks and clogged her throat. She pressed her eyes closed tighter and shook her head, muttering aloud.

No, she wouldn't do this. She wouldn't let this happen again, this slip-slide into melancholy for which there was no cure. Hormones, circumstances, her own choices, the vagaries of fate—whatever it was, she wasn't going to let herself give in to this burst of anxiety again. She just. Would. Not.

Blinking rapidly, Ginny used a clean paper towel to scrub at her face. She drew in a few sharp breaths until the dust made her sneeze. She blew her nose, cleared her throat, got herself under control. She had a closet to clean and lots of other things this house needed. No time to break down over what she couldn't change.

Bolstered, determined, she got back up on the stool and gave the shelf a swift sweep with a handful of paper towels. Something skidded along the wood with her hand, but she was moving too fast, had been too hasty. More than dust and a few dead ants or some dried turds tipped over the edge of the shelf this time.

This time, a dead mouse hit her in the face.

She knew what it was at once, the desiccated corpse with its remnants of fur and dried worm of a tail. She was already crying out in revulsion, not fear, as it bounced off her mouth—oh God, her mouth!—and hit the floor without a noise. Ginny flailed and clutched first at the shelf for support, but the section she grabbed shifted and moved, tipping under the sudden weight of her fist. Something deeper toward the back moved and shifted too, but she lost sight of it as the section slid off its supports and cracked against the light fixture, first blotting the light into shadow and then distinguishing it entirely when the filaments in the bulb broke.

She fell.

Ginny braced herself for the pain of hitting the floor with her ass but managed to save herself, just a little, by stepping backwards and landing on one foot. Her ankle twisted, and she'd have gone all the way down except that the closet was too narrow to allow her the space. She hit the wall with her shoulder instead and left a small dent in the plaster.

With another shuddering cry of disgust, Ginny pushed backwards out of the closet. Panting, she spat the taste, real or imagined, of dead mouse and didn't dare lick her lips or scrub at her mouth with her bare hands. She got to her feet and went to the hall bathroom, where she washed her hands several times under the hottest water she could stand, then scrubbed her mouth.

Mouth dripping, face still twisted from the gross-out, Ginny caught sight of her reflection. Her throat worked—she wasn't sure if she meant to cry again until a deep, low and grinding clutch of laughter pushed past her lips.

Oh God. Oh gross.

Now she was even more happy Barb hadn't come over to help, because if she'd come across a dead mouse in any form, especially one that had touched her face, she'd have gone catatonic and had to be sedated. As it was, Ginny half thought she might puke, but a few sips of water settled her. So did some breathing.

It wasn't the mouse itself, since it was harmless and sad, a caricature of a rodent that had been squashed flat by some chasing tomcat's mallet. It must've died in the closet and dehydrated or mummified. No, it was the fact it had landed on her mouth, her lips… Ginny shuddered and washed her face again.

Of all the gross things that had ever happened to her, including the dead squirrel, she thought this might be the worst. And as far as unexpected contact with deceased rodents went, Ginny'd had her lifetime allotment. Still, the trauma was fading by the time she finished in the bathroom and went back to the baby's room to gather up the poor thing and dispose of it along with all the dirty paper towels.

That task finished, it would've been easy enough for her to abandon the rest of the closet cleaning for another day. Her ankle hurt, though it didn't seem to be swelling, and her heart was still beating a little too fast. Her head felt a little spinny. But if she didn't finish now, she wasn't sure who would.

Plus…something had moved when the shelf shifted. A box, she thought. Or a suitcase. Something solid, definitely not any kind of dead thing. At least she hoped not.

The light bulb in the fixture hadn't shattered, thank God, so she didn't have to clean up or explain broken glass. But she had no idea where to get another one in the mess of boxes downstairs. She'd have to take one from another fixture, though they too were burned out, she discovered when she pulled the chain in the other two bedroom closets, wondering what might be lurking on *their* shelves. Finally, she took the one from her bedroom closet, mentally adding light bulbs to the list that never seemed to get any shorter.

Finally, light bulb replaced, stool settled firmly on the floor so it wouldn't tip, Ginny climbed up again to look at what was on the shelf. It *was* a suitcase, what her gran had called a "train case." Her mom had used one as a makeup case when Ginny was small. Hers had a mirror inside and a removable shelf to separate the top from the bottom. It was blue and bore the initials of some dead aunt.

This case was of a similar size. Olive green, though the dust on it meant the color might indeed be brighter. Ginny pulled it gingerly toward her, careful not to tip this section of shelf in case it was as unsecured as its neighbor had been. The bulb she'd replaced was brighter than its predecessor, bright enough to chase away all the shadows even in the farthest depths of the closet. Even so, she was so focused on the case that she didn't notice the bones until she'd taken it by the handle and was half-turned to step down from the stool.

Tiny piles of bones, at least three, with some random bones scattered in between. Tiny skulls with long teeth. Beside the piles, tucked a little farther back on the shelf and on the opposite side of where she'd found the mouse, the light glinted off several plastic sandwich bags with misshapen forms inside them. Fur, bones, the spread of what must've once been the goo of blood and other fluids but which time had dried.

The smell, she thought, must've been atrocious.

Carefully, she got down to set the case in the middle of the bedroom. Then, armed with the garbage bag and paper towels, the bottle of cleanser close by, she scraped the first pile of bones toward her. She had to stand on her tiptoes to get to the last set. Again, she wished for rubber gloves when her fingertips touched the plastic, and she half expected it to stick to the shelf, but the bags slid without resistance. Hamsters, she thought with a glance inside. Orange and white fur.

She put everything in the garbage bag and went back to the bathroom to scrub her hands. Then she took the garbage bag outside and stuffed it in the can. Back upstairs, she finished cleaning the shelf until the entire length of it, every section, gleamed with the cleanser and the closet smelled of nothing but vinegar.

Chapter Ten

Ginny told Sean about the case, though not about the bones or the dead mouse, or falling off the step stool. She did tell him about the light bulb, since he was sure to notice the one missing in their closet, though all she said was that it had burned out, not that it had broken. She tempered her disclosure over a full dinner of roast beef she'd done in the Crock-Pot with some onion-soup mix and a little red wine, baked potatoes, a nice salad decorated with dried cranberries and almonds and a sprinkling of bleu cheese. Plus, she waited until his mouth was full before she told him she'd found something while cleaning, so by the time he'd chewed and swallowed she could focus the conversation on the discovery and not her actions during it.

"It was there for a long time," she told him, picking at her own salad. It had seemed like a good idea to make it with all the extras, but she'd become so sensitive to smells and flavors that everything was jumbling together in a sensory overload. "It's a girl's case, though. So I don't think it belonged to the owner or his son."

"How do you know it belonged to a girl?" Sean speared another fork of meat. He sighed as he chewed, closing his eyes briefly in an almost-sexual expression of delight.

It amused her, that expression. She knew him so well, after all this time, it felt almost unfair to be so manipulative at keeping his attention directed on something else. But only almost.

"Because," she said with a point of her fork toward him, "it just is. Boys don't use train cases. The kind with a liner and a mirror and stuff inside."

He drank slowly from his glass of wine, savoring it with another of those sighs. Despite an occasional craving, Ginny wasn't a big wine drinker, but he made it seem so delicious her mouth watered in envy. Of course that was her way, wanting what she couldn't have, even though she knew she wouldn't like it if she got it.

"They could," he said.

She laughed a little, though it faded quickly when she thought of the tiny skeletons, corpses that had been kept in baggies. That seemed more like a boy thing, if you were going to go by stereotypes. Puppy-dog tails and all that. "I guess so. But I doubt it. It's a girl's case, I know it."

"What's in it?"

"I don't know."

Sean paused with a crescent roll halfway to his mouth. Both brows lifted. "Why not? You find this grand, secret treasure and you don't open it?"

"I don't know; it didn't seem right." Ginny shrugged and reached for the bread basket. The crescent rolls, at least, seemed appealing, which made sense since of all the food she'd made, they were the only thing she hadn't made from scratch. Full of preservatives, she thought and buttered one anyway, before tucking it into her mouth. Just as she'd thought, delicious.

"After dinner."

"No." She shook her head. "I told you, it doesn't seem right. It's not ours."

"Everything in this house is ours. Bought and paid for." Sean gestured with his fork, looking around the dining room, where Ginny had set up a card table with a fancy cloth and the good dishes, since she'd finally found them in an unmarked box.

She studied him around the wedding-gift candelabra. They'd never used it in their townhouse and here they were, using it again. "Yeah, even the things we didn't want."

He laughed and drank more wine. He wiped his mouth with a cloth napkin that had also been a wedding gift. All these things they'd never really used before, yet seemed so right now. Wine made Sean horny, she remembered that now. She poured him another glass.

"C'mon. It's not that many. The telephone table, that throw rug. The case. That's not so much, when you think about how much stuff was in here when we looked at it, remember?"

She did. The house had been fully furnished, top to bottom, though just the one old man lived in it. He'd had some nice pieces she sort of wished she'd thought to ask for, now that she knew how accommodating the son had been about unloading everything, but at the time her mind had still been awash with modern lines and small rooms. She hadn't been able to think ahead to what it would be like to actually live here and fill all the spaces that cried out for an ornate hand.

"Well. Who knows what else we might find?" she pointed out, meaning that the cleaning service had done a woeful job.

As wasn't uncommon, her husband wasn't on the same track. He woo-wooed with his fingers and made the accompanying sound. "Yessss, we might find something scarrrrry…like bonesssss…"

"What?" Startled, Ginny's fingers twitched and knocked her fork off the table. "Why would you say that?"

Sean gave her a curious glance. "Like in that movie you and Billy are always quoting."

"There weren't any bones in that movie. He killed people and buried them in the backyard."

"But they found bones."

Ginny had to remind herself that Sean had never seen the movie; he knew of it only from what she and Billy said. Still, she hated the way he talked about it like he knew it and she didn't, like she was wrong and he was right. "No. I don't think so." Dammit, now she couldn't really remember if there'd been bones in the movie. Maybe from the dog… Shit, she couldn't remember.

"Anyway," Sean said dismissively, "you knew what I meant. So if we have Gary Sinise living in our attic…"

"Jesus, Sean," she snapped, irrationally annoyed now. He'd listened to her and Billy talk about the movie for years. "Gary Busey. It's Gary fucking Busey."

Silence fell between them as she bit back her anger. He gave her that look she also hated. The one that said she was being an irrational bitch, but he forgave her. He always forgave her.

"Sorry." She sipped from her glass of lemonade, the taste sour enough to pucker her lips but still not as bad as the taste of her anger.

At first he said nothing, but then he shrugged. "If you're not going to open it, what are you going to do with it?"

"Throw it away."

He looked shocked. "You can't just throw it away! What if there's something important in it?"

"Like what? Money?"

"There could be. That would be awesome." Sean grinned.

Ginny's mouth pursed, not quite an answering smile but easing toward one. "A treasure map?"

"Yeah!"

"A winning lottery ticket, never cashed in. Keys to a safe deposit box in Switzerland?

Oh, I know." She snapped her fingers. "The Hope Diamond."

"That's in a museum somewhere, and, besides, it's supposed to be cursed."

"Okay, just some other big-ass diamond, then."

He laughed again. "That would be good, huh? C'mon, babe, you can't just throw it away. At the very least, if you're not going to see what's inside, you should see if the son wants it."

He was right, she couldn't pretend otherwise.

But they were both wrong about what was inside the case. No money, no jewels, no map leading to a trove of buried treasure. There was a key, though, the tiny kind that was meant to fit into a diary. Ginny'd had one of those as a kid, the cover powder blue and fake leather. Her brother had broken the lock with one sharp tug, and she'd never written in it after that.

The diary itself was tucked beneath a sheaf of photos, most of them Polaroids yellowed with age. Some had scrawled descriptions in the white space along the bottom, but most were unidentified. There were a few more of those carved wooden figures, a whole set. There were also a number of childish drawings of typical things: a girl with a pony, a princess, a family, a tree, a rainbow. None of them were signed.

"Hey, look." Sean pulled the diary out and tugged the cover, but the lock held. "Give me the key."

Ginny snatched it up before he could get it. "No! You can't… Jesus, Sean. You can't read it. This belonged to someone."

His puppy eyes did nothing for her. "I told you, it's ours now."

"You obviously never kept a diary." She scowled and curled her fingers tight around the key.

"No. Did you?" He paused, gave her a head tilt, an up-and-down glance. "Do you?"

"I don't now."

He gave up on the diary and sifted through more of the stuff. "Nothing in here looks very interesting."

"Don't sound so disappointed." The key warmed in her palm, and Ginny put it in her pocket, thinking she would have to remind herself to take it out or it would end up getting caught in the washing machine filter. "You know if it really had been money, we'd have felt compelled to give it back to the rightful owner."

Sean reached to tug her onto his lap. He nuzzled her neck, and she let him. "And I told you, babe, we are the rightful owners."

"Pffft." His hands on her hips felt good. So did the brush of his slightly scratchy beard on her throat. She arched into his touch.

"Look. If something happens with the roof or the heating system…" his brows lifted when she pulled away to look at him, "…yeah, I know, don't jinx it. But if something does happen, if that tree out there falls in the yard, we have to cut it up, right? That's our responsibility now."

"Well…"

He settled his mouth back against her, teeth pressing gently as he spoke, "So, I say, whatever we find is ours to keep. If we take the bad, we have to take the good too."

"Isn't it usually the other way around?" She'd said it lightly, meaning nothing, but Sean was silent for a few seconds too long.

Then he said, "Yeah. Usually."

His hands drifted up her back. Pulled her a little closer. He kissed her throat and her slightly exposed collarbones. His breath was warm but made her shiver. When he shifted against her, the bulge of his erection pressing her hip, a flare of unexpectedly strong desire made her draw in a breath.

Ginny looked down at him, her hands caught in his hair as she tipped his face to hers. She kissed him long and slow, before pulling away a little. "Come upstairs with me."

His gaze flickered, the corners of his mouth dipping low. Once more she was both a little sad and a little annoyed that after all this time and all these years, she knew him so well he hardly had to say a word, but he barely knew her at all, even when she was spelling it out.

"I will. Later. I have some homework I need to finish up."

She looked at the clock. "Now?"

"Yeah." He nuzzled against her throat again, but Ginny pulled away.

She got off his lap and started clearing the table. Sean got up and went into the living room. She watched him from the dining room as he rummaged in his bag. He pulled out the leather-bound notebook she'd bought for his birthday the year he started his coursework, and a handful of pens. She watched him tuck his phone into his pocket. When he straightened he threw her a smile she had to force herself to return.

"Hey, beautiful," her husband said.

Ginny cleared the table by herself again.

Chapter Eleven

Ginny didn't tell Sean about the bones in the closet, but that didn't mean she'd forgotten them. For the first week after her discovery, as she puttered around the house and barely managed to accomplish anything, since her husband still insisted she wait for him to "help" her, Ginny kept imagining opening another closet, a drawer, a cupboard, and finding another pile of dead-rodent remains. As she worked slowly, cleaning each cupboard with wet cloths and the baking soda and vinegar mixture that never seemed to clean as well as bleach, she never let her fingers trace the deep places, full of shadow, without thoroughly checking them first with a flashlight.

She hadn't forgotten the case or the diary within. Long ago, before she met Sean, Ginny'd had a college boyfriend. They'd met at a party in the first few months of their sophomore year, and it had been instant love. Well, lust. With the maturity of time behind her, she was willing to amend it to that. At any rate, she'd fallen hard and deep, her feelings for Joseph an abyss with walls so high she could barely see the sky. And with this love came the ever-present knowledge that she loved him more than he loved her. That she wanted him more than he wanted her. That somewhere, someday there would be something that would take him from her, whether it was a sports game, a drunken night out with his buddies…a girl.

Ginny'd become adept at sifting through his drawers without Joseph knowing. In the days before email and texting or even Connex, all she had was the shoebox full of love letters she found on his top closet shelf. The ones from Ginny, and the ones from someone else. Her discovery had led to an argument, the vehemence of which seemed to surprise him, and though it broke her heart to do it, Ginny was the one to end the relationship.

Now, in the life she'd come to after leaving Joseph, Ginny didn't regret the breakup. She never wanted to feel that way about anyone, ever again, that lost and sinking feeling, that drowning. She never wanted love to be a prison. But some part of her did regret, for a very long time, the fact that she'd snooped.

That was probably what had led her to her job of investigating people who lied. Her work had confirmed how easily caught most people are, how little they suspect their secrets will ever see the light of day. It had taught her an unforgettable lesson about the importance of keeping secrets.

Ginny didn't know the owner of the suitcase or the diary or the pictures within it. There was no reason to think that reading the diary would affect her life in any way beyond satisfying her curiosity. Yet even though she'd put the case on one of the built-in bookcases in the dining room and passed it several times a day as she wove through the maze of boxes she wasn't allowed to lift, and though she stopped sometimes to look at it, to touch it with one fingertip, Ginny didn't open the case again.

Sean seemed to have forgotten it, at any rate. He got up in the morning and was off to work just as the light was hitting the sky. In their old place, their morning interaction had been limited to a mumbled "morning" as she stumbled past him on the way to the shower. Here, without a job to force her to wake up, she should've lounged in bed at least until the sun rose, but guilt forced her to head downstairs while her husband shaved and dressed. She made coffee. She made eggs. She made toast and bacon, even waffles, sometimes with a slightly curled slice of orange on the side he never ate and she rescued before the plate hit the trash, tucked away into a plastic storage container and saved in the fridge for the next morning. He never noticed if it started looking a little wilted. Frankly, she doubted Sean noticed much of anything that early in the morning, even with the mug of strong coffee she didn't drink herself yet had perfected the art of brewing.

He noticed her, though. His gaze followed her as she served him his food, sometimes at a place at the table, sometimes pressed into his hand along with a packed lunch as he rushed toward the door. He always took the time to kiss her in the morning, no matter how late he was running.

"How do you do it?" Sean asked, his hands on her hips pulling her closer to press her belly between them.

"A little vanilla in the batter."

He shook his head. "No. Not the waffles, well, I mean, not just the waffles. How do you know what I want to eat, or if I'll have time? You always have it ready just in time."

Ginny smiled and kissed him lightly, pushing up on her toes. The truth was, she had no idea what her husband wanted for breakfast, any more than she had a clue what she should make him for lunch. She guessed, that was all, and figured if it wasn't right he'd tell her. But then Sean had never been the one to press for decisions, happy to go along with whatever pushed him. If she made waffles, he'd eat waffles. If she made an egg sandwich, he'd eat that just as happily.

"I pay attention," she said.

"To what?"

"To everything," Ginny said, and saw this wasn't an answer Sean totally understood. "To what time you get out of bed, and how long you spend in the shower. I can tell if you're on time or not."

"I can barely tell if I'm on time." Sean kissed her again, slower this time, though it was one of the days when he'd lingered with his pillow through at least two snooze cycles. He pressed his forehead to hers, eyes closed for a second before he looked at her. "You're amazing, you know that?"

"Ah. But am I awesomazing? That's the question." She could taste the hint of coffee on his lips. The cream and sugar. Coffee had never appealed to her, ever, but now the flavor sent a tingle through her taste buds. Pregnancy made her crave strange things.

"You are awesomazing," he agreed. "My awesomazing wife."

"You'd better go, or you'll be awesomazingly late."

Sean made a face, but backed away from her. "Remember, I have class tonight."

She'd forgotten, but nodded as though she hadn't. "Oh. Right."

"Need me to pick anything up on the way home?"

"No. I need to get out today anyway. Do you want anything special from the grocery store?"

She could see by the way his brows started to knit that he was going to protest, so she shut him up with another kiss. "There'll be plenty of time for me to be stuck at home, Sean. I can still drive. I can still push a cart."

"Have someone load the groceries for you."

She sighed, but nodded again. "Yes. Yes, I'll go to the fancy-pants grocery store that's twenty extra minutes away, so I can have a bag boy carry my shit for me. Oh, and spend twice as much money."

He laughed, but just a little. "They'll all be fighting over who gets to carry your bags."

"Riiiiight. 'Cuz this is some hot piece of action going on here." She rolled her eyes and stepped back to show him the growing expanse of her abdomen.

Her foot came down on something that would've dug hard into her sole had she not learned her lesson and started wearing hard-bottomed slippers. Instead, her foot slipped forward as her ungainly balance tipped her back, hands flailing. She'd have fallen if he hadn't grabbed her.

Heart pounding, blinking fast as the slight red haze filtered around her vision, Ginny gripped Sean tight as he set her upright. Then the counter, thankfully, was solid under her touch. She shifted her feet cautiously, making sure the floor was solid too.

"Be careful," Sean said like a lecture. "Christ, Ginny!"

As if she'd done it on purpose. Frowning, she looked to see what she'd stepped on. Something metal gleamed. Small and round. She bent to get it before he could stop her, though regretted when she stood too fast and had to again grip the counter to keep herself from wobbling.

"What is it?"

She opened her palm to show him. "It's a button."

"Not one of mine."

As if she'd accused him of dropping it, she thought with a slight curl of her lip. "Not unless you've started wearing things with flowers on them."

Of course he hadn't. This was a girl's button. It looked vintage, tarnished metal with a raised flower design and a small hasp in the back where the thread attached it to the garment. Too small for a coat. A sweater maybe, or a blouse.

She closed her fingers around it. "I'm fine, Sean. I wish you'd go. You're going to be late."

"You should stay home today, take it easy."

"All I've done since we moved in is take it easy," she reminded him with a gesture at the kitchen, still a mess with various boxes full of things he didn't want her to put away but hadn't done himself.

"I have to go."

"Have a good day," she called out after him from the doorway, with a wave he returned from the rolled-down car window.

She thought he was going to say he loved her, but instead he shouted, "Buy organic!"

She watched until the car pulled out of the drive and had disappeared down the street before she shut the front door on a swirl of cold wind. The hall had turned chilly, even through the bulky knit of the sweater she wore over her nightgown, but there'd be little sense in turning up the thermostat since she was going to leave for the store soon anyway.

Upstairs, she stopped in the library and settled the button next to the tiny wooden lady in the fur stole on the otherwise empty bookshelf. In her bathroom, she ran the water hot until steam filled the room, thicker than she expected.

Naked, she stood in front of the mirror and cupped her breasts. Ginny's sister Peg had taken after their mother and been blessed with what she called "an abundancy of bosoms," but Ginny'd drawn the tiny-titty card. At least until now. She'd gone up two cup sizes. Her areolas, always a pale and almost-translucent pink, had darkened to a deep rose that still startled her when she saw it.

Her belly too was a constant surprise. Rounded and firm, still hidable under baggy shirts but straining at the waistband of her "fat" jeans, crosshatched with the first faint silvering of stretch marks she rubbed faithfully with expensive cream but had no hope of avoiding entirely. Her body was changing, and there was nothing she could do about it. No way to stop it. And it would never be the same.

Chapter Twelve

"Ginny?"

Ginny turned with an out-of-season cantaloupe in her hands. She'd been feeling for soft spots and debating if she should put the melon in her basket; she hated the smell of them and always had, but even more so now that she was pregnant. Sean liked them, though, and sometimes that seemed what marriage was all about. Buying things you didn't like for the sake of someone who did.

"Louisa. Hi." Ginny's smile felt a little forced, though it shouldn't. Louisa'd never been anything but kind. "How are you?"

"I'm grand, just grand, doll. But you…look at you." Louisa tilted her head to look her up and down. "My goodness, I guess it's been a long time, hasn't it?"

Ginny could count how long it had been since she'd seen Louisa, down to the day. She let the melon fall gently back amongst its brothers, and her hands went automatically to the mound of her stomach. "Yeah. I guess it has."

"We've missed you. But I see you've been busy."

Ginny's fingers twitched on the front of her coat, thinking she must look gargantuan for Louisa to have noticed. Unless she hadn't, of course, and had meant nothing by her comment. Making small talk. Or she thought Ginny had just gained some weight, maybe, though it wasn't like she'd been skinny before.

"I'm pregnant."

Louisa laughed. "Yes, doll, I see that."

Ginny let out a slow breath that ended in a rueful chuckle as she shook her head. There was no reason for her to avoid Louisa's eyes, but she found herself cutting her gaze anyway. "So. Yeah. I have been busy."

"You know, I still have a few of your pieces left from the show. I've been storing the ones that didn't sell, along with some others, but I'll be happy to get them back to you. They're lovely work. You could think about putting them in the next show, if you want."

Louisa looked again at Ginny's belly, then her face. "Though of course it might not be that easy for you, huh?"

Ginny smiled faintly. "No. It wouldn't be. You could just get rid of them, I guess."

"You don't want them?" Louisa looked shocked, like Ginny'd talked about giving away a baby instead of a couple of self-indulgent oil paintings.

"Not really. I could always paint more. If I wanted to, I mean."

Louisa chewed her bottom lip for a moment. "Well…I hope you do. You made lovely pieces, Ginny. You had a real gift for quirky, fun things. And such great color choices."

"Yeah. Well…" Ginny shrugged, trying to remember what it had been like back in those days when she'd stand in front of a blank canvas and imagine it into a picture, "…it was only ever a hobby."

"We all need hobbies, and if yours is making something beautiful…" Louisa shrugged carelessly and let her fingers flutter in the air. "Nobody said you had to try to make a living at it—"

"Good thing, since I doubt I'd be able to."

"—but you can make beauty, Ginny," Louisa continued. "I hate to see you give it up. You should stop by the shop sometime, pick them up. Or I could bring them to your house. You're over by the high school, right? In that darling little townhouse community. It looks like a European village."

"We've moved." The words sounded too sharp. Biting. Ginny softened them with a smile. "And sure, I'll stop by the shop sometime after we get settled in. Okay?"

She had no intention of doing that. She didn't want the paintings Sean had stashed in the basement; she sure didn't want those other ones back. She didn't care about the pieces she'd spent so much time on. They'd only remind her of disappointment.

"That would be great. Come take a few classes again, if you want. On the house. Before your life changes forever," Louisa advised, with another knowing look and a grin that said she knew just how it would be. "After that baby comes, you won't have much time for hobbies."

"No," Ginny told her. "But I will have created something beautiful."

Louisa looked faintly surprised before she nodded again, more solemnly this time. "Yes. Amen to that. Well, listen, doll, you take care, okay? Stop by the shop. Like I said, we've missed you."

Ginny didn't doubt that was true. The people who hung around the Inkpot were mostly the sort to drink fancy coffee and wear sandals with socks and necklaces of beads they'd made themselves. Ren Faire types, Sean had called them. In to clean living and role-playing games, that sort, though of course there were a few like her, who were totally different. It didn't matter. The only rule in Louisa's classes was that every effort be praised. She encouraged the more talented members to help those less blessed, and even the people who couldn't learn to throw a pot that didn't collapse on the wheel, or sketch anything that looked like what it was supposed to be, discovered they were able to make something by the end of the four-week sessions. People came back to Louisa's classes for more than the instruction—it was a social affair, with everyone often stopping by the coffee shop next door after class to spend another hour hanging out.

Ginny hadn't missed them at all.

Suddenly, she felt worse about that than anything else. Impulsively, she reached for Louisa's hand and squeezed the cold fingers. "I will. Okay? I will."

Louisa squeezed back. "I hope so, doll."

After a few more minutes of chitchat, Louisa pushed off with her cart and Ginny checked her watch. She was in no rush. Sean would be late from class. But it would be getting dark soon, and she didn't want to carry groceries into the house in the dark.

* * * * *

By the time she got home, the sun had dipped low enough that her driveway was cloaked in shadows when she pulled in. In the too-cold house she checked the thermostat, which was, as it had been every other time she checked, set to the right temperature. She bumped it up a few degrees anyway. Scarlett O'Hara refused to be hungry? Well, Ginny Bohn had a bug up her ass about being cold.

She hadn't bought much at the store, but, thinking of Sean's command she not carry her own bags, she'd asked the bagger to parcel out her items into all six of her reusable totes, when three would've sufficed. Unloading the car took twice as long as normal that way but left her only a little winded, so grudgingly she had to admit that maybe he'd been at least a little right.

By the time she got everything inside, the house had warmed up, but only a little, and only in weird places. The front hall was cold but the kitchen stifling, and so was the powder room. The living room had a few warm spots but the other rooms were still chilly—probably because there were still boxes and junk heaped over the floor vents, she discovered. Instead of actually unpacking things, they'd been taking what they needed out of the boxes and shifting them around.

There was definitely something wrong with their "almost brand-new" heating system, and it was pissing her off. Not that her moods were the best anyway. Up and down, up and down. Seeing Louisa hadn't helped that much; now Ginny was thinking of things she'd rather have pushed aside.

Tea might help, both with the chill and the mood swings, but as she leaned over the sink to fill the kettle, Ginny caught a flash of motion out in the yard. Something white fluttered just below the edge of the window, or so she thought. With the light inside reflecting, all she could really see was her own face. It caught her attention for a second or two, her eyes wide and looking like dark hollows in her skull, her dark hair loosing from the pony tail and falling around her face. The pale slash of her lips.

She looked like a ghost.

Disturbed, she turned off the faucet and set the kettle on the stove, but didn't turn on the burner. The high-pitched giggling screams of children wafted to her ears, along with the rattle and rustle of something alongside the house. She looked again out the window and saw nothing, but, dammit, those kids were messing around in the yard again, and it was getting dark. What in the hell were they doing anyway?

She went to the back door and strained to see them, but the only thing within eyesight was that wagon, overturned in the grass. When she opened the door, she meant only to ask them what the heck they thought they were doing—in a nice way, though, not trying to be mean. However, at the first creak of the hinges, they took off in a rustle of leaves and a few dozen whispered giggles and shrieks.

"Hey…!" She let her cry trail off, defeated.

Kids.

She thought of her nieces and nephews, those delightful little hellions who'd turned Peg's hair gray and were going to send Billy, according to him, to the poor house. She put her hands on her belly and rubbed in slow circles against the kick of tiny feet and punch of little fists. She let her fingers press a little harder against the lumps and bumps of her body. She imagined a little bum, the curve of a head or an elbow.

With a sigh, Ginny went out to confront them, but again found nothing but the remnants of childish games instead of the children themselves. The figures that had been lined up along the window well were still there, and she couldn't tell if they were in the same order or not. Something had been added, though. A plastic baggie of Goldfish crackers and an unopened juice box. Kids' snacks, but they didn't look like they'd been lost. They looked like they'd been set there deliberately. Frowning, Ginny took them in the house and tossed them in the trash, thinking again of her gran.

Gran had always been a woman of superstitions, even as at the same time she was utterly derisive of what she called "flights of fancy." In her high phases Gran had left a bowl of milk out on the counter for the Brownies, who were something like leprechauns, from what Ginny remembered, and who'd make mischief in your house if you didn't feed them. Sometimes that bowl of milk went sour and chunky in the bowl, but woe to anyone who touched it. Other times it stayed empty on the counter, a reminder that Gran could be as stingy as she was generous. Ginny's mom had hated that tradition and the story that went along with it, but Ginny had a fondness for the memory.

She had no milk and wouldn't have left a bowl of it on the counter anyway, but something about the way the crackers and juice had been left reminded her of Gran's offering to the Brownies. It seemed like the sort of thing Ginny would like to pass down to her child, one of those weird family things that outsiders might not understand but that meant a lot to the people who did it.

The cat bumping around her ankles was a good reminder that whatever she left had to be more symbolic than nutritious, or at least not tempting to a cat on a diet, with a bad attitude. Ginny bent to scratch behind Noodles's ears, then lifted her. She wasn't any thinner. If anything, Noodles felt even heavier. Ginny rubbed the soft fur under the cat's chin. Usually this jingled the bell collar, but today her fingers found nothing but fur.

"Oh, you bad kitty, what did you do with it?" Ginny sighed and set her down. "Noodles, why are you so much trouble?"

The cat meowed implacably, wound herself around Ginny's ankles some more, and when it became obvious that no food was forthcoming, sauntered away with her tail in the air. Ginny shook her head. In the townhouse, Noodles had always been around, but this house was so much bigger the cat was forever disappearing and showing up again unexpectedly, usually under someone's feet. The bell collar had kept her from getting stepped on more than a dozen times in the past few days alone. Without it, she was likely to get more than her feelings hurt.

Adding a new collar to her ever-present mental shopping list, Ginny pulled a small crystal candy bowl from the cupboard. Also a wedding gift they'd never used, it of course had been one of the first things she pulled out from the packing boxes. Couldn't have been something practical, she thought, like her measuring cups and spoons. Nope, she had to find all the gaudy, expensive things they should've sold at a yard sale instead of bringing along. Well, it had a use now.

She filled it with peanuts, a snack Noodles would leave alone, for sure, and also wouldn't spoil. She added some chocolate-covered raisins too after a moment's thought, because although she was a sucker for most things chocolate, this particular treat was a present from Barb, probably purchased from a fundraising schoolkid. They had left a sour taste in Ginny's mouth, and she had no intentions of finishing them. As a symbolic offering to a mythical group of tiny, sometimes-vengeful creatures, it seemed perfect.

Upstairs in the library, she looked at the boxes shoved against the wall and at her easel propped next to them. Her paints were in those boxes. Brushes, palette, some of the smaller canvases she'd bought months and months ago. Carefully wrapped and packaged solvents and brush cleaners. The paints would surely be dried up by now. The canvases stained, maybe. She remembered packing these boxes months ago, not for the move. Just to put them away. She'd emphatically labeled them not "Studio" but "Art Supplies." She didn't need to open them to find out what was inside, and, really…she didn't want to.

Instead, Ginny threw them all away.

Chapter Thirteen

The kettle screamed.

Ginny got up from the kitchen table to bring it back so she could pour her mug full of hot water. Peg had already helped herself to a mug of Sean's coffee and was setting out the platter of homemade cinnamon buns she'd brought. Ginny chose a tea bag from the box on the table and dunked it in the water, eyed the buns and ran a finger through the thick goo of icing on the bottom of the plate.

"God," she said as she sucked the sweetness, "so good. Why didn't Gran ever teach me how to make these?"

"I was the only lucky one, I guess." Peg rolled her eyes, but fondly. "You know Dana asked her a hundred times for the recipe. Gran never let her have it."

"Has Dana asked you for it?"

"Nope." Peg grinned. "Should I give it to her?"

"I guess if she asks you. I mean, there's no real reason to keep it to yourself, right? Unless you *like* being the only one who can make them." Ginny shrugged and stirred a spoonful of sugar into her tea.

"I don't. It's not that. It's just that Gran gave it to me, only me, and I feel like it would maybe be dishonoring her or something. I mean, maybe she had a reason for not giving it to Dana, right?"

Ginny snorted softly and blew on her tea. "Yeah, spite."

"Cold." Peg shook her head but laughed softly. "Speaking of cold…why is it so freaking hot in here?"

"I know. I know!" Ginny tossed up her hands. "The thermostat's set to seventy. I don't even want to imagine our next power bill."

"Seventy! Good heavens, Ginny. Why so hot?"

"Because if I don't set it that high," Ginny said, "the rest of the house is freezing."

"Have you checked the vents? Maybe something's blocking them."

Ginny gave her sister a look. "Have you seen my house? Of course stuff is blocking them. I hope once I get everything put away…"

She trailed off with a sigh. They'd been in the house for a month and it still looked like they'd just moved in yesterday.

"You know I told you I'd help you." Peg cut one of the buns in half, then again, to put just a quarter of it on her plate.

"I know. But you're busy; you have your own stuff to do." Ginny broke hers into smaller pieces but intended to eat them all. She watched her sister stir artificial sweetener in her coffee and add a splash of skim milk. "Diet?"

Peg looked up, a little startled. "I can't fit into my jeans. Unlike you, I'm not eating for two. It just looks like I've been."

Peg's youngest, Luke, was eighteen. Her oldest, Jennifer, was twenty-eight. It had indeed been a long time since Peg was in Ginny's condition, but she was far from overweight. Ginny watched her sister pluck at the pieces of cinnamon bun without actually eating them. She studied the lines around Peg's eyes. The corners of her mouth. If she looked in a mirror, she'd see those same lines, just a little fainter but unmistakable. When had they started getting so old?

"What's going on?"

Peg sighed. "I'm not supposed to say anything about it…"

Ginny reached to put a hand on Peg's to keep her from further worrying the bun into scraps. "About what? What's going on? Is Dale okay? The kids?"

"He's fine. It's Billy."

"What's wrong with him?" Ginny hadn't spoken to her brother in a few weeks, her move and his work keeping them from connecting. This wasn't unusual, since though she loved her brother, they didn't keep in touch as often as she did with Peg. "Is he okay? Is he sick?"

"No. It's Jeannie."

Ginny frowned. "Spit it out, Peg, I'm not a mind reader."

"Jeannie's going to leave him."

This set Ginny back in her chair. She blinked rapidly, processing this. "What? Why?"

Peg sighed and wiped her fingers with a paper napkin before cupping her mug. She lifted it to let the steam from the hot coffee bathe her face for a few seconds before answering, "She's met someone else."

Ginny's stomach lurched into her throat. She took a bit of bun, too big, and it lodged in her throat so she had to gulp too-hot tea to swallow it. The tea burned her tongue.

"I asked how long it had been going on," Peg went on. "I mean, my God, we just went to the beach with them this past summer, and things seemed fine. I mean, if anything, she was nicer than I'd ever seen her. And, you know, it's not that I don't like Jeannie," Peg added hastily, like she had to explain to Ginny, who knew very well the sort of woman her sister-in-law was.

Ginny stayed quiet for a moment. She and Sean hadn't gone to the beach this summer because all their vacation time and resources had been taken up with buying the house. She hadn't seen Jeannie since the spring, months and months ago. "What does Mom say about it?"

"Oh…I don't think she knows. Billy didn't even want me to tell you, because of… you know." Peg gestured vaguely at Ginny's belly, hidden by the table.

"Oh, for fuck's sake, I wish everyone would stop tiptoeing around me with stuff because I'm pregnant." Ginny tore another bite of cinnamon bun. This one went down much easier.

Peg nibbled at a bite of her own, more daintily. "Sorry. I think he was just being, you know. A good brother."

"Why'd he tell you, if not Mom? Or me?"

"I…" Peg looked caught, eyes shining, glittery.

"You what?"

"I saw her. With him. The other guy."

Ginny paused with her mug halfway to her mouth, then set it down gently. "Oh. God. Peg…you're the one who told him?"

"Well, what would you have done?" Peg frowned. "I saw her out, bold as brass, with some other man. It was clear as anything what they were up to—"

"Why? Were they holding hands or making out or what? Were they dry humping in the middle of the grocery store?" Ginny got up from the table on the unspoken pretense of washing her hands clean of sticky icing, but the real reason was so she could get her reaction under control. At the sink she turned on the hot water and ran it hard, letting it burn her hands while she drew in breath after shaky breath.

"They were at the movies together, in a matinee. Sitting close. I could tell, Ginny. I mean, anyone could've."

Ginny turned from the sink to look at her sister. Peg, the oldest, had always been a little mother to her siblings. It had annoyed the ever-loving shit out of her and Billy when they were younger, and sometimes still did, even though Ginny had come to appreciate her sister's concern, especially since their own mother so infrequently seemed to have any. Still…this…she shook her head slightly. She rubbed her burnt tongue on the roof of her mouth, the pain better than trying to find words. Safer.

"Did you talk to her first?"

"No."

Ginny rubbed at her mouth with the back of one hand. "You just went to Billy and told him."

"He's my brother!"

And Jeannie, as much as Peg might protest she liked their sister-in-law "just fine," had always been a little standoffish. A little…not snotty, exactly, but she'd definitely never tried to ingratiate herself with Peg—or Ginny, who'd decided long ago she didn't care. She didn't need Jeannie for a bestie, or even a sister. However, Peg had always felt a little snubbed.

"But it's not your business."

"How can you say that?" Peg frowned again. "What would you have done?"

Ginny took a cloth from the sink and feigned an intense interest in wiping down the countertops, though she'd done a complete kitchen tidy in anticipation of Peg coming over.

"You're telling me you'd have just let her go on with it? Not told Billy at all? I don't believe you, Ginny."

"You don't know what was really going on, that's all I'm saying. And now, by telling him, Billy knows and Jeannie's leaving him, and maybe if you'd just left it alone…" Ginny bit back her words. Her sore tongue ached as she rubbed it firmly against the back of her teeth. "Forget it. How's Billy?"

"How do you think he is? He's devastated."

"Yeah. I bet he is." Ginny sagged a little, then turned to say something placid, vapid, to turn her sister's attention away from an argument, but found she had nothing to say. Instead, she took her now-cool mug and popped it into the microwave and hit the button to warm it for a minute.

The overhead light flickered rapidly. The clocks on the microwave and stove beeped. The light went out. Came back on. Went out again while Peg looked up goggle-eyed and Ginny sighed a curse. At four thirty, there was just enough late afternoon sunshine to keep the kitchen from being totally dark, but in another ten minutes or so they'd be in complete shadow.

Peg made a face. "What's up with that?"

"Circuit breaker." Ginny glanced at the coffeemaker, still on. "There's something funky with the wiring in the kitchen. Or something. I guess it's the coffeemaker and the microwave together, I don't know. It was blown the day we moved in and has happened a bunch of times since then; we haven't been able to figure out exactly what trips it."

"You should have it looked at. And the furnace too."

"Yes, Mother." Ginny said it with a roll of her eyes, a familiar tease.

"Where's the fuse box? Are you going to go take care of it?"

"Well. Sure. Of course. It's in the basement." Ginny paused. "It will be dark down there."

"You have a flashlight?"

"Oh sure. Somewhere." Ginny laughed and waved a hand toward the dining room, the living room beyond, overflowing with boxes. "Probably ten of 'em."

"Candles?"

"Sure, I have a candle." Ginny opened the drawer but found nothing, no candles, not even the mostly melted stubs of the ones she'd used in the candelabra. "Here, I know. I have one of those lighter things. We'll use that." She found it in the drawer and went with her sister to the basement door.

It opened with a spine-tingling creak. Ginny paused and flicked the light switch on and off a few times, just in case. Of course, nothing. She held the lighter high, but the light didn't shine more than a few feet. The steps, she noticed, were dirty, the wood splintered on the sides. Rubber matting had been stapled to the center of each riser, presumably to keep people from slipping, and dust had collected in all the threads.

Peg clutched at Ginny's shirt. "You should let me go first."

"Because I'm heavy with child?"

"Sarcasm suits you so nicely, sister dear. No. Because I'm older." But Peg didn't move, just peeked around Ginny's shoulder.

Even as kids, Ginny had always been the one who had to go first in the haunted houses at Halloween time. Everyone had always strung behind her while she felt her way in the dark, hands out, ready to be the first in line for the monster leaping out. If she could do that, she should be able to go into her own basement where there was no masked creature waiting to grab her.

Probably.

She had to let the lighter go out for a second to give her finger a rest from holding the trigger. Peg gasped when the alcove went dark. There was still light coming in from the hall behind her, but the stairs were pitch black.

"No windows in the basement?"

"A couple," Ginny said. "Not near the stairs, though."

She lit the lighter again. The shadows withdrew. She put her free hand on the railing, her foot on the top stair. Peg shuffled along behind her until Ginny sighed and stopped three stairs down.

"You're going to knock me down the stairs if you're not careful. Jesus, Peg. It's a basement. It's not quite five o'clock in the afternoon. Serial killers don't come out until at least five thirty."

"Funny." Peg backed up a step. "It's still dark. Be careful! Do you know where the fuse box is?"

She didn't, actually, since Sean had always been the one to go down and fix things. "How hard can it be to find?"

They found out in the next few minutes when they got to the bottom of the stairs and the lighter's glow didn't extend more than a foot or so beyond them. The paintings were gone, Ginny saw that at once. Sean had moved them. She waved the lighter around and caught sight of some of the empty boxes he'd brought down. Too few of them, of course. She had to look away, or be annoyed.

"It's got to be along a wall." Ginny moved toward the wall directly across from her.

Concrete blocks, pale gray. One of the walls, the one on the side that had once been the garage, had been plastered over, probably after the fire. Otherwise, it was nothing special. The walls looked like any other basement she'd ever been in, long and bare and strung with cobwebs along the ceiling, which was open to the beams and hung with wires, tubes and ducts. She understood what Danny the exterminator had meant—the ducts went everywhere.

No fuse box, though. Ginny, Peg shuffling behind, still clinging to her shirt, moved to the left. This wall, the one facing the backyard, also had no windows and no fuse box. The one to the left of that had two windows set deep into wells, through which only the faintest glimpse of failing daylight crept. One of them was the one where she'd found the figurines.

By this time they'd gone around to the back of the stairs, which had been walled off to make a sort of closet beneath them. Another short wall jutted out a few feet, not long enough to reach the far wall. Beyond this, at last, Ginny spotted the fuse box.

"Of course it's on the wall farthest away from where we started. I have to let the light go out again, hold on a second." Her finger had cramped from holding the trigger, and she let it go with a sigh of relief.

Peg let out a squeak as the room went dark.

Ginny laughed and let out a low, groaning ghost noise.

"Stop it, Ginny."

"Where's my golden arrrrrrm?" Ginny moaned, bringing back the old ghost story that always ended with screams. "Where's my—"

"You're a jerk!"

Still laughing, Ginny squeezed the lighter's trigger and headed for the fuse box. Inside, a flash of orange showed her exactly which switch had been tripped. She clicked it over to the right position.

Three things happened at the same time.

One, the furnace kicked on with a whoosh and a flash of blue light. Two, a hulking figure loomed up from around the wall at the bottom of the stairs. And three, Ginny dropped the lighter and plunged them into blackness.

Chapter Fourteen

Peg shrieked; Ginny did too, more in response to her sister's scream than her own fear. In the dark, something shuffled in front of them. The shadows shifted. Ginny reacted instantly, hands fisting, then pistoning out as the dark shape got within reach.

She connected with something soft and felt the familiar skid of corduroy against her hand, but too late—her other fist was striking like she thought she was some sort of Muhammad Ali. Only the sting like a bee part, though, no floating like a butterfly. She'd punched her husband in the face, and he went down to the concrete floor with a muffled shout.

She knew it was Sean because of the jacket and the sound of his muffled grunt, and because, who else would have come down the stairs to find her? With Peg still hollering and Sean letting out a few choice words of his own, Ginny tried to think about how far she was from the dangling light cord and if she dared risk trying to find it.

"Shut up, everyone!" she shouted. "Peg, it's Sean. Sean, honey, are you okay?"

"You busted me in the eye!"

"I'm sorry." She bit back a laugh, her hands still out, still blind, though now she could make out things a little better in the faint blue light from the furnace pilot light. "Baby, I'm so sorry."

Sean got to his feet, more of a felt presence than seen. "What happened to the light?"

"I dropped it. Can you find the cord?" Ginny didn't dare move.

Peg had stopped screaming but her breath was shuddery and she was clutching Ginny's arm so hard she was going to leave a bruise. Peg was lucky Ginny hadn't punched her in the face with that roundhouse strike, and the thought of it made Ginny laugh all the harder. It was terrible, and her laughter definitely had a sobbing edge to it, but there it was.

"Hold on. Don't move," Sean said.

In the next minute, the light from the bare bulb blinded them. Ginny winced. Peg let out a mutter of gratitude. Sean put his hands on his hips and glared at them both.

"The fuck were you doing down here?"

"The circuit breaker popped again," Ginny said.

"You should've waited for me to fix it."

"Uh…look, I really need to get going," Peg said.

Silence. Ginny's sister hugged her and patted Sean's shoulder. She gave Ginny a sympathetic look but ducked away, up the stairs, leaving her alone. Ginny couldn't blame her, really. The temperature in the basement had dropped by about fifty degrees at Sean's statement, and it had nothing to do with the furnace.

He waited until the sound of Peg's footsteps upstairs went out the front door. "You can't be coming down here in the dark, Ginny."

"What was I supposed to do, sit and wait for you to get home? I thought you had class tonight anyway."

"It was cancelled."

She made a face. "And…you told me that? I was supposed to just somehow intuit it? I should've just waited upstairs in the dark and the cold for you to get home?"

"You could've sent Peg down here—"

Ginny pushed past him, heading for the stairs. "It's my house, not hers. I wasn't going to ask my sister to fix my circuit breaker. Besides, it's not like I'm stupid."

"I never said you were stupid," he told her in the kitchen when he caught up to her. "Hey. Stop. Look at me."

She did, glaring.

"I was worried when I got home and you weren't here. That's all. I worry."

She softened a little toward him. Just a little. "I was fine. If you hadn't come down just then, it would've been even better."

His smile quirked. "I really scared the shit out of Peg, huh?"

"No kidding. I'm surprised she didn't pee herself." Ginny smiled too.

"Why didn't you use a flashlight, at least?"

"Why didn't you?" she pointed out and waited for him to get it.

"I didn't have… Ah."

Ginny lifted a brow and made a show of peering around the arched doorway into the dining room. "Yeah. We have one, huh? Right?"

"I think so." Sean sighed. "You want me to unpack those boxes."

"It would be nice. C'mon, we can do it together. You can lift all the heavy things. I'll tell you where they go." She smiled again, watching his face work as he tried to think of a way to get out of the task.

"Fine." He sighed again. "Fine, fine, fine."

But though they unpacked four or five boxes and even managed to shift the furniture around at least sort of the way she wanted it to stay permanently, they found no flashlights. She did convince Sean he needed to run the vacuum cleaner, though, to get up all the bits and pieces of packing paper and dust that had been inevitably kicked up.

"It's way too strenuous," she told him with a very wicked grin as she plopped onto the couch with a book in her hand. "You really should do it."

Grumbling, Sean looked like he meant to argue, but wisely thought better of it. He plugged in the vacuum, a pricey model he'd given her as a gift one year for her birthday— her birthday, for the love of all things holy! Which she'd never really let him live down.

The instant he toed the On switch, the lights went out.

"Shit," Sean said.

In the dark, Ginny laughed.

Chapter Fifteen

"Let me go first. You're gonna love it, I know it. Happy anniversary." Sean pressed a square package into Ginny's hands and stepped back with a grin. "Go on. Open it."

She studied the wrapping carefully. She loved surprises. Loved getting presents. And though they'd both agreed that this year they wouldn't spend any money on each other for their anniversary since they'd just moved into the house, she'd been unable to help herself from buying him something she knew, absolutely knew he wanted. This package in her hands was just the right size for an iPad, which she'd been none too subtly hinting she wanted since her last birthday, when he'd presented her with a vacuum cleaner instead.

Ginny smoothed her fingers over the paper, enjoying the anticipation but feigning concern. "I thought we said we weren't going to do anything for each other."

"I know, I know, but I saw this and knew you had to have it. Go on," Sean said. "Open it up. Let's see."

So she did, sliding her fingers beneath the tape and pretending she meant to fold back the paper in one piece, the way she knew drove him crazy, because Sean liked to tear into gifts and leave the wrapping strewn all over in shreds. She laughed when he danced forward to take it from her, holding it back and away.

"Mine," she told him, and ripped the paper while holding her breath with excitement.

She had to stare at what was inside for a full minute before she remembered to let out the breath. Then another, her eyes not quite connecting with her brain. The paper slipped from her suddenly nerveless fingers and drifted to the floor where Sean crunched it under his feet as he shifted to lean over her shoulder.

"See? You plug it in and it charges up automatically. You can set it to act like a night-light or just when the power goes out, it will come on. And it's a two-pack, so we can put one down here and one upstairs."

He looked so proud, so gleeful all she could do was nod and smile like this two-pack of flashlights from the warehouse club was indeed the very best anniversary gift she'd ever received. "Wow. Yeah. It's…wow."

Sean, clearly pleased with himself, took the package from her to open it, demonstrating how she could plug it into any outlet, how the light-sensitive function worked. How the flashlight itself fit neatly into the holder in any direction, not needing to be lined up any special way.

"It's great," Ginny said around her disappointment. She reminded herself they *had* said they weren't going to buy each other gifts. And that would've been better, she thought. To get nothing because they'd said they were doing nothing, than to get…

"I just want to make sure you're never left in the dark again," Sean said.

Only a selfish shrew could be angry or disappointed when he said something like that. And only a vindictive bitch could take pleasure in seeing his face when she took him down the hall and pulled the sheet off the present she'd had to be so careful to keep a surprise. Ginny guessed she must be both, because she was still a little bitter when she gave Sean his gift.

"What the…" He stared at it. Then her. Jaw dropped. Then he grinned and went to his knees in front of it like a little kid. "Holy shit. How did you do this?"

"I had it delivered. Do you like it?"

He put a hand on the 42-inch flat screen's box and looked down with a marveling shake of his head. "Like it? I fucking love it."

Of course she'd known he'd love it—he'd talked with longing about replacing their ancient television for at least a few years. Sort of the way she'd been talking about wanting an iPad. But hearing the joy in his voice, Ginny could no longer be upset that she'd made such an effort when he hadn't made one of equal size…or expense, she admitted to herself, thinking of his reasons for choosing the flashlights. And when it came right down to it, money should be no measure of someone's affection.

"I'm glad," she said, and meant it. "Let's get it set up, okay?"

"Yeah, yeah." He looked up at her, eyes alight, then got to his feet to hug her hard. "You're the best."

She was far from that, and nobody knew that better than she did. "I'll go clean up in the kitchen. Then we can watch a movie or something?"

"Yeah." Sean was already turning to the TV stand, unhooking all the cords and wires from the old set. "That would be great."

The best. She was the best. Ginny cleaned off the table and loaded the dishwasher. She refilled the Brownies' bowl with wrapped mini candy bars this time, since Sean had seen fit to eat the peanuts and chocolate-covered raisins. She took the fine-linen cloth off the cheap card table and tossed it in the washer, and she set the candelabra back on the old dresser she used as a buffet. She put away the leftovers, making sure to package them in lunch-sized portions for Sean to take to work, because she was the best wife.

The best wife.

Chapter Sixteen

There's a lot of music at this party. Steady thumping. Lots of bass. Someone's strung up colored lights, orange and purple and green. Some are hung with pumpkins or ghosts. Some blink, though not in time with the music.

Ginny knows this place. This party. If she catches a glimpse of herself in a mirror, she'll see she's wearing a Little Red Riding Hood outfit. Blue-checkered dress, short, with a flouncy skirt and petticoat. White anklet socks. Red cape with a hood. She wore it because her roommate, Tina, convinced her that dressing slutty was the only way to attend a college Halloween party. Ginny'd planned to go dressed as a baseball player, in her brother's old uniform.

"Not cool," Tina says when Ginny tells her. "Baseball players are only fuckable by gay dudes."

Ginny sees the logic in this, although the truth is she's not necessarily looking to get laid. She dated Roy, her last boyfriend, from her senior year in high school and all through her freshman year of college, but they broke up over the summer. She slept with another guy after that, just once or twice, to get over Roy, but the truth was that sex had always been something messy, kind of awkward, never the big deal it was all cracked up to be.

Still, it's always better to be fuckable and have the choice of turning a guy down than be the girl at the party, standing alone by the punch bowl. Not that a party like this would have a punch bowl, necessarily, more like a keg, along with various bottles of cheap liquor that are mostly used for shots instead of fancy mixed cocktails, although there are a couple jugs of orange juice and cola on the makeshift bar.

So there she stands in her short, slutty dress and shoes that are pinching her toes. She has an empty basket over one arm, and it keeps getting in the way. Before the night's over she'll lose the basket and never see it again, which is terrible because she borrowed it from Tina, whose grandmother had bought it for her. Tina will always say she doesn't care, but some part of Ginny understands that Tina really does.

"Let me guess," says the frat boy. He's dressed like a baseball player, and now Ginny totally gets why Tina was right. Baseball player as a Halloween costume? Not fuckable. Or maybe it's the guy's beer belly or the rash of pimples across his forehead or the drunken, bleary way he's stroking his gaze all over her cleavage. "Dorothy? There's no place home, right? If I get you wet, are you gonna melt?"

"I'm Little Red Riding Hood, and that was the wicked witch, you asshole," this Ginny says, because this one is dreaming about that long-ago night when she wasn't quick enough with the comeback and had to fend off this loser's pawing grasp for another twenty minutes.

That's the beauty of dreams. If you know what you're doing, you can control them. Ginny's in charge of this dream now, so she can walk away from the horny baseball player and make her way right into the best part of things.

She sees him across the room, like the crowd parted just for her. Just so she can get to him without having to elbow her way past the plethora of tits and ass on display. Instead, she glides. Her shoes don't pinch because her feet don't touch the ground. She floats or maybe swims through the air, thick as water; she pushes it out of the way, scooping it with her hands.

He's the most beautiful man she's ever seen.

He wears a dark suit, a blue- and white-striped shirt, a red tie. He wears a clear-plastic raincoat, and his hair's slicked back. He carries an ax.

"Who's that guy?" Tina says. "Some huntsman."

"It's Patrick Bateman."

Patrick Bateman, played by Christian Bale in the movie version that Ginny's seen, oh, about a dozen times. He's a serial killer, murderer of whores and vapid trust-fund bitches and dudes who get more expensive haircuts than his. He's dangerous.

He's perfect.

He's leaning against the wall with his ax at his side. As she gets closer, Ginny sees it's a real one, though with some sort of shiny metal tape over the edges, presumably to keep it from actually chopping anyone apart. He has no drink in his hand, and his fingers just barely tap his thigh in time to the music. He scans the room like he's looking for someone.

Then, he finds her.

"Do you like Huey Lewis and the News?" Patrick Bateman asks Ginny when she walks up to him in her suddenly ridiculous costume.

The real-world Ginny sputtered an answer to him, trying to be coy, trying to get him to laugh. And he had, the flash of interest in his eyes clear when she bent to set down her basket.

But this is a dream, this is different. Though in the real world his name had turned out to be Joseph and he was nowhere near as smooth…or rich…as the fictional Patrick Bateman, in the dream he stares at her assessingly before he gives her a faint, supercilious smile that widens into a broad, smarmy grin when she says, "Their early work was a little too New Wave for my tastes, but when *Sports* came out in eighty-three…"

He takes her, the way he did then, away from the party. They walk down dark alleys, past stumbling revelers. Drunken, groping couples. One or two sour-faced townies with the bad luck to be out and about in a college town on Halloween night. And then, back to his place. It's nicer in the dream than it had been in real life. Modern. Expensive. He feeds her frozen yogurt from the carton and when she moves to put the spoon on the table, he chastises her quickly.

The dream is jumbled now between real life and *American Psycho* and her own psyche. Patrick Bateman kisses her hard enough to bruise her mouth. She tastes blood. He strips her out of the costume and leaves it on the floor, then takes her up against the white wall in front of a mirror big enough to show the entire room. She can see over his shoulder, his firm ass pumping as he thrusts inside her, the skin of his back marked with swirling lines of black and green. A tattoo. Definitely a product of the dream.

He bites her shoulder.

Ginny stiffens with pleasure, her eyes closing as the room tips and spins. Climax bursts through her. Then again when he pulls away to show his mouth, teeth and lips dripping red with her blood and when he holds up a hand to show off the still-beating heart clutched in his fingers. Her heart.

* * * * *

Ginny woke, panting, the aftermath of her orgasm still rippling through her. She lay on her side with her body pillow tucked between her legs, and though her mind still whirled from the strange, disturbing turn the dream had taken and from her climax, the only evidence of her reaction was the fast beat of her heart. She sipped in some air, slowly, letting her heartbeat slow.

Wow.

Yes, it was weird at the end. Definitely gross and a little scary. But also incredibly sexy. She hadn't been turned on like that since…well. A long time. She shifted under the blankets, suddenly more aware of Sean's light snores. Suddenly aware of the pressure in her bladder and how cold her nose was, how the faint ticking of the air from the vent that had soothed her to sleep was no longer there.

God dammit, the room was cold again. She'd had Sean set and reset the thermostat, even change the batteries. Now her face was like ice. Her toes too, way down at the bottom of the bed. Blinking, Ginny tried to see what time it was, but she'd turned the light completely off on her alarm clock. The clock had a design flaw that set the light from its brightest to dimmest levels, instead of the other way around, which meant hitting the button now would bathe the entire room in an eye-searing arc of blue-white light.

Without the time, all she could do was convince her body to ignore the insistent need to urinate, or risk getting out of bed to pee and discover that the alarm would be going off in about five minutes. Ginny shifted again, pulling her knees up as far as she could to tuck her feet together and try to warm them. This didn't help her bladder at all, and eventually with a small groan she flipped off the covers and eased herself out of bed.

At least in the bathroom the night-light had a clock on it. Even though she felt like she'd been sleeping for hours, it was still only just past midnight. Another six hours before Sean would get up and she'd be up too, making his breakfast and pretending she had important things to occupy her time. She peed forever. The bathroom floor was, if it was possible, colder than the bedroom. Her teeth chattered.

She heard the cries just as she pushed the handle to flush. They were lost immediately in the rush of water, which seemed to echo even more loudly in the dark. Ginny's head went up, eyes wide. She imagined herself as a gazelle, nostrils flaring at the scent of a cheetah in the grass. Ridiculous, and yet she strained to hear as the noise eased.

Nothing.

But she *had* heard it, she was sure. The faint but audible and unmistakable sound of sobs. Now all that reached her were Sean's snuffling snores and then the welcome rumble of the furnace kicking on…except that the air pushing up from the vent next to her wasn't hot. It was far from cold, the way air-conditioning would be, but it was barely tepid.

She was wide awake now. Even with the promise of a few more hours of sleep, even knowing she ought to relish this time before the baby came and interrupted nights would become her life for the next, oh, twenty years or something like that, there was no way she could get back to sleep. Only out in the hall did Ginny remember she hadn't put on her slippers, and winced in advance of whatever it was that she would eventually step on.

Ginny's mom had been a huge fan of warm milk to aid sleep, usually with a liberal dose of cocoa and vanilla sugar added to it. Of course the sugar and caffeine negated any benefit of the milk itself, but that homemade sleep remedy had always been a treat. Ginny made hers the way her mom had, stirring it slowly on the stove so the milk didn't burn or get a skin on the top. A perfect, creamy blend of sweetness and warmth. In her kitchen the light over the stove did little to chase away the dark, and she turned it off as soon as she'd finished making the cocoa.

Maybe she ought to be scared in the dark, she thought with her hands wrapped around the mug as she let the heat from it bathe her face. It was still too hot to drink. She listened to the creaks and groans that were starting to become familiar. She listened for the faint sounds of sorrow, and convinced herself she'd imagined it. Maybe she should be afraid, but there was something comforting instead about standing with her back against the counter, sipping sweetness while the wind rustled the bushes outside.

The brush of soft fur on her ankles made her jump a little, scraping the legs of her chair on the floor. Then, the jingle of Noodles's collar. Sean must've found it, wherever the cat had lost it, and put it back on.

"Hey, puss. C'mere." Ginny reached to pet the cat but got only a waft of air as Noodles ducked out of reach. Her belly made bending under the table too awkward, and, besides, if she grabbed out in the dark, Noodles was just as likely to nip Ginny's fingers as she was to accept the caress. "Fine. Be that way."

She took the mug upstairs with her, but instead of going into the master bedroom, she ducked into the library. Someday, after the garage and the landscaping and the dozens of other things they'd planned, she wanted to add bookshelves to the other two walls to match the built-ins already there. Get some comfy chairs with footstools that matched the Victorian sofa, and good lamps for reading. Maybe they could fix the fireplace in here. She imagined building a crackling fire, the smell of wood burning. Or even a gas insert, Ginny thought as she stood in the center of the room and made a slow circle. That would be cool too.

Or hot, which would be even better, she thought with a shiver before realizing that this room, at least, was much warmer than the hall had been. Or her own room. She moved toward the window next to the fireplace and pressed her fingers to the glass. Definitely cold. But on the other side of the fireplace, the bookcase had warm air puffing out around the edges. Not just warm. Tropical. It felt so good she pressed her palm to the back of the bookcase and let the wood warm her.

But why was it so warm? That was the question. This room didn't face the street, but light from the streetlamps did cut across the side yard here, so with night-adjusted eyes she could make out the hardwood floor. It was also bare, with no rugs, and all the boxes had been stacked along the opposite wall. She found the floor vents easily enough, one on the left side of the fireplace beneath the window. And the other one...

"Here," she murmured and nudged the bookcase with her toe. The other one should be there, but they'd built the bookcase over top of it.

She set her mug on the fireplace mantle to explore. Yep, there was a notch there in the molding along the bottom shelf. When she put her hand there, the air was so hot it almost burned her fingers. She wanted to get down on her hands and knees and bask in it. She wanted to put down a beach towel and pretend she was in the hot summer sunshine, wearing a bikini and tanning oil, frying herself on some beach someplace, instead of getting up to pee at midnight and standing in the dark, freezing, with her belly big and round and full of child.

Instead, she contented herself with sticking one foot against the notch and warming her toes until it felt like they might start to sizzle like bacon. Then the other. Back and forth she shifted with her hands on the bookshelf to help support her weight, and her eyelids grew heavier. Like she was slow dancing, she thought sleepily. Slow dancing with the bookcase.

Ridiculous...

Ginny snapped awake, trying to remember if she'd heard another set of those sobbing cries or if something else had woken her. It took her a good half a minute to realize it was just her body's way of protecting her from falling over, because she'd dozed on her feet, which were toasty warm at least. Stifling a yawn, she shuffled toward the doorway where her foot connected firmly with something furry and angry.

"Noodles," she scolded as the cat ran on silent feet down the hall, making shadows in front of the night-light. "Don't you know better..."

Ginny paused. She'd kicked Noodles because she was sitting, quiet. But when she ran, the telltale jingle of her collar had once again been silenced.

Huh.

Back in bed and coordinated around her multiple pillows, Ginny's lovely sleepiness had vanished. Every time she thought she might actually be able to fall back to sleep, Sean let out another grunt or a snuffle, or he shifted in the bed and pulled the covers off her and made her cold again. He'd always been a restless sleeper, but it seemed to be worse now. Or maybe she was just more sensitive to it. At any rate, at last Ginny had to resort to her old trick of counting backwards from a hundred in order to see if she could trick her brain into shutting down.

She got to eighteen before Sean coughed and her eyes flew open.

Starting over, she got to thirty-seven before he let out a long, ripping fart that had her gritting her teeth.

This time, she got to fifty before he rolled onto his back and started snoring in earnest. Ginny sat up. She leaned over and poked him. Hard.

"Honey," she said, her tone making the endearment a lie. "Roll over."

He did with another snort and snuffle, and she lay back and stared at the ceiling, even though she knew sleeping on her back was going to be impossible and she could only last a few minutes before she'd have to move. When she rolled onto her side to look out the windows, something like the first gleam of sunrise teased her.

She was still awake when the alarm went off.

Chapter Seventeen

With Sean's hands over her eyes, all Ginny could do was laugh as he guided her. "What's the surprise?"

"If I just told you, it wouldn't be much of a surprise, would it?" His breath, warm against her cheek, made her want to nuzzle against him. "Okay. Hold on a second. Don't look until I tell you. Okay?"

"Okay, okay."

She heard shuffling. The scrape of wood against wood. She knew they were in the library because he'd brought her upstairs before making her close her eyes. But what on earth could he be about?

"Open them."

She did, expecting maybe a chair to match the sofa. Instead, Ginny faced her easel—which had been set up in the dormer, with a fresh new canvas in the size she liked best. Beside it was the ugly telephone table. On it rested a new palette. Tubes of paint. A cup bristling with brand-new brushes.

"I know you threw all your old stuff away. I figured you needed some new things."

"Sean…"

"Look, the light's great right there. I mean, I'm not an artist or anything, but the sun shines in that dormer almost all day long."

She knew it did. She'd noticed. Ginny moved forward to look at the setup, then at him. "You didn't need to do this."

"Sure I did. Consider it a late anniversary present." Sean smiled. "Since what I got you was lame, I know."

She didn't want him to feel like he had to make anything up to her. She especially hadn't wanted him to feel like he had to do it by buying her art supplies. Yet, faced with all of this new equipment, the pretty colors, the fresh and untainted brushes, Ginny's fingers did twitch. Just a little.

"I got you special paints and some nontoxic brush cleaner." He sounded so proud. "Natural pigments and stuff. So…you don't have to worry about the chemicals."

It was too much. She should weep, but no tears sparked her eyes. Ginny stroked her fingertips over the canvas gently. Then she kissed him. "Thank you."

"You like it?"

"It's…so nice." The lie hardly tasted bitter at all. "So unexpected."

"Now you can paint again," Sean said. "I know you've been missing it. I can tell. You want to get started on something now?"

"Later," Ginny said. "I'll do it later."

Chapter Eighteen

"I know I have it. I know I have it in a box of things I packed specifically for the house." Ginny put her hands on her hips and looked around the smallest of the rooms on the second floor. No more than a closet really, it would be just big enough to hold a desk and a chair, maybe a set of shelves. Sean's office. If they ever moved everything out of it anyway.

Sean sighed and rubbed at his hair, that bad habit that always left him looking rumpled. She wanted to smooth it, to stroke down the sleek bits that always fell just in front of his ears and stroke it away from his forehead. Too many boxes blocked her.

"What kind of a box?"

"A file box." She indicated the size with her hands, then pointed. "Like one of those. Like any of those, but it's not one of those. I labeled all of them. It should be marked "Linwood." Anything we got from Bonnie would be in there."

"Do we even know if we have anything about the furnace?"

She shook her head and bit her lip. "No. I don't know. Bonnie gave us that entire accordion file of stuff, warranties and receipts and all that. I'd imagine if there was something, it would be in there."

"Dammit, Ginny, the furnace guy needs to know this stuff."

She frowned at his tone. "He can't figure out what's wrong on his own? I mean, isn't that supposed to be what he does? Figure out what's wrong?"

"He says he needs a ductwork schematic so he can compare it to the rooms that aren't getting hot air. He thinks we might have a blockage somewhere." Sean cocked his head and leaned out of the doorway to listen. "I think he's hollering for me, let me go check."

"What kind of blockage?" she asked with a grimace, thinking of the sounds in the walls and imagining some sort of nest.

But Sean was already gone, leaving her among the mess of boxes he'd made when he started tearing things apart. If he'd just looked at the labels, she thought with a sigh, bending to put back a handful of manila envelopes filled with tax returns. But of course he hadn't. He'd expected her to magically hand him what he needed, and when she couldn't, he'd gone willy-nilly trying to find it. And couldn't be bothered to clean any of it up, either, she thought as she put the lid back on the file box.

It didn't solve the mystery of where the box had gone, though. She couldn't even remember seeing it, to be honest, but then why would she have looked for it? The real estate agent had presented them with an enormous, in Ginny's opinion, amount of trash related to the house. Ginny never looked at instruction manuals for any appliances she ever bought, so the chances of her ever reading through those for ones she'd inherited was equally as unlikely.

The repairman had been there for an hour already. Ginny tried not to think about the cost as she went downstairs to the kitchen to finish the brownies she'd been baking before Sean interrupted her for the wild-goose hunt for the schematics. The company charged by the hour, plus for parts, so even if he couldn't find and fix the problem, they were still going to be out some cash.

"Let me just pull it out of the air," she muttered, stirring the batter. Beating it, actually, though the recipe didn't call for such abuse. She slowed her motion, moving the thick, gooey liquid with the wooden spoon.

The kitchen, as usual, was blistering. She tasted sweat on her upper lip. She poured the batter into a baking pan and settled it in the oven, then set the timer. It took her only a few minutes to clean the mess she'd made, and she finished just as Sean and the repairman came up the basement stairs.

Grunting.

Why were they grunting?

Ginny leaned out the kitchen doorway, astounded at the sight of her husband and some stranger wrestling with a table that looked too big to get around the sharp corner. In the way of men, they huffed and puffed commands at each other. "Turn it…tilt it…tip it…yeah, that's it." It sort of sounded dirty, which might've made her giggle if she weren't so astonished.

"What the…what are you doing?"

"Take it down the hall," Sean said to the repairman. With a grin over his shoulder at her, he said, "I got you a dining room table."

"From the basement?" Unable to make the angle in this direction, the men had taken the table down the hall and through the living room, but Ginny ducked into the dining room through the other doorway. "Sean?"

They settled the table in the middle of the room, under the stained-glass light fixture. Her husband looked at her proudly while the repairman-cum-furniture hauler dusted his hands on his coveralls. Ginny could only stare.

"That's a nice piece," the repairman said. "Looks like cherry."

Sean, still grinning like he'd brought her a diamond ring wrapped in a rainbow shat from a unicorn, slapped a hand on it. "Totally solid. Look at it. It was down in a corner, under a tarp."

"I remember seeing it when we looked at the house." It was *not* one of the pieces Ginny'd asked to keep. She bit her tongue in the presence of the repairman, who looked like he might be easily scandalized by a string of inventive invectives.

"Thanks for the help," Sean told him.

The other guy nodded. "No problem. So, like I was saying, the rooms that are too hot are going to stay too hot so long as you've got your thermostat set so high. That's the furnace doing what it's meant to do."

Sean stepped aside to let the guy pass, heading for the front door, and Ginny peeked around the doorway to watch them. "We set the thermostat so high to keep the other rooms, the cold rooms, at least bearable."

"I hear ya, fella. I hear ya. But these old houses, you know, sometimes the heat just goes right out the windows. Through chinks in the insulation, whatever. But I tuned it up and reset the system. You've got a good unit there." The repairman paused at the front door to look at Sean. "It would've been better if I knew who installed it or had a better idea about where some of those ducts went, if they installed all new ducts or if they used the old ones, or maybe piggybacked…whatever. I mean, some of those ducts look like they're not even functioning to me, like maybe they were put in with the old unit or something. If I could tell if they put in new ducts with the new unit, that would help. But you should see an improvement anyway."

"Thanks." Sean shook the guy's hand and closed the door behind him, then turned to the thermostat and fiddled with it before looking down the hall at her. "Hey. He says it should be fixed."

"I hope so." The smell of brownies had begun to permeate the air. She'd been careful not to lick the batter, no matter how tempting it had been, because of the raw eggs. Her stomach rumbled now.

"If it doesn't, we'll have him come back out," Sean said. "Hey. Brownies?"

"They'll be done in a few minutes."

"We can eat them on our new table."

She looked at the new-old dining room table, which was both exactly and nothing like what she'd wanted. "It's filthy."

"You don't like it? I thought you'd love it. You wanted an antique table, you said."

She had mentioned it, yes. After they'd bought the fainting couch she'd looked at a few of the dining room sets in the same antique shop. They'd been sleek, Art Deco, with designs of inlaid wood and matching buffets that had beautiful and ornate drawer handles. Nothing like this square, sharp-edged, utilitarian wooden monstrosity. This table wasn't an antique, really. It was just…old. And well used, she thought, noticing the carved initials along one short side. *CMM.* Someone had been naughty.

"From the basement, Sean? Really?"

He looked at it. "You can polish it up, it'll be great. But if you don't like it—"

"No," she interrupted him. "No. It's fine. We need a dining room table, and this way I can take my time looking for something. Someday."

Until then, they could use this table, even if it was ugly. Even if it wasn't what she wanted. She could make the best of things.

He settled his hands on her hips to pull her close for a kiss. "Have I told you how awesome you are?"

He had, many times, which only made her feel worse about hating the table he'd so obviously been happy to bring her. Ginny pushed onto her tiptoes, just a little, to kiss him back. "Hmm. Because I ply you with sweets?"

"You'll make me fat."

"Then I won't have to worry about any sexy, young chicks chasing after you," she teased, patting his flat, hard stomach. Sean never had to work out.

He looked at her seriously. "You never have to worry about that, Ginny."

She'd meant it only as a joke, but his reply was so solemn it set her back. She cupped his face in her hands and kissed him again. "I love you."

He nodded, eyes searching hers. "You do?"

"Of course I do," she told him, uneasy with the intensity of his expression. "Of course."

"Good," Sean said. "Let's eat brownies."

Chapter Nineteen

The smell. It was repulsive. Thick and cloying, the unmistakable stink of rot.

Ginny sniffed the air, then again. "Ugh. God. Sean, you need to check the glue traps."

"I did, yesterday. Nothing." He rattled the paper instructions for the TV stand with a growl. "Insert rod A into slot B. What the hell? There is no slot B."

Ginny sniffed again, walking slowly around the living room, which was still cluttered with a few boxes, even though it felt like they'd been unpacking forever. Sean had decided this was the weekend to put together the new television stand he'd insisted they needed for the new flat screen. He'd been cursing at it for the past hour and a half.

"Can't you smell that?"

He sifted through a bag of small metal parts and plucked out a screw, then cursed some more when it didn't fit into the right hole. "No. Smell what?"

"I smell it." She sniffed again, nosing along the wall and over the vent. "I can't believe you can't smell it. Something died in the walls, Sean. I'm sure of it."

"I thought you told me the exterminator said mice wouldn't smell that bad."

"I know what he said, but I'm telling you, I smell something disgusting. It's..." She leaned over the vent blowing warm air that was nowhere near hot, and grimaced. She pulled her sweatshirt sleeve over her fingers and held it over her mouth and nose. "It's stronger when the heat's on."

"Could be something in the ductwork." Sean shrugged, clearly unconcerned as he struggled with the TV stand's legs. "God dammit. Why do they have to make these things so hard to build."

"We could've paid someone to put it together in the store," she reminded him, and wished she hadn't when she saw the set of his shoulders.

"They wanted to charge a hundred bucks for set-up and delivery."

"I know they did." But if they'd done that, they could now be watching a movie together or doing something else instead of this.

"I can do it anyway."

She sighed. "I know you can."

The smell, thank God, had faded. Or she'd become immune to the stench. Either way, she could breathe with the filter of her sweatshirt. She watched him for a few more minutes, but knew better than to offer her help.

The next time the heat kicked on, though, the smell was back. She coughed from it, and Sean gave her a curious look. Ginny waved a hand in front of her face.

"You really don't smell that?"

Sean stood and took a long, deep breath. "Yeah. I smell something. It's faint, though."

"Please check those glue boards again. I'm sure something's dead on one!"

He sighed. "Sure, babe. Can I finish this first?"

Her look must've been answer enough, because Sean let out another sigh and hung his head. Without another word, he left the living room. She heard the slow tread of his feet on the stairs, in the hall, and finally into the nursery. She heard the creak of the cubbyhole door opening. More footsteps in the hall, then in their bedroom. She couldn't hear the cubbyhole door in their closet opening or closing. He came down a few minutes later with empty hands.

"I told you. Nothing. I mean, the guy said he didn't see any signs of anything, right?"

"I still hear things," Ginny said stubbornly. "In the walls. I told you."

Sean sighed and came closer, rubbing her upper arms to soothe her. "I'm sure you do…"

"I just heard it the other night," she pointed out. She did not add that she'd heard it while she was wakeful, unable to sleep, and he was snoring away.

He hugged her, stroking her hair. His shirt was damp. He smelled of sweat; she had to turn her head.

"All I can say is, I checked the traps. He said he'd be back to check the bait boxes. Right?"

"Yes."

"So," Sean said, "the next time he comes, ask him if he can smell it."

"Fine," she said, though it wasn't fine at all.

He worked in silence while she flipped through a couple of magazines. When he'd finished, he stood and waved at it. "All done."

"Looks good."

Shit, now they'd been reduced to single syllables. Ginny sighed. "You want some help hooking up the TV and stuff?"

"No. I got it."

She went to the kitchen while he worked and made him an ice-cream sundae as a peace offering. She took it to him in the living room, then stood and shivered while he ate it. He offered her some, but she shook her head.

"I'm freezing." Ginny rubbed her arms and went to the vent in the floor, feeling a waft of lukewarm air. "The kitchen's sweltering. I don't get it."

Sean sighed and handed her the empty ice-cream bowl. "I'll call the repairman again tomorrow. Okay?"

Ginny looked at the bowl, then at him. "Yeah. That would be great."

Sometimes, he did get it. Sean got to his feet and hugged her, acting like he didn't notice that she'd turned her face when he tried to kiss her. "Can't have my honey being cold, can I?"

"It's just that it should work," Ginny said. "It's supposed to be an almost-brand-new system, right? We just had the guy out here to check it out. It should just work."

"Lots of things should just work, but they don't." Sean looked at the TV stand.

Ginny knew that was certainly true. Marriage was one of them. Or maybe it was the other way around; marriage shouldn't work but did.

She looked toward the kitchen, then the bowl. "You want anything else?"

Sean, engrossed in his task, just grunted.

Ginny took the bowl into the kitchen and put it into the dishwasher. She stretched, slowly, droplets of sweat pearling on her forehead. The kitchen was still so stinking hot. The clock on the microwave blinked from their last power outage, and as she set it to the correct time, she noticed two things. The first, that it was getting late and she was getting tired. Second, Noodles had not yet been fed.

The reason she hadn't noticed was because the cat, who normally made her demands well known with a variety of vocal yowlings, had not seen fit to demand Ginny's services as head can opener. This was definitely not normal, but not entirely unheard of. Noodles could be cranky and sometimes suspicious, and Ginny was convinced the cat could also hold a grudge. If being shooed off Ginny's pillow this morning had sufficiently put her little pink nose out of joint, it was possible she was still hiding upstairs, even at the expense of her empty belly.

Opening the can would bring her running, at least it usually did. Not this time.

Ginny opened the can and scraped the gloopy, stinky contents into a bowl and set it on the special mat by the back door. No Noodles.

"Noodles! *Ssss, ssss, sss!*"

No cat. In the sweltering kitchen, Ginny licked the sweat from her lip and fought off a wave of unease. She went through the dining room to the living room, where Sean still fought with the TV stand. She didn't bother asking him if he'd seen the cat. She went past him, into the front hall, up the stairs, into the bedroom. She got on her hands and knees and looked under the bed.

Nothing.

Ginny sat up, her breath coming a little too short in her lungs. She closed her eyes, trying to remember the last time she'd seen Noodles. This morning. The cat had been making herself at home, not just on Ginny's side of the bed, but on her pillow, and Ginny had clapped her hands and shouted to chase her away. She hadn't seen her since.

"Shit. Shit, shit…" Ginny rubbed her face, got up and went downstairs.

"Sean. Have you seen Noodles?"

He looked up at her, the building instructions crumpled in his fist. "Huh? No."

Ginny sat slowly on the couch, which was still nowhere near where she wanted it to be. "She's missing."

"What do you mean, missing?" Sean wasn't paying attention to her, his focus still on the TV stand, which now at least looked as though it could hold the TV. "I'm sure she's around. Did you call her?"

"Yes. Of course. I opened her food, she didn't come running. I'm worried she got out of the house, maybe when I went out to get the mail."

"I'm sure she'll turn up." Sean turned back to fussing with cords and wires.

This answer didn't suit Ginny, who went through the house, calling the cat's name over and over with an increasing amount of desperation. Ginny looked in every closet, every crawl space, under every piece of furniture, behind every door. No Noodles. She opened the front door and called out into the night, thinking that if the cat had run out, she'd be more than eager to run back inside to her safe, warm house, but the only answer was a car passing by, splashing up a puddle from the day's earlier rain.

"She's gone," she told Sean in the living room, where he'd finally finished his project. "I can't find her anywhere."

He looked up with a frown. "She'll turn up. Even if she ran outside—"

"I called for her outside. She didn't come."

"Someone will find her." Sean looked at the TV, then at her. She could see the struggle on his face, the desire to finish getting his new toy set up and the knowledge he should somehow comfort her.

At least he thought he should. Ginny wasn't interested in being comforted. She backed up a step when it looked like her husband meant to come and hold her. She wanted to find her cat. Not be woo-wooed and petted.

"She'll come home," Sean said. "If she's outside, someone will find her, or she'll come home."

The floor vibrated beneath Ginny's bare toes as the furnace kicked on. The curtains blew gently. Ginny took a breath, her hormone-enhanced sense of smell working hard. The faint scent of rot swirled around her, and she clapped a hand over her mouth and nose.

"What if she's not outside?"

"Then she's fine," Sean soothed. He moved toward her but the cords tangled on his foot, and the television leashed him in place.

"No, no. I mean, what if she's in the house, but...trapped somewhere? Don't you smell that?" Ginny cried, shuddering. "Christ, Sean. Tell me you smell it."

He took a long, deep breath. "I smell it. But it's hardly anything, honey. It's a mouse, like the guy said. Got stuck in the walls. It's not Noodles."

Sean dropped the cords. This time, Ginny didn't move away when he came to hold her. She pressed herself against him, her eyes closed, as he rubbed her back. Her belly made a bigger distance between them than she was used to, really noticeable for the first time.

"We'll find her. I promise."

She knew he couldn't promise anything of the sort, but she let him anyway.

Chapter Twenty

Ginny's gran might not always be completely locked in the present day, but she never looked anything less than her best. Compared to Ginny's mom, who wore a sweatshirt with a stain on it, her hair frowzy, her jeans out of style, Gran was the epitome of a classy lady. From her carefully coiffed perm to the shoes that matched her bag that matched her belt, Gran looked like she'd just stepped out of a salon run by fashion elves slaving to dress her. There was no such thing, of course. Ginny's mom had been the one to make sure Gran had everything she needed, and she wasn't afraid to make sure Ginny and everyone else knew it.

"Hours," she said. "Hours it took us to get ready."

"Well, Gertrude, if you took some care with your own appearance, perhaps mine might not be such an offense," Gran said with a sniff and held her hand out for Sean to take as she hobbled through the front door.

He looked at it as though he wasn't sure if she meant for him to kiss it, and Ginny stifled a laugh. Gran had never approved of Sean, who'd shown up to his first family function wearing a black-leather jacket and a week's worth of beard scruff, riding a Harley-Davidson motorcycle. That he'd sold the bike and kept the jacket in the back of a closet now wouldn't make a difference. Gran could forget what she had for breakfast that morning, but she'd never forget that Ginny's "boy" was of the bad sort.

"Virginia. You're looking fat."

"Thanks, Gran." Ginny stepped aside so Sean and her mom could ease Gran into the living room and onto the couch, which stuck out awkwardly in the middle of the room because they'd stacked up all the still-unpacked boxes behind it.

"Mother, Ginny's not fat. She's pregnant," Ginny's mom said too loudly. "Remember? We're here for Ginny's baby shower!"

"And I'm old, not deaf," Gran retorted. She gave Sean an up-and-down look before turning back to Ginny. "Virginia, have your boy bring me something to drink. Two fingers of Scotch, no ice."

"Mother," Ginny's mom began, but Ginny waved her quiet.

Sean backed up a step. "I'll get it."

He already knew to make the drink only half the alcohol Gran requested, the other half water. She complained it was too strong the other way and wouldn't finish more than a few sips.

Ginny gestured for her mom to sit in the armchair while she took the other. They both looked at Gran, who stared back.

"Are you going to give me food, or what?" Gran asked suddenly. "It's mashed-potatoes-and-meat-loaf night at home. What are you going to feed me?"

"There's plenty of food, Gran." Ginny smoothed her shirt over her belly, feeling self-conscious though she wasn't any fatter now than she'd been this morning when she got dressed.

Gran snorted as Sean brought the drink and pressed it into her hand. She stared up at him. "You look much better clean-shaven."

Sean passed a hand over his cheeks and chin, then gave Ginny a brow-raised glance and a quick smile. "Thanks."

"I liked his scruff," Ginny blurted. "I liked it when he looked a little ragged."

Sean looked surprised. Then pleased. Gran, however, sniffed and daintily sipped from her glass before making a face and holding it out for him to take.

"This drink tastes like a ruffian made it."

"Can I be a ruffian if I'm clean-shaven?" Sean said it with a straight face but a twinkle in his eyes.

Before Gran could reply, the doorbell rang and Sean went to answer it. Soon the living room overflowed with guests, and Ginny wished, hard, she'd been more demanding about unpacking the boxes Sean had insisted would be fine shoved up along the wall under the windows. She cringed as Billy's daughter Kristen, running after her brother, ran into a box that made a definite jingling sound when bumped.

That made her think of Noodles and the bell on her collar, and how the cat would've hated this crowd, and how they'd have had to lock her in a room to keep her from darting out the front door. How she'd probably have peed on something out of spite. Maybe, Ginny thought suddenly, with the door opening so often, Noodles would make her way back home, reappearing underfoot like the triumphant small queen the cat had always been.

She didn't, though, and playing hostess gave Ginny little time to think about it further. The present opening was an extravaganza of paper and ribbon, onesies and booties and diapers and plush toys. Such generosity moved Ginny to tears more than once, but it seemed quite acceptable for the expectant mother to cry when she opened a handmade and embroidered quilt it must've taken her mother more than a year to make. Ginny didn't point out what that meant, not when they were all there to celebrate. But she knew.

It was a big party, bigger than Ginny wanted, but her mom and Peg had insisted on inviting everyone who could possibly be invited, plus some people Ginny wasn't even sure she knew. Sean's mother hovered around making sure the food was all set up and drinks poured, which was nice but gave Ginny nothing to do but sit and hold court. Barb had also brought along all the paper products and baked a cake with plastic babies riding carrots on the top that looked like something out of a horror movie. Now she nursed a glass of white zinfandel and laughed too loudly at whatever Ginny's mom was saying to her.

Ginny had filled a plate with beef barbecue on a roll, macaroni salad, red beet eggs. The same food that had been served at every baby shower she'd ever been to. She'd been starving and ate too fast; now her stomach rumbled and ached, and she wondered if it would be bad form to ask everyone to leave so she could take a nap. She leaned in the parlor doorway, looking at the stacks of gifts she'd opened. Babies needed so many things.

"Look at all the loot." Sean appeared beside her.

"Yeah, I know." She leaned against him. "Don't be a ruffian and run off with all of it."

He put an arm around her shoulders and kissed her temple. "That's me, hooligan to the core. Maybe I should grow my beard again, you think?"

"Beard. Ha. You never had a beard." She turned to face him. "You only ever had that three days' worth of stubble. I could never figure out if you thought it made you look like a badass, or you were just too lazy to shave."

"Now you know, huh?"

"Yeah. Too lazy," she teased, and kissed his mouth.

He tasted of Scotch and, more faintly, of cigarettes, but that had to be her imagination because Sean had quit smoking a few years ago. The first time she got pregnant. She kissed him again and slid her hands, flat, up the soft corduroy of his jacket to cup his shoulders.

"Were you...smoking?"

He looked briefly guilty, then...not defiant. More like daring. "I was out back with your brother, showing him where I wanted to put the shed."

Surely the size or expense of a shed wasn't that important or stressful that a discussion necessitated cigarettes. "Sean."

"Yeah. We were smoking. Drinking a little too. It's a party, baby." He nuzzled her, his mouth finding the sensitive spots on her neck and below her ear, making her shiver. "Can't a guy get a little happy at his wife's baby shower?"

Ginny had never been the one to tell Sean he had to quit smoking, he'd done that on his own. Of course she'd been glad he quit. Of course she had. But now, his kisses flavored with liquor and smoke, his hands sliding up her hips to cup her waist, Ginny had a flashback to the first night they'd fucked. You couldn't even have called it making love. No bed, no soft music or candles or slow, sweet undressing.

The first time she'd had him inside her, they'd been at a party thrown by someone she didn't know. A house she'd never been inside before. There'd been loud music, a table laden with food, the air thick with smoke and even the tang of marijuana. Sean had introduced her to all his friends as "his girl," though they'd only been seeing each other for a week or so and Ginny wasn't even sure she meant to keep going out with him. His fingers had linked with hers, his other hand free to hold his cigarette, but he was so careful to never blow the smoke at her. Considerate that way, and also in how he made sure she always had a fresh drink, a plate full of goodies if that's what she wanted. He remembered that she liked pepperoni and not shrimp, that she preferred her drinks without ice. He'd paid attention to her back then.

The revelation had hit her, watching him laugh with a guy whose name she still didn't know. Sean's hand in hers, his focus on someone else, the sheen of colored lights from the Christmas tree making pretty patterns on his face and against the soft fringes of the hair he always, always, always wore in front of his ears. She'd tugged his hand and he'd turned to her at once, making her the most important person in the room to him.

They'd fucked in a tiny powder room, her ass slipping on cold porcelain, his jeans around his ankles. His hand over her mouth when she started to cry out. She could still taste his skin.

"Come with me," she whispered now and took his hand, but when she tugged him toward their powder room, Sean hung back.

"Ginny. What are you doing?"

No, she wanted to say. *Don't speak. Don't refuse me. Just come into the bathroom with me and shut the door, and put yourself inside me and put your hand over my mouth so nobody hears me cry out your name.*

She laughed instead, shaky and self-conscious, her humor insincere. "Nothing. Just playing."

"Later," he told her. He kissed her temple.

But there would be no later, because it wouldn't be the same. And that was the problem, wasn't it, Ginny thought as she watched her husband walk away from her. Things changed. Nothing stayed the same.

"Time for caaaake," Barb trilled, appearing in the arched doorway between the kitchen and dining room. "Everyone, come and have some cake!"

Ginny put on a smile. Sean's mom, for all her useless fluttering, did make a mean red velvet cake, with icing to die for, and Ginny fully intended to take advantage of her eating-for-two status. Despite the weird plastic babies—riding carrots, of all things—the cake was pretty, all white and red and presented on the special cake platter Barb used for every special occasion.

"You cut it," Barb said. "I tried something new, a special recipe, because I know how much you like cherry pie, Ginny."

They had a cake knife, but of course it was still in a box somewhere, so Ginny took the cleaver Sean handed her. Someone made a joke about never getting between a pregnant woman and cake. Everyone laughed. Ginny pressed the blade slowly through the white icing, the dense red cake...and into something else.

As she lifted the first piece of cake, the insides oozed and dripped with sticky red goo. Thick clots of it clung to the cleaver. One plopped onto the table. Ginny recoiled.

Blood.

So much blood.

"It's a cherrvelvet!" Barb clapped her hands. "A cherry pie inside a red velvet cake! I thought if it worked out, I'd make a cherrpumple for Thanksgiving. That's a cherry pie inside a pumpkin pie inside an apple pie."

Ginny swallowed against a thin sting of bile. "It's...great."

"Looks like something that got squashed on the road," Gran said. "And why do those cherubs have such gigantic private bits?"

God bless Gran for distracting the crowd. Ginny handed the knife to Sean. She backed away from the oozing, dripping cake.

"We'll need some more plates," she said faintly. "I'll get some."

In the still-unorganized pantry, Ginny let the spring-loaded door close behind her.

The small room was blisteringly hot, and the stench that had so plagued the rest of the house earlier still lingered here. She put a hand over her mouth and nose and gripped the shelving with the other as she sagged.

* * * * *

Blood.

There's so much blood.

She goes to the toilet, her back aching, her belly cramping. Ginny knows what this means. She's always known. She could tell from the beginning. Something didn't feel right, it never had. She never told Sean. She didn't want him to worry. He's been so excited.

When she goes to the toilet and puts her hand down between her legs, her fingers come away covered in blood. Dark, thick blood. Clots of it cling to her skin. Another rush of cramping squeezes her, and Ginny cries out. There's a woman in the next stall, so Ginny bites her lip against another cry.

The pain is worse than it was the other times. Like her insides are tearing. Shredding. *Which…they are,* she thinks as another wave of pain washes over her.

She is losing her baby.

Everything inside her goes tight, tangled, twisted; her belly tenses. Hard like a rock. She's not even in maternity clothes yet, just wearing a size larger, and she lifts the hem of her T-shirt to press her hands against her bare skin. The blood smears on her pale skin. There is so much of it, it's everywhere.

She needs to find her phone. She needs to call for help. She needs to have this not be happening, but it is. Even as she fumbles for the phone and presses the emergency number, another series of contractions push through her. She can't speak through gritted teeth. She can only groan.

"Are you…okay?" Someone outside the stall raps softly.

"No," Ginny manages to say. "I'm losing my baby. Please call for help."

The sound of running feet. The slamming of the restroom door. Oh, how she wishes she'd stayed home today instead of going to the grocery store. Then she would be at home, in her own bathroom. But she's not, she's here, and the blood keeps coming.

Something soft and loose happens between her legs. Something tries to slip out of her, and Ginny holds it back with one hand while she leans to unlock the stall door with the other. There are paramedics there on the other side, one young man, one older woman.

"We're here, hon," says the woman and locks her gaze with Ginny's. "We're here now. You can let go."

And Ginny does.

She lets her daughter go, and there is more blood. Always more blood. And they take her away to the hospital, where Sean doesn't show up for hours and hours. When he does, his face is pale, his hair is mussed, he stinks of cigarettes and alcohol, maybe even the faintest hint of perfume. Ginny doesn't even care. She can't look at him when he's there at last, because he'd been so convinced it would all be okay, and she'd known it wouldn't, but she'd let him believe it.

* * * * *

Hours have passed in her memory, but only minutes in the pantry. She needed to hurry before someone who meant well came in here after her and she had to blow off her tears as more sentimentality. Ginny scanned the shelves for paper plates and napkins and found a plastic bag she remembered buying at the store. The paper goods were inside.

As she moved to pull the bag from the shelf, her toe nudged against a bulk bag of rice she'd brought from the townhouse and dropped in the pantry without using once since they'd moved. The bag shifted, revealing the vent it had been covering, and fell on its side with the contents spilling. With a curse, Ginny bent to sweep up the grains with her fingers, too aware of the party noises from outside and expecting Sean's mom to poke her head inside at any minute.

Some of the rice skittered across the floor and into the vent pulsing hot air. More spilled as she tried to lift the bag and close it. Ginny grabbed a handful, debating about just tossing it back in the bag and throwing the whole thing away—the chances of them ever eating any of it seemed pretty slim at this point.

Something moved in her hand.

Startled, Ginny looked down at her palm. Some of the white grains of rice were... moving. Wiggling. Too stunned to even drop it at first, the low, angry buzz of something else distracted her. As she watched, a fly forced its way out of the vent. Bobbing on the currents of hot air, it tumbled drunkenly toward her.

Ginny dropped the rice and maggots to swat at it, but the fly dive-bombed her. Disgusted, she backed up, still crouching. More flies came out of the vent, at first one by one, then in twos and threes. Twenty flies circled her. Then more.

Ginny scrambled backwards and hit the door, which opened inward and made it impossible for anyone to open, though by now she'd started screaming. Covering her face against the flies' assault, she tried to find the doorknob with her other hand, but her fingers skidded on the wood and missed the metal handle. She heard muffled shouts. The door bumped behind her, moving her toward the flies. She had to move forward into the thick of the buzzing swarm still pouring out of the vent so the door could open, but in her terror found it almost impossible to do it.

"Ginny!" Sean hollered, pounding then shoving on the door hard enough to force her forward a few steps.

The flies swept past her and into the kitchen, where the much larger space dispersed them from a thick black cloud to a more widespread swarm. Party guests screamed and ducked, running. Someone ran into the table, shaking it hard enough to topple the cake stand onto its side, spattering red velvet cake and cherry pie all over. Billy, always a quick thinker, grabbed a swatter from the hook on the side of the cabinet, and started flailing.

"You okay?" Sean looked into her eyes, holding her upright.

Ginny nodded, swallowing her disgust. "Yes. Gross. What the hell?"

He looked past her into the pantry. "They must've been breeding in that bag of rice or something. You sure you're okay?"

Ginny nodded again, straightening. "Yes. Go help my brother. Get rid of them."

Ginny's mom opened the back door, letting in a swirl of icy wind, but allowing the men to shoo the flies toward it. Some fell dead under Billy's swatter and the rolled-up catalog Sean grabbed from the counter. Others flew off into the house, God only knows where, the thought of finding them later making her shudder.

In just a few minutes, everything had calmed down, except for Sean's mom, who sobbed over the broken cake like she'd given birth to it instead of her son. Peg and Dale made their goodbyes, while Billy wrangled his kids into the powder room to get them clean from eating the cake with their bare hands. Ginny's mom took Barb to the living room so she could get herself under control. Sean went to the alcove to find the mop and bucket, leaving Ginny and her gran standing in the middle of the now-empty, but at least flyless, kitchen.

Gran still clutched her glass of Scotch. Her lipstick had smudged, her carefully styled hair a little rumpled. She looked smaller than she ever had, her shoulders and back hunched. She lifted her glass in Ginny's direction, and Ginny waited for the scolding or the accusation that Ginny had a filthy house.

"That girl did it," Gran said.

"What girl? Kristen?"

"Who's Kristen?"

Ginny sighed. "Billy's daughter, Gran. You know Kristen. She's ten? Blonde?"

"Looks like her mother, oh that one." Gran nodded. "Same sour face."

"Oh, Gran." Ginny bit the inside of her cheek to keep from laughing.

"Not that one. The other girl. The one with the dark hair. Like yours when you were small. I saw her upstairs." Gran sipped from her glass with a grimace and shuffled to the sink to pour away the liquid. "Nobody knows how to make a decent drink anymore."

All of Billy's kids were as blond as Kristen, all taking after their mother, as Gran had pointed out. Peg's daughter Maria had dark hair, but she was away at college, not at the party. Ginny moved to take the empty glass before Gran could drop it.

"You saw a picture of Maria? Upstairs?"

Gran looked contemptuous. "Not a picture, Virginia. Listen to me. That girl. Upstairs."

Gran stabbed a gnarled finger, the nail painted bright red, at Ginny. "That girl looked like a hobo. Hair a mess. Wearing rags. Shameful, really. A girl like that would bring filth with her."

"I don't understand." Unease dried Ginny's throat, so she filled Gran's glass with water from the tap and drank it, tasting a hint of Scotch. "There was no girl, Gran."

Gran sighed. "I saw her, just like I'm seeing you right now. You mark my words, Virginia. She's trouble."

"Who's trouble, Mother?" Ginny's mom came into the kitchen and gave Ginny a sympathetic glance. "I came to get Barb a cold compress."

"Oh. God." Ginny grimaced and moved aside so her mom could pull a clean dishcloth from the drawer. "She's that bad, huh?"

Ginny's mom lowered her voice. "I swear she almost passed out."

Again, Ginny bit the inside of her cheek to keep from laughing as Sean reappeared with the cleaning supplies. He held them aloft triumphantly, then caught sight of her. His brows raised.

"What? They weren't where I thought they'd be." He looked from Ginny to Gran, to her mom. "Where's my mom?"

"She's calming down in the living room," Ginny's mom said.

Sean sighed, shoulders slumping, and set the mop and bucket down. "Right. Okay. I'll be back to take care of this."

"You never mind," Gran said firmly. "The day a man can clean a kitchen floor better than a woman can is the day we all get taken up to heaven on the back of a unicorn farting rainbows."

"Mom." Ginny's mom sighed and shook her head. "For God's sake."

"No, Gran. You're not cleaning my floor. It's time for Mom to take you home anyway. You go." Ginny shooed her. "I'll take care of this."

At first, Gran didn't move, but then she nodded and allowed Ginny's mom to shuffle her toward the front door. There she hung back to look askance into the living room and mutter something about "ridiculous biddies," before Ginny's mom helped her into her coat and tied the scarf around her throat.

In the doorway, the cold air making Ginny shiver, Gran paused and wouldn't be moved along, even by her daughter's arm-tugging. "You listen to me, Virginia. Get yourself a priest."

"Mom. What does Ginny want a priest for?"

"That girl is trouble, Virginia. You get yourself a priest and get her out of your house."

Then Ginny's mom was moving Gran off the porch and along the sidewalk toward the car, Sean's mom was up and in the kitchen, insisting on getting on her hands and knees to take care of the mess, and Sean was pouring himself a full glass of Scotch.

"What the hell was your grandmother talking about?" he said in an aside as Ginny tried her best to just stay the hell out of Barb's way.

"I have no idea. Can you get rid of that rice?"

"Sure." He drained the glass and set it in the sink. Then he took Ginny in his arms. "Hey. You okay? You look pale."

"I feel a little woozy," Ginny told him. "I'm going upstairs to lie down, okay?"

* * * * *

The nursery was still bare, though soon enough all the gifts they'd received today would be brought up to fill it. Ginny stood in the empty room, remembering how she'd imagined what it would look like when it was finished. When they had a baby cooing and crying in the crib Sean had not yet put together. When she would rock her child in the chair they'd not yet bought. She put her hands on her belly.

"A girl…with dark hair…like yours when you were small."

Ginny closed her eyes and whispered, "Baby, are you here?"

But when she opened them, the room was still as empty as it had always been.

Chapter Twenty-One

"Have you seen my mug?"

Sean didn't even look up from his iPhone, where he was busy tapping away at some zombie game he'd become obsessed with. "No."

Ginny looked again into the cupboard. She ran her fingers along the collection of mugs. None of them matched, which had never bothered her before but suddenly irritated her. Their plates matched. Their silverware matched. Their glasses even matched, a full set of tumblers, drinking glasses and wineglasses in a pattern she'd picked out for their wedding registry and sometimes regretted because it had been the most expensive one. They'd had to spend a fortune to finish the set after getting only a few pieces, and the cost to replace any that broke was ridiculous.

Ginny started pulling out the motley collection of freebies from banks and charities, lining them up on the counter until Sean finally bothered to look up and ask what she was doing. "I'm looking for my mug. I told you. Have you seen it?" A sudden uncharitable thought made her eyes narrow. "Did you take it to work and leave it there?"

"No."

"Think hard." She kept her tone as pleasant as she could, as nonconfrontational, but she couldn't keep it entirely sweet. "Did you take my mug?"

"I don't even know which mug you're talking about." Sean stood. "I gotta run."

And run he tried, without bothering to put his dish in the dishwasher. Or even the sink, which would still have been an affront, but would've at least been something of an effort. Ginny stared at the plate, the fork still soaking in the mess of fried eggs and last bit of jelly toast he hadn't eaten.

She'd be damned if she cleaned it up. She'd cooked him that breakfast when the very smell of frying eggs still made her want to heave. She'd even spread that toast with jelly, grape, which she also loathed, because he'd been running late in the shower and she didn't want him to have to rush. And now he not only got up without bothering to pretend he intended to clean up after himself, like any adult would, but to add another insult, he was ducking away from her inquiries about her mug.

"Hey!" she cried, stopping him at the front door. The cold swirled in, but she didn't care just then. The house was going to be too damned cold anyway. A few minutes of wintery air pummeling her hardly mattered. "My mug."

Sean sighed and turned. "Which one?"

"The one with the pink skull and crossbones on it. The one my sister bought for my birthday." She eyed him, still suspicious. "You know, the tall, skinny one?"

She saw a flicker of recognition in his eyes. It made her frown. She liked that mug because her sister had picked it out for her on a weekend trip away a few years ago. They'd gone to a bed-and-breakfast and done some outlet shopping, eaten in nice restaurants that weren't kid friendly. It had been the last time they'd done anything like that—life had gotten in the way. Ginny had spent her next birthday in the hospital, miscarrying.

She liked it because it reminded her of good times. Sean liked it because the tapered bottom fit neatly into his cup holder. She'd bought him a travel mug, but he still took hers. He didn't see the problem, after all. There were plenty of mugs for her to use, and of course her insistence that he leave "hers" alone made her out as some unreasonable shrew.

"I didn't leave it at work."

"Did you use it?" The accusation rang out, too loud, too harsh for this early in the morning and the enormity of the offense. Or lack of.

His gaze skittered from hers. "I…if I did, I put it in the dishwasher. Look, I have to go. I'm going to be late."

"Fine. Go." She flapped a hand at him, already turning to swallow her anger, to shove it down deep so it couldn't come out in another outburst.

"Maybe you left it somewhere," he said from the doorway, but was gone before she could reply.

Left it somewhere?

It could've been a dig. At least, in the mood she was in, Ginny wanted to take it that way. It was true; she was more apt to be the one leaving her belongings strewn about. Her shoes, car keys, a sweater draped over the railing instead of hung in the closet. It was a flaw, she knew it, but because she knew how it irritated him to find her stuff all over the place, she'd been trying harder to make sure she was better about it.

Because she listened to him, she thought bitterly as she yanked open the dishwasher. The mug wasn't in there, and she wasn't surprised. She hadn't used the fucking thing.

Yesterday she hadn't made tea because even the decaf seemed to be wreaking havoc with her sleep. She'd been up every night for the past three. Counting backwards from one hundred did nothing. Neither did lavender on her pillow, though it did give her varied vivid and intriguing dreams during the few hours she did manage to sleep.

Ginny closed the dishwasher and moved again to the cupboards to search them all in case someone had put it away in the wrong place. Nothing. Anger simmering, she drew in a slow breath and let it out, reminding herself to keep her blood pressure from rising. She could drink her herbal, decaf tea from a different mug. No big deal.

Except that it was, and she wanted to cry when she filled another mug with hot water and let the tea bag steep. Even as she swiped her tears with the back of her hand, Ginny knew she was being ridiculous. But that was the deal with pregnancy and lack of sleep, wasn't it? Emotions running high and close to the surface, ready to spill over.

Tonight if she didn't sleep she'd think about making an appointment with the doctor, she decided when she took her tea into the living room to look through the old issues of her magazine subscriptions that had finally caught up to the address change and arrived in bulk. She'd suffered this before. Not quite insomnia. She had no trouble getting to sleep when she went up to bed. Hell, there were some nights that if she hadn't had to wait for Sean to get home from class so they could have dinner and spend some time together, she'd have put her pj's on and hit the sheets by eight. No, her trouble wasn't falling asleep, but staying asleep, then getting back to sleep once she woke up. Every night between midnight and 2:00 a.m. She told herself her body was preparing for the baby. It didn't make the mornings come any later.

In the living room, the slick pile of magazines slipped from her fingers and the tea scalded her when she tried to keep from dropping them. She stubbed her toe on a box that had been nudged out of place, even though she'd specifically shoved it up against the wall, hard, last night. Ginny let out a muttered curse and set her mug down on the end table that should've been an inch or so to the left but instead had also been shifted so the mug toppled to the floor and soaked the magazines. It didn't break, at least there was that.

"God damn it," she said, then louder, "son of a bitch."

She yanked a roll of paper towels from the cupboard and got on her hands and knees to blot up the mess. Her magazines were salvageable. She could make more tea. But, damn it, Ginny thought as she looked around the chaos of her living room, when the hell was Sean going to finish unpacking all these boxes the way he'd promised he would weeks ago? Months, now. It had been more like a couple of months.

"Screw this," Ginny muttered as she got to her feet. Her knees hurt, and so did her hand from the hot tea. For the first time in weeks, she'd been planning on just sitting with her feet up, the way her husband insisted, now that she had something to do while she sat, since everything else she might've occupied her time with was mostly still packed away in boxes. All she'd wanted was to read through the accumulated weeks of gossip from the celebrity magazines and maybe check out a few new recipes. Hell, learn a few things from *Popular Science* or the news magazines she'd ordered from her nephew's school fundraiser.

But nope. Instead, she looked around at the mess and could no longer ignore it. Couldn't avoid it. She was done waiting for him to "get around to it."

By lunchtime, Ginny'd managed to unpack every box in the living room and move the ones that still needed to go upstairs into the hall. She'd been ruthless. If she took something out of the box, it either found a place in the living room or was designated for some other specific place in the house…or put into the trash. She'd hauled two full trash bags out to the curb and half filled another.

She even moved the furniture. Slowly, a little bit at a time, but she did it. It helped that they didn't have much. The furniture that had filled the living room in the townhouse left plenty of space when divided between the living room and dining room, and she wasn't quite sure that everything was placed exactly where she wanted it, but it would do. At least they could freaking *use* the room, she thought as she took a few minutes' breather by settling on the couch, her feet on the ottoman, the now-dry magazines on her lap and a fresh mug of tea on the end table.

Yes. This. She looked around the room with satisfaction, ignoring for the moment the boxes in the hall that would need to be carried upstairs and her rumbling stomach, which would be soothed only for so long by the liquid. For now, she was going to sit and enjoy the results of her hard work.

She woke up an hour later, her neck stiff, the magazine article only three-quarters read and the tea long cold. Blinking, wincing, Ginny stretched and rubbed her furry tongue on the roof of her mouth. She looked outside, where the skies had gone gray enough to make it seem later than it was.

She'd needed the rest, that was for sure, but it would've been nicer to take a nap in her bed. Or at the very least, lying down on the couch instead of sitting up. Now everything ached, joints popped, and she didn't feel very rested at all. She was hungry, though. Starving, in fact, which was a nice change from the intermittent nausea that had plagued her with enough frequency that even when she didn't feel sick to her stomach, she worried enough about feeling sick that she kept herself from eating too much.

Now she felt like she could down an entire twelve-inch hoagie, a whole pizza, a couple of cheeseburgers with an order of fries and a thick, creamy milkshake. Chocolate, she thought as moved through her now completely uncluttered living and dining rooms toward the kitchen. No, mint chocolate chip. Yes. Maybe there was some ice cream in the freezer, and she'd treat herself to a scoop. Or two.

She hadn't felt this good, aside from the creaking joints, in ages. Even the nagging loss of Noodles wasn't weighing on her. She actually hummed under her breath as she pulled out the makings for a sandwich and lined it up on the kitchen table. Bread, turkey, roast beef, lettuce, pickles, mayo. She sliced some tomatoes and added them to the growing tower of lunchy goodness. No true Dagwood sandwich would be complete without some good spicy mustard—her mouth watered at the thought—and a few slices of Swiss cheese.

Except that when she looked for the mustard, the spot where it should be on the fridge door was ostentatiously empty.

Huh.

Ginny looked again. Then at the other shelves. Then at last she found it, shoved way to the back behind the bottle of lemon juice and an expired carton of half-and-half she took out to toss in the trash. She pulled out the deli package of cheese too, frowning. Sean didn't use mustard. He liked mayo or, shudder, margarine on his sandwiches. She'd even known him to spread white bread with ketchup before adding bologna, a combination that had made her gorge rise even when she wasn't fighting the pregnancy nausea. He didn't use mustard, so she couldn't blame him for putting it away in the wrong place, because how hard was it, exactly, to put things back in the place where they'd been found. Right? Even Ginny, who admittedly sometimes left her shoes by the front door until she had more pairs there than in her bedroom closet, knew enough to replace the mustard in its slot on the door. Next to the ketchup and mayo and salad dressings, that's where the mustard went, and since it wasn't there, she had to assume she'd been the one who hadn't put it back.

Uneasily, thinking of her lost mug, Ginny opened the mustard jar and found it so empty she could barely scrape enough out of it to spread on her bread. This was annoying, but not tragic. What she found when she pulled the cheese out of the package, though, was enough to make her throw it down on the table with a low cry of outrage.

It was bitten.

Someone, and it could only have been Sean, because who else would've done it?

Someone had taken a bite out of the entire block of sliced Swiss cheese and put it back in the package. The tooth marks were clear, rippled around the edge of one of the larger natural holes in the cheese. The entire package was ruined, and why? To what freaking purpose?

"He doesn't even *like* Swiss cheese!" Ginny cried aloud.

Which probably explained why he'd taken only one bite, though it didn't come close to making sense of why he'd bitten it in the first place. Grumbling, Ginny threw the cheese and the half-and-half into the garbage, then finished her sandwich. Sans cheese it was still good, but her appetite had been cut in half. She finished only part of the sandwich and wrapped up the rest for later, tucking it back into the deeper realms of the fridge so Sean wouldn't accidentally take it for his lunch tomorrow.

"He'd take it and complain about how it had mustard on it," she groused to her sister when she called a few minutes later while Ginny was cleaning her mess. "Gah. Peg, I'm so annoyed."

"I hear that." Peg's sigh filled up the phone. "It's like a war zone in my house right now. Between indoor lacrosse, Dale's triathlon training and work, oh yeah. Work, 'cuz everything else we do is 'leisure.' We barely have time to breathe."

Ginny's hands drifted over the mound of her belly. "It was different when I worked. I didn't notice the mess or care about it as much, I guess. Or maybe he was just more in to helping out, we both pitched in. But now that I'm home full time..."

Peg snorted a chuckle. "Oh, just wait until the sprout arrives. You'll look back on this time as your glory days."

"You're not helping."

"Sorry." Peg sounded anything but contrite, but she did try again. "I guess my best big-sister advice to you is to take it easy. Let Sean do the unpacking, like he wants to."

"Like he says he wants to. But then never does. I understand he's tired when he gets home from work, and school's been harder than he thought it would be. I get that too. But, Jesus Christ, I'm the one who has to maneuver around everything in boxes, try to find stuff..." She trailed off.

"You need to take care of yourself. Should I have Dale talk to him?"

"No," Ginny said, thinking of how little Sean would appreciate a lecture from his brother-in-law. "You guys are busy enough. Anyway, I did it all down here, and he won't be home for a few more hours. I'll do some more and it won't even be an issue."

"It sounds like it is an issue, though. And, Gin, you need to be careful..."

Irritation flared. "Sean says the same thing. You're supposed to be on my side."

More silence.

Ginny sighed. "I had an appointment just last week. The doctor said everything was fine. I'm not on any restrictions. I'm not high risk. There's absolutely no indication of any problems. At. All. I'm not running a marathon or lifting barbells, for crying out loud, Peg. I'm just putting away books and knickknacks."

She didn't mention the huffing and puffing of pushing the couch and chairs into place, or the boxes of books that were meant to be taken upstairs. Her sister's pregnancies, all six of them, had gone off without a hitch. By the last one, she gave birth at home in her bed, with all the kids around her, cheering on the birth of their new baby brother, and it was over before the midwife even arrived.

Her sister didn't have any real idea what it was like to know that the life inside her had died and was decaying, or what it was like to crouch in a public restroom, knowing there was nothing she could do to stop her body from rejecting it. Her sister understood grief and could probably understand the loss of a child more fully than Ginny could yet grasp, but she couldn't really understand what it was like to lose one in the womb.

Peg also couldn't understand how important it was to Ginny that her loss did not define her. Not her life, and not this pregnancy. This child was still clinging to life inside her and had not yet shown any indication of giving up, and Ginny refused to surround herself and this baby with fear.

"I'm not overdoing it," she told her sister. "Trust me."

"I just worry for you. That's all. I remember how devastated you were—"

"I'm fine." Ginny cut her sister off. "Really. But I have to go. I've got to defrost some things for dinner and stuff."

"I guess you won't be serving any Swiss cheese," Peg said, and Ginny found some laughter at what just a short time ago had made her so angry.

"I should serve only Swiss cheese," she said. "And mustard."

They said their goodbyes the way sisters do, without a lot of mush and gush, but a lot of love nevertheless.

Then Ginny went back to the task she'd set herself.

Chapter Twenty-Two

By the time Sean got home that night, bringing flowers for no reason he'd admit to but which Ginny suspected had something to do with her missing mug, she'd carried all the books upstairs and put them away in the bookcases. She'd cleaned them all first, of course, and swept the floors. Dusted the mantel, that sort of thing. But what had transformed the room was the addition of her collection of hardcovers and paperbacks, many she'd owned since childhood, all arranged and displayed. Those books adorned the shelves like they'd been meant for them.

She took him by the hand after feeding him a slow-cooker beef bourguignon and homemade biscuits. When she led him upstairs, his confusion was obvious. And when she pushed him gently forward, inside, to show off her efforts, his face first fell. Then he scowled.

"What the hell is this? I thought maybe you were going to show me something you painted."

"It's my library," Ginny said calmly. "I know you said you wanted it to be a studio, but I can paint in here just as well this way…"

"That's not what I meant."

She crossed her arms, aware of how they rested now on the shelf of her belly in a way they hadn't even a few weeks ago. "What did you mean, then?"

He gestured. "This. The books. Where are the boxes? How did you get them all up here?"

"I carried them." The flavor of sarcasm was bittersweet. She didn't tell him that she'd done it a few at a time rather than lifting each heavy box. It had been easier to make many trips with lighter loads. It had taken her most of the rest of the day and left her sweaty, but satisfied.

"Christ, Ginny. I told you I'd do this."

Frustration boiled out of her. About the books and the boxes, the unkept promises.

The mug. The mustard. The cheese. And other things, months and years of things that had eaten away at her and been shoved down or pushed aside because it was always easier that way, because she owed him something greater than her anger.

"But you didn't, did you, Sean? You didn't do it! You promised and promised and promised, but every night you come home and you eat dinner, and then you disappear conveniently into the bathroom for your nightly dump while I take care of the cleanup, and then you have to read the mail, and watch some TV or do your homework, and by then it's time for bed, so you never get around to it."

"I'm tired when I get home! What do you think, I work all day and then can just come home and have all this energy left over to do your projects for you?"

She seethed, her fists clenched. "They're not *my* projects, Sean. They're part of living in this house, together, which I could easily do by myself, as you can see, because I did. And the only reason I didn't before was because you insisted that you'd do it. But you didn't. So I did. Why are we even fighting about this?"

Before he could answer, she turned on her heel to leave the room, relentless in her desire to get away from him before she said something she regretted. She'd done it before, used her tongue to cut him, and he didn't forget. Sean might forgive, but he never, ever forgot.

She thought he wouldn't follow her. He didn't like confrontation, which was why they hardly ever fought, why whenever they did argue it was because of something she said, she did, her choice. She was the one who fought, never Sean.

So when he reached out to tap her shoulder, she whirled, startled. "What?"

"Don't walk away from me," he said.

Her back stiffened. "I'm tired, Sean. I want to take a hot shower and go to bed."

For another second or two, she thought he was really going to keep up with it, but he just shook his head.

When she came out of the shower, though, he'd already turned down the sheets and sat on the edge of the bed, still fully dressed. He looked up at her when she came in, her skin still damp and flushed from the heat, her hair pulled on top of her head.

"I just don't want anything to happen to you, Ginny. That's all."

She sat beside him and thought about taking his hand, but the effort at that moment was too great. She couldn't tell what was raw between them, just that something was, and she didn't have the energy to deal with it.

"I can't sit around here doing nothing all day long."

"You could paint."

She sighed and rubbed at her eyes. "It's not that easy, you know. Besides, painting was just a hobby."

Painting had only ever been an excuse, something she'd taken up to fill in the long and lonely hours she'd wanted to spend with a husband consumed with work and school and things he wouldn't talk to her about. That she'd discovered she loved it was a bonus, something unexpected but lovely. But it hadn't started out that way. It hadn't been something she'd dreamed of doing as a kid. To see that she had some small talent for it had never pushed it beyond anything but a hobby. It had never quite become a passion.

"You could work on the baby's room."

Ginny said nothing.

"We could get a kitten," he said suddenly.

Ginny flinched. "What? No? The last thing I want is another kitten, right before…I mean…you can't just replace Noodles! You can't just get another one because the one we had ran away."

Silence, this time from him. Her words hung in the air between them, uncomfortable. Awkward. Bad memories threatened, of similar but more horrible conversations, and she pushed them away.

Sean looked at his hands, clasped lightly in his lap. "You should take advantage of this time to rest and relax. Because you won't have this free time in a few months. If we're lucky."

Bile scratched at her throat and a burning pressed in her chest. Heartburn. Stress. The taste of long-simmering anger.

"If we're lucky," she repeated in a low voice. Then, louder, "Lucky? Don't you think we'll be lucky? You think I'm going to lose this baby."

"Don't you think…" he hushed himself, then turned to look at her, "…don't you think I have a right to worry? Even the doctor said—"

"The doctor said there was no way to know if anything I did would've made a difference. She said that the body knows what's necessary, even if the mind and heart don't agree, do you remember that?"

He huffed. "Yes. She was a jerk."

"She was maybe a little brusque." Ginny had appreciated the obstetrician's assessment of her miscarriage, better than if she'd joined them in the hand wringing and breast beating. "She also said that there's no reason to think this time is the same, or that we'll have any problems. We haven't, Sean. This baby is healthy. I'm healthy. I'm seven months along, and there are no signs of any problems like the last time."

There'd been genetic abnormalities. Ginny'd had every test possible this time through and been given the all clear for Down's, spina bifida, everything else. She and Sean had been poked and pinched and prodded, their DNA scanned, the probabilities of their conceiving a child with abnormalities factored, and the results had all come up the same, just like the doctor had said.

"Is that why you won't decorate the nursery, then?" he challenged her suddenly. "Because you're so convinced there's nothing wrong, that it will all be all right? Is that why you've left every single thing we got in the wrapping with the receipts attached… just in case?"

Ginny got up, looked with longing at her pillow and the warm blankets, then at her husband. She lifted her chin. "I'm going to read," she shot at him before he could say a word. "With my feet up. I'm not tired now."

Which was a lie. She was exhausted. She was melting with it, the desire to sink into her bed and pull the blankets up, to lose herself in vivid dreams of old flames and movie actors. She wanted to sleep and end this fight, erase the knowledge that her husband did not believe in this child. That he didn't believe in her.

"Ginny. Wait."

In the doorway, Ginny paused. "We have no reason to think there will be any problems, Sean."

"We have every reason," he said in a hard, low voice totally unlike his normal tone. "Don't you get that? We have every reason."

The terrible thing was, no matter how hard she tried to convince herself otherwise, she knew he was right.

Chapter Twenty-Three

She was cold again.

The house had been warm when she went to sleep, and with her flannel pajamas, the pregnancy hormones and the knitted afghan, Ginny'd fallen asleep toasty warm. Now she woke, cold and disoriented. The blanket had bunched beneath her, pressing her flesh into an ache.

She was on the Victorian couch. She put a hand down to touch her book on the floor beside her. The lights were out, she realized as her fingertips brushed the smooth hardcover. She'd found an old favorite, Clive Barker's *Imajica*, in one of the boxes, and the dust cover had raised letters she could trace.

The lights were out.

She hadn't turned them out before falling asleep, she knew that much. She'd been reading by the light of the pendent lamp, which was too dim to make any dent in the shadows but cast a perfect pool of brightness for reading. She'd been on her side, the book propped on a pillow and the couch's firm, upholstered back providing a delightful pressure against her back. She remembered letting the book close, even recalled setting it gently on the floor. But she had not turned out the lights.

Sean must have come to check on her, seen her sleeping and turned off the lamp to leave her in peace. Ginny smiled at this thought of domestic kindness, until she remembered they'd been fighting. And at any rate, it wouldn't have been like him to leave her sleeping on the couch. He'd have insisted she come to bed to be more comfortable.

But if it wasn't Sean, who was it? The boogeyman, she thought with a small laugh. A cool gust of air swirled from beneath the couch and tickled her fingers, and suddenly the idea of the boogeyman didn't seem so laughable. She didn't quite snatch her hand up and out of the dark…but almost.

Ginny sat, pushing at the tangle of the afghan in frustration and not quite able to get herself free. She had no idea what time it was, but it felt like her normal midnight or

1:00 a.m. rising. Her bladder was telling her that anyway.

Something scratched and rustled inside the wall behind the bookshelves.

Ginny paused, thinking it was her own shuffling, but a second later the noise came again. The distinctive scritch-scratch of claws or nails against the inside of the drywall. She held her breath. Faintly, faintly, came the far-off jingle of a bell.

"Noodles?" It came out as a whisper; she couldn't force her voice any louder than that. "Noodles, sweetie…"

Through the darkness came the sound of breathing, soft and fast and faint. Ginny froze, unable to move, incapable of closing her eyes though she was straining them so hard into the blackness that small, bright flowers had begun blooming around the edges of her vision. She'd put one foot on the floor a minute or so ago and now drew it up under the blanket she clutched to her neck. She had to pee so bad she could taste it, as her gran would've said.

Ginny swallowed, then again, her throat so dry she thought she might choke. What had shifted in the walls, what was now breathing so close to her? Or maybe not what. Maybe…who.

"A girl…with dark hair…like yours when you were small."

"Maeve," she whispered, because that was the name she'd wanted to give her daughter, the one she'd lost. "Maeve, honey? Is it you?"

Ginny tensed, waiting for something to touch her. Weeping, she reached into the darkness and found nothing but the night. She listened in the dark, but the bell didn't jingle again.

Chapter Twenty-Four

"A blank canvas is only intimidating if you don't let yourself imagine what you might paint on it."

Louisa had been fond of saying that as she walked around the room, looking at what they were working on. Ginny knew she was trying to be helpful, but it was never that she'd found the blankness intimidating. If anything, she always had too many ideas about what to paint and never enough skill to re-create what was in her mind's eye. Not intimidating, frustrating.

The canvas in front of her was now frustratingly and intimidatingly blank. She'd dutifully kept it set it up on the easel near the window, where the light was best. She'd sketched out on a notepad the shapes of what she thought to paint, her pencil making a scritch-scratch noise that was uncomfortably like the noises she'd heard in the walls.

She looked around the room, waiting for inspiration to strike. And it did, but not to create anything. The fainting couch called to her. That, and a mug of tea and the rest of her book. That was a much better prospect.

There was nothing that said she *had* to paint. It should never have become something forced upon her, the way she felt forced now. But Ginny didn't feel like painting.

The truth was, Ginny was sure she'd never really feel like painting again.

Children's laughter caught her attention, and she looked out the window to search for them. As she watched, the boy pushed through the hedge and bent to pick up what looked like a badminton birdie. It must've flown over the bushes, though why those kids would be outside playing badminton at this time of year... Ginny shrugged. Not her kids, not her problem. Well, except for the fact they were in her yard again. The boy ran through the pile of leaves just down the hill, his sister following, and she lost sight of them.

The sky had gone gray again. Ginny shifted her weight from foot to foot and dabbed her paintbrush without enthusiasm into a blob of a color called Azure Sky, which was nothing like the color she could see through her window. Despite the chill in this room, it wasn't cold enough outside for snow, which meant the clouds covering the sun meant rain. Cold November rain, just like in that Guns N' Roses song. The faint rumble of thunder proved her right a minute or so later.

Autumn thunder always felt strange, not like summer storms that sprang up after a hellish day and broke the heat. Storms in the fall were creepy, not sexy. The rain would be cold, not warm.

* * * * *

Warm rain. The sound of thunder. Ginny closed her eyes, remembering how the sky had opened, how everything had come down. Steady, unyielding rain, hard enough to sting her bare arms as she ducked between the tents, wishing she'd thought to bring a sweater or an extra outfit. She would be soaked by the end of the day, her carefully styled hair flattened, her makeup smeared, her pretty shoes bloated with wet.

Her paintings hadn't looked the same in the glare of strung light bulbs instead of sunshine; nobody's had. They'd strung some on wires in the tent. Others leaned on unsteady easels, posts sinking into the rain-softened ground.

The crowds came, despite the rain. They splashed in the puddles and trekked through the mud. They carried shopping bags of crafts and paintings carefully wrapped in plastic to shield them from the ceaseless downpour. They waved giant tubs of French fries and apple dumplings and ignored the ice-cream truck and cotton-candy vendors—cotton candy dissolves in the rain before it can be eaten. It leaves behind a sticky film as the only reminder of its sweetness. Ginny knew this because she'd watched a young mother pushing her toddler in a stroller, unaware of his tears as his treat washed away before he could get it to his little mouth.

Lots of people had come to the art show, and it had seemed to Ginny that at least most of them took a turn through the tent she shared with the rest of Louisa's students. Lots of strangers took the time to ask about her work, some even complimenting it. A couple even bought a piece. Lots of faces, lots of smiles, but no matter how often she looked up hopefully to the tent entrance, waiting, none of them had been his.

* * * * *

Blinking at the next rumble of thunder, farther away now, Ginny came back to herself. Her back ached, and so did her fingers from clutching at her paintbrush so hard. She'd been standing there so long the small dabs of paint she'd put on her palette had started to dry, a thin sheen of darker color covering the brightness beneath. She took a deep breath and put everything down.

She didn't want to paint today, or maybe never any other day, but she left her supplies where they were so that perhaps when she returned they might taunt her into feeling creative.

Ginny went downstairs to make some tea. As she filled the kettle at the sink, the first fat drops of rain splattered the glass. She leaned to crane her neck, trying to get a glimpse of the sky but couldn't quite make it.

The kids from next door ran across the yard, kicking at the leaves and shrieking with laughter. The wind picked up strands of the girl's blonde hair as she twirled and fell down into a pile, her arms and legs moving like she was making a snow angel. Her brother tossed the birdie at her, hitting her in the forehead. She sat up, indignant, and shouted something at him Ginny couldn't make out. Then she got up to chase him, and they ran out of sight again, down toward the creek.

The kitchen was broiling hot again, even as the library had been chilly. Her memories had left her flushed, but the temperature in here was unbearable, too hot for hot tea. She settled the kettle on the stove but didn't turn on the burner, and instead went to the fridge for a cold glass of orange juice.

The carton was empty, not even a swig left. Fuming, she tossed it in the trash and wrote "orange juice" on the list clinging beneath a magnet, advertising window treatments, on the fridge. She drank some water instead, then wet a paper towel and used it to dab at her face and the back of her neck, the swell of her cleavage.

It was too damned hot here. Too cold in other rooms. The damned furnace, Ginny thought, needed a kick. She didn't care what the guy said about it, there was something wrong.

Determined, she pulled the rechargeable flashlight from the wall dock. Sean would be happy to know she'd found a use for it, even if she didn't want to admit that it had been an eminently practical present.

The basement door creaked as she opened it. Behind it was the set of spindly, creaking and open wooden stairs with a splintery railing she gripped firmly. The floor below was concrete and unforgiving of a tumble. For a moment she considered taking off her slippers, but she wasn't wearing socks with them and the thought of going in bare feet into the filthy cellar was as unappealing as taking the time to go upstairs and put on socks. Instead, Ginny just made sure to settle each foot firmly on the stairs before she took another step.

The bulb swayed a little when she pulled the chain, and the pool of light at the bottom of the stairs shuddered. Just beyond it was another pull chain, though, and a few feet more, another. They were hung all over the basement, none connected by a light switch but all close enough that you never needed to pass through any darkness to get to the next…unless, as she discovered now, several of the bulbs had burned out.

But that's why she had the flashlight. Ginny clicked the button. The blue-white light flashed rapidly, like a strobe, before she clicked it again to put it on the regular setting. A steady beam of bright light shone ahead of her, looking almost solid with the dust she'd kicked up swirling in it.

Ginny held the flashlight in her palm and slowly waved the light from side to side. "Whommmmm. Whommmm."

Lightsaber.

The effect was ruined when the light bent along any objects in the way, but still it was good for a giggle as she oriented herself. She swept the room with the flashlight. All the corners the light from the bulbs wouldn't reach, even if they were all lit.

The furnace was in the far corner, in a little jig-jog that upstairs was part of the dining room. Ginny flashed the light above her, into the ceiling joists. She remembered too late the sound of nails and claws, and screamed when the shivering shadows tossed a pair of bright eyes at her, a flash of teeth.

Seconds later, of course, with her heart pounding and palms sweating, she had to laugh. It wasn't a raccoon—or worse, a rat—but a child's stuffed toy shoved into the space between the rafters and close to the silver ductwork.

That was creepy and gross, but not terrifying and not as weird as some people might think. She could remember as a kid hanging out in her grandma's basement with Peg and Billy and their cousins, trying to scare each other with stories or playing hide and seek. As a teenager, Ginny's uncle Rick had built a rec room of sorts in the basement, using spiffy 1970s paneling and cast-off furniture he and his friends had salvaged from the garbage. There'd been plenty of weird things tucked into the rafters of Gran's basement, including the gape-mouthed plastic face of a decapitated blow-up doll Peg and their older cousins had convinced her was a "princess mask." Compared to that, a kid's teddy bear was hardly strange at all.

To her right was the concrete wall that had been repaired in the long-ago fire. It was just as dirty and hung with cobwebs as the other walls, but of slightly different brick. Sean had stacked their ski equipment along it but left bare the metal shelving unit she'd meant him to use. Ginny shook her head, biting her tongue and refusing to let herself get worked up over it.

The furnace kicked on with a rumble when she approached. That had to be a good sign, right? She didn't know much about furnaces, other than how to change the filter, but the repairman had mentioned that Reset button and whatever he'd done to it had worked, at least for a little while, so it seemed like it was worth a try again.

Over in this corner, the bulb had not just blown, it was missing entirely. Ginny touched the chain and set the fixture swaying anyway as she passed, but she used the flashlight to look over the furnace. She regretted, now, playing the role of little wifey while Sean went with the repairman to check things out. She'd always made it a point in the past to be aware of everything, the basics of what she considered necessary adult skills. How to change a tire, balance a checkbook, change a fuse, mix a basic cocktail. In the days before she'd gone to a Mac, how to defrag a computer. Yet when the repairman was here, she'd hidden herself away in the kitchen like some sad parody of June Cleaver, complete with apron and bare feet.

What the hell had happened to her?

A sudden sob threatened to strangle her, but Ginny forced it back. No crying. Not here in the dim and dirty basement. Christ no. She wasn't going to lose it. She bit her tongue and rubbed the sore spot against her teeth until the urge to cry went away enough to ignore.

The Reset button. Where would it be? She shone the light over the entire furnace, but there was no helpful marking. The furnace itself still rumbled comfortingly but also deceptively.

"Let me heat your house," the furnace's rumble said. *"Or, you know, make you think I'm going to. But then you wake up freezing your tits off while chocolate melts in your cupboards."*

Just to the left of the furnace was a small window set high in the wall. It opened into a well framed with a half circle of metal and a patch of gravel at the bottom. She could see nothing through it, but some pale light filtered through, enough that when she went around the side of the furnace she could click off the flashlight.

And there it was. At least, she assumed the switch on the side of the furnace, tucked between two sections and just above the place the filter nestled, was the right one. What else could it be?

What's the worst that could happen, Ginny thought, and flicked it off.

At that moment, the light from the window cut out completely, leaving her in shadow. Ginny turned, the flashlight tumbling from her fingers as she spun. Framed in the window was a face, eyes wide and mouth yawing.

It screamed, shrill and high and piercing. The sound ripped at her eardrums and set the hair on the back of her neck on end. She dropped the flashlight, screaming herself, louder and more frantically than when the stuffed bear had startled her.

The face disappeared. More screams echoed. She heard the faint rustle of feet in the leaves.

Ginny collapsed against the furnace, no longer rumbling, and let herself dissolve into relieved laughter. She pressed a hand to her heart to slow the beating. The other went between her legs, praying she hadn't lost control of her bladder. She seemed safe enough there, though there'd been a moment when she was sure she was going to piss herself. At least she'd managed to avoid that.

It was one of the kids from next door, the face in the window. For whatever reason, they'd been peeking in her windows. Well, they'd had a scare, hadn't they? Maybe it would keep them away from her house, she thought, even as she laughed again at how they'd terrified her too.

She bent slowly, carefully, to find her flashlight, but it had rolled away somewhere. It was gone. She'd have to look for it later, in the brighter daylight or at least when she'd replaced all the burnt-out bulbs, but for right now her bladder was protesting the strain she'd put on it. She'd be lucky to make it upstairs.

Somehow, with her knees knocked together, Ginny made it to the bathroom in time to avoid an accident. Washing her hands, she caught sight of her reflection and laughed again at the memory of the neighbor boy's terrified face. Of her own fear. She laughed, loud and long.

And then she was weeping, both hands gripping the porcelain while she bent forward, helpless against the onslaught. Her shoulders heaved. Sobs racked her. She opened her mouth and almost expected to puke, that was how fierce the tears burned, but, instead, snot and saliva dripped into the sink. Fat, hot tears splashed. Her fingers curled and gripped, tight and tighter, because if she let go of the sink she was surely going to fall onto the floor.

It didn't pass with ease, this sudden burst of grief, this madness. It didn't fade or taper off into sniffles. It ended abruptly, like someone had slapped the hysteria out of her, and it didn't leave her feeling better, the way tears were supposed to. Everything about her face felt hot and swollen, and when she dared to face her reflection again, she looked how she felt.

Ugly.

With a determined shake of her head, Ginny gathered up the sorrow and the crazy, and she folded it like origami. She pushed it away, pushed it aside. Pushed it inside.

Deep inside.

Chapter Twenty-Five

"What the hell were you doing in the basement anyway?"

As predicted, Sean hadn't been amused by the story she spun as humorous so she could forget how it had ended. Ginny sighed and pushed her fork through the spaghetti noodles and sauce. It was a lackluster dinner, at best. Overcooked pasta and sauce from a jar, garlic bread she'd cobbled together from some leftover hamburger buns and garlic powder. She wasn't hungry anyway.

She looked at him across the dining room table. He seemed so far away, compared to their seats at the old table in the kitchen, but she figured if he was going to surprise her with this ugly table, she could insist they use it. "I told you. I was looking at the furnace."

"If the furnace isn't working," Sean said, "tell me about it, and I'll call the repair guy to come back. We paid him enough, he should make good."

Ginny frowned. "I can call the repair guy. I'm not helpless."

Sean said nothing, just dug his fork into the pile of noodles on his plate and slurped them up. Sauce splattered. He washed down the mouthful with a swig from his glass, then forked a bite of salad. He chewed. Loudly.

He'd always eaten that way, openmouthed, slurping and smacking and crunching. It suddenly repulsed her. Stomach twisting, Ginny broke off a piece of bread and forced herself to nibble it. She hadn't eaten all day.

"And you should've told me yesterday." He pointed at her with his fork.

He had sauce around his mouth. Once upon a time, she'd have leaned to wipe it with the corner of her finger and tucked it in her own mouth. The thought of that, tasting something from his skin, suddenly repulsed her more. Ginny swallowed convulsively.

"You weren't home until late last night. I didn't think about it."

He'd come home after she was already in bed. He'd smelled again of cigarettes and liquor. He'd wanted to make love. They'd done it in the dark, without words, his hands roaming over the changing mountains and valleys of her body. It had been like making love to a stranger, which was why she'd been able to come and why she'd gone to sleep with silent tears soaking into her pillow after.

"Did you turn the furnace back on?"

"I…" Ginny hesitated, "…I'm not sure. I don't know."

"No wonder it's so frigging cold in here." Sean frowned. "I'll take care of it after dinner."

"Fine. Thank you." The words sounded stiff and ungrateful, but what did she have to be grateful for, exactly? Making her feel like an idiot? Or that he might actually complete this chore, instead of merely promising to do it?

"So," he said after a few minutes of nothing but the sound of silverware clinking on the plates, "how was your day?"

"Fine."

He leaned back in his chair and wiped his mouth with a paper napkin; bits of paper clung to the scruff of his goatee. He didn't notice. Ginny had to look away.

"Just fine?"

"Just fine," she told him. "How else would you expect it to be?"

"Did you paint today?"

She frowned. "No."

"Why not?"

Said that way, it could be a genuinely curious inquiry. Or it could be a dig. Either way, she had no answer for it, no good answer that wouldn't lead to more questions.

"I didn't feel like it."

Sean wiped at his mouth again, this time with his fingers. It was the gesture of a man trying to hold back words with his hand, but he didn't try hard enough. "Why not?"

"Christ, Sean. I don't know. I just didn't." Irritated, Ginny stood to take her plate into the kitchen.

She'd baked cookies earlier today when she was not painting. She'd dusted the living room and changed out the towels in the bathroom She'd run a couple loads of laundry. She'd read half a book. She'd napped. She'd watched a couple hours of television. She'd paid some bills. She'd done a lot of things that were not-painting, so why was she letting him make her feel like she'd squandered her day, when he was the one who kept telling her to relax?

"I just thought, you know. With all your time you'd be getting back into it by now."

She turned from the dishwasher. "All my time?"

"Yeah. All your time. I don't have all the time you have."

Both her brows went up. "Everyone has the same amount of time, actually."

"Not actually." His half smile was supposed to charm her, but it didn't look genuine. "Some of us die before the rest. So technically—"

"I was busy," she cut in. "And I didn't want to paint. Okay? I just didn't feel like it. You act like it's some kind of crime."

"It's just that I wouldn't have bought all that stuff for you, if I'd known you weren't going to use it. I'd have spent the money on something else. In case you didn't notice," he added in a tone more sarcastic than she'd ever heard from him, "we're not exactly floating in extra money."

"I never asked you to buy it!"

Sean didn't say anything at first. They stared at each other across the kitchen until he dropped his gaze. Scuffed his toe on the floor she'd spent a good forty minutes sweeping today. Muttered something.

Her senses of touch, smell, taste had heightened in this pregnancy, but her hearing apparently hadn't. "What?"

He looked up at her, somehow defiant. "I said, 'you used to like it'. You used to love it. But when I try to help you with it, all of a sudden, you don't want to have anything to do with it."

Her jaw dropped. She turned to the sink to wash her hands so he wouldn't see them shaking. "Wow. What a selfish, self-absorbed thing to say."

"What's that supposed to mean?"

She ran the water too hot, but refused to flinch as she rinsed away the soap. Her skin went red. She didn't turn to look at him. "Why would you think my painting has any goddamned thing to do with you at all?"

"That's the trouble," Sean said. "It *doesn't* have any goddamned thing to do with me, and it never did."

Time ticked past, one second at a time, the way it always did. An eternity passed in the span of one, two, three breaths. Ginny swallowed her words and refused to let his become bruises.

"I'm going to take these cookies over to the neighbors," she said finally when it became apparent that Sean was neither going to speak nor leave the kitchen until she did. "It's about time we met them anyway, and I want to make sure the kids are okay."

"Tell them to stay the hell out of our yard."

The vehemence was so unlike him, it almost made her turn. Ginny kept herself still. She didn't want to look at him. Didn't want to see his face. She was afraid of what he'd see on hers.

"I'm going to take care of the furnace."

She waited for the sound of his footsteps moving away before she turned. Then she pressed her fists to her eyes until colored sparks danced. She drew in a few deep breaths. She didn't cry.

Ginny took the cookies out the back door, across the grass but not through the hole in the hedge. She walked all the way around to the sidewalk, then up the neighbors' driveway. She knocked on the front door, her knuckles stinging in the cold air.

The woman who opened the door looked surprised and a little suspicious, even when she saw the platter in Ginny's hand. She looked younger than Ginny by about five or six years, her hair in a messy topknot and faint lines of exhaustion around her eyes. She had a baby gnawing its fist on her hip, a spit rag tossed over her shoulder. "Can I help you?"

"Hi. I'm Ginny Bohn. From next door." Ginny twisted to point.

The woman looked at her belly, obviously just noticing the bump. "Oh God. Yes, of course, come in, please! I'm Kendra. This is Carter."

She waved the baby's fist in Ginny's direction. "Oh, cookies. Yum, thanks."

Ginny followed her into the house and down a hall to the kitchen. This house was newer than theirs, laid out more like a raised ranch than an expanded bungalow. It was bright and airy, decorated with furniture from IKEA and plenty of childish artwork. Also, toys all over the place she discovered when her toe nudged a couple of matchbox cars.

"Oh God. Sorry. Sorry," Kendra said as she settled Carter into a heavy plastic high chair and set a rubber hammer in front of him. "No matter how many times I tell him... CARSON!"

She turned to Ginny, who was still holding the cookies. "Oh, let me take them. Can I get you something to drink? Coffee? Oh no. You're probably off that for now. I had to quit it when I was pregnant, even decaf gave me heartburn, I couldn't stand it. I could make some hot tea?"

"That would be great, thanks." Ginny slid into a chair at the table across from the baby.

Peg had been frazzled like this when her kids were smaller, and Ginny had no trouble imagining herself equally so. She put the cookies on the table and smiled at baby Carter, who gave her a solemn, somehow accusatory stare in return.

"You have three?" Ginny asked.

Kendra put a kettle on the stove, then turned. "Oh yeah. Three monsters. CARSOONNNNNN!"

There came the pounding of feet on the stairs. A minute later, Carson skidded into the kitchen on sock feet. Red cheeks, tousled blond hair—that was the face she'd seen in the window, all right. Close on his heels was his sister, hair in pigtails but otherwise a smaller version of her brother.

"You can't tell they're related at *all*," Ginny said lightly.

Kendra laughed. "They take after their dad. I swear we had a third just so I'd get one that looked like he belonged to me."

The baby in the high chair didn't seem excited by this. His face scrunched up in silent despair. His mother sighed and rubbed the top of his head, waiting a full five seconds before the first wail hit. She looked at Ginny with a faint smile of apology.

"He's…cranky."

"He's a cutie. And these two," Ginny said, still keeping it light, well aware of how protective her sister could be about her children, "I think I already know. Carter and…?"

"Kelly," their mother offered with a curious look that became suspicious again, this time leveled at the children. "What did you guys do?"

Ginny shook her head. "Nothing bad. I don't want you to think that. They've been playing in the yard, but—"

"Carson James Wood! Kelly Madison Wood! What did I tell you about that?"

In his high-chair prison, Carter let out a longer, louder wail and pounded his fists until Kendra scooped him out with a sigh. Plunked on her hip, the baby stopped crying out loud, though the silent tears of outrage still coursed down his fat little cheeks. His mother kept her attention on the other two.

"But, Mama…"

"Don't you 'but Mama' me. I told you both to stay in our yard… Oh God." She turned to Ginny. "Were they down by the creek? They were down by the creek, weren't they?"

"I don't…know," Ginny hedged, annoyed as she'd been by their repeated trespassing, but not willing to send the kids down the river, so to speak. Yet she also felt something like a mother's kinship with Kendra, like there was some sort of code she'd be breaking if she didn't take the mother's side. "And really, it's okay. I know the leaves can be tempting. And honestly, if my husband actually put them in bags instead of just raking them into piles, they probably wouldn't even be tempted to come over and jump in them. Right, guys?"

Kelly's eyes had gone wide, her lower lip atremble. She shook her head. "We were looking for the little girl. We were leaving her snacks because she's—"

Carson elbowed her. "Shhh!"

"Oh, for crying out loud." Kendra clapped a hand to her forehead. Behind her, the kettle started to whistle. "Both of you. To your rooms. I don't want to hear it," she said before either of them could protest. "Go. Now!"

She turned off the burner with one hand, twisting her body expertly to keep the baby away from the heat. She took a couple of mugs from the cupboard and put them in front of Ginny, then a small box of loose tea bags. Finally, the kettle, which she also kept far away from the baby. She put the kettle on a trivet and took the seat across from Ginny.

"I'd pour," she said, "but this guy here has grabby hands."

"I can get it," Ginny assured her. "What would you like?"

Kendra shook her head. "Nothing for me, thanks."

An awkward silence fell as Ginny prepared the tea, but only for a couple seconds because Kendra snagged a cookie and bit into it. "Oh wow. Fantastic! No, baby boy, not for you." She grinned at Ginny. "He's nursing, doesn't even have a tooth yet, but he keeps trying to get at our food. Monkey see, monkey do. I guess that's how it is for the youngest."

"I guess so." Ginny dunked a tea bag and let it steep, then took a cookie. The dinner she hadn't eaten seemed delicious now.

"How many do you have? I mean, is this your first?"

"Ah…" Ginny paused, caught off guard though she knew she shouldn't be. It was a complicated question with a simple answer. "Yes. Our first. But my sister has six, so I've got my auntie card."

"Not the same as having your own, let me tell you that." Kendra blew out a breath and looked tired again. "When you can't give 'em back…"

Another few seconds of strained silence. Ginny sipped her tea. Kendra bounced Carter on her knee.

"I am sorry about Kelly and Carson," she said finally. "I've told them to stay out of your yard. I don't want them down by the creek. I know it's not deep or anything, but kids can drown in just a few inches of water, you know? And besides, they shouldn't be in your yard. I'm sorry."

"It's okay, really." Hearing Kendra apologize over and over made it harder for Ginny to be irritated by the kids coming through the hedge. "Really, they mostly just jump in the leaves."

She thought about mentioning the stones they'd tossed at the house, the noise of their shrieking, the offerings they left in the window well, but in the end decided that would just get them into trouble and make her sound like exactly the sort of cranky neighbor she didn't want to become known as. Besides, she reasoned, someday not so far in the future she might have the kid who ran into the neighbors' yards and did naughty things.

"Still. I'm sorry. It's just that they're sort of obsessed with it."

Ginny's brow furrowed. "The house?"

"Yeah. Your house. My husband, Clark…" Kendra sighed and shook her head. "Men. They can be such idiots, right?"

"Umm…sure. Right."

Kendra laughed a little. "Yeah. Anyway, Clark was trying to get them into bed one night when I was out with some of my girlfriends for ladies' movie night… Oh hey, you should totally come! Stacy from down the street, that blue Colonial on the corner? They fixed up their basement pretty nice, big-screen TV and stuff, and her husband likes to have the guys over for poker and beer and sports or whatever, so she told him if he was going to do that, she was having chick-flick-and-wine nights, and it's been great. Maybe your husband would be interested?"

"In…chick flicks and wine?" It took her a second, but she laughed once she caught up to Kendra's train of thought. "Oh. Sports and poker. He might be. I don't know. He's pretty busy."

"Oh. Travels a lot? I thought I saw that he was gone a lot. Not," Kendra said, "that I'm a Sneaky Pete or anything, just that, you know, you guys being the new neighbors and all, in that house, we just all wondered what sort of people you were."

This pricked at Ginny's ears. "That house? What do you mean?"

"Oh…just that most of these places in the neighborhood have sold two, three, four times over in the past few years. I mean, we've been in here…five? Yeah, five years. And we're old-timers. But Mr. Miller from next door, he built that house before he got married. It was one of the first in the development. And he was the only owner. Until now, you guys. That's all I mean." Kendra looked vaguely guilty. "I mean, it's not like someone died in the house or anything."

Something in the way Kendra said it sent up a flare. Ginny leaned forward. "They told us he died in the hospital."

"Oh, he did, he did, totally," Kendra assured her. From upstairs came the sneaky, sly sliding of feet. "You'd better be in your rooms!"

The noises stopped. Carter giggled suddenly, as though pleased by his siblings' punishment. Kendra chucked him under the chin.

Ginny's head spun a little from trying to keep track of Kendra's conversation, but then she *was* used to Sean's mom, who was the queen of non sequiturs. "So…your husband?"

"Is an idiot? What?" Kendra laughed again, looking confused.

"He was trying to get them to go to bed…?"

"Oh, right, right. Yeah, so he was trying to get them into bed, and he told them that if they didn't go to sleep, he was going to tell the ghost next door about them, and she'd come over and get them." Kendra's mouth twisted, her smile rueful. "Like I said, he's an idiot. Those kids didn't sleep for a week."

Noises in the walls.

Cold spots.

"A girl…with dark hair…like yours when you were small."

"The…ghost?"

Kendra laughed again. "Oh, he just made that up. It's not true at all. I mean…" she looked suddenly doubtful. "It's just that Mr. Miller's daughter, Caroline. Well. You know about her, right?"

"I don't." Ginny sipped more tea and took another cookie, suddenly ravenous.

"Oh. Well, she went missing when she was about fourteen or so. They never found her, so far as I know." Kendra's eyes gleamed for a moment. Her expression suggested she was both disturbed and solemn with the responsibility of being the one to share this story, but her gaze told a different, gleeful truth. "Mr. Miller had an older son, Brendan. He'd be the one who sold you the house, right?"

"Right. Yes."

"You know he built it himself? Old Mr. Miller?"

"I didn't know that."

Kendra nodded. "Yep. Custom-built. That's why it has so many nice features. I mean, all those built-ins, right?"

The house did have nice features, but Ginny didn't care about them now. "So…what happened?"

"Oh right. Right. Well, old Mr. Miller's son and his wife, not the son's wife. Mr. Miller's wife. They moved out after about a year of not being able to find her. The story is that both of them refused to ever come back or set foot in the house again." Kendra lowered her voice, conspiring, though Ginny had no desire to share secrets. "Mr. Miller lived there all alone for the past fifteen years. Nice guy. Always seemed super sad, though. And no wonder, right?"

"No wonder," Ginny murmured. The tea had a flat taste she didn't like, but she sipped it anyway to give herself something to do. "So…if they never found the girl…?"

"I heard, just a rumor, you know, but I heard that someone found her on one of those Internet sites, living out in California or something. Runaway."

"So…she definitely didn't die."

Kendra looked guilty again. "No. I mean, I don't think so. And surely not in the house. It was before we moved in, of course, but stories like that…"

Got exaggerated, Ginny thought. Inflamed. But that was exactly the reason why she should find it easy to believe the girl hadn't died in the house. "Something like that would surely have gotten around."

"Well…yeah. I mean, like I said, Clark was being an idiot. He was just trying to scare the kids, which was stupid. I'm sorry they were in your yard, though. I'll have a talk with them."

"They were peeking in the basement windows. They scared me. I scared them, pretty bad, I think."

"Ohhhhh Gawd. Well, that explains why Carson came tearing in here the other day like wolves were chasing him. I'm sorry!"

Ginny found a smile. "Really, it's okay. I think they learned a lesson, didn't they?"

"Still, I'm going to make them come down here and apologize." Before Ginny could stop her, Kendra had gone to the bottom of the stairs to shout up, "Carson! Kelly! Get your butts down here, now!"

The pounding of feet came again. The children looked caught and guilty, scuffing their feet on the linoleum. Kendra took them both and shoved them forward in front of Ginny. Carter grabbed a handful of Carson's hair and pulled hard enough to twist the older boy's head. There was a kerfuffle.

Ginny was already exhausted.

"You tell Mrs. Bohn you're sorry for going in her yard and for peeking in her windows."

"We just wanted to see the little girl," Kelly said through a lisp Ginny hadn't noticed before. "She lives in the basement."

"Kelly, enough stories! Apologize right now."

"I'm sorry." Kelly's lower lip trembled.

"Me too," Carson added. "We just wanted to see her, because sometimes she looks so sad."

"That's enough," Kendra snapped. "Enough stories."

Ginny held up a hand. "Wait a second. What do you mean, Carson?"

"We always ask her to come out and play, but she—"

"Enough! Up to your rooms!" Kendra yanked his sleeve to turn him toward the stairs, even as her son tried to finish his sentence. She cut him off with a swat to the rear, earning her a sullen glare, but both children obeyed. Kendra turned with a heavy sigh, Carter still bouncing on her hip. "Honest to God, I'm going to kill my husband."

"It's fine. Really." Ginny stood. "I have to get going anyway."

"I'll let you know about girls' night, okay? And I'll have Clark give your husband... What's his name?"

"Sean."

Kendra nodded as though she'd already known. "Right, right. I'll have Clark give Sean a call about boys' night. Okay? Sound good?"

"Sounds...great," Ginny said, though her head was already awhirl from just forty minutes in this woman's presence. She couldn't imagine how it would be to spend any longer amount of time. She was nice and all, but...scattered.

Kendra led Ginny to the front door. "Thanks for the cookies. I'll make sure to keep the kids out of the yard."

Ginny paused in the doorway to look over her shoulder. "Oh, you know what? Don't worry about that. I like seeing them there. They can come over anytime they want."

"Are you sure?" Kendra looked doubtful.

Ginny thought of Carson's earnest face, his sister's lispy lilt. Both of them had seemed pretty convinced there was a little girl in her basement. "Yes. Absolutely."

Chapter Twenty-Six

CMM

Ginny traced the letters on the diary. At least now she knew who the diary belonged to. It stayed locked, though. Caroline Miller might be dead, or she might be alive and living on a commune in California with a husband and a bunch of kids. But this was her private diary, and Ginny still didn't feel right breaking into it.

"You should just read it," Peg said. "Maybe there are some clues!"

"Like what kind of clues?" Ginny put the diary back in the train case and closed the lid.

Peg rolled her eyes. "About what happened to her, duh."

"She obviously hid the diary away so nobody could find it because she didn't want anyone reading it, Peg. I feel like maybe I have to honor that."

"So her ghost doesn't get you?" Peg lifted a brow and sliced into the chocolate cake Ginny had put in front of her. "God, so good. When did you get in to baking?"

When I stopped being in to anything else, Ginny thought but didn't say. She pressed her fork into the crumbs on her plate. "I told you there've been some strange things happening."

"You think it's a ghost, really? Because of what Gran said? C'mon, Ginny. That's just…stupid." Peg gave herself a quick sign of the cross.

"Gee, thanks," Ginny said dryly. "Glad to know my older sister's on my side."

Peg sighed and reached to pat Ginny's hand. "Everything you told me about could be explained. Noises in the walls? The exterminator came, right? Cold spots? The furnace is fixed."

"Not really."

"So, it's still broken. Besides, it's more like your house is cold with hot spots, not cold spots, right?" Peg pulled the front of her blouse away from her throat and fanned it back and forth. "I mean, your kitchen's like a sauna."

"Yes. I know."

She hadn't told Peg about the other things. The mug that went missing. The figurines that turned up in random places, like the ones lined up in the window well. The distant sound of a jingle-bell collar from a cat that had been missing for weeks.

"Listen…" Peg squeezed her hand again and waited until Ginny looked at her before continuing, "…how are…things? With you and Sean."

Ginny gently extricated herself and got up from the table, ostensibly to carry her plate to the dishwasher, but really so she didn't have to look at her sister's face. "Fine. They're fine."

"You know, when I was pregnant with Jennifer, I thought I might actually end up in prison for killing Dale. It was that bad."

Ginny turned. "You never told me that."

"What could I tell you? That I was crazy? That I dreamed, actually dreamed…" Peg paused, her voice cracking just a little. A glimmer of tears was swept away before they could fall. Peg cleared her throat. "Jesus help me, Ginny. I dreamed about taking a knife to his throat and just slitting it open like he was a pig."

Stunned, Ginny leaned back against the counter, gripping it with her hands on either side. "Jesus."

"I know, I know. It was terrible. I'd have these explicit, vivid dreams like I've never had before. And sometimes, in some of them…"

Ginny watched her sister blush. Peg, an emergency room nurse, dealt with everything imaginable. Bad language, bodily fluids, objects inserted and stuck in orifices that were meant to be exit only. She had a bawdy sense of humor, so long as it wasn't sacrilegious. She'd been the one to tell Ginny about the intricacies of blow jobs and warn her about possibly crapping herself on the delivery table, so what could possibly be so bad, so strange, that it could fluster her?

"Sometimes, I'd dream that I'd…you know," Peg said in a low voice.

Ginny had no clue. "You'd kill him?"

Peg shook her head, then nodded. Shook it again. "Yes. I mean, no, yes, I dreamed that, but there were other dreams, not the same ones, usually. But sometimes. Yes, okay? I admit it. Once or twice, I dreamed that sort of dream, that violent dream, a big knife, lots of blood squirting. Once I woke up laughing."

Ginny thought of her own dreams, those slick, slippery, delicious visions of lust that had been visiting her almost nightly. "Don't worry, I think that's normal. I mean, not the part about killing your husband, but if you want to analyze it, that big knife probably wasn't a knife. If you know what I mean."

"Sometimes," Peg said darkly, "a cigar really is just a cigar, Ginny."

"Are you saying you really wanted to kill Dale? I don't believe it." Ginny pulled a glass from the cupboard and filled it with orange juice from the fridge.

Peg waved away the glass Ginny offered. "God help me, Ginny. I really did want to…well, maybe not kill him. But I sure did want him out of my life, away from me. I couldn't stand the sight of him. Everything about him drove me insane. The way he breathed at night, I'll tell you the truth, I had visions of putting a pillow over his face."

Ginny stifled another laugh, though it sounded slightly horrified. "Oh, Peg."

Peg shrugged. "I had Jenny, and after that everything was fine. And it didn't happen any of the other times, just with that first. So I thought, you know, maybe…"

"It's not my first time," Ginny said gently.

Peg flushed again. "I know. I'm sorry, that was stupid."

"No. It's okay." Ginny was tired of having to feel sorry for other people's grief surrounding her pain, but this was her sister, and she was trying to help. "You want to know if I'm having crazy dreams too?"

"Are you?"

"I've been having my share of sexy ones," she admitted. "Honestly, I don't mind. A nice wet dream once in a while? What's wrong with that?"

"And the…other?"

"No," Ginny said firmly. "I don't dream of slicing my husband open with a knife, Peg. I think that was just your particular brand of crazy."

Peg didn't seem offended. "I just wanted you to know that if you were having some problems, I'd be willing to listen. Pregnancy can put a strain on any marriage, and so can a big move. And especially, hon, when you have the considerations you do—"

Ginny threw up a hand to stop her. "Honestly, Peg, I'm completely burned out on this type of discussion. Yes, I had some problems before. But that was then, this is now. And I'm damned tired of everyone waiting with bated breath for me to lose this baby. That's it, that's all."

"I'm sorry," her sister said quietly. "That's not what I'm doing. But can't you understand why Sean might be worried?"

Ginny looked at her with narrowed eyes. "What's he said?"

"Nothing to me. He talked to Dale. Said he thought you weren't really facing things, that you wanted to forget what happened, and he was worried it was affecting how you were dealing with this pregnancy."

"I haven't forgotten!" Ginny cried. "As if I could ever forget!"

"He says you won't decorate the nursery."

Ginny shook her head, refusing to get herself worked up over this. "That's not forgetting. That's being practical. The baby will come home from the hospital and stay in our room for the first few months anyway. And we don't know if it's a boy or a girl, so why should we spend a lot of time and effort on something that might turn out to be…wrong? And babies have personalities," she continued. "What if we go with a jungle theme and our daughter turns out to be a princess sort of girl? What if we have a boy who'd really like trains? Or, hell, the other way around, I don't care. I just want to focus on the baby."

She stared at Peg, who stared back.

"I just want to think about the baby," Ginny said quietly. "Not the color of the fucking walls. Okay?"

"Okay," came Peg's equally quiet answer. "Okay."

Chapter Twenty-Seven

Ginny wears gartered stockings.

High heels, black patent leather, red soles. Shoes she'd never buy in real life, but here they fit her perfectly. Here she walks like a queen in expensive stilettos, and she never thinks of falling.

The stockings swish, swish as she walks. The bare skin of her thighs rubs together. She wears silk panties. Red, she thinks. Yes, red. A matching bra of red and black, pushing her breasts forward, giving her cleavage that turns men's heads.

Oh, she wants to be that woman. The one who makes men stare. She wants to walk into a room and have them stop whatever they are doing. She wants their eyes to bulge out, their tongues to loll, to make them cartoon wolves with an *AROOOOGA* noise. She wants to be desired.

There's power in this. These clothes, this walk. The sway of hips, the jiggle of her breasts. She is all woman. She is not just desirable, she *is* desire.

What will he think when he sees her? When her shirt unbuttons, one at a time, to reveal the slope and swell of her breasts? When she unzips her straight black skirt and lets it fall on the floor? When she steps out of her clothes and stands in front of him dressed like a wet dream, will he get hard for her right away, or will she have to kiss him first?

Oh, how she wants to kiss him.

It's all she can think about. That first kiss. How his mouth will taste, how his tongue will feel stroking hers. There have been nights when she can't stop from touching herself to the idea of that mouth, those lips and teeth on her flesh. He will kiss her mouth. He will kiss her face. He will kiss her jaw, her throat, the slope of her shoulder.

He will kiss her all over, every place she wants him to, and his hands will follow along the path his mouth makes. He will part her thighs and find her heat with fingers, tongue, cock, and she'll take him into all of her body's secret deep places.

She will take him all in.

* * * * *

Ginny woke without opening her eyes, pleasure coursing through her and the shreds of the dream slipping away. She moaned before she could stop herself. When she opened her eyes, Sean was staring at her over the edge of his iPad.

"Nightmare?"

A nod made the lie easy. It would've been harder with words, but since she couldn't manage to find any, she settled for sitting up and scrubbing at her face.

"Must've been a doozy," Sean said. "You were really wriggling around."

Embarrassed, Ginny let her fingers pressing her eyes keep her from meeting his gaze. "I don't really remember it. What are you still doing up?"

"Reading." He tipped the screen to show her, though she couldn't possibly read the text from this far away. "You've only been asleep for about an hour."

"It felt like a lot longer."

He looked concerned and pulled her closer, though it wasn't comfortable for her to snuggle up to him the way he wanted her to. "You want to talk about it?"

"No."

"Was it about the baby?"

"Sean, no." Ginny sighed and pushed away. "I have to pee."

She padded to the bathroom, her habit, as always, to leave the light off and needing it even less with the light from the bedroom. She peed with her elbows resting on her knees, her face in her hands.

She remembered that lingerie. The bra and panties, expensive and sexy. An impulse purchase. They'd fit her perfectly. She'd tried them on about a dozen times but worn them only once. They were still in her drawer. She'd never wear them again, she knew that, but she hadn't been able to get rid of them, either.

At the sink she washed her hands and looked up without intending to see anything. Usually she averted her eyes anyway in case the irrepressible urge to shout out "Bloody Mary" three times overtook her. That old story had scared the bejesus out of her as a kid. Tonight, though, she was more awake than usual and there was more light. She saw her silhouette, the flash of her eyes and flip of her hair as she bent to the sink.

And then, something else.

A figure, a shadow, drifted past the bathroom door. Indistinct, but definitely there.

Startled, Ginny whirled, ready to confront a sneaky Sean trying to scare her, but there was nothing there. She was frozen for a minute or so, waiting to see it again. She stared, hard, but saw nothing. Ginny cocked her head to listen for the sounds of anything from downstairs. Was that the creak of a footstep? The squeak of a cupboard. Ah. A late night snack. Satisfied she'd solved the mystery, Ginny headed back to bed.

He'd turned the light out before going down, at least he'd done that. Ginny crawled into bed with a sigh and settled into her pillows. The dream had faded but the memories lingered. Closing her eyes might bring them even more into focus, so she stared instead at the wall, the darkness…

Something touched her.

Not something, someone. A hand stroked down her back, cupping her rear. Ginny shrieked and fought against the blankets and the touch, trapped by the tangled sheets at her feet and the pillows she'd propped herself up with.

"Hey, hey! Honey! Ginny, babe, it's me!"

Sean snapped on the bedside lamp, but it took her a few seconds to stop fighting him. Ginny blinked rapidly. "When did you get into bed?"

"What do you mean, get into bed? I've been here the whole time. I got tired while you were in the bathroom. I figured I'd—"

"You turned off the light!" she accused. "I couldn't see that you were in here!"

Sean frowned. "Where else would I be?"

"I saw you go into the hallway. I heard you go downstairs. I heard you in the kitchen," Ginny insisted when she saw the incredulity of his expression.

"Honey, you had a nightmare, maybe you just…"

"No." She shook her head. "No, I saw it, Sean. And more than that, I heard someone downstairs walking. I heard cupboards opening."

Sean reached behind the bed to pull out a golf club. He never played golf, but he'd kept that club behind the bed as long as she'd known him. "Stay here."

She clutched his arm. "No! What, are you crazy? Are you going to go downstairs? Sean, no. Call the police first."

The second she said it, she knew why he didn't want to do that. Then the police would come, and if there was nothing… Ginny let out a frustrated sigh. He wanted to reassure her, but he didn't believe her enough to call the cops.

On the other hand, he believed her enough to take the golf club.

"I'm going with you."

"No you're not. You stay here."

They could fight about it all night, or she could let him go. Ginny let him go, but as soon as he went down the stairs, she was up and out of bed, looking over the railing. Not that she could see anything, but she had her cell phone clutched in her hand, ready to dial 911.

"Sean!"

No answer.

Oh God. It was like that story from when she was a kid, one from that same Bloody Mary book, about the headless roommate in the fur collar. She'd hide up here in the dark and reach out to feel him when he came back to bed, and instead of her husband, she'd find a decapitated corpse...

"SEAN!"

No answer again. Her finger swiped her phone to unlock it, her finger hovering over the keypad. "If you don't answer me, I'm calling the police!"

He appeared so suddenly at the bottom of the stairs that she screamed. He waved the golf club at her. Ginny tried to remember to breathe.

"Nothing down here," he said.

"Are you sure?"

"Babe, I'm positive. All the doors are locked and everything. There's nothing, I promise. It was just a bad dream."

He had one foot on the stairs, but she was already heading down. "I want to see."

Sean sighed but stepped aside, humoring her. "I'm telling you, honey, there's nothing."

In the kitchen, she looked around suspiciously, but he was right. Nothing. No *sign* of anything anyway. No door hanging open, no bloody splatters on the wall, no butcher knife missing from the block. Even the chairs weren't out of place.

"See?" He came up behind her and kissed her hair. "I told you."

She sagged against him, finally calming down. His hands traced circles on her belly. Warm, slow, soothing circles. Within a few seconds, she was giggling at the memory of how she'd jumped and screamed. Ridiculous.

"My hero," she murmured, turning in his arms to kiss his mouth.

"That's me." Sean's hands drifted lower to cup her butt again and pull her close. She could feel him through the thin material of his pajama bottoms. They rocked a little slowly together.

The body didn't separate the source of pleasure the way the mind did. When he kissed her neck, it felt good. When he rubbed against her, that felt good too. With the remnants of the dream lingering, Ginny was more than willing to see where this might go, but first she needed a drink.

"All that screaming," she explained.

"I'll be happy to make you scream some more," her husband offered with a naughty grin.

She was laughing too when she opened the cupboard to pull out a glass, but the laughter stopped like it had been slapped from her. So did every bit of desire. She turned to show him what she'd found.

Her mug, the favorite black-and-pink one with the skulls.

"The least you could do is put it back where it belongs," Ginny said coldly.

Sean looked confused. "I didn't put that there."

She gave him her back, too angry to even look at him. "Someone did, and it wasn't me."

"I'm telling you, Ginny, it wasn't me."

"I didn't do it!" she shouted and slammed the cupboard door hard enough to make the dishes inside rattle. She whirled on him. "Why don't you just admit it, Sean? You took my mug to work and you forgot it, and then you brought it home and tried to sneak it back before I noticed. Well. I noticed. Why don't you just admit it?"

"Because I didn't do it!"

"So, who did?"

He was silent for a while, staring. He shrugged and cut his gaze from hers, his expression sullen. Stubborn. Then he looked back at her almost boldly, like a challenge.

"Maybe you did and just forgot."

Ginny's lip curled. "I didn't forget. How could I forget something like that?"

She knew by his next silence he was thinking of all the times she had forgotten things, all her absentminded times. Ginny turned back to the sink so she didn't have to look at him. "That's not fair, Sean."

She wanted to pull away, to storm from the room and ignore him, but his fingers insisted on soothing her. Working at the aches and knobs of pain and tension in her neck and back. He knew all the places to touch her. He always knew.

"All I'm saying is, you're distracted. You're pregnant. Pregnant women can be forgetful."

"Did you read that on the Internet?" She sounded bitchy and knew it, but couldn't force herself to care.

"It's true, isn't it?"

With a sigh, Ginny let herself relax against him. His lips pressed her temple and his hands slid down to rub her belly. She closed her eyes and put her hands over his, feeling the baby press upward against the touch. "Yes. It could be."

But it wasn't. She hadn't seen that mug in weeks. The last time she remembered using it was the night she'd made tea and fallen asleep in the library. Surely if she'd used it since then and put it back in the wrong cupboard she'd remember, and it wasn't like she'd have done it on purpose to fuck with her own head.

"Things happen, that's all. Give yourself a break," Sean said.

What he really meant was give him a break. Wasn't that what he always meant? And, because that's what she owed him, that's what Ginny did.

Chapter Twenty-Eight

They'd never had a lot of extra cash, even when she was working, but they'd always had enough to go on vacation, eat out a few times a week when neither of them felt like cooking, stop for an expensive coffee drink on the way to work instead of brewing it at home. Lots of little conveniences, that's what having enough money brought. And now…well, they weren't in debt, at least not beyond what Ginny considered "normal"—mortgage, one car payment with the other vehicle paid off. She and Sean both tried hard to pay off their credit cards every month so they didn't carry a balance.

They weren't in debt, but they simply didn't have anything extra.

Next month might be better, without the unexpected expense of the furnace repair and an electrician who'd looked at the fuse box but hadn't been able to figure out why they kept blowing fuses. She'd have to start holiday shopping in earnest, a task that always fell squarely on her for both sides of the family, and which she'd usually have finished by now. The move had taken up so much time over the summer she just hadn't had time. Or felt like it either, she thought as the baby moved inside her.

She tallied up the income and expenses, balancing the accounts. Then she logged into their credit union's online banking site and transferred some money from their savings, cringing at the remaining balance. It had been at least a week since she'd gone online, too busy with unpacking and everything to even think of it, but since dinner was already in the oven and Sean wasn't going to be home until after class, she had some time.

She looked up instructions on how to reupholster dining room chairs, then how to make slipcovers, then local places that would do it for her. The DIY sites made it seem deceptively easy, but she knew better. The businesses that specialized all charged too much for her budget, at least for now. She shifted on the seat, listening to it creak.

She flitted around the Internet, browsing some of the email shopping offers that had come in, watching a video her sister had sent a link to. Somehow, without thinking much of it, she ended up logging in to Connex. It had been weeks since she'd checked it, and she didn't even try to get caught up on the entire contents of her updates list. The site had changed a bit too, she noticed with a frown. She couldn't seem to find her inbox or how to upload a photo without stumbling around and hitting something by accident, and a bunch of status updates referenced opting out of new settings she didn't have the time or energy to care about.

Her sister had uploaded a bunch of new pictures, though, and Ginny looked through them absently. Her fingertips found the edge of the table, tracing the letters over and over as she scrolled through her nieces and nephews mugging for the camera, modeling new outfits, whatever. One link led to another, to another and another, until she ended up on the page belonging to a friend of her niece Maria. The girl had posted a lot of personal stuff, much of it TMI. It was like a train wreck—Ginny knew she shouldn't look, but did anyway.

People used to put that stuff in journals. Now they put it on the Internet. She thought of the box upstairs in the library, the diary inside it. Her fingers traced the letters carved into the table, over and over.

CMM

Caroline. Her diary. Her name on this table. That girl had lived in this house, and disappeared from it too.

Ginny's fingers tap-tapped on her keyboard, running a Connex search for Brendan Miller. Of course, about two dozen names came up, but when she narrowed her search, she came up with just three names. She could tell nothing from the profile photos, since she had no idea what Brendan Miller looked like, but she knew he lived in Lancaster somewhere.

"There we go," she murmured to the screen. She brought up his profile and found an email address but no phone number.

One thing she'd learned in her business was that even people who should know better often didn't appropriately privacy-protect their online information. A quick further search discovered Miller's address, which was current and confirmed by the most recently updated white pages database. In under ten minutes, she had everything she needed to know to get in touch with him. It was one of the easiest searches she'd done in a long time, but now Ginny sat back in her seat and wondered what she would do with that information.

He had a right to know. He obviously didn't care about the furniture or other things in his father's house, but surely he'd have wanted something personal of his sister's. Even if he hadn't wanted anything to do with his dad when he was still alive, he at least deserved the chance to have what his sister had left behind.

She dialed the number as she went upstairs. A woman answered just as Ginny entered the library to look at Caroline's box.

"Hi, can I speak to Brendan Miller, please?"

The beat of silence lasted way too long. "Who's calling?"

"This is Ginny Bohn, I—"

"Who?"

Ginny paused. Brendan Miller hadn't come to the settlement. She had no idea if he was married, but this woman sounded like a suspicious wife. She tried again. "My name is Ginny Bohn. I bought his father's house?"

Another long pause. "Yes? What about it?"

"Is he there?"

"No. He's not. Can I help you?" The woman's clipped tone didn't sound the least bit helpful.

Ginny tried anyway. "I've found something in the house."

"He doesn't want anything from there, he told me." Another pause, then a resentful sniff. "I told him there were a lot of lovely things in that house that we could use, but he refused to have any of it. I said that even if he didn't want it, maybe the kids would, someday. I mean, it was family heirloom stuff."

"Oh, honestly...I don't know anything about that, really. There were only a few things we asked remain in the house anyway." She thought suddenly of the ugly table she didn't like, but the thought of offering it to this unhelpful and snide-sounding stranger was suddenly unpalatable. "But I'm not talking about—"

"Whatever. It was his father's stuff. I guess if he didn't want it, who am I to say a word?"

Ginny had been on this ride before, the up-and-down roller coaster of marital resentments. She understood how it felt to feel marginalized, she totally did. Yet nothing in this woman's attitude made Ginny sympathetic.

"It's not furniture," she said quickly before the woman could continue complaining. "It's something personal."

The pause this time was longer. "Like what?"

"I'd really like to talk to him about it, if you don't mind."

That was the wrong thing to say. An audible, choking gasp poked Ginny's eardrum.

The woman spat her words like bullets, "I do mind, as a matter of fact. What did you say your name was again? What sort of personal business do you have with my husband?"

"It's his sister's suitcase," Ginny said before the woman could go off on her some more. "I thought he'd want it."

"My husband doesn't have a sister."

"No, well...um, so far as I know, she's...gone."

"Who did you say this was again?"

Irritated, Ginny sighed. "Is there a better time I can reach him?"

"No. Don't call here again. My husband didn't have a sister."

With that, Mrs. Brendan Miller hung up and left Ginny's jaw hanging open.

What a bitch.

Chapter Twenty-Nine

The Ouija board had been spectacularly easy to get. Ginny simply ordered it online, and it arrived within a couple days. It was different than the one she remembered from slumber parties as a kid. This one was smaller, with glow-in-the-dark letters and planchette. Still, it had the same setup with *YES, NO, GOODBYE* and the alphabet curving across it.

Peg, on the other hand, could not be convinced to use it. "No. No way."

"Peggy, c'mon. We used to do it all the time as kids. Remember?"

"I remember. But I'm not doing it now." Peg shook her head and then her finger. "And you shouldn't, either. What are you thinking, bringing that into your house? Don't you know that you could attract…something?"

"There's already something." Ginny put the box aside and set the board in the middle of the dining room table.

Peg huffed. "Oh, Ginny. Come on."

Ginny paused to look at her sister. "I'm serious."

"You have mice or squirrels in your attic, that's all—"

"Mice and squirrels might get into the food in the pantry," Ginny said. "But they wouldn't use a mug and then put it back in the cupboard."

"Well, neither would a ghost, for crying out loud."

Ginny raised a brow. "How do you know?"

"Ghosts are spiritual entities or whatever. They don't need to use a mug." Peg waved at the Ouija board. "And this is just asking for trouble."

"You used to love this game!"

"It's not a game," Peg said seriously. "I mean it, Ginny. Father Simon spoke about it a few months ago, because of the kids getting in to stuff like that for Halloween. It's a bad tool. It invites bad things."

Ginny sighed and pulled the board toward her. She put her fingertips on the plastic planchette and moved it experimentally around the board. "Father Simon is kind of hysterical."

Peg made a snuffling noise of protest, but her expression said she knew Ginny was right. "Don't be disrespectful."

"Didn't he also give a sermon about how couples should watch more television together because it prevented arguments?"

Peg's mouth worked on tamping back a smile. "Yes. He did."

"And how's that working for you and Dale?"

Peg didn't answer for a moment, then said reluctantly, "We fought over the remote."

Ginny slapped the table in triumph. The planchette bounced and slid, skewed toward the board's grinning sun. "See?"

Peg shook her finger at Ginny again. "He's the authority on spiritual matters, and if Father Simon says Ouija boards are dangerous and bad, I believe him. Besides, didn't you see *The Exorcist?*"

"It's a movie, not real life."

"*Paranormal Activity?*" Peg asked, as though that somehow was less fictional.

"Did they even use a Ouija in that?" Ginny scoffed. "Also, just a movie."

Peg frowned, her expression shadowed. "You don't remember, do you?"

"What, the movie? Not much. I fell asleep, except for the last couple of minutes. Which were some of horror cinema's finest," Ginny admitted. "But no, I don't remember the rest."

"Not the movie. The Ouija board. The one at Gran's house."

"I do remember it. That's why I got this one."

Peg sighed. "But you don't remember what happened with it. Obviously, you don't. Or else you wouldn't be sitting there with that thing in front of you."

This had the flavor of a story. Ginny perked, leaning closer to her sister. "What happened?"

"I don't really want to talk about it."

Ginny tossed a ball of the plastic wrapping that had been on the box at her. "Bitch!"

Peg laughed, though it trailed into an uneasy sigh. "It was some creepy, scary stuff, Gin. You were maybe...ten? Eleven?"

Which would've made Peg seventeen. Ginny remembered being ten, vaguely. It was the year of the short haircut. Being mistaken for a boy was the most traumatic thing for Ginny that year, certainly no strange paranormal thing.

Unless she'd just forgotten about it.

"We were at Gran's for Christmas. The big party, and we were staying over for the rest of the week, along with Roberta and Dana and Carla." Peg paused. "Or maybe Dana wasn't there, I don't remember. No, I think she was on some youth group trip. Or had she already gone off to college? No, she had to be there, because—"

"Is it important?"

Peg shook her head, focusing. "Oh no. Anyway, we were all staying over until New Year's."

"Gran had another party, didn't she?" Now Ginny was remembering a little more. "She always had the Christmas Eve party, but she had that New Year's thing one year."

"Just the one," Peg said ominously.

Ginny rolled her eyes. "She had other New Year's Day things. I remember going there for pork and sauerkraut."

"Sure, just the family. But not a big party with neighbors and stuff. She always said it was because having two big parties so close together was too much work." Peg gave Ginny a significant look. "But I think it was because of what happened."

"Jesus, Peggy. What happened?"

Peg frowned. "Ginny, please."

"Sorry." Her apology was automatic but sincere; she didn't have to drink the Kool-Aid to understand that her sister liked the flavor.

"We were all playing with that thing." Peg gestured at the board. "Roberta found it in one of the closets upstairs. It was probably Uncle Jimmy's."

"What, along with the collection of biker mags?" Ginny snickered.

Peg laughed too. "Yeah. Anyway, she brought it downstairs after Gran went to bed. We were all supposed to be in bed too, but you know we never were."

Nighttime in Gran's house during Christmas vacation had created some of Ginny's favorite childhood memories. Sneaking cookies, playing endless games of Monopoly and Clue by the light of the tree. Everyone had new pajamas, the fabric still stiff. The older kids played their portable boom boxes, fighting over who got to pick the next cassette.

"So Roberta brings this thing down into the living room, and we set it up near the tree. By the train set. Dana and Carla went first. They held it on their knees, sitting crisscross applesauce."

Ginny laughed at the term. She hadn't heard that in years. Her cousins, fraternal twins, were usually the first to try anything new. "You're taking a long-ass time to tell this story."

"Do you want to hear it or not?" Ginny nodded, only slightly chastised, but Peg was determined to draw it out. "I need a refill."

"Oh, Peg. C'mon!" Ginny's protests were met with Peg's unwavering stare and her raised coffee mug. "I'm the pregnant one."

"And you know I don't know how to use that fancy coffee thing you have."

Ginny narrowed her eyes, but got up. In the kitchen, she fussed with the coffee pods to brew her sister another cup. On a whim, she opened the cupboard to see if any other of her dishes had gone missing or been moved around, or if any other gifts had been left in their place. Today there was nothing.

Maybe she really was just crazy.

Peg came into the kitchen. "You're a terrible hostess. I need something to eat."

Ginny removed Peg's full mug and replaced it with hers while she brewed some cocoa from another pod. Then she took both mugs and sat at the table while she watched her sister dig into the fridge. "If I didn't know any better, I'd say you were trying to stall." Ginny gave Peg a significant look over the rim of her mug. "So come on. Spill it. What, you think I'm going to get too scared or something?"

Ginny had always been the kid who stayed up late reading scary books under the covers with a flashlight, who snuck downstairs to watch horror movies after her parents went to bed. Halloween had never seen her in a princess tiara or a cowgirl hat. Halloween was for zombies and witches and vampires. One year she was a werewolf, complete with ears and furry paws, a bloody and mangled red cape around her neck like a scarf. She'd won first prize in the parade. There wasn't much Peg could tell her about supernatural things that would scare her.

"You're the one who thinks she has a ghost," Peg pointed out. "I don't want to freak you out."

"I've faced worse fears than ghosts." Ginny meant to say the words lightly, teasing, but they came out solemn and serious and heavy. She swallowed hot cocoa too fast, and it burned her tongue. She turned her face from her sister's.

Peg reached for her hand anyway. "Right. Sorry. I wasn't thinking."

Ginny shrugged again and blew on her cocoa, though now she no longer had the taste for it. "So. This story?"

Peg grimaced. "Fine. So we were all downstairs playing with the board, and you'd been upstairs sleeping or reading or something, I don't know. But you came down when we were doing it, and you wanted to play. So, you sat down across from Carla and put your fingers on that plastic thing—"

"The planchette." Fascinated by this story she couldn't remember, Ginny leaned forward.

"And it started to move."

Ginny waited, but Peg didn't say more. "And?"

"It started to fly all over the board, all wild. Carla accused you of moving it, but you said you weren't! And it went all over; it started spelling out words and stuff. We all got freaked out. You took your fingers off it, and it stopped. You put your hands on it, and it went again, crazy, until it flew right off the board."

"Wow." Ginny laughed. "Sounds like I was pulling a fast one on you all."

Peg was silent for a couple seconds. "Maybe."

"Or what? Maybe it was Satan?"

"You *were* a devil," Peg told her.

Ginny tossed a balled-up paper napkin at her. "Hyuck, hyuck, hyuck. Very funny."

"You don't remember?"

"Vaguely. But probably only because you just told me about it." Ginny turned her mug around and around in her hands, pressing her palms to the heated porcelain. "I'm not sure what was so freaky about it."

Peg hesitated, but pressed on. "You said it wasn't you doing it, making it move. That it was the lady in the blue dress."

"Sounds terrifying."

"You insisted it was the lady in the blue dress, and she wanted to tell Carla something important, but Carla was so scared by that time that she wouldn't put her hands on the planchette. You were sitting there and it started moving again, we assumed you were pushing it of course. Trying to scare everyone. But it was going slower, more controlled, and we could read what it was saying. Over and over, 'Don't go to Boston'."

"Wow. Weird."

Peg nodded and took a minute to sip from her coffee like it gave her strength. "You know what happened, right?"

"If I knew," Ginny pointed out, "would I be asking you?"

"Carla was supposed to go to Boston for a dance competition. Which you probably knew. I mean, everyone was talking about it. But she got so freaked out she didn't go."

"And what happened? Let me guess, the plane she was supposed to go on crashed or something." Despite herself, Ginny got a shiver.

Peg shook her head. "Nope. Nothing happened."

"Well…what on earth? Why would that mean anything then? I was probably just messing with her!"

"She didn't go to Boston that weekend, and, instead, she went to Buffalo with her mom, shopping. They were in a car accident. Carla was driving."

Ginny wrinkled her nose. "I remember that."

"The car was totaled but they were okay. But, one thing they never talked about, Carla only told me once and it was just after Peter and June got married, and they had that reception in that creepy inn, remember? And everyone was talking about how it was haunted, and what weird things happened, and Carla refused to stay there, she went and stayed at the Holiday Inn?"

There were benefits to having a large family—all the stories that started and ended with "you remember?" being one of them—but not right now. Ginny waved an impatient hand. "Yes, I remember."

"Carla told me that a steel rod from the truck that hit them went all the way through their windshield, all the way through the car. If her mom had been driving—because her mom's a few inches taller, right?—she'd have been decapitated. But Carla was driving because—"

"She didn't go to Boston."

"Yes!" Peg crowed, triumphant, and slapped the table hard enough to make their mugs jump. "Because you told her the lady in the blue dress said not to!"

"Oh, Peg."

"The lady in the blue dress, by the way, is in a picture in Gran's house. It used to hang up in the dining room, but she took it down when she remodeled."

"So, I saw a picture of a lady in a blue dress and wanted to freak out Carla, and I made up a story that happened to have some weird repercussions." Ginny waved her hand again. "You can't say it had anything to do with it. I mean, you can never know what might've happened. Only what did."

"I thought you of all people would be excited to hear that story."

Ginny laughed. "But you're the one saying it's the devil's tool! Sounds to me like it saved Aunt Dina's life."

Peg clearly hadn't thought about it that way, because she opened her mouth to say something, but stopped. Then started. Stopped again, while Ginny laughed. "It's still not a toy," she said finally. "And I think if you use it to contact whatever's in this house, you'll regret it."

"So you believe me, there's something here."

Peg hesitated again. "I don't know."

"Fine. Don't believe me. But if there's not a ghost or spirit or something in here…" Ginny paused to draw a shallow breath that wanted very much to be a sob, "…then it must be my husband trying to gaslight me. Which do you think I'd rather have it be?"

Peg didn't have an answer for that, at least not one that came out of her mouth. Ginny's sister's thoughts rolled over her face in a series of twitches and glances that required a lifetime of interpretation to understand. Fortunately, Ginny'd known her sister for her entire life. Peg didn't believe Sean was trying to drive Ginny crazy, but she didn't quite believe Ginny's stories, either.

Ginny frowned and got up to dump her cooling cocoa in the sink. "I don't care if you believe me or not. I'm telling you, weird things are going on in this house."

"Maybe you should have Father Simon come over."

Ginny turned, brows raised. "What? Why… Oh, Peg. Really? Look, I know you're trying to get me back into the fold and all that, but this is a really crappy way of doing it."

Peg had the grace to look guilty, but then defiant. "It wouldn't kill you to get a little religion."

"I don't go to church. Period. Why on earth would Father Simon come over to investigate my missing mug?"

"He'd just come over to talk to you, that's all. If you and Sean are having issues…"

"I'm not taking marital advice from a man who's not only not married, but will never be married and in fact has never, in all likelihood, ever even had sex," Ginny added. "And besides that, it's not his business if Sean and I are having problems. I didn't say we were having problems!"

She rinsed her mug and put it in the dishwasher, refusing to look at Peg. Her sister's mug scraped on the table. Then her chair skidded on the floor.

"It was just a suggestion," Peg said.

Ginny turned, not wanting to fight with her sister. "I know."

"I'm not saying you're having problems. Just that it wouldn't be a surprise if you were. I mean, this is a stressful time. A move, new house, you're not working. The baby," Peg said quietly. "I wouldn't be surprised at all if it was affecting your sleep or making you susceptible to strange ideas."

"Did Sean tell you that? That I haven't been sleeping?"

Peg looked caught. "He said he was worried."

"I'm fine. And it's not my lack of sleep, I'm not imagining these things, and we aren't having any problems." Ginny scowled. "I can't believe you're going to believe him over me anyway."

"Because you think he's gaslighting you? Oh, Ginny. Really? Sean?"

Ginny stabbed a finger in the air. "I don't want to believe it, no! But knowing he went and talked to you behind my back about how crazy I am only makes that seem more likely, doesn't it?"

"I'd believe in a ghost before I'd believe your husband was trying to drive you crazy."

"Aha!" Ginny cried triumphantly. "Yes! You see what I'm talking about?"

"I'd also believe you were crazy before I believed you had a ghost." Peg smirked and took her cup to the dishwasher. She studied her sister up close, seriously. "Talk to Father Simon, Ginny. Do it as a favor to me."

"Do *me* a favor and stop trying to foist him on me."

Peg sighed and closed the dishwasher. "Fine, fine. Whatever. But don't ask me to do that devil board with you, and get rid of it. Don't have it in your house. Even if you think it can't do anything bad, it's a bad influence. And don't do it by yourself."

"Oh, like in *Witchboard*?" Ginny hadn't thought about that, she'd been focused on the idea that two people were required to use it.

"I don't know what that is, but it sounds bad. Promise me you won't use it alone. That's how the demonic influences get inside you. Promise me!"

Peg seemed so serious that Ginny nodded. "I promise. Of course. Fine. I'll toss it in the trash as soon as you leave. I promise, Peg."

Peg eyed her suspiciously, but then nodded. "Good. Call me later, okay?"

"Fine. Yes." Ginny ushered her sister to the door, accepted her hugs and more advice, because that was what her sister did. But when the door closed, she didn't call her sister's priest to come over for dinner, and she didn't dump the Ouija board in the garbage either.

It wasn't the first time she'd broken a promise.

Chapter Thirty

Candles were supposed to be romantic, Ginny thought. But when the power went out and your husband had misplaced the rechargeable flashlight and blamed you for it, candlelight was only annoying. In the kitchen she'd lit a series of tea lights in every single holder she could find. In the living room she'd lit a couple of jar candles, and in the dining room, collected in the center of the old, scarred table on a porcelain platter, she'd lit three huge pillar candles. The scents—pine needles, vanilla, cinnamon and something called Misty Memories—warred with one another. With her stomach too.

The light was pretty, golden and flickering over the old, polished wood. It hid all the flaws in the plaster, the dust in the grooves of the carved wood. It made shadows, though. Moving, deceitful shadows.

Ginny looked at the board in front of her. She should put it away, get in the car and go anywhere until the power came back on. But she didn't have the strength to face the Christmas mall crowds, frenzied by all the sales. She wasn't hungry and didn't want to sit by herself in a restaurant. And coffee shops had soured for her. Besides, Sean would be home in an hour or two and by then she'd be ready to eat. He could take her out to dinner if the electricity wasn't back on. Buy her a new rechargeable flashlight. Hell, a generator, if this was the sort of thing that was going to keep happening.

For now, she studied the board in front of her. Her fingers curled and pressed the cool plastic. She closed her eyes and drew a breath, anticipation tingling in her fingertips as she waited for the planchette to move.

Nothing.

Maybe she had to say something. Some sort of greeting? "Hello."

Still nothing. She inched her fingers toward her and the planchette moved easily enough on the little felt pads at the ends of its legs. No friction or resistance. Ginny moved it around in a circle, then a figure eight, but she could tell it was her making it go. Not spiritual forces.

"Is there…anyone here?"

For a second it seemed like the planchette twitched, but as she waited, breathless, nothing else happened. With a frown, Ginny sat back and stared at it. In the flickering light, the shadows beneath the planchette made it look like it was wiggling, just a little, but when she touched it, she could feel nothing.

She tried again, letting her fingertips rest so lightly on the plastic she was almost not touching it at all.

"Caroline? Caroline Miller. I'm talking to you." Ginny hadn't meant to let her voice drop so low and growly, but speaking at full volume seemed silly. She took a breath and held it for a second before letting it seep out through her nostrils. The smells of the melting wax made her want to sneeze.

The Ouija board did nothing. Frustrated, Ginny thumped her fist on the table. The planchette jumped and skewed a little, the pointer facing her.

"C'mon. I know there's someone here. I know you're in this house. Caroline," Ginny said. "I have your suitcase. With your things in it. With your diary. I haven't read it yet, out of respect, but maybe…maybe you want me to read it? Why did you put those things up there in the closet? Why didn't you want anyone to find them?"

That was a dumb question, she realized. Of course Caroline wouldn't want anyone to find her box of secrets. Ginny wouldn't have wanted anyone reading her diary when she was thirteen or fourteen either. She thought of her own little secrets. She wouldn't want anyone knowing of them now, though hers had been much more easily hidden and erased.

But not forgotten.

"Do you want me to read this journal?" Ginny put her fingertips back on the planchette. "Will it tell me what happened to you?"

The candles flickered as though someone had blown a breath across the flames. Ginny froze, catching sight of motion from the corner of her eye. She turned, slowly, slowly and saw only shadows growing longer and shorter as the candle flames moved. Still, there was a presence here. She felt it, didn't she? The weight of someone's gaze. She strained to hear the sound of breathing, the creak of floorboards. The back of her neck prickled.

She whipped her head around, preparing to scream at the sight of some ghostly figure floating toward her with its mouth yawning wide to eat her up.

Nothing.

With a shuddery sigh, Ginny pushed the board away from her. Maybe Peg had been right. It was dangerous to do this alone, if only because of the things it made her imagine.

She was sliding the box back into its place on the shelf in the living room when the lights splashed across the front windows and tires crunched in the drive. She pulled the curtain enough to peek out, then met Sean at the door, opening it wide and stepping back out of the way so he could come in.

"Creepy." He unwrapped his scarf and hung it on the coatrack, then set his briefcase at the foot of the stairs where he'd forget it repeatedly until she bugged him about it.

"What's creepy?" Ginny rubbed her arms against the chill breeze he'd brought in with him.

"The way you opened the door, like nobody was there." He leaned to kiss her, but absently. "What's with the candles? Did I miss something? It's not our anniversary…"

"The power's out."

He grinned at her, his teeth flashing white in the dim light. "You're kidding, right? Here I thought you were planning some romantic dinner surprise. I got excited there for a minute, thinking about heart-shaped meat loaf."

"I couldn't cook anything without power." Guilt groped at her like a drunken prom date. It had been a long time since she'd surprised him with anything like that. The fact she hadn't even thought about it felt worse than the fact she hadn't done it.

Sean looked over his shoulder. "How long's the power been out?"

"About an hour."

"Well…" he shrugged and gave her a confused look, "…are you sure? I mean, did you check it?"

"It's dark outside, Sean. I think I'd notice if the lights suddenly came back on."

"No, I mean…did you call the electric company or anything? Because everyone else on the street seems to have power."

This first stunned her, then annoyed her. She went automatically to the wall switch, already squinting against the flare of light she expected when she flipped it. But, like the Ouija board's reluctance to perform, the lights didn't respond either.

She couldn't keep the triumph from her voice. "No. See? Out. Just like all those other times."

"Shit." Sean reached around her to flip the switch on and off several times. "The whole rest of the street's lit up. Nobody else is dark. Must be another fuse."

"Of course it is."

"Still, why'd you sit here in the dark?"

"Because the last time I went downstairs to look at the fuse box you told me I shouldn't. So I didn't," Ginny said carefully. So carefully.

Sean said nothing.

"I'm getting really tired of this, Sean."

He rubbed her arms gently. "Yeah, yeah. I know."

"I mean, the power goes on and off if a squirrel sneezes in the yard. It's winter; it's dark a lot earlier and cold." She was getting ramped up and wanted to stop, but couldn't. "It's ridiculous, Sean! We just bought this house; we paid more for the extra-detailed home inspection. Why does this keep happening?"

To give her husband credit, he took her near hysteria in stride. He pulled her close and pressed his lips to her hair. With her cheek against the front of his jacket, the heat in her face faded. She fisted her hands in the material and closed her eyes, willing herself to remember this was not that big a deal.

"I'll get an electrician in here."

"We can't afford it," she muttered against him. "Those guys charge an arm and a leg just to come through the front door, not to mention, God forbid, he finds something wrong."

Sean's back straightened. "I wish you'd quit worrying so much about money."

"I wish we had more," Ginny said. "Then I wouldn't worry."

For a moment, his hands tightened around her. Then he let her go, stepped back and headed for the kitchen. Ginny followed.

"I know you don't want me picking up a part-time job—"

He stopped in the kitchen so fast she almost ran into him. He turned, and even in the shaky, dim light from three-dozen tea lights, she could see his look of scorn. "Ginny, get real. Get a part-time job? Like that?" He gestured at her jutting belly.

"Pregnant women work all the time."

He put his hands on her upper arms, but unlike the soft caress of earlier, this time his fingers pinched a little too hard. "I don't care."

"You're hurting me."

He softened his grip and rubbed to take away the sting. "I'm sorry."

She knew he hadn't done it on purpose, but moved away from him anyway. "I've always worked part time during the Christmas season. And it would help, Sean. A lot."

"I don't want anything to happen to you. That's all. Can't you understand that? Jesus," he added so suddenly, so fiercely, she jumped. "I can't believe we even have to go over this again."

"I understand why you wouldn't want me to work doing what I was doing. I get that. But a few shifts here and there at the bookstore, or—"

"I'm going to check the fuse box."

"Fine." Ginny pushed past him and into the dining room, ostensibly to get her now-cold tea, but mostly to avoid snapping at him. She braced herself for the question about the flashlight, already biting her tongue, but all she heard was the thud of his shoes on the basement steps.

A couple minutes after that, the lights came on.

The sudden brightness stung her eyes, the perfect excuse for tears. Ginny blinked them away, went to the kitchen to pour her tea in the sink. She wet a paper towel and dabbed her face with it too.

"It was a fuse again," Sean said from behind her.

She hadn't heard him come up, and startled, a hand on her heart. "God. You scared me."

He had the flashlight in one hand, unlit now. "Sorry."

"Where'd you get the flashlight?"

Sean gave her a funny look as he ducked out of the doorway, presumably to hang it back on the nail and plug it in. "What do you mean?"

"It was gone." He had to remember the argument. Or maybe he didn't. Sean had a way of pushing things to the back of his mind that he didn't want to remember.

"I just figured you put it back."

"I didn't."

Sean sighed, looking weary. "Ginny, I'm starving and exhausted. Can we just…not do this now?"

"Do what?" Tears threatened again. Knowing it was pregnancy hormones didn't help. She hated this up and down, this constant topsy-turvy. "Talk? Discuss how this is the same flashlight that went missing and you accused me of taking it, or, what, I don't know, hiding it from you or something, but when it was my mug that was gone, you wouldn't even—"

"Enough!" he cried too loud. "Christ. Just…enough. Okay?"

"Fine." She looked away from him and breathed in. Somehow, she found it within her to reach for his hands, to link their fingers. She looked at him, her husband, the man she'd bound herself to until death did them part. "Want me to make you something to eat? I can heat up some pot roast. I know there's some in the freezer. Why don't you go take a hot shower and I'll make dinner. Then maybe we can watch a movie or something?"

"I have some homework…" He hesitated. She let go of his hands, but he grabbed hers back. "No, pot roast sounds good. And a movie. That sounds great."

He went upstairs, and Ginny went into the kitchen to pull leftovers from the freezer and put them in the microwave. She hesitated before pushing the button, but this time the lights stayed on. No blown fuses.

She rinsed the empty Brownie bowl and held it to the light for a moment. She hadn't filled it for a few days because she'd been meaning to pick up some of the licorice treats Sean liked, but hadn't remembered the last time she was at the store. She did have some wrapped butterscotch candies—Sean didn't like them, Ginny thought with a small smile, but maybe the Brownies did. They were in the pantry, and she steeled herself out of habit before she went in.

Ginny had avoided the pantry closet since the baby shower, unloading her weekly loads of groceries and cleaning supplies as fast as she could or making Sean do it. Every time she went inside it, she couldn't stop her skin from crawling with the memory of the flies swarming all over her. Worse now was the fact that the closet was so narrow— with her increased bulk she could go in but could barely turn around enough to get out without backing out.

It was hot, as usual, though, thank God, the smell had gone away and there was no evidence at all of flies of any kind. Still, Ginny kept a foot propped against the door to keep it from swinging shut as she reached for the bag of candy on the shelf. It was right where she'd left it. But there was something else too.

A red collar with a jingle bell.

With a cry, Ginny clutched it, mindless that the door shut behind her. She pressed it to her heart. "Oh, Noodles."

The cat had gone, and unlike the folk song, it didn't seem like she was coming back. But there was this, at least. Ginny closed her eyes against tears for a moment. Then she opened them. She kissed the collar and rubbed the soft leather for a moment, making the bell jingle. Then she tucked it away inside an unused kitchen crock and tapped the lid gently.

Sean wouldn't understand. He might even think she put the collar there, which would raise uncomfortable questions about where the cat had gone. What had happened to her. What part Ginny had played in her disappearance.

"Thank you," Ginny said aloud. "Thank you, Caroline. And…please…keep Noodles safe with you. Love her a lot…for me."

Chapter Thirty-One

"The house looks amazing. How did you do it?" Kendra bounced Carter on her hip as the baby looked goggle-eyed at the lights strung along the molding.

"A little at a time. That's all." That was the truth too. A little bit every day for the past three weeks. A few strings of lights, a couple batches of cookies. Nothing too strenuous, nothing Sean could chastise her about.

Nothing, in fact, that he'd noticed. He'd come home from work and class every night, sometimes too late to even eat dinner. Sometimes he smelled of the bar. Sometimes he didn't. When he did get home early, he watched TV and went to bed. He hadn't so much as put a hand on her in weeks. Barely kissed her in the mornings. It was just like it had been…before, only this time she didn't have the Inkpot to distract her.

"Well, it looks great. Thanks so much for inviting us."

Ginny found a smile. "Glad you could make it. Help yourself to food, drink, whatever." She looked at Carson and Kelly. "I have games set up in the den, if you want to play them. There are some other kids in there."

Watching them scamper off as Kendra took the baby toward the buffet table, Ginny scanned the room for sight of her husband. He'd gone into the carport to put some beer in the giant tub of ice. She needed him to get some more napkins down from the high pantry shelf.

"Talk about a white Christmas." This was Peg, a plate of food in her hands and a set of festive reindeer antlers on her head.

"Are you kidding? It's been snowing since the end of November. I'll be surprised if we ever have spring."

"Pessimist." Peg bit into a sugar cookie. "Ooh. Gran's recipe?"

"Yes. Of course."

Her sister laughed. "You've become ridiculously domestic."

"Wow, and you look ridiculously festive." Ginny looked at her own maroon, dropped-waist dress. It had a white-lace collar. She *felt* ridiculous. Like a pregnant toddler.

"You look gorgeous," Peg said. "That dress is the perfect color for you."

Ginny rolled her eyes. "Yeah. Thanks."

Peg laughed. "Oh stop. Great party, by the way. Who are all these people?"

"Beats me. Word must've spread around the neighborhood." Ginny waved a hand toward the dining room, where she'd set the table with the vast display of food. "Neighbors. Some people Sean works with. You guys. Friends. You know, the usual Christmas open house crowd."

"Who knew you were so popular?"

Ginny laughed and shifted, wishing she'd gone with her sneakers instead of these too-tight black flats. Her dogs were barking. "Not me."

The door opened, bringing in a swirl of frigid air and whirlwind of pine needles from the decaying wreath on the front door. More people. She knew them. Louisa from the Inkpot, along with Tiffany, Michele and Becky. Ginny would've stepped back in surprise, but the wall was at her back and she had no place to go.

"I'll let you go play hostess. I'm going to find Dale," Peg said and abandoned her.

Not that Ginny should've felt abandoned. These people had been her friends once, or at the very least acquaintances. Louisa, in fact, had made quite the effort to stay in touch. Guilt stabbed her. She'd never returned Louisa's calls or messages, and though she'd promised her that day in the grocery store, Ginny had never gone back to the Inkpot.

"Ginny! Oh my God, you look so great!" Tiffany had a loud voice and a bright smile, and she was a hugger. She came for Ginny with both arms open wide, engulfing her before patting and making baby goo-goo noises at her belly. "Congratulations!"

"Thanks. Umm…"

"Your husband invited us," Tiffany said. "Came by the Inkpot with a cute, little printed-out invitation and said to make sure that the whole gang came. All of us."

Of course Sean hadn't mentioned it. He probably thought he was doing her a favor. Ginny smiled and nodded, accepted their hugs and congratulations, directed them toward the food and drink and where to hang their coats. She moved to close the door behind the last person, but someone pushed it open from the other side.

And there he was.

"Hi, Ginny," Jason said. "Merry Christmas."

The world whirled out from beneath her, but Ginny didn't fall, and she didn't spin. She would never do that again for him. Never.

"I came with Becky," he said quietly. Standing a little too close. Voice a little too low so she had to strain to hear him. His gaze held hers a little too long. "I didn't mean to surprise you."

Ginny blinked rapidly. She took a breath. "Oh, Jason. Yes you did."

Then she turned on the flat heel of her pinching shoe and went upstairs, leaving him behind. It was quiet up there, the sounds of the party far enough away to make it clear to her she had responsibilities as a hostess to get down there and make sure everyone had enough to eat, enough to drink. Enough to make merry.

"Fa la la la fucking la," she whispered with the bedroom door shut tight behind her back. She put her hands on her belly as the baby inside squirmed and kicked. Her heart hurt, and it hurt to breathe, but, no, she was not going to cry. She was not going to lose her shit here and now. Not tonight, not because of him.

He'd come with Becky. Of course he did. Becky had always had her sights set on him. Becky, with her low-cut shirts and tits hanging out, her tiny, tight ass and skinny jeans tucked into knee-high boots, her blonde hair hanging down from underneath her trendy little caps.

Ginny's jealousy was huge and ugly and unrepentant. It came with sharp teeth and jagged claws and venom, and it tore her up from the inside out. She panted with the effort of keeping her tears locked up tight, but her mouth opened in a silent, yawning scream she stopped by biting the meaty part of her palm. She closed her eyes and breathed.

She breathed.

In the darkness by her closet, something moved.

With the lights off, the push of air as whatever it was moved gave it away, rather than anything she could actually see. The only light came from beneath the door, and it crept only an inch or so along the floor around her feet. Then, the flash of something.

Eyes.

Now was not the time to fuck with her. Ginny stepped forward. "Who's there? What are you doing in here?"

And then, more softly, "Caroline?"

It moved again, dark on dark. A hint of swirling hair, an outstretched hand. Ginny reached suddenly frigid fingers into the darkness. The room had gone so cold she was sure that in the light she'd have been able to see her breath.

"Ginny?" The door bumped into her, closing at once. She stepped away as Sean pushed it again. Light spilled into the room, bright enough to make her squint. "Are you— Hey. What's wrong?"

"Nothing. It's too hot downstairs. I came up to change." She tore at the hideous dress, moving toward the open closet door. She turned on the light, looked up and down, but whatever it had been was gone. If anything, it was colder in here than in the bedroom, and in a moment she saw why.

The cubbyhole door was open. Not a lot. Just a crack, but it was enough to let the tendrils of icy outside air seep into the closet. Ginny closed it, hard. She traced the outline of the door with her fingertips and turned to look at her husband who'd come in behind her.

"I'll be down in a few minutes. I just want to put on something more comfortable."

"I thought maybe you weren't feeling good. Peg said you just disappeared."

Ginny straightened, looking him in the eye, searching his face, that lovely face, for any sign. Anything at all, any glimmer or hint that he'd known what he was doing when he invited her "friends" from the Inkpot.

But no matter how well she'd always been able to read him, Sean had never been transparent. For all the times she'd spent wishing he knew her, there'd been an equal number in which she'd been unable to understand him. Her husband stared back at her, his expression concerned but otherwise implacable.

"No. Just too hot. And this dress, I never should've put it on. It makes me look like Laura Ashley puked all over me." She swiped at the collar and then the casual French twist of her hair.

"You look beautiful."

"I look enormous and blotchy and disgusting!" Ginny shouted.

The words rang in the closet, softened only a little bit by the hanging clothes. They echoed. They stung.

"You look," her husband told her, "beautiful."

Then he backed out of the closet and left her there.

She was going out of her mind. That was all. The simplest and easiest explanation— she was crazy. There was nobody in the room; there had been nobody in the room. There was no ghost haunting this house.

But there was a ghost haunting *her*.

With shaking, swift fingers, Ginny used the mirror over her dresser to put on some lipstick and swipe some shadow on her eyelids. She dabbed perfume on her wrists and at her throat—lilac and vanilla, a special-blended scent she ordered from an online *parfumerie*. She put on a pair of black-velvet pants, not maternity but of material stretchy enough they still fit. Then a dark-green sweater from the back of her closet, also not maternity but cut with a swing to the hem that meant she could leave it untucked to her thighs and have it look like it was meant to be worn that way. She twisted her hair up again, but left a few loose curls to frame her face.

Then she went downstairs.

The party had grown while she was gone. More neighbors, her brother and Jeannie, hesitantly reconciled. A few more people from Sean's office. It was too much to hope that Jason had gone. Ginny saw him standing next to Becky in the far corner of the living room, next to the Christmas tree. Becky was laughing, tossing her hair. Jason was looking everywhere but at her, both his hands full of crystal punch glasses.

Ginny moved through the guests and played hostess, ignoring them both.

Chapter Thirty-Two

Since finding the collar, Ginny no longer feared the pantry. She wasn't tall enough to reach the napkins Sean had not yet managed to get down for her, though she'd reminded him a couple times. People were pulling paper towels off the holder, not that it was a big deal, but she was going to run out of those soon too. Now Ginny stretched up onto her tiptoes, reaching, her fingertips skating along the plastic-wrapped package of napkins she'd purchased specifically for the Christmas party because they had snowmen on them. Festive napkins, perfect for a party, except by the time she managed to get them down the party would be over and she'd be stuck using holiday napkins until the Fourth of July.

The door opened, then shut.

"I can get that for you."

She knew that voice without turning, and there was scarcely enough room for her to whirl around. So she didn't. With her back to him, Ginny said, "I can get it."

"You can't. Let me."

She could feel him against her back, a heat she'd imagined a hundred times. No, a thousand. He didn't touch her, but then he didn't have to, did he?

"I can get it," she repeated firmly, voice neutral, like she was speaking to a stranger.

Jason cleared his throat. Ginny's fingers curled in the wire shelving in front of her. She willed herself to stay still as he reached over her to grab the napkins down and hand them to her. When it was done, he didn't move away.

He said her name in a low voice, full of longing. More heat. Her cheeks flushed with it, but this was not the fire of lust kindling in her breastbone.

In all the times she'd imagined seeing him again, all the ways she'd thought about how this would go, never in one of them had she faced him with her belly pushed out in front of her as proof she was tied to another man. She'd never pictured him in her house. Her own fucking house.

Ginny turned, the expanse of her body pushing him back a step. "What are you doing here, Jason? Really. What the hell are you doing?"

"I wanted to see you."

"It's been almost a year."

He nodded, his eyes fixed firmly on her face like he was afraid of looking anywhere else. He was looking at her, but not really seeing her. "I know. But I wanted to see you, and when Becky asked me...I just..."

One of the things she'd always liked best about him was the way they could talk to each other. Whatever else had failed, it had never been their words. Watching him now, his mouth working with nothing coherent coming out, Ginny wanted nothing more than for him to shut up before he ruined every memory she had of every conversation they'd ever shared.

"You shouldn't be here, Jason."

"I know."

They stared in silence beneath the bright, bare bulb of the pantry. It was unforgiving, that light, shadowing his face and make the lines of it harder than she remembered. It highlighted the glint of silver in his hair, the lines at the corners of his eyes and mouth. He'd aged since she'd seen him last. Well. She supposed she'd changed more than he had, and in a far less flattering manner.

Incredibly, he moved a step closer. Once, standing this close would've sent electricity arcing between them, a palpable spark. Now, there was nothing for her except the slow and dull throb of the grief she'd tried her very best to shed. The anger, rising.

Jason's voice rasped when he spoke, "I'm sorry, Ginny."

Sorry he wanted to see her? Or for that other thing she'd worried over and picked apart until it had left her raw? Or for something else she'd never figure out, she thought, looking him over. It didn't matter. It was over. That cake was baked.

That door was closed.

She couldn't squeeze by him. "Move."

Jason backed up, hands out but not touching her, to let her pass. He snagged her sleeve before she could totally get away. She stopped, but didn't turn. There wasn't enough room.

"I'm sorry, Ginny."

She couldn't keep her voice steady, though she tried. "You should have come to Philadelphia."

"I wanted to."

"Not enough." She shrugged to show him how little she cared, and it must've worked because from behind her, Jason let out a small sigh.

"Well…you look great. And…I guess I'm glad to see that you decided to…you know. Stay with your husband."

At this she turned, her incredulity passing in a heartbeat.

"Jason," Ginny said with something close to pity. Something more like condescension. "I never, ever intended to leave my husband."

That was it. All she had to say. He let her go, and she took the napkins in her trembling hands, into the dining room, where she opened the package and filled the basket she'd placed there for just that purpose. She focused, focused, eyes blinking to keep them dry, swallowing hard against the tightness in her throat that could've been tears or a scream, she couldn't tell the difference.

"Great party." Becky lifted her glass of wine. "And you, wow, Ginny. You look so…happy."

There might've been smug satisfaction on the woman's face, or it might've been Ginny's imagination. Either way, she straightened with a smile. "Thanks."

"I mean it. You're really glowing." Was that something wistful in Becky's tone?

"It's hot in here." Ginny made a show of fanning her face. "But thanks."

Behind her, Sean appeared with a platter of mini corn dogs from the oven. He put them on the table with a nod toward Becky and looked at Ginny. "I was going to get the napkins for you. But I saw you already got them."

Before she could answer, Kelly and Carson pounded through the dining room with Ginny's nephew Luke fast on their heels, though at eighteen, Luke was old enough to know better. She reached as he thundered past, and brought him up short.

"No running, it's too crowded in here."

Luke looked sheepish. "Sorry, Aunt Ginny. Just playing with the little kids."

"Play something else," she suggested, but not unkindly. "I don't need my whole house torn apart."

Becky was gone by the time she finished scolding, but Sean was still there. He watched Luke head out after the kids, then looked at her with an expression so odd her heart thumped in response. But if there was something he wanted to say, he wasn't going to do it there.

The party went on. Food eaten, beverages drunk. Some people danced in the living room. Some kissed beneath the mistletoe. The front porch became the haven for the smokers, including Jason, whose profile Ginny could see through the kitchen window when she filled the kettle for tea. Sean was there too.

"Kelly? Carson?" Kendra came into the kitchen without her little baggage on her hip. She wore her coat and a worried expression. "Ginny, hi. Have you seen my kids?"

"I saw them earlier, playing with my nephew." She turned from the sink and put the kettle on the burner but didn't turn it on. A look at the clock told her it was late, probably past the kids' bedtime. Close to her own, actually.

"I can't find them." Kendra gave her a weary smile. "I think they're playing hide and seek."

"Oh." Ginny chewed the inside of her cheek. "Umm…well. Let's find Luke and see if he knows where they are."

Luke had abandoned the play of little kids in favor of facing off with his dad in Guitar Hero. The rapt audience of freshman girls from down the street made the reason for his decision obvious; nevertheless, a thin, helpless bite of annoyance stung her.

"I don't know where they are, sorry," Luke told her with an apologetic shrug. "I haven't seen them in a couple hours."

It wasn't like Kendra was the queen of keeping an eye on her children, Ginny thought uncharitably at the sight of Kendra's panicked expression. Still, having once misplaced Luke in a department store when she was supposed to be taking him to pick out a birthday present for Peg, Ginny knew the rush of panic. She put a hand on Kendra's arm.

"We'll find them. They have to be in the house somewhere. Right?"

Kendra nodded, looking doubtful. She pulled a cell phone out of her pocket and pressed a few numbers. "Clark. Are the kids there with you? No, not Carter, I know he's there. No, well…they didn't go with you? No," she snapped. "They're not missing. They're just…they're here somewhere. I just wanted to make sure they hadn't gone with you before I started hollering for them. Yes, we'll be home soon. Just put him in the crib, for God's sakes! Give him a bottle, whatever!"

She disconnected and gave Ginny an embarrassed shrug. "You'd think he'd never put the kid to bed before."

"We'll find them," Ginny repeated so she didn't have to comment on Kendra's marital discord. God knows, Ginny shouldn't judge. "Let's look upstairs."

Sean had come back inside the house, his nose and cheeks flushed pink with cold. He smelled of smoke. Ginny pulled her husband aside to explain the situation. He didn't get it, she saw that clearly enough.

"I'm going to take Kendra upstairs and check around. Keep an eye out down here."

"Carson!" Kendra cried, because at that moment her son ambled out of the dining room with a cookie in each hand and chocolate around his mouth. "Where have you been? I've been looking for you everywhere! Where's your sister?"

"Don't know." Carson lifted a cookie to his mouth but didn't bite it. He looked suddenly alarmingly green. "Don't feel good."

Oh hell no, Ginny thought. "Bathroom's down the hall."

God help Kendra if her son puked all over Ginny's brand-new area rug, she thought, but Kendra at least had this part of parenting down. She hustled Carson down the hall so fast he dropped both cookies before he could toss them. The bathroom door slammed behind them.

Ginny looked at Sean. "I'll go look upstairs."

He lifted his eyes to the ceiling at the sound of pattering footsteps. "Someone's up there."

Running. Back and forth along the hall and in the baby's room. Also the library. Ginny and Sean tracked the noises with their eyes for a minute before she gestured at the fallen cookies. "Can you get that? I'll be back."

He looked first surprised, then annoyed, but said nothing as he bent to clean up the crumbled mess. Ginny left him to it, not interested in an argument, though his response had rubbed along her skin like a shark's scales being stroked the wrong direction. She climbed the stairs with one hand on the railing to help heave her bulk along, and by the time she reached the top she had to stop and catch her breath.

She flicked the switch on the wall, but the ceiling fixture stayed dark. Colored light from the outside Christmas bulbs came in through the window facing the street, but it was filtered even further by the stained glass. Some other light drifted into the hall from the bathroom night-light, but that was it.

Shadows moved, whispering and giggling. The patter of feet slapped the floor beyond the railing across from her and slipped around the corner into the nursery. The door shut with a click, cutting off the childish laughter.

"Kelly?" Ginny put her left hand on the railing, but didn't move toward the nursery.

She could go to the left, past the bathroom and her bedroom, to get there, or she could go to the right and pass the library. The door was closed there too. If Kelly came out of the nursery, she could jog either left or right and avoid Ginny altogether, depending which way she ran. Ginny didn't feel like chasing her, especially not in the dark. As she hesitated, her decision was made for her.

The door to the library opened, and Kelly tumbled into the hallway on a couple stumbling steps before she stopped with her back to Ginny.

"Come out, come out, wherever you are!"

Ginny put out a hand to snag the girl's dress. "I'm right here."

Kelly whirled with a shriek that startled Ginny into echoing it. Her scream scared Kelly into another wail, and the girl ran back into the library. Ginny managed to gather her wits, though, and pursued her. The light in this room worked, though both of them put their hands up against the sudden brightness when she turned it on.

"Enough," Ginny snapped, her patience worn thin by the unpleasantly behaved neighbor children. "Kelly, stop it."

Kelly's screams trailed into a whimper. Her terror faded visibly, though at the sight of Ginny's face, her eyes widened and she looked like she might start to sob instead of scream. "You scareded me!"

"You scared me too. You shouldn't be running around up here in the dark, especially alone."

"I'm not alone. I'm playing with the little girl."

"Which little girl? From the party? What did she look like?"

Kelly looked evasive. "Umm...she has dark hair."

"What's her name?"

"I don't know her name, I think it's Carrie."

Ginny froze. Her gaze narrowed as her heart set up a quickened, nervous thumping in her wrists and the base of her throat. "It's not nice to tell stories that aren't true, Kelly."

"I'm not telling stories." Kelly looked chastened, but unrepentant. She scuffed at the floor with one of her patent-leather shoes. "Carson quit with us because he wanted some more cookies, but she kept playing."

"Kelly," Ginny said warningly. "Don't make me tell your mom that you were lying to me."

"But I'm not! I was playing with the little girl, I was. You can ask her yourself!"

Ginny looked around the room, half expecting to see a floating ghostly form. "Where is she?"

Kelly looked shifty-eyed again and shuffled her feet. "She probably ran away."

"Where would she go?"

"I don't know." Kelly shrugged.

"She was in here with you? Playing hide and seek?"

Kelly nodded, looking a little relieved that Ginny's tone had gone a little softer. "Yeah, she was hiding in the cubby, and I found her, but she ran through."

"In the…" Stunned, Ginny looked toward the small door set into the wall. There was another identical door in the nursery, but she hadn't known the storage space connected the rooms.

It made sense, of course, but another surge of irritation rose. The one peek she'd taken had shown her a slanted, narrow space with nails sticking through the roof and a gap in the floorboards under the eaves, stuffed with insulation. Not the place to be running and playing.

"Where is she now, Kelly?"

"I don't know, I told you, she ran through…"

The girl kept talking for a minute or so, but Ginny was looking past her to the easel and paints she'd set up weeks ago and had been ignoring ever since. The painting on the easel had only been a few strokes, just a couple blobs of color and some light pencil sketching. She hadn't touched it since then, or even looked at it. But one thing Ginny knew for sure—she most definitely had not been finger-painting.

Anger, real anger now, instead of just annoyance, bubbled out of her. Stalking past the sniffling child, Ginny looked at the painting. Jaw set, she glared at Kelly.

"What did you do?"

"I didn't…I mean, me and Carson…and the little girl…"

"Why would you touch this? What made you think this would be okay, to go into someone else's house and touch their stuff?" Ginny snapped a hand toward the mess on her canvas.

Someone had streaked it with color in broad, thick lines. There was a pattern to it, but no shape, no form. It wasn't a painting that meant to look like anything specific, not a dog or horse or person. Not even a rainbow. If anything, it resembled some of the most offbeat pieces of modern art she'd ever studied, and Ginny loathed modern art.

"Answer me!" She took a step toward Kelly, who must've rightly assumed it was threatening though Ginny hadn't so much as raised a hand.

"I t-t-told you, it wasn't me or Carson. It was the little girl, she painted it!"

"Let me see your hands."

Kelly tucked them at once behind her.

Ginny's mouth twisted, but she kept herself from shouting. She took another step toward Kelly. "Kelly, I don't want to have to tell your mommy you've been naughty."

Reluctantly, Kelly held out a hand.

Ginny snagged her wrist to study the girl's palm for telltale signs of paint. That was how Kendra found them.

"Kelly? What's going on?"

"Mommy!" Kelly screamed and ran into her mother's arms, burying her face against Kendra's stomach. Her shoulders shook with sobs.

Kendra gave Ginny a narrow-eyed, frowning glare. Peg had once revealed to her younger sister that no matter how terrible her children had behaved, if another adult was the one disciplining them, something protective and feral reared its head. Ginny saw it in Kendra's gaze now, the sharp glance at Ginny's hands and then how she took up her daughter's to go over the wrist. Checking for bruises, maybe.

Ginny didn't care. She'd seen the evidence on Kendra's hands. She kept her voice sickly sweet, though. Concerned, not accusatory. She felt more than able and happily willing to take on Mama Bear, but the tiny, still-rational part of her held her tongue.

"She got into my paints. Be careful she doesn't get it on your pretty blouse."

Kendra yanked Kelly's grasping hands away from her at that news, peering harder at her daughter's palms. She sagged, then looked at Ginny, embarrassed. "Oh God. Kelly. What on earth?"

"You should take her home," Ginny said firmly enough that Kendra blinked. "Now."

"Right. Yeah, I'm sorry. I'm really sorry, Ginny." Kendra paused. "I cleaned your bathroom for you, though. Carson's okay now, but…yeah, I took care of it."

As though Ginny should be, what, grateful? She smiled thinly but kept her voice as sweet as sugar cookies. "Thanks for coming to the party."

Kendra nudged Kelly forward; the girl went as reluctantly as she'd offered Ginny her hand. "Say thank you to Mrs. Bohn."

Kelly hesitated.

Ginny smiled at her. She couldn't really get down on her knees to be eye to eye, but she bent forward so the girl had no choice but to stare her in the face.

"Merry Christmas, Kelly."

"Thankyouforhavingus." Kelly'd rushed the words and ducked back behind her mother, who gave Ginny another apologetic look.

"Merry Christmas. Thanks for the party, it was really lovely. Umm…yeah." Kendra fumbled when Ginny didn't return the smile. "We'll just…okay. Good night."

In the doorway, Kelly looked over her shoulder at Ginny. "Merry Christmas, Carrie!"

Kendra shushed her, shoving her along, but Ginny turned to look behind her. The cubby door was cracked open, just a little, and she couldn't remember if it had been that way before or if that squeak of Kelly's patent-leather shoes had masked the creak of it opening.

Ginny stared at it for a long time as the sounds of merriment drifted up from downstairs. It wouldn't take much for her to cross the room and open that door. At the very least, she should shut it tightly to prevent drafts.

She opened the door the whole way, her fingers reaching for the pull chain on the light she remembered was inside. It, like the light in the hall, didn't come on. Ginny muttered a curse for ancient light bulbs. She looked along the low space, into the darkness, forcing herself not to be uneasy. There was nothing in there but dust and the nose-tickling smell of pink insulation, and maybe a mouse or two that had been smart enough to avoid the bait left by Danny, the exterminator.

Except there *was* something back there, in the deep and shifting shadows. Something small and crouched. And something on the floor too—spots of green, the same color that had been on Kelly's palms and splashed across Ginny's canvas. She looked hard into the darkness and willed her eyes to find a face, hands, toes, but the figure remained solid and lifeless, without a glimmer of eyes or teeth. It remained a nothing.

She leaned in just a little to take another look at the floor, the small curved imprint of a bare foot. Unmistakable as anything else, just this one, the others more spattered and uneven. She was reaching to touch the paint and check to see if it was wet, when someone called her name. Startled, she jumped and smacked her head on the inside of the doorframe. With a muffled curse, she backed out of the cubby.

"Your friends are getting ready to leave. I thought you'd want to say goodbye." Sean leaned in the library doorway. "What are you doing?"

"Oh. That little heathen from next door was messing with my stuff. She was inside here, running from room to room."

"In the crawl space?" Sean came up behind her to look over her shoulder. "In the dark?"

"Apparently."

He snorted soft laughter. "Brave kid."

"Stupid kid. She could've fallen through, broken a leg. Or worse. Not to mention that she got into my paints and…" Ginny broke off with a sigh and a shake of her head. "Never mind. Just remind me, next year, when I say I want to have a party…that I don't."

His laugh sounded a little more like his usual, this time. "Right. You say that now, but…"

"Next year we'll have a little one of our own. I probably won't even have time to plan a party."

He gave her a curious look and put a hand on her belly, rubbing. A tiny foot, a little hand, pressed against his touch. He put his other hand next to it, his strong fingers curling against her flesh. "You'll want to see everyone."

Ginny put her hands over his. "Honestly? The only people I need to see will be the ones I already see all the time. I don't need to host a big shindig and invite all kinds of people over and feed them and stuff."

Sean said nothing for a moment or two. Then he leaned to kiss her. "Your friends," he reminded. "They said they were leaving. I thought you'd want to say goodbye."

Ginny knew then whom he meant, and why exactly he'd gone to such lengths to invite them. It was a relief, in a way, not to wonder anymore if he knew. She said nothing at first, letting the sounds from downstairs drift up to them…but not come between them.

Finally, she pushed away just enough to look at him. "They can find their own way out."

After a moment he nodded. Then he hugged her again, his hands moving in small circles over her back as her belly made a bridge between them.

It wasn't until later in bed, when she'd woken once again in the night with wide eyes and the idea that someone had spoken her name, that Ginny recognized what had been so odd about the paint in the crawl space. It had looked like the print of a bare foot, a child's foot. But not Kelly's she remembered, because Kelly had been wearing patent-leather shoes.

Chapter Thirty-Three

More snow. Inches of it on top of the mountains they already had. Sean had made it to work, even though the radio stations were all warning motorists to stay off the road. His class would be cancelled, or so she thought, but he'd told her he had to make it in or forfeit some of the paid time off he wanted to take after the baby came. She had to weigh the anxiety of imagining him swerving into a ditch against knowing how much help it would be having him home, and in the end Ginny'd had no choice anyway. If her husband said he was going to work, he was going to work. It was stupid to make them all come in when they could just close the offices. It served no purpose to have people risk their lives to come in and pound away on keyboards, entering data.

"Not all of us have the benefit of working for ourselves," he'd reminded her this morning, early, when she'd rolled over in bed with a groan at the sound of his alarm.

He hadn't pointed out that Ginny wasn't working and hadn't been for months. She said nothing about it either, just got up and made him breakfast while he showered and the lights flickered, and she hoped the power wouldn't go out again.

It did, of course, blipping on and off a few times before finally cutting out altogether. Ginny sighed, frustrated and thinking of the three loads of laundry she had yet to do, the full dishwasher. Her rumbling stomach and the soup she'd intended to heat up for her lunch.

Her cell phone rang, Peg on the other end inviting her over for lunch and to watch movies. Peg's house had power. Peg had a four-wheel-drive vehicle and wasn't afraid of driving in the snow, because, as Peg said, she'd survived teaching six teenagers how to drive.

"I'll come pick you up. We'll hang out. I'll bring you home when Sean gets home, or he can stop here on his way home from work. I'll make goulash. It'll be good." Peg paused. "I never see you anymore."

That wasn't true—Peg had stopped by on her way to what she called the "fancy" grocery store on Ginny's side of town just two weeks ago.

"You're just not used to having all your kids out of the house, that's all. Makes you feel like you're missing stuff you aren't."

"Not true," Peg said. "What, I can't miss my baby sister? And besides, you know...I worry about you, a little bit. In that big house alone."

Ginny was silent for a second or two. "You don't have to worry about me."

"But I do."

Above her, the lights flickered, but immediately dimmed and went dark. Ginny sighed. "Yes. Please come get me. I can't stand it here without power; it's so gray today I can't even get any decent light to read."

"I'll be there in half an hour."

It took forty minutes, actually, the roads worse than Peg would admit at first. Her SUV handled everything okay, but it was eerie riding the snow-covered streets, the wind so bad the traffic lights swung. Not many other people were on the road.

"The smart ones," Ginny teased.

"Yeah, yeah. I can take you home, let you sit in the dark eating cold cereal."

But Ginny knew Peg wouldn't do anything like that, even if they'd been closer to Ginny's house and it would've made sense for Peg to turn around. As it was, by the time they got into Peg's driveway, the wind had kicked up further and the snow had become so thick it turned the afternoon to dusk. Peg pulled into the garage and shook her head.

"I hope *we* don't lose electricity."

Ginny made a face. "You'd better not. The only reason I came with you was for the food and the warmth."

"And the entertainment," Peg pointed out. "C'mon. Let's get inside."

It hadn't been as long Peg seemed to think, but it had been long enough that nostalgia crept over Ginny as she sat at her sister's kitchen table with a mug of Peg's homemade cocoa in front of her, along with a plate of shortbread. Instead of watching movies, they played cards and laughed about old stories. They filled themselves with cocoa and cookies, and Peg never did get around to making the goulash, which was okay since every time Ginny called Sean's number she got a message saying his number was unavailable.

She called her house four or five times as the afternoon wore on, becoming night, but each time the phone rang and rang without the answering machine picking up. That meant the power was off. The sixth time, she was able to leave a message for Sean, saying she was on her way home and would be there soon.

"The power's back on. Can you give me a ride home?"

Peg looked at the clock. "You're not staying for dinner?"

"Couldn't get ahold of Sean," Ginny said, already gathering her coat. Her back ached from sitting in the hard kitchen chair, but she wasn't going to tell her sister that. "He should be almost home by now. At least the lights will be on for him."

* * * * *

All the lights were on, blazing forth from every window, when Ginny got home. She waved as Peg backed out of the driveway. The snow had tapered off drastically an hour or so before stopping, so the roads were passable.

Humming, pleased with the afternoon despite how it had begun, Ginny let herself in the front door. Sean, who seemed to come from nowhere, his face a strained mask and his hair askew, swooped down on her immediately.

"Where the hell were you?"

Taken aback, Ginny shrugged out of her coat and hung it on the coatrack by the front door before looking at him. "I was with Peg. I left you a message."

"I didn't get any messages!"

"I tried your phone," she said patiently, biting back her own instant anger that had been jerked upright by his tone. "I kept getting an error message. But I left one on the answering machine."

She saw at once by his expression that he hadn't even checked, but before she could point that out or make an explanation, he'd launched into her again.

"God dammit, Ginny! You pissed and moaned about me going in to work today because you said the roads were too bad, then I come home to find you gone, every freaking light in the house on...your car still in the driveway. What the hell was I supposed to think? You couldn't leave me a goddamned note?"

Oh, how tempted she was to snap back at him, to curl her lip. Instead, she pushed past him and down the hall to the kitchen, keeping her pace steady. Not running, not giving him that effort. In the kitchen, she looked at the answering machine, blinking merrily with one message. Hers, it had to be.

She turned as he came in after her. "I did leave you a message. It's not my fault you didn't listen to it. And I told you, your cell phone—"

"There's nothing wrong with my fucking phone."

Ginny blinked, slowly. She took a step back from him. "Are you calling me a liar?"

His shoulders heaved and his fists clenched, lightly, but clenched just the same. He said nothing. Her gut twisted. Her heart became stone. She had a thousand words to say to him, perhaps many more than that, but she bit them all back, chewed and swallowed them. Ginny shoved them deep inside her to join everything else she'd pushed down.

Sean scowled. "I came home and you were gone. All the lights were on, and you weren't here. No note, nothing."

Her chin lifted, just a little. "So…what? You thought I just ran off and left you? With all the lights on? Without my car?"

"Someone could have come for you."

"Someone *did* come for me," she told him. "My sister."

Sean shook his head, just barely.

Ginny sighed and shifted to ease the ache in her back. Her belly rippled with Braxton Hicks and the baby's kicking. She winced as she tucked her hands beneath it, wishing she could lift it in a sling and somehow relieve at least some of the weight.

She pointed at the blinking answering machine. She sounded weary, because that was how she felt. "I left you a message. I'm sorry you were worried."

"I thought you'd gone off with him."

She'd had a hard-enough time catching her breath lately, but at this every molecule of oxygen left her. She sagged, fingers clutching at the countertop. Her tongue had gone thick, her lips numb. "Oh, Sean. No."

"I thought, well, this is it. She's gone. She finally did it. But the least…" his voice broke, and she saw with growing alarm that her stoic husband was close to tears, "…the least she could fucking do is leave a note!"

"I went to Peg's, that's it!" Her own voice rose, razor-edged with hysteria. "I didn't go off anywhere. I wouldn't. Sean, I—"

He turned from her when she tried to touch him, and Ginny let her hand fall to her side. She had no right to force him to let her soothe him. She had no right to anything, really, and she would take none.

"Just tell me something, because it's been driving me crazy thinking about it."

She swallowed hard, prepared to give him all the details, the few there were. "What?"

Sean scraped at his eyes with the fingertips of one hand, the other's fingers tucked into his belt loop on his hip like he was afraid what it would do if he didn't keep it tethered. "Did you love him?"

It wasn't the question she'd expected, but as soon as he asked, she knew she'd been foolish to think he'd ask anything else. "No."

He looked at her, his expression horridly naked. "Then why?"

"Because you wouldn't touch me," she told him simply. She spread her fingers and gave a half shrug, her words the truth, with nothing to redeem them but that. "You stopped hugging me, kissing me, touching me. You stopped all of it, Sean. It was like living with my brother...no, worse than that, because I've never doubted, even when he was being mean to me, that my brother loved me. And for a long time, with you, I wasn't sure."

"I never stopped loving you," he said hoarsely.

She hated the sound of tears in his voice. She hated that she'd done this, broken him somehow. Tearing off the scab was supposed to help an infected wound leak its poison, but this...she'd never wanted this.

"I wanted my husband there for me. I needed you. And you just...went away." She wanted to touch him, but mindful of his last reaction, kept her hands at her sides. "I know you were grieving. But you wouldn't talk to me."

"I was. I couldn't bear it, how much you'd gone through. How I almost lost you too." He shook his head and began to pace. "Seeing you in the hospital, knowing I'd done it to you..."

"You didn't do anything to me." She wanted to empathize with him, or at the very least find an edge of sympathy for his agony, but all she heard was him burdening himself with what had been her pain. Making what happened to her, somehow...his, not even theirs. But just his.

Typical, she thought. Turning the loss of their baby somehow, into his private torture. That he'd somehow been responsible, or that he could've done anything differently. It was typical of his need to fix things, regardless of what had broken them or how much worse his efforts at tinkering made them.

"I got pregnant. We both wanted kids. Something was wrong. We lost the baby." She took a deep breath, hating that she had to be the one, once again, to walk him through this. "It happens to a lot of people. We're far from the only ones. And it was a blessing, I think, because we weren't prepared to have a child with special needs, or even to lose a child after it was born."

He shuddered, still pacing. Every so often his hand crept up to tug through his hair.

"I couldn't stand to think about it happening again."

"So…you just stopped…" she shook her head, trying to piece this together, to make sense of it, "…you stopped touching me."

"I had to."

"Despite what the nuns might've told you in the third grade, Sean, hugging doesn't lead to pregnancy."

He stopped his pacing, thank God. He looked at her. "You just…you were at me. All the time."

This was not how she remembered it, not at all. Ginny remembered needing to hold him and be held. To grieve together. And later, when her body had healed enough for it, to make love to him again and find that closeness that had always been so much a part of their marriage.

"I was at *you?*" She tried hard to think on it, to recall if she'd been some sort of vamping siren, skimping around in lingerie or accosting him in dark corners. "You think wanting to have sex with my husband is…what…wrong? Weird? Abnormal?"

"You were at me about having another baby."

With the counter behind her, Ginny couldn't move backwards. Her fingers slipped and gripped on the laminate. One nail bent and broke. Wincing, she held it in front of her to watch a small bead of blood form beneath the nail she pulled off and tossed into the sink drain. She sucked at the blood, and it was only half as bitter as all the things she wanted to say.

"And I couldn't do it," Sean said. "I just…couldn't."

Again, Ginny racked her brain to think if she'd been the one pushing for another child. All she could think of was telling him, at the time, it would all be okay. They could try again. They could always try again. She remembered saying it from the hospital bed. She remembered saying it in the shower with the hot water pounding over her aching body as the blood leaked down her legs and into the drain. She'd said it to comfort him.

"I thought you wanted a baby," she told him and reeled with the idea that all this time she'd been trying for something he didn't even want.

"Not enough to risk losing you."

She'd been wrong to think Sean had never feared losing anyone, she saw that now. But, try as she might, she couldn't make herself sympathize with his choices.

He started pacing again.

This time, she reached out and grabbed his sleeve, hard enough to stop him. "Stand still. Look at me."

She waited until he did, his gaze naked and horrid and hard to face, but she forced herself to do it. "I am fine. This baby is fine. Nothing is going to happen to this baby, or to me. You're not going to lose me."

His sharp bark of laughter surprised her enough to let go of his sleeve. Her husband's mouth twisted—not quite a smile, not quite a sneer. He closed his eyes for a long couple of seconds, and when he looked at her again, his gaze was flat and hard and assessing.

"I already did." He gestured at her belly. His shoulders sagged. He let himself sink into one of the kitchen chairs and buried his face in his hands, squeezing his head like a man in the grip of a migraine. "Didn't I?"

She sat across from him and took his hands, forcing him to let her hold them. She squeezed his fingers. He didn't look at her, but that made it easier and she was grateful for that.

"No. Never." There'd been times when Ginny was uncertain of what would happen and where her path would lead, but of this she had never been unsure. "You did not lose me."

He looked up at her. "I didn't want to watch you go through that again, and I was right, wasn't I?"

Disturbed, she squeezed his fingers again. "No. You'll feel differently when the baby comes. You'll see, it will be all right, and we'll be okay—"

"I don't know if I can," he said quietly.

Her heart started breaking. "You don't know if you can what?"

"Love it. Be a father to it. I figured I'd try, you know? I'd do my best. But I'm not sure I can."

"Oh, Sean. Of course you can. You'll love this baby. Lots of people are scared about becoming parents, but…you'll see. You'll be an amazing father."

"But I won't," he told her steadily, "be the father."

"Of course you—" He wasn't talking about being afraid. Being incompetent. "What? Oh— What the hell?"

She snatched her hands from his. It would've been her turn to pace, if she'd been able to push herself away from the table, to get her bulk moving quickly enough. Instead, she sat, trapped by her inertia.

"I wondered if you were going to tell him," he continued conversationally, like they were discussing the day's mail. "But he didn't seem to know. I saw him look at you at the

Christmas party when they came in. He was surprised. Why didn't you tell him?"

"Because it was none of his business," Ginny snapped. Her heart raced. Her stomach churned. She thought she might vomit or pass out; her hands trembled. "Sean, you are the father of this baby."

He shook his head, pushing away from the table, and she grabbed for him, snagged his sleeve but couldn't keep him there. He jerked from her touch and stood so fast the chair tipped over behind him. She jumped at the crash and put her hands on her ears for a moment. She closed her eyes.

"You are the father of this baby," she told him, not wanting to see him not believing her. "I swear to you."

"I can't be."

"You are!" Ginny shouted, glaring at him.

They stared at each other. She shuddered. He backed up to the doorway as though he meant to flee, but stayed.

"I can't be," he said again. "I had a vasectomy."

Ginny tried to draw a breath and could find nothing but dust in her throat and lungs. She choked on it, gasping. This was…this was…

She became aware of him shaking her. Her head lolled. Sean cradled her, slapping lightly at her cheeks until she shoved him away from her. She struggled to her feet, facing off with him.

"What in the actual fuck do you mean, you had a vasectomy?"

He looked as she imagined she had when confronted with the acknowledgment of her infidelity. Guilty and somehow defiant too. The world tipped, but she refused to slide with it.

"I couldn't take the chance of getting you pregnant again. I couldn't." His tone had turned pleading, and he held out his hands to her.

She refused to take them. "I can't believe you'd do something like that without even telling me!"

"I knew you'd say no."

She spit to the side, her disgust so thick it was like some living thing she needed to eject. "You should have told me. We should have talked about it. We could've talked about lots of things!"

"I knew you wanted a baby—"

"No!" The word slashed at her throat. "You wanted to fix the situation, Sean, the way you always do. You wanted to fix it so you didn't have to worry about me getting pregnant, so you didn't have to worry about anything. It was all about you, like it always is!"

"That's not true!"

She shook her head and made a shoving gesture with her hands, though she was nowhere near him. "When? When did you do it?"

"The weekend you were gone to the art show."

"In Philly." She laughed dully. "Oh Christ, Sean. Jesus Christ."

"I know you were with him. And it was almost eight months ago. You do the math."

"You don't know shit," she told him flatly, her rage undiminished, but finding herself incapable of raising her voice. "And *you* do the math, you son of a bitch. I came home from Philly and we made love. Remember? After we went to that Italian place. You couldn't even wait until we got upstairs. We did it in the living room. Remember that?"

The sex had been some of the best they'd ever had, and, now, even the memory of that pleasure was destined to become pain. Ginny pressed her hand to her breast, pushing on her heart, willing it not to burst. She swallowed around the lump in her throat.

Without looking at him, she shook her head. "You know it takes a few weeks after a vasectomy to be completely sterile, right? They did tell you that, didn't they?"

He didn't answer at first, and when she forced herself to look at him, she saw another combination of guilt and defiance.

"Did you even read the paperwork or pay any sort of attention, Sean? Did you? No," she said before he could, "because you never do. You never pay any fucking attention!"

"I went back a week later, like they said. I was all good."

"Yeah, well, we fucked before that, didn't we?" She straightened. "This is your baby, and you want to know how I'm so sure?"

He said nothing.

"I didn't fuck Jason in Philadelphia, that's how I know. In fact," she added as though it were a casual admission, when it was anything but, "I never slept with him. Not once. I never even kissed him, so how's that for being absolutely sure he's not the one who knocked me up?"

Sean blinked. She held up a hand to stop him from speaking. His mouth opened, then closed.

"I did not have sex with him. Never. But I did have sex with you and, vasectomy or not, you are the one who fathered this child. So I would suggest you pull up your big-boy pants and start dealing with it. Because this is...this is how it is," she gasped, breaking down at last. "This is how it fucking is!"

Somehow, he was holding her, rocking and stroking her back. She didn't want to be in his arms, but didn't have the energy to push him away. He comforted her, but it was his own comfort he sought, and Ginny was just too damned tired to stop him.

"But I thought…" Sean murmured. "I mean, I saw some of your emails…"

She didn't have the strength to even confront him about his snooping; at any rate, she'd sent the emails and had been wrong to do it. She always knew she would own up to what she'd done, if she had to. But that was before she found out about Sean's betrayal, which was somehow bigger than what she'd done. Or maybe it wasn't, maybe it only felt that way to her and would be the opposite to him. It didn't matter.

"You didn't sleep with him," he said happily, as though that made everything okay. "Good. Oh good."

She pushed away from him and went on clumsy feet to the sink to splash some cold water on her face and the back of her neck.

"I'm glad," Sean said from behind her. "God, Ginny. You don't know how glad I am."

"Well," she said coldly without turning, "don't be that fucking happy. I didn't sleep with him, but I wanted to. And I was going to. He didn't show. That's the only reason I didn't."

The lights went out again.

Chapter Thirty-Four

Instant darkness fell over them.

Ginny heard the scrape of a chair on the linoleum and Sean's muttered curse. The table bumped, the glass salt and pepper shakers in the center of it rattling. Sean cursed again.

"Don't move," she said crossly. "You're going to get hurt."

"Where's the flashlight?"

"I don't know. It should have turned on when the power went out."

"Did you use it today?"

She could sense where this argument was going and her answer came out clipped, "No. I didn't have to. It was daylight when Peg came for me."

"Are you sure you didn't use it and then not put it back?"

That he could accuse of her this, of all things, while they stood together in the dark, after having the worst fight of their marriage…Ginny lost it. She started to laugh, at first low and then louder. Her laughter cycled up and up, becoming a series of hiccuping, frantic guffaws that hurt her throat.

"Jesus, Ginny! Stop it!" His hand passed by her close enough to brush her sleeve, but he missed her.

"I didn't use it!" she shouted into the shadows. "You're the one who used it last. Remember? You took it downstairs to check the fuse box the last time it blew. That's the last time I saw it. You left it down there, probably."

"Well shit." Sean sounded miserable.

She didn't want to take glee in it, but she did. If she'd been able to caper with it, she would've. She wasn't proud of that, but it was the truth. The full and awful truth. She was glad he'd been the one to lose the flashlight, that his accusation had bounced back and hit him in the face.

"You left it down there," she crowed. More laughter, this time cut off with her hand over her mouth because the sound of it disturbed her. It would've been better to vomit than keep laughing that way.

"I'd better go get it."

"How are you going to do that in the dark?" she said derisively. Disgusted by this, by everything. And so suddenly tired all she wanted to do was lie down and close her eyes and maybe not wake up.

"Let me use your phone."

The baby moved inside her, a reminder of why Ginny couldn't give in to selfishness. She sighed and fished in her pocket for her phone. When she thumbed the screen, the dull blue gleam provided at least a little illumination. A thought snagged her; she pulled her hand back before he could take the phone.

"Where's yours?" A beat of silence proved her right again. Ginny sighed, no longer gleeful. No longer glad to be proven right. "You lost it?"

"I dropped it," Sean said. "I think I did something to the battery. It won't turn on."

"But there's nothing wrong with your goddamned phone," she quoted. "Wow."

"Just give me yours. I'll go get the flashlight and we'll figure out what to do next." Sean took the phone from her limp fingers. "You stay here. Don't move."

Ginny said nothing. She watched the blue light move out of the kitchen. She heard the basement door open, then the creak of Sean's feet on the stairs.

She sat in the darkness.

She sat for a long time.

She wasn't sure when the tears began, only that they started in silence. They burned in her eyes and slid down her cheeks. She tasted salt. She put her face in her hands and sobbed, shoulders heaving, body racking.

In the darkness, Ginny broke.

And in the darkness, a small hand touched her.

She didn't startle from it, because somehow she'd been expecting this to happen. Small fingers curled over her shoulder, then slipped down her arm. A small hand held hers. The fingers were cold and slender, the nails ragged when they pressed lightly into Ginny's palm.

"Carrie?" Ginny whispered, and got no answer but a squeeze.

Then the hand withdrew as the sound of Sean's feet came up the stairs. The cellar door opened with a familiar creak, and in the next moment the white glare of the flashlight cut through the dark and pierced her eyes. Shadows danced behind her.

Something crashed.

"Ginny?"

"I'm right here."

"I told you to stay put." Sean shone the light around the kitchen.

Ginny put up a hand to block the glare, but not before she saw a glass of water she'd left on the edge of the counter had fallen and smashed on the floor. She twisted in her chair, but whatever had knocked it off the counter had disappeared. She closed her fingers over the residual feeling of that cold touch.

"You could've cut yourself," Sean said.

"I didn't do that." Outside, the wind howled and a spatter of snow hit the windows over the sink.

It startled Sean, who crunched glass under his feet. He muttered another invective and swept the light over her. "It just fell?"

Ginny shrugged.

"Don't tell me it was a ghost."

She said nothing, told him nothing. His shoes crunched more glass and he swept the light around the room again. He grunted.

The lights came on as all the appliances beeped. Sean clicked off the flashlight. Ginny didn't move.

"It's broken," Sean said unnecessarily, and she didn't know if he meant the glass or everything else.

Chapter Thirty-Five

"Mr. Miller?"

The man getting ready to cross the street paused, brow furrowed as he tightened his scarf around his neck. "Yes?"

Ginny had been good at her job, back when she did it. Good at getting people to talk to her without alarming them. Something in her face, she thought. Something pleasant and deceptively innocent. She wasn't investigating Brendan Miller for insurance fraud, so, really, he had nothing to fear from her, but he looked at her warily anyway.

"I'm Ginny Bohn."

It took him a second or two, but he figured it out. From his expression, Ginny thought he might bolt, and what would she do then? Waddle after him? The thought was laughable.

His gaze fell to the bump of her belly beneath her puffy coat. "If there's a problem with the house, you need to talk to the realtor about it. We signed papers; you took it as is…"

"It's not about the house. Well. It sort of is about the house." She stepped to the side, in front of him, when he moved to go around her. She'd stopped working because she was pregnant, but now realized something—he might've shoved her aside if not for her belly. She held up the train case. "I have this."

Miller stopped trying to get around her. "What is it?"

"It belonged to your sister."

The cold wind had rubbed two pink spots in his cheeks. Now they grew brighter. His mouth worked for a few seconds before he actually spoke. "Impossible."

"I found it in the house. I thought you might want it."

He fixed her with an angry, sullen glare. "I don't want it. I don't want anything to do with anything from that house. Okay?"

"Okay. Okay." She knew how to soothe, how to gentle. Like taming a skittish horse or a strange, tooth-baring dog. "I'm sorry. I just thought you might like to read it."

"Read it?"

"There's a diary," Ginny told him. "At least, I think that's what it is. It has your sister's initials on it. Look, can I buy you a cup of coffee or something? Get in out of the cold?"

She pointed down the street. "My treat."

For a moment, she thought he'd say yes. She was so certain, in fact, that she'd already taken a few steps in that direction. But Miller shook his head and backed up.

"No. I don't think so."

Ginny paused. There was an art to working people, getting them to agree to things they didn't want to do, or to admit to what they'd prefer to keep a secret. "I know what happened to your sister."

It was the wrong thing to say. His gaze flickered. His mouth thinned. "Nobody knows what happened to my sister."

This time, he did push past her. Ginny managed to snag his sleeve, not hard enough to stop him but enough to give him pause. "There's something in the house, Mr. Miller."

He'd just stepped off the curb, and stood between two parked cars. Everything about him vibrated the urgency to flee across the street. He looked at her over his shoulder.

"I told you. You bought it as is. If you have a problem, talk to your realtor." Then he stepped out into the street.

"I think it's your sister!"

That stopped him. He turned. He wasn't much older than Ginny, though the lines on his face and gray in his hair made him seem so. He was good-looking, behind the scowl and the furrowed brow, but there was nothing welcoming about him. Not at all.

His gaze dropped to her belly. "What is it that you want, exactly?"

"I just want to know what happened. That's all."

She'd gotten to him. Everything about him sagged. He put a hand over his eyes, briefly, before looking down the street to the coffee shop.

"Fine. I'll give you half an hour, but that's it."

Chapter Thirty-Six

"She was always scribbling." Miller looked at the case Ginny had pushed across the table in front of him, but he didn't touch it. "My dad called her Doodle. She'd draw for hours in these big notepads, that soft white paper…what was it called? Newsprint. She'd draw cartoons and landscapes and people, animals, just whatever. And when she got older, she'd write stories to go with them."

"Did she keep a diary?"

He shrugged. "I don't know. I didn't pay attention."

Something in this sentence seemed to break him again, because he put his elbow on the table and his face into the comfort of his hand. Ginny had learned the trick of seeing when someone was faking pain, but everything about this guy's anguish was real. Her fingers crept over the table toward him, but she stopped herself from touching his sleeve. He didn't seem the sort to welcome it.

"I didn't pay attention," he repeated. "I didn't want to know. I didn't want to see."

"See what?" Ginny asked gently.

"My mother didn't either, though that's not really an excuse." He shuddered. His fingers dug into his skin. His hand covered his eyes, so she couldn't see if he was crying, but his voice had gone rough and hoarse.

Ginny was silent, giving him time.

When he finally looked at her, his eyes were rimmed red but dry. "She was always his favorite. I was the son, right? He should've been taking me out to play ball in the backyard, toss around the pigskin. He should've been taking me fishing, camping, all that shit. But nope, Caroline was his favorite. They'd spend hours tucked up together in his big chair, reading books or looking at those stories she wrote. She could do anything and get away with it. Once she carved her initials in the dining room table, can you believe it? I thought my mom was going to murder her, but my dad just told her to leave it alone. Caroline was a daddy's girl, all the way. My mother called her 'the little wife.' Like she was joking, but I don't think she was."

A worm of nausea twisted inside her. Ginny's fingernails scraped at the table as she withdrew her hand. She linked her fingers, squeezing them tightly together on the table in front of her.

"Yeah," Miller said, though Ginny hadn't spoken. "You know what I'm talking about. It was cute when she was little, right? But not when she started to get boo…breasts. She shot up a few inches, started to get curves and wear makeup."

"How old was she?"

"Thirteen. And, Christ…" He pressed the heel of his hand to his forehead for a moment, then shook his head. "I have two daughters. Seventeen and fourteen. I know what it's like, you know, when they start developing. It gets weird. *They* get weird."

Distaste rippled across his face, and he gave her a look of such loathing that she'd have recoiled if it had been directed at her instead of his memories.

"You have to make some distance between you. You just have to. They're not your little girls anymore, you can't be having them sit on your lap and whisper in your ears. It's just…that's not what a dad does." His lips drew back to reveal perfectly straight but yellowed teeth. "I have daughters. I know."

Ginny had a flash of a summer night years ago. She'd been what, twelve? Thirteen? She'd worn a thin, sleeveless nightgown with flowers on it, and it had shrunk in the wash. More likely, she'd grown. It hit her midthigh instead of reaching her knees, and the fabric had grown faded in the wash. It had been her favorite for a long time. She'd come out of the shower, her hair still wet, and gone to sit with her dad on the couch to catch a rerun of some comedy program. He'd been annoyed, told her to go change her clothes or stay in her room. She hadn't understood then and maybe not ever, until just now.

"What did your mother do?"

Miller grimaced and looked down at his hands, which had linked much the same as Ginny's. "She had her favorite too, I guess. Even if by default."

"And then your sister disappeared."

"She never came home from school." He kept his voice low and his gaze on his hands. His fingers twisted tighter, knuckles going white with the pressure. "She went in the morning and stayed all day. Her friend Laura was the last person to see her, and she was crossing the park, heading for home. She never made it."

"And they never found out what happened?"

Another shrug. He looked out the window, toward the street. "No. Someone reported they saw her getting into a white van, but, really, that's such a cliché; who knows if it's true. We had some other reports of her being spotted in different places across the country. California, Montana. None of them ever panned out. She was just…gone."

"What did your parents do?"

He looked at her. His smile was terrible, thin-lipped and more like a snarl. "They fell apart. They'd been on rocky ground for a while before that."

"Fighting a lot?"

He shook his head. "Oh no. They never fought, at least not where I heard them. No. They stopped talking to each other before Caroline went missing. After she was gone for a while and the news started to taper off and the investigation went cold, they stopped even seeing each other. It was like they were invisible to each other. They'd pass in the hall, not even look at each other."

"It must've been horrible for you. I'm sorry."

His laughter was worse than the terrible smile. "It could've been worse. I could've been in the back of someone's van, right?"

"How old were you?"

"Sixteen." The cup in front of him had stopped steaming, and now he drank. "We stayed there for another year after she went missing. We never talked about her. I mean, I tried, but I wasn't allowed to."

"They told you that?"

"They didn't have to. I wasn't stupid, and I wasn't heartless. I could see it upset them. So it was sort of like…I'd never had a sister in the first place. They took down her pictures. They put away her things. I wanted to save some of them…I tried."

He cleared his throat once, then again. He looked at her, his gaze naked. "She always wanted a cat, but my dad hated them. Said he was allergic, but he wasn't. He just didn't like them. It was maybe the one thing he didn't give her that she wanted, you know? But he let her have hamsters instead. A whole bunch of them, they just kept having babies. Well, after she was gone, nobody remembered to take care of the hamsters. They started eating each other."

Ginny swallowed, thinking of the plastic bags in the closet. The bones. The fluffs of fur. "Oh."

"Yeah." Brendan Miller gave a short, sharp laugh. "I didn't want them to take them away, though. I kept thinking, hey, maybe she'll come back. If she ran away, right? She'll come back for them. She loved those stupid hamsters. So I took them, and I hid them.

But they died anyway."

She didn't have to ask what he'd done with them; she already knew. But she didn't know why. "You hid them in the closet?"

He nodded, looking guilty, then lifting his chin as though daring her to accuse him of something. What, she didn't know. "Yeah. I was a kid. A dumb kid. I thought maybe, even though they were dead, she'd want them. So I put them away for her until she could come back."

"But she never came back."

"No. Then my mom left him, and I went with her."

Ginny's cup was long empty and her bladder had begun its protests. "And you never went back? Or had anything to do with your dad ever again?"

Miller shook his head. "No. And that bastard…he never…"

She waited for him to compose himself, embarrassed not just by his story but by the somehow confessional nature of it. She shifted in her chair, needing the bathroom and not wanting to get up before he was finished. Miller swallowed hard and gave her another of those bright, hard stares.

"He never bothered trying to see me, I mean. We left, he never bothered or cared about us after that. He sent checks on time; that was all my mother cared about. And that was it." He drew in a shaky breath and let it out. "Like I said. He had his favorite, and it wasn't me."

Before Ginny could say something, even to offer sympathy, Miller had pushed the train case back toward her.

"So I don't really care to read my sister's journal or whatever it is. Throw it in the trash. It's old news. She's gone, and she's never ever coming back."

"You're sure of that?"

He shrugged. Then nodded. Stood. He tossed a couple dollar bills on the table, though she'd offered to pay for the coffee he'd barely touched. Miller stared down at her.

"I'm sure of it. All those stories about seeing her in California or wherever are bullshit, and you think so too, or else you wouldn't have come after me so hard. You think my sister's haunting your house, Mrs. Bohn? Well. You might be right. But, guess what, I don't care. And I don't want to know about it. Never contact me again, or I'll have no problem going to the authorities. And if you find anything else…" he paused to give the box a sneer, "…consider it yours. I don't want it back."

She didn't want to shout after him, but it took her two or three steps for every one of his just so she could catch up. Ignoring her suddenly violent urge to pee, Ginny caught him again at the curb. "You think your father did something to her, don't you?"

Miller gave her the side eye. "I don't *think* it. I know he did."

Then he stepped off the curb and crossed the street, leaving her behind.

Chapter Thirty-Seven

This was it. She was going to open it and read it. Ginny plucked the key from beneath the stack of faded pictures, and fit it into the lock. She turned it. She opened Caroline Miller's diary and started to read.

Four pages of random thoughts scrawled in an uneven hand. Nothing important, no revelations. Then…nothing. Blank pages.

"Wow. So that's kind of a letdown, huh?" Sean leaned over her shoulder. "Bummer."

Ginny had told him the entire story, come clean about everything. The things she'd seen and heard and felt and thought. The time for secrets had ended, for both of them. Sean didn't believe her about there being a ghost in the house, but he did believe that Ginny thought it was true. That was enough for her; it had to be.

In the past, Ginny hadn't asked him to quit smoking or sell his motorcycle. He'd decided those things on his own. She didn't ask him to stay, either. She hadn't asked Sean if he'd thought of leaving her, but she'd faced the idea of leaving him and hadn't done it; now she waited. Some things that were broken could be repaired, good as new. Others, even if they worked again, would always bear evidence of the damage that had been done. That was their marriage. Broken, repaired, working somehow. But not unscathed. Perhaps someday they'd both stop tiptoeing around each other, or maybe they'd always hold what each had done between them for the rest of their lives. The baby would make a difference. Or not.

"I love you" was all she'd said, over and over, as Sean paced and ran his hands through his hair and when he'd asked her if it was his fault, any of this. *"I love you,"* she'd told him. *"That's what matters."*

She wasn't sure if he believed in her love, any more than he believed in the ghost of Caroline Miller, but it seemed as though he believed Ginny believed in it. And that also had to be enough.

Now, he squeezed her shoulders before withdrawing. "I'm sorry. I know you hoped it would give you some clues. Or something."

"It's okay. I'm not sure I'd have learned anything I didn't already know. Or couldn't guess." Ginny closed the diary and put it back into the train case, along with the pictures and all the other bits and pieces of things that had once belonged to Caroline Miller. She looked at him. "And maybe...maybe someone in a white van really did carry her off. Or maybe she's okay."

"We'll just never know," Sean said.

And maybe it was better that way.

Chapter Thirty-Eight

The worst winter in twenty years was turning into the worst spring. While usually an early thaw would've been welcome, this year the massive amounts of snow that had accumulated were melting too fast for the earth to handle it. Water rushed day and night, down the street and into the drains, which overflowed and made lakes across the sidewalks and into the yards. Kids sloshed in it and ran paper boats down it.

Ginny looked for Pennywise, the clown.

Not really, though she did avoid the drains when she went out to get the mail. Debris had clogged many of them, making the problem worse. So did the gray skies dumping more rain every day. She was sick of the sound it made on the roof. Sick of sloshing. Sick of everything being damp.

She was sick of waiting, waiting, for things to change.

She could see the star of her due date on the calendar now. The obstetrician told her she could go early. She could go late. This wasn't her first pregnancy, but it was her first to go to term and there was no predicting what her body was going to do. The baby would come when it was ready, the doctor told her. That was the way babies worked.

From the nursery window, Ginny watched Kelly and Carson duck through the hedge and into her yard. The snow had gone, replaced by mud and the grass that had been overlong before winter came. They ran through it in their rain boots and slickers, slashing at the overgrowth with long sticks. Then back through the hedge, widening the hole for a moment before the brush closed behind them again.

The rocking chair Sean had struggled so hard to put together still squeaked, but rather than finding this annoying, Ginny took comfort in the consistent noise. She closed her eyes and rocked in the nursery she'd finally allowed herself to decorate, both hands on her big belly. She listened to the squeak and the creak of wood on wood.

She listened for the sound of footsteps.

Something like a sigh brushed past her on a swirl of cool air. They'd turned off the heat at the beginning of last week, and even in an unseasonably warm late February, it was not yet time for air-conditioning. She wanted to open the windows at least, but the rain prevented it. Instead, Sean had turned on the house fan.

Ginny rocked and breathed. Another whisper, another sigh, the soft pad of footsteps in the hallway. If she opened her eyes, she'd see nothing but shadows. Ghosts never showed themselves in the daytime. But she felt a presence, eyes watching. She felt a hopefulness. It was the only way to describe it.

So, she sang.

Her gran had sung this lullaby to her when she was small. Like the best of Grimm's fairy tales, the song about a pair of children lost in the woods had delighted her childhood love of all things macabre, and it wasn't until Ginny got older that the horror of the lyrics had become clear. She sang it now anyway, to the baby in her womb and for those she'd lost.

For the one who seemed unable to leave.

In the yard, Kelly and Carson chased each other again. Their screams snapped open Ginny's eyes. She sighed herself, annoyed that they couldn't seem to stay in their own yard, that they had to be so loud. Her child would never, she thought mildly. Never, never.

They disappeared around the side of the house, heading back toward their yard again. Ginny's eyes drooped. She drifted. She'd been sleeping better at night, but now it seemed all she wanted to do was sleep. Her body's way of getting ready, she supposed.

Sleeping, she dreamed.

* * * * *

She stood next to the crib Sean had so painstakingly put together. It had been dressed in pale-green-and-yellow linens decorated with jungle animals. She recognized it as the pattern someone had given her at her baby shower—though, as was the way of dreams, she couldn't remember who'd given it. Cartoon lions and elephants and monkeys capered next to palm trees all over the sheets and bumpers. Over the crib hung a mobile, and it spun lightly and tinkled out a classical tune she couldn't recall the name of.

There was nothing scary in this dream, but a sense of unease twisted inside her, getting strong as she crossed the room to look into the empty crib. She touched the mobile with one finger to stop its turning, and the music ground to a sudden, unlovely halt. One, two, final notes plucked at the air and fell silent.

Gauzy curtains blew inward, reminding her again this wasn't real. She'd never have such long curtains. They were dangerous. Could tangle around a curious toddler's neck. And ugly, she thought. Pink and purple, sheer, tab tops.

These were not her curtains.

Ah, this, then, was not her baby's room. Ginny turned in half a circle, looking around. Again, in the way of dreams, she looked down at her flat belly and mourned the loss of it, even as she knew it had to mean she'd given birth. That meant there was a baby here, somewhere. Not in this room, which clearly belonged to an older child. A girl who favored pink and purple, a white-painted bed hung with netting Ginny would also never allow because it could strangle a child in the night.

Everywhere she looked, she saw danger. A tangle of too many electric cords plugged into a socket. A bookcase laden with toys and books, unsecured to the wall, just begging to be toppled over onto a soft head. In the closet, a pull string, too long, and an empty socket, tempting a child's curious fingers to probe. Too many things that could cause harm. Her heart pounded. She clutched at the air, but touched nothing.

Somewhere, far away, her baby cried for her. Ginny's nipples got tight and hard, burning. She covered them with her palms and felt the sharp points, but the pressure didn't relieve the tingling and hot fluid leaked through her shirt. An answering pull tugged in her womb, deep inside. Like menstrual cramps, but harder and more painful.

She turned around and around, but this room had no door. She was trapped here, and she ran her hands over the walls, now a garish pink. Like the inside of an organ. Like a wound. The steady thud-thud of a heartbeat throbbed in her ears as the floor beneath her shifted and pulsed.

The crying didn't stop. Desperate, Ginny pushed at the walls, feeling for the door or a window, and found nothing. She turned around and around. She punched at the walls and felt an answering pulse of pain deep inside her. She kicked, she punched, she swore and got nothing but more pain for her efforts.

Ginny quieted. Listening. The baby—her baby, she had no doubts—still wailed and wept. Ginny pressed her fingers to her forehead. This was a dream. She knew it, yet couldn't quite control it.

She was sitting in a rocking chair by the window but couldn't wake herself. She tried, with a leap and a howl, but the room stayed the same. She heard the creaking of the rocker on the wood and imagined her foot pressing. Releasing. Her breathing, soft and slow. But she could not wake herself.

The baby was still crying.

There was a door in this room, she remembered that. A small door, child-sized. It went from one room to the next. She didn't need to get out another way, if she could get through there…and suddenly it was there, that little door. That tunnel strewn with mouse shit and insulation, the hazard of nails poking through the roof, ready to score her scalp and make her bleed.

Then she was in the library. She still heard the baby, though it was farther away now. Harder to hear.

Ginny's baby was crying, it was somewhere in the house, it was lost and she had to find it. Ginny had lost her baby. She'd lost her baby. She had lost her baby, and it was crying, it was screaming for her, it was crying and there was a pounding…a pounding…

A pounding at the front door, and the bell rang. Steadily, insistently demanding she wake up, wake up, wake up.

* * * * *

Ginny woke, startled, gasping, her hands pushing out instinctively to ward off the touch of whoever was shaking her awake. She was alone. She blinked and ran her tongue over her sleep-sticky teeth. She'd been asleep in the rocking chair, her head drooping, and now her neck hurt.

She rubbed it as she listened. No baby crying, but the doorbell rang again. Then a moment after it. Then there was a knocking.

With a sigh, she heaved herself up from the chair, ready to pound whoever was banging so fiercely. It had better be a special delivery package of something expensive, she thought as she lumbered down the stairs and shuffled to the front door. But it wasn't.

It was Kendra, hair wild, eyes wide. "Ginny. I knew you were home, I saw your car."

"I was sleeping." It was a pointed response, but Kendra didn't get it.

"Are Kelly and Carson over here?"

Ginny stifled a yawn with the back of her hand, noticing that Kendra looked soaked. Her jeans were black to the knees from wet, her shoes sloshing. She had no umbrella and her pale-pink T-shirt had gone semitransparent. She needed a sweatshirt.

"No."

"No?" Kendra looked past her into the hall. "Are you sure?"

Annoyed, Ginny leaned against the doorway to relieve some of the pressure on her back. Her entire pelvis ached, along with her hips. Her joints were separating, according to the doctor. She was lucky she could stand upright at this point, that's how it felt.

"Yeah. I'm sure." Ginny paused. "I saw them earlier, in the backyard."

This was also a pointed statement Kendra didn't seem to get. She shook her head, water splattering. "I told them to stay in the yard. Not to come over here. But they just really like your yard, I guess…"

"I guess they do, but they're not inside, I'm sure I'd have noticed that. Did you go around the back of the house and check? Maybe they're peeking in my windows again."

"They're not there." Kendra heaved a breath and burst into tears.

Ginny watched her impassively for a moment. Surely this was still a dream. Part of a nightmare that was worse than the one she'd been having. But it got worse, because Kendra let out a low, sobbing breath.

"OHMYGODTHECREEKTHEYWENTDOWNTOTHECREEK!"

The words came out in a rush, one butted up against the other so that Ginny needed a half minute to parse out what the other woman had said—but when she did, her resentment and snark fled as swiftly as a hare chased by nipping hounds. She reached for Kendra and found her wrists. Tugged them.

"Stop." She sounded calmer than she felt. "Stop, we'll find them. We will go look, okay? I'm sure they're fine."

Kendra, panicked, shook her head so fast her hair stuck and clung to her cheeks. She moaned, a brittle, fragile noise that set the hair on the back of Ginny's neck standing upright. She bore down on Kendra's wrists, pinching the skin and maybe even crunching the bones. Kendra cried out, but looked at her.

"We will find them. Okay? Come on. Let's go look."

Kendra resisted. "Noooooo…"

Ginny wanted to slap her. "If they're really down there, don't you think you'd better haul your ass and get to them?"

"What if they *are* there?" Kendra cried through chattering teeth. She jerked free of Ginny's grip and crossed her arms over her stomach, bending as though she might puke. "What if they are there, and we find them?"

Ginny stepped out of the way, no patience left for this woman whose terror she could empathize with, but whose uselessness she could not. "We want to find them—"

Kendra shook her head again and looked at Ginny with wide but somehow sightless eyes. "WHAT IF THEY'RE DEAD?"

"They aren't dead," Ginny said solidly and looked past Kendra to the pouring rain. "I'm sure they're wet and cold and scared of getting into trouble, but you won't ever know if you don't move your ass."

Kendra still didn't move, not until Ginny grabbed up her coat from the rack and pushed past her. She'd forgotten boots and had none anyway, her feet too swollen for anything but these slippers. Sodden grass squelched under her feet as she stepped off the porch and sidewalk, with Kendra finally following. They should've gone through the house and out the back, but too late now. Ginny hunched against the rain, which sent chill, dripping fingers trickling down the back of her neck.

The yard sloped gently but in her ungainly state she needed support and grabbed Kendra's arm to get it. Fortunately the woman didn't let her topple. She gripped Ginny by the arm, and then with a handful of her jacket in the back. She barely kept them both upright when Ginny slipped in the mud, though. The sudden shift in her weight sent pain rippling through her thighs and deep inside.

Ginny groaned. "Oh God. Kendra, seriously, I'm like eleven months pregnant here; you're going to have to go down the bank yourself."

The creek had already risen up and over, flooding the lower yard. Ginny hadn't realized how close to the house it had crept, even in the few short hours since last she'd looked out the window. The grass floated like seaweed in the cold brown water. Rippling waves pushed some debris, newspapers or junk mail, it looked like, against Ginny's calf and she wrinkled her nose in disgust.

"I can't!"

Ginny stood as straight as she could and backhanded Kendra across the face. The slap wasn't nearly as hard as she'd meant it to be, but it still cracked Kendra's cheek and left a red imprint.

Kendra gasped and put a hand to her face.

"Look at me!" Ginny demanded. "Should I be out here going after your kids? No! What the hell is wrong with you? Get your ass down there and look for them!"

Kendra stepped back, and Ginny wavered in the squishy muck. More rippling water washed over her legs, splashing the hem of her nightgown. She looked to where the creek had once burbled and chuckled along over smoothly polished stones, as cheerful and dangerous as a fluffy kitten. It rushed and roared now.

Just across it, in a pond like the one in which Ginny and Kendra stood, was a figure in a red hooded coat. It turned at the sound of Ginny's shouts, and Kendra let out a wail of relief.

"Kelly! Kelly! Where's Carson?"

He was there too, a little farther on. Both children waved at their mother, who set off at a run through the overflowing creek toward them. She went down in a minute as her foot plunged into a hole or something. Kendra face-planted into the water and flailed.

Ginny wanted to laugh in that horrid way she always wanted to chuckle when someone fell, not because she really thought it was funny, but because there was no helping it. She cut it off into a strangled yelp and moved a step or two forward. She stopped herself from going farther.

She was pregnant, for God's sake, and already this was a bad idea. Kendra had fallen into the water, and Ginny didn't want to do the same. She'd never get up. She'd drown in her own backyard.

Besides, Kendra had made it to her feet, soaked and muddy, but seemingly unscathed. Until she started to scream, that was. She screamed and flailed some more, backpedaling and falling again. She rolled, desperate to get up and out, while the kids stared at her with goggle eyes. Kelly got too close to the edge, where the water was rushing instead of just rippling, and her feet got taken out from under her.

Ginny watched in horror as Kelly went under, nothing but the red hood showing. In seconds she was downstream a few feet and sputtering up out of the water, but she couldn't get to her feet. Kendra screamed. Carson had put his hands over his face.

Ginny was moving without thinking, one hand on her belly and the other held out to balance herself like a tightrope walker with a pole. She slipped in the soggy grass but made it to water up to her knees before Kelly went under again. The girl had snagged on a tree branch that had fallen into the water, and it was the only thing keeping her from being pushed farther downstream. It was also pressing her under the water.

"OHMYGODMYBABY!" Kendra shrieked.

Ginny was actually closer to the girl. Her slippers had come off. Her toes dug into the mud and grass, which gave her a better grip. Just a foot or so in front of her was where the creek normally ran, and she had no idea how deep it was. Just that it was fast. Beside her was a part of another branch that had fallen during one of the snowstorms, thick and heavy enough that she had to strain to lift it.

"Help me!" she ordered Kendra.

Miraculously, the other woman moved without fuss. She grabbed the end of the branch and lifted it as Ginny guided it toward Kelly. The girl grabbed at it. Missed. Grabbed again.

This time, she caught it. Her mother yanked it, moving Kelly just a few feet closer so she could grab the red coat.

It was over in minutes. Ginny found herself clutching a sobbing and shaking Kelly, both of them higher up on the lawn and away from the creek, while Kendra waded across using the branches and grabbed up Carson. By the time she got back to Ginny's yard, all of them had blue lips.

But they were alive.

"Oh my God, oh my God!" Kendra clutched at both kids. "What were you doing! What were you thinking?"

"We...we...we wanted to see the..." Carson could barely speak through his chattering teeth.

Whatever it was he'd wanted to see, his mother wasn't interested. She shook him, then grabbed at his sister and started hauling them away from the water.

Ginny, exhausted and shivering, followed. Every part of her ached, and all she wanted was a hot shower, clean clothes and the comfort of her bed. Instead, she slipped on the sopping grass and went to her knees. Her fingers dug into the soft mud.

Ahead of her Kendra wasn't even looking back as she bustled her kids home. The three of them were sobbing and screaming. Ginny thought she should be offended her neighbor wasn't even bothering to look back and check on her, but that would mean she had to deal with Kendra and her two spawn. And didn't she understand, anyway, the force that moved a mother to forget everything else but her children?

The baby moved inside her, protesting the position and kicking out so hard the little feet stole Ginny's breath. She gasped, then coughed as she pushed herself along the muddy slope and struggled to get herself upright. Her fingers dug again into the soil and grass and slipped, scraping along a tree branch. Or something. Not a tree branch.

Ginny dug a little deeper and came up with something shorter than the length of her forearm. Knobbed on the end. It must once have been white, but time in the earth had turned it dark. She cradled it against her for a moment and looked behind her at the rushing water that had eroded so much of her yard. Then at the thing in her hand. She knew what had so captivated Kelly's and Carson's attentions, what they'd been looking at.

It was a bone.

Chapter Thirty-Nine

She'd showered and changed her clothes and tied her wet hair up on top of her head, but that only left the back of her neck exposed and vulnerable. Sean's fingers squeezed, squeezed her there. He meant the touch to be gentle and soothing, but every press against her sent a ripple of irritation down her spine, until finally she shrugged her shoulders to squirm away.

The officer who'd come to the house was young and fresh scrubbed. His uniform had been crisp and polished when he came to the door, but now shoes were spattered with mud and his trouser legs, sodden. He'd gone down to the creek, but in the dark and with the rain coming down more heavily than before, he'd come back in the house.

"How long will it take?" Ginny asked. "Until you know if it's human?"

The officer looked uncomfortable. "I'm not really sure. I've never had to deal with anything like this before. It could be a…week? Maybe?"

"A week?" Ginny sounded as outraged as she felt and turned away to keep him from seeing her face.

"Well…forgive me, but it's not like it's an emergency," the officer said quietly. "We'll do the best we can and let you know, okay? In the meantime, if you find anything else, you let us know."

"We're not going to find anything else." Sean said this to soothe her, not the cop. He rubbed her shoulders again. "Thanks for coming out, Officer."

When he'd gone, and they were in bed, trying to sleep, Sean kissed her shoulder. "It's going to be okay, Ginny. All of this will be okay. I promise you."

She knew about his promises, and wanted to believe him. Or at least that he meant it. But how could he promise her something like that?

"Maybe now you can just forget about all this stuff." Sean's voice rose beside her in the dark. He sounded sleepy.

Ginny was anything but tired. She breathed in the scent of lavender, faint now but still lovely. She needed to buy some more before the baby came. She had to do a lot of things before the baby came.

"It's over," Sean said. "You have to know that, right?"

Sean loved horror movies as much as she did, maybe more. He had to know that finding the source didn't make the ghosts go away. Not if you hadn't yet figured out what they wanted. Ginny breathed. She breathed.

The bed dipped as he rolled toward her. His hand rested on her hip, then slipped around to caress her belly. His heat covered her back as he nuzzled at her shoulder.

"You don't believe me," she said. "Even after what we found."

"We don't know yet what you found."

"Bones, Sean."

"They could be anything. Animals. Someone's pet cemetery, probably."

Ginny shivered, though her flannel pj's, the blankets and her husband's warmth had made her anything but cold. "They're not animal bones."

Sean sighed. "Honey…even if they're not…"

"What?" She'd have turned to face him, but her body was too unwieldy. "If they're not…what?"

"Even if they're not animal bones, they're not hers."

"And that's supposed to reassure me?" Ginny huffed and tossed his arm off her so she could heave herself upright. The floor felt very far away when she sought it with her toes. "Jesus, Sean. If they're not Caroline's bones, whose are they? Do you think that makes me feel *better*?"

He shifted to sit next to her, his legs long enough that his feet had no trouble finding the floor. He took her hand. "I just think you've let yourself get too worked up about this Caroline Miller business. You said yourself there were reports of her being sighted in California and Idaho and a whole bunch of places."

"Her own brother thinks something happened to Caroline here, in this house. Something her dad did. Well, I think her dad killed her."

"And buried her down by the creek."

"Yes." Ginny shook her head. Her bladder panged. She might as well get up and go to the bathroom. She couldn't sleep anyway, and she'd be up in an hour, even if she peed now.

"That bone was small. It was really small."

A Braxton Hicks contraction rippled across her belly, and she bit back a gasp as she put a hand on the bedpost to keep herself from doubling over. It wasn't painful, just surprising. Her fingers gripped the wood.

"It didn't belong to a fourteen-year-old girl. That's all I'm saying."

Ginny put her other hand on the lump of her belly. The baby was quiet, not moving. Did it dream, she wondered suddenly. Or did it share her dreams the way it shared what she ate?

"It was a baby's bones."

"We don't know that either."

But she knew it. She felt it. She rubbed her belly, but the baby didn't move. When was the last time she'd felt it move? She'd lost track. So close to the end now, it seemed the baby was always squirming, never still.

"I know it, Sean. *I* know it."

She didn't realize she was weeping until he pulled her close to stroke her hair and his T-shirt felt damp under her cheek. Ginny knuckled her eyes, pushing hard enough to make brightness bloom behind her eyelids. She drew one hitching breath after another but couldn't seem to get enough air. She rocked, and he rocked with her.

"It's a baby. I know it's a baby..."

He hushed her, but she couldn't be soothed. Tiny bones in the closet, bigger bones in the yard. So much death in this house, and the baby hadn't moved, hadn't moved in hours.

She realized she'd said it aloud when he answered her.

"Does it hurt anywhere?" Sean rubbed her back. "Ginny. Are you...bleeding?"

She shook her head, then wondered if he could see her in the dark or just feel the motion of her body. "No. It's not that."

She'd spent the last few months telling him over and over that this was all going to be fine, but no matter how much she'd pummeled him, Sean had never quite believed it. Had she been wrong, and he right? Her hands moved over her belly again and again, seeking any motion beyond the tightening of her muscles.

"It doesn't hurt. They're not regular. It's Braxton Hicks, not regular contractions."

"It's too early for you to be in labor."

"I'm not in labor, Sean." Ginny swallowed snot and salt; the taste nauseated her.

"Should we call the clinic?"

At two in the morning, calling the doctor for a little hysteria seemed unreasonable, unless you were a pregnant woman nearly due to give birth, one who'd found bones in her backyard.

"I'm just upset. Give it a few minutes."

Together, they waited in the dark, their hands linked, but the cramps and contractions eased.

"It's going to be okay, Ginny. I promise you," Sean said again as morning light eased through the windows.

She didn't believe him, but she believed he thought it was true, and this also had to be enough.

Chapter Forty

Ginny didn't want to look out into the backyard. Caution tape sectioned off the lower portion of the yard where the creek still ran deep and fast. The rain hadn't stopped, either. She didn't want to look out and see the churned mud and torn-up grass, or all the places the investigating team had dug. It was only a yard, the damage could be repaired.

And they'd found nothing.

They were going to keep looking. Moving downstream, as well as starting farther upstream. There wouldn't be a single infant bone buried in her yard; that just didn't make sense. But it could've come from anywhere, not her yard, or its companions might've been swept away.

If only the rain would stop. Off and on for the past week and a half, sometimes a steady downpour and others a faint drizzle, the water refused to sink into the ground already oversaturated from the melting snow. Everything was wet. Nothing would dry.

Ginny didn't really want the tea she'd made—even thinking about drinking it made her feel like she had to pee. The never-ending patter of rain on the roof didn't help. Her back hurt. Her feet hurt. All her joints ached and creaked. Sitting for too long made her rear end numb, but lounging on the couch left her too lethargic to finish all the tasks that had suddenly become so important. The books called it "nesting," and Peg laughed when Ginny told her on the phone how she'd gotten the overwhelming urge to run every single washable item in the house through the laundry.

Ginny hadn't laughed. The need to make everything clean for the arrival of her baby was pathological and embarrassing, but she was also helpless against it. The problem had become lugging the baskets up and down the stairs, difficult enough earlier, before she'd become so huge and clumsy. Now impossible.

She comforted herself with folding and refolding the tiny shirts and pajamas. With stacking diapers and packages of wipes. She arranged and rearranged the plastic shelves full of baby items and organized the selection of stuffed toys on the wooden bookcase. She rocked in the chair, which, with its hard wooden back, should've been uncomfortable, but which offered her just the right amount of support.

She rocked a lot.

She dreamed.

She woke to darkness, sorry at once she'd allowed herself to nap in the chair instead of in bed or at least on the couch. Her head spun for a second or two when she stood, gripping the arm of the chair, and blinking to orient herself. The night-light in the hall reminded her where she was, but for a good few minutes she had to think about it.

The nursery. She was in the nursery. In her house. Sean was gone; he'd be home later, after work, after class. Later. Everything would be later.

Discomfort rippled across her lower belly. She stood for a moment, legs planted slightly more than shoulder-width apart. Something twinged inside her, and she winced.

She needed a drink. Her mouth had gone dry. Her stomach was a little upset, and the thought of a cold glass of ginger ale was all at once the most perfect thing she could imagine.

She shuffled toward the door out of habit and was glad for it when her foot kicked something small and metal. There was no way she could bend to pick it up, but she heard it skitter across the floor and land somewhere close to the soft throw rug. When she turned on the light switch near the door, the lights seemed to take forever to turn on. Those stupid fluorescent bulbs she hated. Too dim at first to see what she'd kicked, and she didn't want to wait until they got bright enough.

It was a button. Struggling, she managed finally to grab it and tucked it in her pocket. By the time she got downstairs, she had to pee. Again. The sound of rain had infiltrated everything, so that the splash of urine in the bowl was drowned out. She flushed, washed her hands, and in the kitchen poured herself a tall glass of ginger ale. The first sip went down easy, cool and sparkling. The second tasted bitter. She poured the rest down the sink.

From the basement came the juddering sound of the sump pump going. The floor rumbled a little under her feet. Ginny put her hand on the counter for a moment, feeling off-balance. Her hair fell in her face, and she brushed it away.

The phone rang, and she thought about ignoring it, but answered anyway. "Hello."

"Hey, sweetheart. It's me."

The sound of Sean's voice relieved her more than she knew she needed to be relieved. "When are you coming home?"

"Soon. The professor was late, and he's going over stuff that will be on the final. I was going to duck out early, but…"

"No. You shouldn't miss it." This class was breaking him. He needed all the help he could get. Ginny took a deep breath, but her lungs barely filled. Too much baby, not enough room for anything else.

"What's going on there? You okay?"

"It's still raining. And it's dark," she added.

He laughed. "Turn the lights on?"

"I don't know, I kind of like it in the dark. It's peaceful, with the sound of the rain."

"I thought you'd be sick of that by now. I am. How's the sump pump?" Sean coughed lightly, then murmured something to someone on the other end of the line. "Sorry, honey, I have to go. The break's over."

"Go, go." Ginny made a flapping gesture with her hand, though of course he couldn't see it. "I'm fine. Everything's okay here. So long as the power stays on."

"Right." Sean paused. "Shit. I should come home."

She laughed. "No, no. I'm fine. Really. Be careful coming home, the rain's horrible."

"And you…the baby? You're still okay?"

His question annoyed her less now that she was so close to the end, because he was asking something she could answer with full confidence and have him believe her.

"A few Braxton Hicks. That's all. I love you. Be careful," she added, trying to get him before he could disconnect, but he already had.

The floor vibrated again as the sump pump went off. Ginny peeked out the back door at the glitter of rain slanting down. The entire backyard had become a swamp. They wouldn't have to bother going to the beach this summer, they could simply pitch an umbrella off their back patio.

Her stomach had settled a bit, which was good, though now the first tingles of heartburn were tickling the base of her throat. Ginny took a handful of saltines and a glass of milk with her upstairs to the library, where she picked up the book she'd been trying to finish for the past few weeks. There was nothing wrong with the book, it was all her. Easily distracted and having difficulty focusing. She thumbed the pages and settled her milk on the small wooden table she'd set up next to the chaise lounge. Then she tucked herself under the knitted throw and tried to concentrate.

The problem was the rain. Constant, ceaseless, drumming. She'd turned the heat up and now the room had become almost stifling. Ginny couldn't stand against the triple threat of heat, white noise and pregnancy. The book dropped from her fingers and she knew it as she let her head fall back against the chaise, but she was simply too drowsy to care.

She woke up when the electricity went out. The sudden black pounded her eyelids as thoroughly as if she'd been in the dark and the lights had snapped on. Ginny pushed herself upright, forgetting about the book, which crashed to the floor. She looked automatically toward the windows to see if theirs was the only house without power, but the outside was as dark as in. So, the whole neighborhood then.

Fortunately, she'd grown so used to moving around this house in the dark that it was no big deal for her to make her way downstairs, though she made sure to take her time and place each foot solidly and carefully on the step, to be sure she didn't tumble down. The rechargeable flashlight had turned on when the power cut out, so she had no trouble seeing her way to grab it from the dock.

Beneath her feet, the floor did not vibrate. The sump pump wouldn't run without electricity, of course. Which meant water in the basement. Ginny moved to the back door again, but the light from inside reflected on the glass and she could see nothing but her own silhouette. She shielded the light and tried to see outside.

That couldn't be the creek, could it? Lapping at the edges of the flagstone patio? Ginny opened the back door, heedless of the rain, and held up her light.

"Oh shit." It *was* the creek, or maybe it was just that the saturated swamp of her backyard had joined with the still-rushing creek waters to make one vast pond that seemed to be creeping toward her house at an exponentially fast rate. "Shit, shit."

Her phone rang from her pocket. "Sean? Where are you?"

"I'm stuck. The roads are closed. The bridge is out." Sean sounded panicked. "The state police are redirecting everyone; they said almost all the back roads are flooded out. I don't know how I'm going to get home. Are you okay?"

Other than the nausea now rumbling through her? "Yes. I'm fine. But the power's out. And the water…Sean, the water's going to come into the basement."

"Don't you go down there!" he warned. "Not in the dark. It'll be fine."

Ginny moaned, imagining the water pouring in, rising. Ruining. "But the water…"

"It's too dangerous for you to go down there. Promise me you won't. In fact, you should go across to Kendra's house."

"They don't have power either," she told him. "It's not just us. And frankly, I would rather drown."

This forced a laugh from both of them, and the small bit of humor made her feel better. Ginny looked into the backyard again, then went to the front of the house to look out the front door. In the driveway, the water was up to the middle of her car's tires. Fear, real fear, plucked at her.

"Everything's flooding here, Sean."

"You stay put. I'm going to ask the cop what to do. But you…don't you go out and try to drive in it." Sean sounded fierce, determined. Helpless. "You stay there, Ginny. Get upstairs if you think it's going to come in the house."

"Oh, it won't, will it? Just the basement. It's not going to come in the house, Sean." But even as she said it, a vision of gray waves of water washing over her kitchen floor and down the hall filled her head.

Her stomach muscles went tight. Hard. Ginny put a hand on the table, bending forward with her legs slightly spread. This felt different than the other times. This felt more…real.

"Ginny! Are you okay? What's going on?" Sean had been talking to her, but she hadn't heard.

Ginny shook herself as the contraction passed. She blew out a slow breath. "I'm fine. Just a contraction."

"Shit! What?"

"Nothing to worry about," she soothed him, though in fact she was starting to wonder if there would be something to worry about very soon. She put a hand on her belly, low, then over her crotch. She ached down there. Inside, deep. "Just get home when you can. Be careful—"

But again, she was cut off, this time not because her husband had a quick-draw disconnect thumb, but because the signal had been dropped. Ginny breathed in, breathed out, until the pain in her belly eased. She still ached inside, something like the worst sort of menstrual cramps. But when it passed she could stand upright and breathe easily again, at least as easily as was possible with her child doing the cha-cha against her ribs.

In the bathroom, though, the paper slid too easily against her flesh after she urinated. Something thick and wet spilled over the sides of the paper, and with a grimace Ginny maneuvered the light so she could see what it was. The doctor had warned her about the mucus plug, but truthfully Ginny hadn't quite understood what it was or what it would look like until she saw it there.

"Oh. Shit," she said softly and let the paper fall into the toilet. She flushed and struggled back into her panties. She washed her hands, forgetting that with the electricity off, the water pump wouldn't work until the tap sputtered and burped, going dry, and the toilet tank didn't refill.

Another contraction hit her at the base of the stairs. Still mild, she almost could've walked through it, but she didn't want to take a chance on the stairs. Ginny held the newel post until the pain passed and tried to remember how long it had been since the last one. She'd better start keeping track, no easy task with all the clocks stopped and no clue where her watch was.

Upstairs. Sean had told her to go upstairs. She heaved herself up one at a time and went into the library, where she set the flashlight on the table. It wasn't bright enough to read by, but it cast enough light to show her the plate she'd left there earlier was empty. Ginny touched the crumbs with her fingertip and put them to her tongue. Salt. She wasn't hungry, which meant she'd probably eaten them. Right?

But she knew she hadn't.

She looked into the shadows, toward the small door of the crawl space. Of the closet. She'd have bent to look beneath the fainting couch if her body would bend that way, which it wouldn't. Instead, she sat, her knees slightly spread and her hands on top of them. There was nothing to do here but wait. She thumbed her phone and brought up Peg's number, but that call rang on and on without answer. Ginny typed in the net address for the local news channel, but the page stuck halfway and refused to load so that all she could read was "Roads closed, police direct traffic to alternate".

She waited for another contraction, but none came. She waited for the lights to come on, and that didn't happen either. In limbo, waiting, starting to get chilled as the house cooled, Ginny curled up under the blanket and let herself float in the darkness. Not quite dreaming, but not really awake.

* * * * *

In front of her, a child.

A girl. Long dark hair, bedraggled and tangled. Big dark eyes shadowed with darker circles in a pale, pale face. She wore a dirty, shapeless sack of a dress that had been cut from a flowered pillowcase and a tattered cardigan, the buttons of which were missing or hanging by threads. Scabs and dirt encrusted her legs and bare feet. She stared at Ginny as her mouth worked, but nothing came out.

Ginny blinked and sat, slowly. The flashlight had dimmed a little. She should have turned it off to conserve the charge. How long had she been sleeping?

"Come. Please." The girl held out a hand.

This was not the girl in the photos Ginny'd found, though there was something of her in the shape of her face. And this girl was too young. Ginny had never seen this girl, but she knew who it was, just the same. "Caroline."

The girl said nothing.

"What do you want?" It seemed the right question to ask a ghost who'd at last been brave enough to show her face. "Are you here because I found...I found you?"

The girl stepped forward. The floor creaked. Ginny frowned. Why would the floor creak beneath something that had no weight?

"Come. Please. Please?" The girl held out her hand, the tiny fingers dirty, the nails ragged. She opened her palm, faceup. There was a button there, like the one Ginny had found earlier. It fell from her hand and hit the floor with a clink before rolling under the lounge.

Ginny was up and off the lounge, her arms pinwheeling, as fast as she could move. It wasn't fast at all. Her breath sharp in her lungs, she put the chaise between her and this wraith, this vision, this shade that was no ghost.

Oh God.

It wasn't a ghost.

"Who are you?" Ginny's voice came out high, strained, not like her own voice at all.

"Water." The girl looked toward the bookcase, which made no sense. Then at Ginny. She pointed down. "Water is down there."

"In...the basement?"

The girl took another delicate, hesitant step toward Ginny. In the flashlight beam, her skin looked almost translucent, her dark eyes somehow filmed. Ginny was reminded of pictures she'd seen of cave fish and mushrooms, things grown in the dark.

"Down there. It's coming in. It's coming up!" The girl shuddered and jerked. She turned and ran for the cubbyhole door while Ginny stared in stunned silence. "Please come! Please come help!"

"We want to see if the little girl can come and play. The little girl in the basement. I was playing with the little girl."

Ginny thought of what Kelly and Carson had said. She remembered what they'd called her. She spoke, her voice on the edge of a cough, but loud enough. "Carrie."

The girl turned. Incredibly, she smiled. Her teeth were black and skewed, but the smile was sweet and shy. She held out her hand. "Please come. Hurry. Come!"

You think your father did something to her, don't you?

I don't think it. I know he did.

She thought about things going missing and being returned. Of a waving silhouette in a window. Food set out in a bowl and being eaten.

She thought of the sound of footsteps in the night.

She thought about the place where the garage had once been, and the basement wall that looked different from all the others.

And then she knew what had happened all those years ago.

Chapter Forty-One

Carrie gestured frantically and ducked into the cubbyhole. Ginny bent to look inside. The rain sounded much louder here, and she shivered at the waft of damp, cold air.

"I can't fit in here, honey." The endearment slipped naturally from her lips. That was how you addressed a child. "I'm too big. And I don't understand…"

Carrie disappeared. Only for a second, because after that her small head peeked out from a dark place in the corner. Ginny strained to look. It was an air duct.

Not all of it made sense, but this did. Still, she shook her head and waved at the girl to come closer. Carrie's wide eyes blinked when Ginny shone the light too closely on her, and she put up a hand to block it.

"I can't fit in there, honey. Listen, you need to come out here, okay? I'll…I'll call someone. We'll go across the street, or next door." Ginny hesitated, thinking of the water rushing down the street, as swift and deep as the creek in the back. "I will help you."

Carrie let out a low, moaning cry of desperation. She wriggled from the air duct and dropped almost soundlessly to the dirty plywood. She moved toward Ginny, who backed up as instinctively as if a raccoon or a rat was coming at her, though the girl had shown no signs of antagonism.

"I'll take care of you," Ginny whispered.

Another contraction hit her. She groaned at the suddenness, one hand on her belly and the other grabbing at the easel. It tipped, spilling her unfinished canvas.

Carrie cried out and covered her face. A second later she peeked through her fingers and moved closer. She put her small hands on Ginny's belly, and Ginny didn't have the concentration just then to recoil.

"Water, coming up. Down there." Carrie pointed again to the floor, to her bare feet, to something Ginny couldn't see. "Mama says, come get help."

Ginny choked. Everything inside her seemed to be tensing, and the sharp ache inside her intensified. She counted the seconds—one, two, three, four—before everything eased.

Her fingers had gouged the inside of her palms. She swallowed, hard.

"Your mama is down there?"

Carrie nodded and tugged at Ginny's sleeve. "Please come. Mama says, the lady is nice. I tell her, the lady is nice. She says, you help us."

Carrie looked pleading, then terrified. She shook so hard her teeth chattered and looked around the room, though there didn't seem to be anything to see. She looked back at Ginny.

"Mama says, he is gone!"

"Who? Who's... Oh God, oh God," Ginny muttered. She managed to stand up straight. "Your mama and you in the basement. And he...yes, honey. He's gone. And I'm going to help you. But I can't get into that air duct, I have to call someone. We'll call, okay?"

But her cell phone still wouldn't pick up a signal, and the power was out, and though she knew there was a landline phone somewhere around, she didn't know where it was or even if it would work if she plugged it in.

"How high is the water, Carrie? How far up?"

Carrie hesitated, then ducked low to the ground and held her hand to just above Ginny's ankle. Then she put it higher. Higher. To Ginny's thigh.

Surely it couldn't be that high, could it? If the basement was flooding that much, it would come into the first floor, wouldn't it? Ginny didn't know. All she could think of was a foundation where there'd once been a garage and the concrete wall in the basement below it.

"You come." Carrie tugged her sleeve, pulling Ginny toward the bookcase to the right of the fireplace.

All the pieces were falling into place. The figure she'd seen in the window upstairs—not the one by the easel, but another window on the other side of the fireplace, one that she'd assumed was built for symmetry. The one behind the bookcase.

Carrie reached along the molding and pressed something with her small fingers. The bookcase creaked. It shifted.

It moved.

Ginny cried out, not so much in surprise as a twisted sense of victory. She was not crazy. She was not crazy. And this house was not haunted, at least not by a ghost.

Carrie grunted, shoving at the bookcase until Ginny hooked her fingers into the now-open slot and pulled. Even with the weight of the books, the case moved smoothly, on oiled tracks like a sliding glass door. It was an ingenious design, but the space behind it proved even more so.

There was a window here, identical to its sister on the other side of the fireplace, though this one was hung with a cloak of spiderwebs, the sill decorated with a multitude of dead flies. The narrow space between the outside wall and the back of the bookcases was just wide enough for Ginny to stand in, though even without the baby bulk, she'd have brushed both sides with her shoulders. Directly to the left of the opening was the brick side of the chimney, while about four feet to the right was an opening in the floor.

Just a hole, no safety railing or anything to keep an unwary stumbler from falling into it. But then, Ginny thought, anyone entering this space would've had to know exactly where they were going. Carrie ducked around her and leaped toward the hole, too fast for Ginny to catch her.

Ginny, imagining the girl plummeting into an empty space, cried out.

Carrie looked over her shoulder and stepped into the darkness. She didn't fall. She gestured for Ginny to come closer.

It was a metal spiral staircase, the first step a few inches below floor level. It circled into darkness, though when she hung the light into the opening, Ginny could see that the stairs continued without a break down to a small landing.

She'd never have thought she could fit into it, but she could. And did. There wasn't enough room for her to fall either forward or back, so even without a railing to grab she could put one foot at a time down on each step. She couldn't see Carrie below her, but she could hear her. When Ginny got to the landing, there wasn't much more room. She held the flashlight as high as she could to look around the narrow column of space.

She was behind the pantry that should've been an extra foot or two wider, but wasn't. "Oh God. He did this. He built all of this…"

She didn't have time to break down or dwell on the sickness that had led George Miller to build this house with a prison inside it, though that was what she was sure she'd find. Ginny gave herself a shake that set her head spinning. She braced for another contraction. Everything about her pelvis felt loose and wobbly, like her hips weren't hinged quite right. A contraction eased and passed, and she drew in a few shaky breaths.

Carrie had already gone down the first few steps of the other spiral staircase, moving without fear or pause into the inky blackness that reached beyond the dimming glow from Ginny's flashlight. She spoke over her shoulder, "Come."

Ginny followed, slowly and carefully. Her hand shook, which sent the light tipping back and forth. Shadows, light and dark. She eased down, step-by-step. The air smelled damp, thick with must that wanted to make her cough, if only she could draw a breath deep enough.

"Wait," Ginny whispered. Then louder, "Carrie. Wait for me."

The narrow corridor bent at a right angle and ran along what must've been the back of the house. The exterior concrete wall was black with wet, and water was actually trickling in fast streams down from the ceiling. Water on the floor too, a couple inches that got deeper the farther she went, as though the passage was on a downward slope.

Ginny put one hand on the inside wall, also of concrete. George Miller had really done his work well. There was no sign from the basement that this section was two feet shorter than it should've been. She shuddered, stopping, her gorge rising. Her muscles tensed again as she leaned against the wall to let the contraction pass. Ginny swallowed bitter saliva, trying not to puke. Still, no pain. Just discomfort. Yet there was no denying it—she was in labor.

"Carrie. Wait." The spasm passed, Ginny straightened and pulled out her phone again. Upstairs she'd fluctuated between one and two bars. Down here, with multiple layers of concrete and earth between her and the sky, there was nothing.

The water had risen another inch while she stopped. Carrie danced in it, impatient and frantic, while Ginny slogged toward her, grateful for her slippers. Even heavy and soaked, they were protection against whatever might be on the floor under the water.

The flashlight dimmed drastically before rallying and returning at half its former brightness.

Ginny shook it, knowing even as she did the effort was silly. It didn't have batteries the way old flashlights did. You couldn't rattle it into another burst of energy. Instead, the beam of light shook around and went even dimmer.

"Shit," she breathed.

What the hell was she doing? Nine and a half months pregnant, no power, no phone, a faulty light, following some feral child into a basement that was flooding. She didn't even have a weapon. It was the classic stupid move from every horror movie, and suddenly she was choking with laughter. Bent with it, shoulders heaving as the flashlight swung dangerously close to the water and she fought the grip of another contraction.

No, no. Don't fight. Don't fight it.

Ginny tried to breathe through it the way the classes taught, but the laughter wouldn't let her. All of this, so ridiculous. So surreal. She'd have gone to her knees right there in the water if the passage weren't so narrow there wasn't room for her to fall.

The laughter and the contraction passed. Ginny wiped her face—tears or sweat, she couldn't tell. Carrie had moved even farther down the passageway, around another corner. Ginny followed with the lamp, the light now the strength of a guttering candle, held high.

The corridor came to a dead end. Not a concrete wall here, but something shiny. Metal? Shit, the wall was metal, smudged with handprints and splashed with water where Carrie must have kicked. The girl turned as Ginny rounded the corner. She gestured.

"Come. Please." She tugged at a metal handle and the wall moved the way the bookcase had, sliding like a pocket door into a recess in the wall. Carrie put her back to the door and braced her feet against the wall on the other side. She grunted with the effort.

Ginny sloshed closer. The flashlight swung in her hand, back and forth. Dark and light. She could see nothing beyond the sliding metal door.

"Honey, I won't be able to get through there. There's not enough room."

Carrie pushed harder, forcing the metal door farther into the recess. Her legs shook, and she bit on her lower lip. There was still no way Ginny could step over Carrie's legs and shove her bulk through the opening. Ginny put a hand on the door just above Carrie's head. She could feel it threatening to move the moment the little girl ceased her counterpressure.

Ginny wedged herself into the space as far as she could, her breasts and belly crowding against the girl. "I got it. Go."

Carrie moved at once, slipping from the space and letting the door move against Ginny's weight. Ginny had a vision of an elevator door slamming shut on an unwary passenger—but somehow she guessed this door wouldn't spring open. It would cut your fucking fingers off instead.

The door sprang shut behind her the instant she left off the pressure, but she wasn't all the way through. It would've snapped her ankle had she not shoved the flashlight between the door and the wall just long enough to get her foot out. That was the end of the flashlight, which cracked with a snap and plunged them into perfect darkness.

Ginny closed her eyes and tried to catch her breath. Sounds became magnified without sight to counter them, she knew that. She heard the soft swish of Carrie's feet in the water and felt the push of it against her calves. Carrie's chilly fingers slipped into hers and squeezed. She probably could see much better than Ginny could, but even cats needed some amount of light in order to see in the dark. Carrie was still human.

Wasn't she?

Ginny grabbed her phone from her pocket and pressed the Home button to bring up the menu. Instant bright-white light. She slid her thumb along the screen to unlock it and tapped quickly, looking for a flashlight app. "I can't believe I didn't think of this before."

She found it. More bright light, using her phone's LED flash set to a permanent glare. It lit the corridor, even narrower on this side of the door, and threw giant shadows on the walls. The ceiling was lower, hung with shiny ductwork and wires that cast weird patterns of shadow. Ginny ran her hand along the door. This side had no handle. Nothing but smooth, cold metal reflecting the light from her phone.

Then, up near the top, higher than a child could reach, higher than Ginny herself could reach, she saw a small dark circle. She stretched to touch it, and her fingertip felt a rough edge before dipping just barely inside. A hole. Probably for some sort of key, which she did not have.

She was trapped down here.

But she would not be afraid. She would not let herself give in to terror. All the creepy, scary things that had happened since moving into this house had not sent her gibbering, and neither would this, especially since she knew the cause was nothing supernatural. She would not be afraid.

She was a liar.

She followed Carrie down the corridor and the ceiling got lower and lower. The light from her phone was eye-achingly bright and far-reaching, yet like the high beams of a car, limited in scope. They'd only gone about four feet when the corridor jogged again, this time to the right.

The smell hit her first, hard as a fist, thick like smoke. The musty, earthy smell of the water had been nose-tickling but normal. Natural. This stench, of unwashed bodies and rotten teeth, of food left to spoil…of human waste… Ginny retched, turning her head and certain she was going to vomit. She hadn't eaten anything in hours. Nothing came up but bile she spit into the water that was now up to her knees. She heaved again, then stood to shine the light.

The room was no larger than her bedroom and built on a cant that left her thinking of those haunted house rooms with the strobe lights, usually painted black and white, the kind with tilted floors to screw up your perspective. The ceiling was so low she had to bend her head, and the light showed her there were at least two slanted fun-house doorways. A small, domed refrigerator took up space in one corner, with what looked like a tiny two-burner stove next to it and a spindle-legged sink. Beside that, a child-sized wooden table perfect for tea parties in which every cup was poisoned. The furniture wasn't all she saw in this nightmare room.

There was something else too.

Chapter Forty-Two

Carrie splashed through the water to reach a low metal bed frame and stained mattress shoved against the far wall. The water licked at the mattress's bottom edge. It would be sodden in minutes. There were four of them. Or five. Ginny could not yet look at whatever they were, those crouched and shivering things with pale faces and grasping, skeletal hands.

Ginny switched the phone from one hand to another. The light shifted. Shadows loomed and swooped from the shaking of her hands. She closed her eyes. Pain, this time fierce and deep and seemingly unrelenting until then…it was gone. She opened her eyes.

Whatever was on the other side of the room had moved closer.

Ginny couldn't speak. Her breath came short and sharp as dizziness assailed her. She almost dropped the phone, but then clutched it so tight her fingers hurt.

She gave a breathless, gasping scream. They were in front of her, two of them, with Carrie hanging back with the other three still huddled on the bed. One stood, up and up, curving and hunched, its neck and head tilted at a strange angle to show her a smooth, pale face with dark eyes. It held out a hand to Carrie, who linked her fingers with it. They stood in front of Ginny, saying nothing. Just watching.

And… Oh God. They were not monsters, they were not things made of shadow and fear. They were children. A boy of maybe thirteen, grown too tall for this cramped space. A girl a little older than Carrie but not much bigger, her dark hair as tangled and dirty but pulled back from her face with a length of frayed ribbon. And there too, thinner and without her collar, but purring as she was cuddled—Noodles.

"Oh," Ginny said in a broken, hesitant whisper. "Oh, you poor things."

From beyond one of the dark doorways came a low, rattling hiss that turned the heads of all the children, those in front of her and the ones who'd hung back on the bed. Something slithered through the water, and Ginny saw a snake before she recognized it as something more sinister. A length of chain coiled and moved, disappearing into the water, now just past Ginny's knees.

"Mama, I brought the lady." Carrie turned with another shy smile, and the shadows shifted.

The figure in the doorway moved toward her, one shoulder higher than the other as the weight of the shackled wrist kept one hand closer to the floor. The shaved skull and hollow cheeks made it impossible to guess its gender, though the worn dress gave a hint. Ginny knew at once who she was.

"Caroline. Oh my God. Caroline Miller."

Caroline gave a hoarse croak. She was weeping, Ginny saw, though it was too dark to see if there were any tears on her wasted cheeks. She drew Carrie to her and kissed her head. She looked at Ginny.

"Is he gone? He's really gone?"

Ginny pushed closer, carefully, through the water, though the small room was mostly bare. "He's gone," Ginny said, and let Caroline's withered hand take hers. "I'm here."

Caroline's body racked with silent sobs, but when she raised her face to Ginny's again, her eyes were dry. She licked her cracked lips. "The water's coming in."

"Yes. I know." Ginny tried not to shudder. She failed.

Caroline might look weak, but her grip was so tight it became painful. She leaned closer, her breath sour but her eyes bright. "I sent Carrie for you. She said you were a nice lady, that you left things for her."

Ginny nodded, though that wasn't quite the truth. "Yes. I didn't know... Oh my God. I'm so sorry. I didn't know."

Caroline's bright gaze didn't dim as she shook her head. "Nobody knew. It's all right. It's all right. You're here now. You can help us. You can help us?"

"The door closed behind me." Ginny tried to breathe shallowly so she could avoid the stink. "How do you open it?"

A rough and grating noise came from Caroline. Incredibly, a laugh. "From this side? You don't."

Ginny watched as Caroline's children gathered silently around her, staring with wide eyes and open mouths. There were four children altogether. The oldest, a girl, hunched like her brother, put a hand on Caroline's shoulder and murmured something Ginny didn't understand.

Caroline replied, her voice pitched low and mumbling, the words not only indistinct but not quite right. Strung together in a pattern Ginny couldn't recognize, like tuning in unexpectedly to a foreign radio station. Whatever Caroline said seemed to satisfy her daughter, because the girl nodded and stepped back, just outside the circle of light.

Ginny's fingers cramped, and she switched hands again. She looked at her phone's battery indicator. The water had risen impossibly higher, up to her thighs. "My light won't last forever. We have to get you out of here. All of you. How do we open that door, Caroline?"

"He had a key. Always a key. It was shaped like a…" Caroline's mouth worked, her expression momentarily blank before her eyes focused again, "…a T. It was shaped like a T and that's how he opened the door. There is no other door."

"Of course not." If they'd been able to get out through that door, wouldn't they have done it long ago? "Carrie. She was small enough to fit through the ducts—"

Before Ginny could speak again, a swift and hot gush of fluid ran down her legs. She clutched her belly and held out the phone, blindly, hoping someone would take it from her before she dropped it. Someone did, and she put both her hands between her legs, terrified she'd feel a baby's head bulging against her giant cotton panties.

"The baby," she said, and a groan took the place of any words she might've said next.

"Your baby is coming," Caroline said flatly. "Here and now? Don't worry. Don't worry."

Worry was not the name for this vast and roaring terror, this overwhelming fury of anxiety and fear. Ginny gasped as the contraction peaked. She breathed with it, incapable of embarrassment though she'd bent over to put her hands on her knees and was panting like a dog on the street in August. Everything inside her pressed down, down. Only the rising water kept her from squatting right there, because she would not, could not push her baby out into that filthy wetness.

She became aware of Caroline on one side of her, the oldest daughter on the other. They walked Ginny in mincing crab steps, the largest she could take, through the doorway and into a smaller room the size of a closet. The light from her phone shone over their shoulders, illuminating a full-size bed and a dresser. As the light slanted crazily along the walls, Ginny saw they'd been hung with countless childish drawings like the one that had been left on her easel. The stick figures seemed to dance, and, nauseated, she closed her eyes while they took her to the bed.

She put both her hands on the damp mattress and bent forward. She breathed. And finally the contraction passed.

"My water broke. I'm having contractions," she said without opening her eyes. "The baby is coming, yes. Here and now."

Tears came, shaking her. A firm hand squeezed her shoulder. She looked up to see Caroline.

"I will help you. Linna will help you. We know…we know about babies, lady."

"My name is Ginny."

"Ginny," Caroline said, and smiled. "Ginny, we'll help you. It's going to be all right."

Nothing could be all right about this. Water up to their thighs, the stink overpowering everything else. Her baby born in this hovel? No. No. Ginny shook her head, but another contraction ripped its way through her, and there was nothing but pain to think about just then.

It passed.

There was something amazing about how much it hurt and how suddenly the pain ceased, and she'd have been able to think about it more if only the world would stop spinning. It was because she wasn't breathing, Ginny knew, and braced herself to take a long, stinking gulp of fetid air. It helped only a little.

"You need to get on the bed. Lie back. Lift your dress, and let us look." Caroline gestured. "Deke. The light."

Ginny'd prepared herself mentally for knowing that in the hospital it was likely she'd have a whole slew of strangers staring at her vagina while she pushed this kid out. In no realm of her imagination had one of those staff been a teenage boy. There was no shielding of her body, though, no way even for her to protest, because she was too busy bearing down against the sudden pressure in her womb.

Hands helped her back onto the disgusting mattress, propped her with pillows. Hands lifted her nightgown and pulled her panties off. Ginny wept, not from pain or shame, but from knowing there was no way her baby could survive this filthy place.

"Mine did," Caroline told her, and Ginny realized she'd spoken aloud. "The ones who got born alive, they all made it. Yours will too."

Ginny opened her eyes. "My phone. I have to see if…there's a signal."

Deke handed over her phone without argument. Ginny thumbed the screen, with no luck. She tried anyway, first with a call that wouldn't even send and then a text. After that, another. Each time, a small, angry red exclamation mark showed up next to her message, proving it didn't go through. Her fingers tightened on the phone with the next contraction, and Caroline gently pried it from her hand.

"Let Deke hold the light, Ginny."

Ginny panted and gasped, then gave in to a shriek. This embarrassed her more than anything else had, but Caroline patted her shoulder.

"It's okay to scream," she said. "Nobody can hear you down here."

"You…all…can."

Caroline gave another rusty laugh, as cutting as knuckles on a grater. "Screams don't bother us."

The pain faded. Ginny drew a breath. She shifted on the bed, against the pillows, and tried to see the floor. "The water?"

"Still coming in." Caroline turned her head and coughed, then spit.

The chain on her wrist jangled. She didn't use that arm at all, Ginny saw. The fingers of that hand looked curled and useless. Caroline saw her looking and gave her a smile that showed straight, even teeth that could only be the product of expensive orthodontia.

This detail drove home the horror of this girl's…no, she was a woman now…this woman's life more than anything else could have. Ginny remembered that smile, flashing bright with metal. The curly permed hair, the fashionable clothes. Caroline had been smart and bright and beautiful once. All of that had been stolen from her, replaced with… this.

"When the pains get worse, one on top of each other, it will be almost time. You'll feel like you have to push the baby out. Like you have to use the toilet. You won't be able to help it. But until then, you should rest and try to get through each pain as it comes." Caroline said this calmly, as though it were the most normal thing in the world to be giving birth in a flooding basement, in the dark. "Linna and I will be here to help you."

Ginny waited for the next pain, but her body seemed to have gone quiet. "I can't feel it moving."

Caroline said nothing at first. Then, softly, she put her good hand on Ginny's belly. "It doesn't matter. Your body will push it out, no matter what."

More tears came, but Ginny forced them back. She clutched at Caroline's hand. "I'm so sorry. So, so sorry I didn't figure this out sooner. I didn't put the pieces together, they were all right there. I should've known. I should've…"

"How could you have known anything?" Caroline looked surprised, then sad. "My mother didn't know. My brother didn't know. Nobody ever did. But you're here now. And this will all be okay. But first, your baby—babies don't wait for anything."

More contractions came and went, some longer than others. Ginny waited for them to form some sort of pattern, but they refused. Some were short, others long. She tried counting the minutes between them and lost track with their irregularity.

Ginny had no idea how much time had passed and asked to see her phone. Only half an hour since she'd come into this room. An hour, maybe a little longer since she'd last spoken to Sean. Not soon enough for him to worry. Not soon enough.

"Mama. Water," the girl a little bigger than Carrie said.

"Yes, Trixie. I see it." Caroline never lost her calm, flat tone. She sat on the bed next to Ginny and took her hand. "It won't be long now."

"Until the baby comes?"

"Or the water." She'd proven her ability to laugh, but there was nothing like humor in Caroline's voice now.

Ginny tried to think, to focus, to fixate on something her brain wanted to tell her was important. Something about…Carrie. Something about…the water.

And then she couldn't think of anything but the agony. It tore at her. It consumed her. As though from far away, she heard Caroline murmuring to Linna, something about blankets. Something about a basin. But then the all-encompassing urge to bear down took over, and all Ginny could think about was pushing.

Hands moved her again, lifting her hips, in the almost nonexistent break between contractions, to slide something beneath her. Hands pressed on her knees, parting and pushing them back toward her hips. Hands cradled her feet, bare, the slippers lost.

It had never been like this. The pain had been a familiar echo, vaster but still not entirely foreign. But this grinding, desperate need to strain and push and expel…Ginny was helpless against it. She couldn't stop it. Her body did what it was meant to do. If she died, she thought, her body would continue to birth this child.

She felt the baby move down the birth canal, inch by agonizing inch. Too slow, and too fast at the same time. A bright, red-hot center of pain burned between her legs as she screamed. The sound spiraled up and up until her voice broke.

"The head. I see the head," Caroline told her. "The baby's almost here."

Ginny looked down between her legs to see Caroline and Linna both poised there, hands ready. The light from her phone had no delicacy. It made everything harsh. Ginny saw the flash of the other children's faces, but Deke was solid and steady; he held the light focused firmly between Ginny's thighs.

The inexorable need to push cycled back, and Ginny rode it. Her fingers clutched the bare mattress, digging into the now-sodden material. She growled with her efforts, her teeth gritting so tightly she thought a tooth cracked.

The baby was born.

For a breathless, eternal moment, the emptiness inside confused her and Ginny sagged against the pillows. There was no cry, no wail. She struggled upright, desperate, and croaked out a wordless plea.

Caroline bent over the child, then lifted it. The baby hung limply in her hands. Then it moved. Then it screamed.

Ginny had never been so happy to hear anything in her life.

Chapter Forty-Three

Ginny dozed with her baby tucked up close to her naked skin, both of them covered in a blanket and Noodles purring by her side. She was too exhausted to care how dirty it was. Caroline and Linna pressed on her belly, eliciting a fresh burst of pain and another hot slosh of something from inside her. They talked to each other in that mumbled, mangled language, ignoring her, while the other children were dispatched on errands Ginny didn't understand.

She didn't care.

For now, her son was safe. They were warm, though anything but dry. And Ginny was tired...so tired...

She didn't want to, but forced her eyes open. Her vagina burned and ached. Someone had pushed a folded bundle of material between her legs. The baby snuffled against her, then went quiet. Ginny was bleary, but awake. Her mouth tasted sour, dry. She'd have given almost anything for a drink of cold water.

Ginny smoothed her hand over her baby's soft head and marveled at the hair there. It was pale, not dark like hers. He took after Sean. Ginny wanted to know the color of his eyes, but didn't want to shine the bright light directly on him. "You have electricity down here."

"Yes. Sometimes. But it was better to use a flashlight with batteries, when we could. It's so good to have light." Caroline's low voice drifted through the darkness. "We have two lamps, but the outlets down here are bad. When we try to use the stove, sometimes it blows the bulbs."

Ginny thought of all the times the power had gone out. "It blew our fuses too."

"He said he'd fix it. That and the heat, he got that directed in to us because it was so cold. But it never worked as well as he wanted. He said he could build things just fine, but he didn't understand electricity. We have a couple candles, but the matches got wet. They were your candles..." Caroline paused and sounded almost shy. "He stopped letting us have them, and no matches, either. Because we might start another fire. And that would've been very, very bad."

"Caroline, why did you wait so long before you sent Carrie to get me?"

There was a long, long silence.

"We had to know," Caroline said quietly, "if we could trust you."

The simple way she said it broke Ginny's heart. She found the other woman's hand, the one weighed down by the chain and shackle. "You can trust me."

"He didn't know we were saving food. He didn't know we'd eat only half of what he brought us, eat the things that would go bad. I made us put the rest away, in case. He was getting old, you see. He said he'd be around forever, that no matter what happened he'd be there, but I knew better. So I made us put the food away. Batteries. The light bulbs, though he'd yell about how careless we were to break so many." Caroline coughed again. The noise was rattling and thick. She spit to the side, into the water. "He always threatened not to bring more. To let us starve, or sit in the dark. But I always knew he wouldn't. He didn't want us to die, you know. He didn't want us dead."

Ginny shivered. "But…I don't understand, Caroline. Why would you stay here? If Carrie could get out through the ducts to get food, to find me, why wouldn't you send her earlier? I would've helped you sooner."

The bed dipped as the children gathered around. Their mother looked around at them, then at Ginny. "You're here now."

A pulse of hot fluid leaked from between Ginny's legs. She grimaced, but there was nothing to do for it. "My husband is on his way home, but the roads are closed. He might not get here for a while, but if he doesn't hear from me, he will worry. He'll send someone or do something. But, Caroline…we can't wait for that. You have to send Carrie out again."

Caroline said nothing at first. She looked around at faces focused on hers. All of them were so quiet. They sat so still.

She looked at Ginny. "Yes. Carrie should go out."

Carrie let out a low wail and shook her head. She ran from the room. Caroline held up a hand when her sister moved to go after her. "No, Trixie. I'll go after her."

Dragging her chain behind her, Caroline went into the next room, leaving the light behind. Ginny stared at the foot of the bed. Deke, the tall boy who'd held the phone while she gave birth. Linna, the oldest girl. Trixie, a little bigger than Carrie.

The circle of light stretched to the wall, and Ginny could clearly see a few of the drawings she'd noticed earlier. This one had six stick figures. One, the mother. Five children around her. She looked again at the group.

"One of you's missing."

"T-T-Tate." Trixie had a stutter, either nerves or a speech impediment. "Huh-he got stuck. Huh-he was t-too big."

"He said bad things would happen if we tried to get away," Deke said flatly, the "he" in question clearly referring to George Miller, and not Deke's brother. "Tate pushed him. He hit Tate's head, and Tate wasn't sure what happened. Then Tate said we need to try, Mama. We need to try. And he went—"

"Deke," Caroline said sharply, a dark silhouette in the doorway. "That's enough."

The water, at least, seemed to have stopped rising. It sloshed against Caroline's thighs as she moved toward the bed. "Carrie will go. But she's very afraid. She's not sure what to do."

"Do you have a pen? Paper? Something to write with?"

"Everything's wet," Linna said. "The crayons are broke. The paper was in the cabinet. It's ruined."

Trixie let out a sob at that, and flung herself onto the bed while Linna rubbed her back.

Ginny was struck with inspiration. "My phone. I'll type a note in it. She can take my phone and find someone. Go next door, give them the phone. They'll see it. If not, at the very least, they'll know it's my phone, or figure it out. And she can tell them, can't she? Where we are?"

Caroline hesitated. "Carrie is…special."

"She's very special," Ginny said softly, seeing Carrie creeping up behind her mother. "Very special and very brave. She'll know just what to do. Won't you, Carrie?"

Carrie stepped out from behind her mother, and into the feathery edges of the light circle. "Scared."

"Bad things happen!" Deke cried suddenly. "Bad things happen when we try to go outside! Don't let her, Mama. Don't let her go!"

"Deke, hush!" Caroline shook him by the shoulders. "You're going to scare your sisters. Stop. It will be fine. We have to do this. You don't understand, but we do."

Horribly, Ginny thought she understood. Caroline remembered a life on the outside, but none of these children did. After living their entire lives down here, was it any wonder they might be afraid of what waited for them in the outside world? What horror stories had George Miller told them to keep them willingly imprisoned?

"Tate went out! Tate went out and he never came back! He got lost! Tate didn't come back!"

The back of Caroline's hand cracked across Deke's face hard enough to send him splashing to his hands and knees in the water. He came up sputtering, backing away, across the room.

Ginny's stomach churned at the violence, and she cringed, covering her baby as best she could.

Nobody else seemed surprised at Caroline's actions. She spoke calmly, "Deke. I don't want to make you go to the corner. Not now, like this. But if you can't get yourself under control, you will go to the corner even if you have to sit up to your ears in this water. Do you understand me?"

In the white light, Deke looked extremely pale. Water sluiced over his face, mimicking tears. He nodded after a moment. "Yes."

Caroline sighed. "Carrie, can you take this lady's phone up through the ducts. Out of the house? Can you go outside?"

Carrie shuddered visibly. She hadn't been splashed with water; her tears were real. She shook her head.

Again, Ginny was inspired. "Carrie. You know the other children? The ones you were playing with here in the house? Kelly and Carson, the night of the party."

Carrie looked fearful, then nodded.

"They live in the house next door to me. You can go to their house and see them. Their mother is very nice, she's a nice lady. Like me. You can trust her too."

Caroline pushed the hair from Carrie's forehead and cupped her cheeks. The chain clanked. "You have to be brave and strong, like Miss Ginny said. You have to do this for us, baby. It's...well. You just have to. Okay?"

Carrie nodded again. Ginny gestured for the phone. Carefully, so she didn't disturb her sleeping, still-unnamed baby, Ginny tapped a message into her phone. She saved it as a note, sent it as a text that failed, and added it to an email that also failed. It didn't matter, once Carrie got the phone into a place where there was a signal, all of the messages would be sent. She checked the time too.

Five hours since the last time she'd spoken to Sean.

It seemed so impossible that all of this had happened in so little time, but she didn't need a pinch to prove she wasn't dreaming. She had the pain between her legs and the child snuffling lightly in her arms. She had the splash of water and five pale, wide-eyed faces staring at her.

"Do you have a plastic bag?" Ginny asked. "The kind for sandwiches. One that closes at the top. In case she drops it, so it doesn't get wet."

"No. We have a few plastic bags, but we used them to line the toilet." Caroline shook her head.

"Never mind. She's going up, right?" Ginny took a deep breath, determined to be positive. "Carrie. You hold it tight. Is there something else we can put it in for her? A purse or a bag we can tie to her?"

"I have a stocking," Linna piped up shyly. "It got a hole. We didn't mend it yet. She can use the match for it. It's long enough that we can tie the end to her shirt somehow."

"Yes. That will work." Ginny held up the phone. "But once she takes it…we won't have any light."

Caroline smiled. "We've sat in the darkness before. We can do it again."

Ginny cringed at the idea of sitting here in the pitch black with four feet of water all around her, the bed like a boat in an unstable sea. But it was the only option. She needed to get her baby out of here.

She checked the message one last time, hoping something had managed to get through, but nothing had. She thumbed the screen and tilted it to show Carrie. "See? Like this. You just push this button when you get there, you show it to them. Okay? That's all you do."

The phone looked twice as big in Carrie's tiny hand. Ginny lost her breath when it looked like the girl was going to drop it over the side of the bed, but she caught it. Carrie pushed the button and held up the phone for Ginny to see.

"Yes. Like that." Ginny took the phone, then the sock Linna handed her. "Okay. Are we ready for the dark?"

"Yes. We are," said Caroline.

It was instant and total and unyielding, that darkness. But it wasn't unfamiliar, and it was no longer terrifying. Carrie found her way into the ductwork. The rest of them huddled on the damp mattress, piled with equally damp blankets, trying to stay warm. The baby woke, wailing, and found Ginny's breast. The sharp pull of his lips and tongue on the sensitive nipple stung, and Ginny had no milk yet, but the baby sucked anyway and seemed content.

Ginny blinked, eyes straining, but the darkness here was total. It was something of a comfort, actually. She closed her eyes and let herself drift for a minute or so before forcing herself back to consciousness.

Caroline's rusty laughter gritted out of the darkness. "Ginny. I lied."

Ginny roused, trying to push through the wall of her weariness to understand. "About what?"

"Being ready for the darkness," Caroline said. "Nobody is ever ready for it."

Chapter Forty-Four

"I was thirteen when I figured out I could get my daddy to give me anything I wanted." Caroline's words drifted out of the darkness.

Ginny had no idea how long they've been sitting in silence. Someone had moved onto the bed to cuddle next to her. She thought it must be Trixie by the size and the flow of hair. Trixie snored lightly.

"Caroline, you don't have to tell me this now."

"Now," Caroline said, "might be the only time I ever tell it."

That would not be true; Ginny knew that. Caroline would have to tell her story a lot of times very soon. To the police, certainly. To her brother. To the media, if she wasn't careful, or if she wanted to earn something for her pain. Still, Ginny thought she knew what the other woman meant. What better time to tell a story like this, but in the dark?

"All my friends liked my dad the best because he was always around to do whatever we needed. He could always drive us to the mall, or he'd drop us off at the pool and pick us up. And he'd sometimes stop on the way home to treat us to ice cream. He didn't try to talk to us like the other dads did. He just listened. He let me pick the music. He was… cool. He was the cool dad.

"When I was thirteen, I wanted a bikini for the summer. My mother said no. She wanted me to wear a one-piece. But all my friends had them. She made me buy a babyish suit. I was the only one. The only one without a cool swimsuit. And my dad noticed."

Caroline's voice was low and warm, like melting butter. Or maybe Ginny was melting, dissolving into the darkness and shadows. She put a hand between her legs and it came away wet, the smell of copper strong on her fingers. She was bleeding. A lot.

"He took me to the mall and gave me money to buy a new suit. He saw all my friends wearing them. He wanted me to have one. To be like them. They fought about it, really loud. Brendan hid in his room with his music playing loud, but I could hear them in their bedroom. He won the fight. He always won the fights. And he brought the suit to me; he tossed it down on the bed, and told me to try it on. To show him how it fit. So I did."

Pause. A breath. Silence, but for the sound of water, trickling.

"I figured out then that I could get whatever I wanted out of him. Out of boys, in general. With just a little show of T and A."

The phrase seemed oddly innocent, but fitting.

"Do you know," Caroline asked suddenly, "if she knew there was something going on? My mother, I mean. She had to have known. Didn't she?"

Ginny couldn't tell if Caroline was desperate for affirmation or denial. "I don't know."

"She knew," Caroline whispered. Then, even softer, "Do you think she misses me? Will she be happy to see me again?"

"Oh, Caroline. I'm so sorry. But your mom passed away."

More silence. The baby made a meeping grunt, but settled. Ginny's thighs stuck together when she moved.

"So…I'm an orphan." Rusty, grating laughter became a sob. "Just as well. Just as well."

Ginny had lost track of time long ago. She listened for the sound of shouts or voices, but heard nothing. "These rooms…soundproofed?"

"Yes. He built this house like this, you know. Back before he even met my mom. He built this house himself."

Ginny's lips pulled back from her teeth. "Jesus Christ."

"He told me he was taking me to the beach for the weekend. As a special treat. We weren't supposed to let Mom know. He said nobody could know, or they'd want to come along. That's why he picked me up on the way home from school. I was walking. I was just scuffing my feet along in the leaves and thinking about going to the football game the next day. He pulled up in a van. I didn't know it, and I would never ever have gone inside." Caroline paused. Coughed. She coughed for a long time, and when she stopped, her voice had gone rough and thick with phlegm. "But I saw it was my daddy, so I got in."

"Someone reported it. The van. They saw you get into it."

"But they didn't know it was him. Obviously. They thought a stranger took me."

"Yes," Ginny said.

Caroline snorted. "They were right."

A sound like distant thunder rumbled, then stopped. Ginny felt the vibration in the bed, or maybe just thought she did. She strained, listening. They all did. But nothing else happened.

"When he showed me the bookcase, the hidden stairs, I thought it was amazing. So cool. And then when he showed me this little space, like a playroom, I thought it was so much fun. He told me this was our place, our special place, that nobody would ever know about it, and until he left me there and didn't let me out, I thought it was going to be great." Caroline sounded tired. "Also, he lied. Because it wasn't just our special place. Not until later. Not until after."

"After what?"

"After she died," Caroline said wearily, casually. "I wasn't the first one."

"Oh. Oh God." There should've been more words than that, but Ginny had none.

"Her name was Terry. She was jealous of me, right from the start, because I had long hair and pretty teeth. She didn't have teeth. He'd pulled them so she couldn't bite."

"Please. You don't have to tell me this."

"I have to tell you this!" Caroline hissed. "I have been waiting for too long to tell someone this!"

Ginny shut up after that. Caroline talked. Ginny listened.

"He never touched me, not until she died." That seemed to be an important fact. "He promised he'd let me out. But I saw what he did to Terry. I didn't want to lose my teeth, or have him cut my hair. I thought someone would find me. I mean, I was in the house. In the goddamned house, right? How could they not know? How could they not hear me screaming? I did try to get away. So he put on the chain. And then...a baby."

At every pause, Ginny hoped Caroline wouldn't say anything else. She prayed for someone to find them. But other than another rumble that sounded like distant thunder, there was only blackness and Caroline's voice.

"He took it away from me. It was a boy. He said I wasn't old enough to take care of a baby. I was fifteen by then, or...I think I was. I lost track of time. I made marks, for a while, on the wall. But he saw them and erased them. So he took the baby. It was small anyway. I think it would've died. I think...it did die. Didn't it, Ginny? Did my baby die?"

Ginny thought of the bones in her backyard. "I think so, honey. Yes."

Caroline gave a shuddering sigh. "Then came Tate, and he let me keep him. Said I needed something to keep me occupied when he couldn't visit me. Tell me something. When did my mother die?"

"I'm not sure, Caroline. But I know that she and your brother moved out of this house about a year after you went missing."

"Oh. Oh. Oh," Caroline said. "Oh. She didn't stay? So she didn't know. Really? She didn't know I was here?"

Mrs. Miller might have suspected something, but it couldn't have been this. "I don't think so, honey. I'm sure she didn't know. I think she really thought you were…gone."

"She thought I was dead."

"Yes. I think so."

Caroline gave a barking sob. "Oh. Okay. That's good. That's good, you know? Because she just thought I was dead, she didn't leave me here on purpose."

"No. I don't think so." Ginny reached blindly to find Caroline.

Caroline turned and pressed herself to Ginny's shoulder. Her tears were hot and wet on Ginny's neck; the baby gave a startled cry. Ginny put her hand between Caroline and the baby, but didn't push the other woman away. She cradled her as best she could.

"No, Caroline. She didn't leave you here on purpose. I'm sure of it."

They sat that way for another interminable amount of time. Ginny had never known kids to be so quiet for so long, but thought perhaps they'd all fallen asleep. Her muscles were stiff, and her back ached. Every movement sent another hot pulse between her legs, and her head spun.

"I'm bleeding," Ginny said. "Too much, I think."

"I thought once the children came, he'd leave me alone. He promised, after each one, he would take us all upstairs. After the ones that didn't make it, he always said he would take me to the hospital. But he never did."

"How many times?"

"I don't know," Caroline said, but Ginny knew that was a lie. No mother who lost a child could ever forget it, no matter how many times it happened.

"Caroline, I feel really bad. I feel really sick. I'm losing too much blood."

"Wait."

The bed moved as Caroline got up and returned a few minutes later. She took away the material bunched between Ginny's legs and replaced it with another. Ginny forced her mind from thinking of germs. Sepsis. Her breath shuddered. Oh God. Where was Sean? Where were the police?

"Shh. Shhh, listen." Ginny sounded drunk. She wished she were.

Deke spoke up. "It's Tate!"

"Tate's gone," Linna snapped. "Don't be a dumb-bum. Tate went up and he didn't come back. He's dead!"

"Tate knew he was getting old. Tate said, what happened if he died? What would happen when he didn't bring the food? So Tate tried to get the key, the special key, but he pushed Tate down so hard it cracked his head open. And then he went crazy." Deke was sobbing, shouting as Caroline and Linna tried to shush him.

His shouts startled the baby awake. He began to wail. Ginny rocked and soothed, but nothing would calm the infant.

"Tate said the only way out was through the walls! And we didn't have food anymore, it was gone, and the heat was off, the 'lectric was off, it was cold! Tate went up," Deke said, more quietly, "and he didn't come back."

"When did Tate go up?" Ginny asked. "Not so long ago. After we moved in, right? It was after that. George died in the hospital, and we bought the house four months after that. Your food ran out. Your power ran out. And Tate went up, into the duct, and didn't come back."

The furnace. The flickering lights. Oh God.

The flies.

Ginny heard herself muttering, though her words were a slurred jumble of sounds she couldn't distinguish, even to herself. She struggled to move, to get up, and felt herself falling into a different sort of darkness. She clutched her screaming baby. She would not drop the baby. She would not drop her son.

The sound of thunder wasn't distant this time.

"Ginny! Wake up! You have to get up! Now!"

Ginny fought the waves of black and red, the swirling descent of gray. Someone shook her. Someone tried to take her baby from her arms, and she screamed, fighting.

The roar grew louder. So did the sound of water. Someone pulled her, got her standing, pushed her toward a spindle-legged chair shoved in front of the dresser. Which she could see.

There was light.

Faint, from the room outside this one, but after so long in the dark, any speck of light was bright as a star. Ginny put one hand on top of the dresser, the other cradling her shrieking child. Screams were good, better than silence. Better than a baby who made no sound. Someone shoved her from behind, and her muscles protested as she tried to lift her leg and get on top. Something ripped inside her, something slid down her thighs, something thick and tearing her on the way out.

Clarity hit her along with the pain. The rumble and roar had been the basement wall collapsing. The water was rushing in, frothing and foaming and rising.

The ceiling in these rooms was not high.

Trixie was already crouched on top of the dresser. There was no room for Ginny there. Instead, Ginny put her baby there, one hand on her son to keep him from toppling off. The naked infant squalled in fury.

The water rose.

Caroline and Ginny clung to the dresser. On the opposite side of the room, Linna, clutching the cat, and Deke had scrambled on top of the table. The water had already reached their shins and was still climbing. Their backs pressed to the ceiling, necks angled.

Impossibly, the water rose.

It was up to Ginny's chest, and filled with rubble. Something sharp hit her leg and sent her swirling into the muck, her head under the water with barely enough time to grab a breath. She came up choking, flailing with one hand, the other hooked into the dresser's metal handle.

"Asher!" Until that moment, she hadn't known what she wanted to call her baby. But now she knew there was nothing else to call him.

Ginny got to her feet and put a hand on top of the dresser, found her son and held him in place. She didn't need a chair to get to the top of it now, because the water buoyed her. Trixie shuddered, and Ginny took her hand. She looked into her face, realized she could make out the sight of the girl's dark eyes, her open mouth.

The water rose and pushed her upward, to the low-hung ceiling. She clung to the dresser. She kicked to keep herself from being swept away. She focused on Trixie's face.

"I'm here," she cried. "I'm here. I'm here."

Someone shouted her name. More light poured into the room, bright and glaring and focused in beams. Flashlights. Men in boots and yellow overcoats.

And Sean.

He grabbed her, but she wouldn't let go of the dresser without Asher safely cradled against her. Firemen, the other men were firemen. They shouted, pointing, grabbing at Linna and Deke. Sean, hair plastered to his face, reached for Trixie and pulled her from the dresser, into the water that was now neck high. Ginny held her son over her head and moved, following him, the front of her nightgown gripped tight in Sean's hand.

Somehow, he pulled them out, over the remnants of the collapsed basement wall and the dirt that filled the space. Down the corridor that rose at the slight incline so that by the time they reached the metal door, propped open with a large metal shaft, the water was only to their knees. Then they were through the door, the stairs in front of them and the firemen with the other children close behind them.

Then they went up.

And they didn't come back down.

Chapter Forty-Five

Ginny rocked.

Asher, warm and clean, sucked sporadically at one breast, rosebud mouth going periodically lax. Ginny smoothed her hand over the baby's soft, downy hair. She sang him a lullaby, soothing her son to sleep. In the next room, her husband slept too.

In another house, another place, Caroline Miller and her children were also warm and fed and safe. But did they sleep? Did they dream? Ginny didn't know. The police and Social Services and Brendan Miller and lawyers and the media had all taken their pieces of Caroline and the children from the basement. Ginny had visited them in the hospital just once, right after they were found, and then only because she and Asher had been admitted as well.

She and Sean had managed, so far, to keep the reporters camped out in front of the house from bothering them too much; she supposed at some point they'd have to talk to them, or they would all give up and go away. They bothered Sean more than they did her, if only because Ginny clung to the idea that somehow sharing what happened might help Caroline and her family more than keeping all of it as yet one more secret.

Ginny was tired of secrets.

In her arms, Asher stirred and let out one small cry, then fell further into sleep. Ginny rocked, her eyes closed, smiling at the sound of Noodles's collar jingling as the cat padded into the library and jumped onto the Victorian couch where she'd taken to spending most of her time. She was still too thin, but she never got underfoot anymore, and she never ran into places she wasn't supposed to go.

Ginny rocked, dozing in the dark. There came the creep of small bare feet, the whisper of cold air swirling, the soft brush of fingertips against her own. Maybe those things would always be in this house. They'd never go away. But Ginny didn't open her eyes, because she knew it was all a dream. That was all, just a dream.

She wasn't haunted any longer.

About the Author

Megan Hart writes books. Some of them use a lot of bad words, but most of the other words are okay.

She can't live without music, the internet, or the ocean, though she and soda have achieved an amicable parting of ways. She can't stand the feeling of corduroy or velvet, and modern art leaves her cold. She writes a little bit of everything from horror to romance.

Find her at: www.meganhart.com, www.twitter.com/megan_hart, and www.facebook.com/megan.hart!

Live fast, die young, and leave a bloodthirsty corpse!

Ghost Heart
© 2016 John Palisano

Live fast, die young, and leave a bloodthirsty corpse. That's the saying of a new pack of fiendish predators infesting a New England town. They're infected with the Ghost Heart, a condition that causes them to become irresistible and invincible…as long as they drink the blood of the living. But these vampires don't live forever, and as the Ghost Heart claims them, their skin loses color and their hearts turn pale. When a young mechanic is seduced by the pack's muse, he finds falling in love will break more than his heart.

Enjoy the following excerpt for Ghost Heart:

We headed outside, toward the alley behind the bar; we walked into the nice, cool drizzle. I loved the change in climate. The bar had been so hot and stuffy, so being outside was welcome. Mike hiked up the collar of his leather jacket and couldn't walk fast enough.

Once we made it around the corner I spotted the Whistleville River just beyond the bridge. I thought about how, a few miles up, on the east side of town, the Jeep in my shop had plunged over that same bridge. I imagined the bodies of the kids stuck there, tangled in the water grass, decomposing, and slowly turning into fish food. I shook off the idea— just chalked it up to collateral damage from a nice Anchor Steam buzz.

We rounded the old brick building and made our way toward the parking lot in back. Rain filtered through the street lamps, falling in curtains, shifting and moving in the crosswinds. A new spotlight lit the rain from the side. Headlights. Tires screeched a few hundred feet in front of us.

There was a Jeep. *Another damn Jeep*, I thought. It raced toward us, stopping with a hard jerk. The rainfall increased.

A window rolled down, but I couldn't see inside.

A raspy, deep voice, said, "Hey."

"What do you need, man?" I asked. "Come on."

"You know exactly what you did," he said. "Disrespecting me and my girl."

"I don't know you, man," I said. "I think you're mistaking me for someone else."

"So you're calling me a liar?"

I pulled my collar up. "Look, friend," I said. "I don't have time for this. I'm drunk.

I want to go home."

"Oh, sure," he said. "You just want to go home and forget all of this."

His door opened. It was the big, bald guy that had been next to Minarette. "Too late," he said. "The damage is already done. Talking about me." Two others got out of the Jeep. They looked like normal, clean-cut guys in their 20s, only there was something wrong with their expressions. I thought they had to have been high on something. Their eyes seemed so vacant.

"Like I just told you, man—I'd have no reason to. I don't even know you."

One of the cronies said, "Come on, Damian. Get him already." I had a name.

I looked over to Mike, who was staring at the other two guys—guys we didn't know—who'd found their way over toward him.

I got shoved. Damian. He was in my face. "What're you going to say now?"

My head got real dizzy. Too much booze. I wasn't in any kind of shape to fight.

He shoved me again. I tried to stay up, and did so barely.

A holler, and Mike was against a wall.

"Leave him alone," I said. "This isn't his fault."

"Well," Damian said, "I don't care."

He pushed me, but I stepped back.

"This is bull," I said. "And I sure as hell ain't gonna apologize for something I didn't do."

He swung for my face–and just barely hit my shoulder.

He was way stronger than me. I was in trouble. My shoulder thudded. There'd be a nasty bruise. The bastard.

I put up my fists while Damian hovered.

Mike was on the ground. One of the goons was on top of him. Looked like they were robbing him.

"Get off him," I said. "You bullies. What the hell?"

His fist, my face.

Every color exploded—like I was in the middle of a mortar shell.

I tried to put up my arms to block him, but I'd been knocked for a loop.

And he hit me again.

I felt incredible pain.

I felt nothing.

My feet failed first—my legs followed.

Down for the count, the others cheered.

Everything felt like it'd turned slow motion. Reaching behind, I sat myself down. The world spun. The hit was too much for me to brush off.

Damian kicked me in the chest. My breath forced out, the hit knocked me to the pavement.

I heard more cheering, and more laughing.

My breath wouldn't catch.

Damian leaned over me. His pug-like face looked inches away, then, miles away.

He said something, but it didn't register. Everything sounded like we were inside a tunnel.

More kicks to my middle.

My body and mind were separate. There was nothing grounding me.

I turned my head to check for my friend.

The two goons were centered on his head. They'd leaned down and it looked as though they were eating him. What the hell?

They were on his neck. They held him down with their hands. The veins on the backs of their hands were puffed out, like they'd done steroids.

One lifted his head. He looked so normal, other than those vacant eyes. The ghoul could've been anyone. Blood rimmed his lips and dripped from his chin: it was Mike's blood. Our eyes met for a moment and from between the ghoul's lips a worm-like thing slipped out. The tip was pointed and sharp. It twitched just a bit and I knew it was his tongue, although it was different than any other I'd ever seen or heard of.

He lowered his head again. When he connected, Mike jerked. It seemed more like a reflex than a reaction. Mike's eyes were shut. His skin had gone pale.

They were draining him of his blood.

One of their shirts had come undone in the front in the scuffle. His chest looked so white it was almost clear. I swear I could see his insides moving...could make out the faint movement of a beating, translucent heart. A stream of red entered the chamber, blossomed, and then colored the cradle of veins surrounding the organ. Blood. Mikey's blood–drained from him and taken inside the ghost-like heart of the ghoul kneeling over him. *How could the blood get from its tongue to its own heart so damn fast?* I thought.

I tried to yell and scream, but nothing came out. I was in shock. Nothing worked. I looked up to see where Damian was. He'd walked away from me and stood a few feet away from his creeps; he watched them work. Damian's skin was the same pasty white as his consigliore.

I turned my head and every nerve inside me seemed to explode at once. Mike laid still a dozen feet from me. Rain ran from his forehead, down his cheek. Only it wasn't just rain, I noticed. A good stream of blood ran within the rain. There were unnatural gaps in his throat where they'd fed. Moon-shaped bruises marked his flesh.

Those bastards. I'd get 'em. Somehow, some way, I knew I would. They stood over him, both of them wearing goatee-shaped smears of blood. Formerly empty eyes glistened. The blood—Mike's blood—had reinvigorated them.

The sons of bitches.

Damian looked lit up from the inside. That sounds funny, because people don't glow. It's just that the rain seemed not to touch him. His skin didn't look well at all. Maybe it was because he was so pumped from the fight that he just looked that way. Who knows?

He'd won. They'd won in no time.

I considered myself a big guy, but I'd been outgunned. I was shocked at how fast Damian had taken me down. It was inhuman.

Drugs. Had to have been drugs. Maybe coke. Definitely some kind of upper. That'd explain it.

Then? One final insult—a swift kick to my balls.

The blinding pain knocked me down from space, and back inside my beaten husk.

Bile rose. I turned my head, spewing hot, half-digested beer everywhere.

"You should take a picture," one of the goons said.

"Don't need to," Damian said, "I won't forget this."

Neither would I.

Damian laughed and looked down at me. "You loser," he said. "You got something smart to say now?" He spat at me, turned, and walked away. I heard them get inside the Jeep, turn it on, and drive away.

He and his crew were gone, leaving Mike and me lying broken in the rain.

Once I could no longer hear their Jeep leave, I pulled myself up. Everything hurt and stung. My wet clothes clung to me. I crawled over toward Mike.

Nudged him.

Got nothing.

Kept pushing, tapping, and calling his name.

No response.

I used my thumb to try and open an eye.

No reaction.

I checked for a pulse.

Found one, but it was faint.

The skin of his wrist was cold.

I tried CPR, but never really learned how, so it was for naught.

Reaching inside my coat pocket, I found my phone in pieces. One of Damian's kicks must've smashed it. Still, I tried to turn it on. Just in case I could make one more call. No dice.

I screamed at Mike.

A few folks had made their way over, probably after hearing my yelling. I hollered for them to call an ambulance, and the cops. They didn't have to, though. Blue and red lights arrived moments later, just as the rain let up. I got myself to a bench, and sat.

When I finally got my head on straight, I watched as the EMTs put my friend on a stretcher. They rushed, going as fast as they could. Mike was in big trouble.

So was I.

It's all about the story...

Romance

HORROR

www.samhainpublishing.com

CPSIA information can be obtained at www.ICGtesting.com
Printed in the USA
LVOW07s2131240116

471955LV00004B/47/P